Nia

Nia

Allan Wargon

PIED PIPER
BOOKS

Library and Archives Canada Cataloguing in Publication

Allan Wargon
Nia / Allan Wargon

ISBN 978-0-9865671-1-7

1. Title

PS8595.A7734N53   2011   C813'.54   C2010-904751-6

Typeset by Gordon Robertson Design, Toronto, Canada.
Printed and bound in Canada by Friesens

10 9 8 7 6 5 4 3 2 1

Published by Pied Piper Books
825941 Mel-Nott TL, R R 2, Shelburne, ON LON 1S6 Canada

This novel, though it is fiction, is dedicated
to a wonderful woman who actually lived,
died, and left indelible memories.
The world is very much richer for her
having been in it.

Part One

A few evenings ago I was lying here,
just as I am now. We'd had supper here
on the porch and Nia was sitting on the edge
of the cot, the small of her back against my thigh.
   I drew her down and she came meltingly,
her body to mine, her mouth to my mouth.
I touched the sweet hollow between her breasts,
held their warm heaviness, nuzzled her soft cheek,
kissed the hair beside her temple. All yielded to me.
   You have changed, I said.
   She sat up then, her hands in her lap,
and looked out over the water. Stars were in the sky
beyond the porch rails, the trees on the far shore dark,
stirring, doubled with star glints in the glimmering pond.
Nia, her hair unpinned and loosely off her neck,
sat looking at the quietly moving water. I waited,
wanting to hold her, yet not wanting to intrude.
   After a moment she said, I guess when you
belong to somebody, you belong completely.

Yes. But everything is more complex than it seems.

1

The rising tide carried off a dory that was vital to the scene. It had been drawn up on the shore but no one had thought to secure it. There was no other boat; the motor ship that had brought them to this isolated cove was not due back for another three hours. The actors shrugged and sat down, while some of the crew, delighted by this divine rebuke to their director, began dismantling the equipment. But Robert, frowning fiercely, told them to leave everything as it was. Stripping to his shorts he plunged into the waves and swam after the dory, which an offshore breeze was swiftly driving seaward. He was all but out of sight, had swallowed some water, and was beginning to thrash, when he reached the boat and pulled himself aboard it.

Nothing was said while they finished the scene, but that evening, when the director was working alone in his room — he wrote reports on each day's filming, explaining how he meant the shots to be edited — the others discussed the incident. The crew held there had been something *weird* in Robert's feat, while the actors, who recognized swagger when they saw it, nonetheless wondered why he'd taken such a fearful risk.

*

Robert had dragged his crew though continual discomfort and danger. They were chilled by rain, burnt by the sun, cut by rocks;

5

they were seasick, they went without meals and slept on bare boards. The men grumbled and occasionally shouted; once one wept, others reproached Robert to his face. And secretly they plotted to denounce him when they got back. But they obeyed — overcome by his sheer stubbornness, by what seemed his absolute devotion to getting the best-possible shot.

None of the crew had worked with Robert before, and had assumed from his reputation that he would be slow, moderate, even timid. Indeed, some suspected the assignment was meant to ruin him: why else, they had argued, would Eldon have recruited an arty director to shoot such rough stories? They could not believe that the producer simply wanted to exploit Robert's talent, for these crewmen, more than most — they'd been chosen for their toughness — looked upon talent as an erratic and somewhat unmanly quality. So they had not been at all prepared for the person they now had to deal with, and feeling that something singular was at work in him they were wary and scornful, and sometimes a little afraid.

*

There were some nuns in the Cape Breton village where the crew was staying. These half-dozen sisters made up the teaching staff of the Catholic high school, and they lived together in a drab wooden house leaning at the low corner of a rambling plot that also held the brine-pitted church, the old graveyard, and the rectory. This last building, like the first, was coated with weathered clapboard, but it was graced by three tall columns and a wide verandah. Standing at the high end of the property, it had a commanding view of the village and its curving harbour.

Robert had been shown through the nuns' house at the request of the priest, a robust passionate man with heavy hands and a ruddy face, whose strangled love of life constantly threatened to break through his piety. The son of a coal miner, the good father had been one of that dedicated group of students, fostered by St. Frances Xavier University, who had become leaders in the cooperative movement. This priest could be moved to tears by the mystery of the mass, but with the film people Father Jovian was as little pontifical as a playful puppy. He invited them to huge dinners of lobster, which was out of season, blessed their beer to give it an extra kick, offered prayers for the success of their movie, and served them holy water that turned out to be contraband ninety-proof whiskey. At first the cast and crew were astonished at this freedom, but they soon took it for granted, and began to treat him familiarly, and with a tinge of contempt.

If the priest felt slighted he didn't show it; he forgave the others for the director's sake. In Robert's intensity he sensed a loneliness as deep as his own, and he could not do enough for him, even to satisfying his eagerness — passed off as a naïve interest in Catholicism — to see the inside of a nunnery.

Actually, Robert had been motivated by a mischievous, yet humble, romantic longing. He had been told that the mother superior, who was briefly absent, was young, good-looking and well educated, and it was to penetrate her surroundings, to see and feel and smell some of the details of her existence, that he had asked to be shown the house in which she lived. He was in luck: hers was the only bedroom door open, just at the top of the stairs, and while they stood there — the nun conducting them was pointing out to Jovian a jagged crack in the ceiling — Robert could see that on her desk the superior had some dainty writing paper of the sort women sometimes use for intimate correspondence, and that there were modern novels among the books that filled the shelves under her window. These personal touches enchanted him; sight unseen he became infatuated. Two nights later, when he saw her window lit and partly open, he wanted to climb to the woodshed roof under it and whisper in to her — stand-in though she was. On the hill, in the dark, he struggled with this fit. Finally he went on his way.

Was he aware of what drove such exaggerated desires? Yes, partly; it was a sort of delirium trembling within him. But vanity would not let him admit he was so little in control of his own behaviour. He liked to think of himself as inflexible in his purpose, ready to do anything to further the cause. This lofty self-regard prompted him to help with the most menial tasks; he would even carry equipment and drag cables. But often he only got in the way, and his zeal was galling to those who were simply trying to do their job.

*

Their next location was Sable Island, called *the graveyard of the Atlantic* because of the many ships wrecked on its shifting shoals. The filmmakers were put aground there, in waist-deep water, during a blustery dusk, with high seas heaving. Two of the landing boats were swamped and half filled with sand, littering the surf with kegs and cases. The drenched sailors cursed the wind, the waves, the boats, the cargo, while in the bewildering dark the flickering lanterns held by men from the rescue station, who were eagerly awaiting their provisions, particularly the bottled sort, only added a final bizarre touch to the scene.

*

In the morning the crew searched for a lost set of earphones, and though it was a spare set, which the soundman said he could do without, Robert set off alone in the evening to see if its wooden container might have beached farther up shore. Engrossed in looking at scallop shells, seaweed, and the skeletons of ships buried in sand, he failed to notice the fog coming in. Suddenly it engulfed him, and was soon followed by night. The rescue station, where they had slept, was on the other side of the island; in the haze and darkness he could not find the path by which he had come.

Once he turned inland, but swiftly sank into soft ground and drew back, for he had been warned that the bogs were *bottomless*. A fine mist was seeping from the fog; by midnight he was wet and chilled. However, he had some paper matches, and in the shelter of a dune, using his pocketknife, he dug small splinters from a dry core of driftwood, and then, carefully shielding this tiny kindling,

8

set it alight. When he had a good blaze going, wild horses came up to the circle of light and stood staring and snorting round its wavering edge. In these fantastic circumstances he felt he could give himself up to thinking of *her*.

He'd heard that the producer had a new assistant. But he had not expected a beautiful woman, open, frank, free of restraint. Her impact was immediate. It was all hugely upsetting. He felt it could only interfere, and perversely, chaotically, he resented it.

*

Yet his work took on a new tenderness. He tried to capture every fleeting effect, filling the background of his scenes with wild horses, with the colonies of lazy seals sunning on the sand, with the thousands of terns wheeling overhead. *Oh, let's get it!* he would cry, as if in rapture — but the crew, who felt they were already labouring beyond reason, heard it as only another brutal command, condemning them to even greater effort.

Most of their rushes — each day's exposed film that was rushed to Montreal to be hastily processed, screened, and reported on to the crew — were well received, and Eldon's comments were encouraging. Then one day Robert got a telegram, relayed by radio from the mainland, which went beyond the usual expressions of approval. It said 'Terrific!' and was signed Nora. The director quickly replied to Eldon, stating that he did not want to hear from her. Eldon was surprised — he had told Nora to send the wire, but deciding not to make an issue of it, he explained to her that *because you are new* . . . and *the guy is under a lot of pressure*, and so on.

She smiled her quick smile and said *Oh, I understand* — And indeed she did.

From then on Robert heard only from Eldon, but when he thought of them reading his reports, or looking at rushes, it was Nora's face he watched for the reaction.

*

Much of the whale hunt footage they sent from Newfoundland was simply too strong to use. Everyone called it a hunt, but the big school of black whales had been driven into a shallow arm by government whaling ships, and trapped there by long nets strung between rocks. The whales could easily have broken through the nets, but they were gentle animals, not given to aggression. Then, under the dull glare of the declining sun, with the tide going out, the local fishermen quietly lined up their boats. On the signal of a sudden single shot, they charged the whales. Shrieking, shooting, striking large cans, they drove the terrified creatures towards the beach, from which the water was rapidly receding.

It was an explosion of lust, fury, murder. All the fishermen's desires, irritation, anger and hate went into it. The men screamed as they speared with their long lances, and the whales, spurting blood, thrashed and gasped in agony. In their frenzy some pregnant ones gave birth to immature whitish babies three or four feet long. The salty, fishy smell of the water and boats mingled with the warm, heavy, living odour of blood. Sometimes Robert could not make himself heard over the roar of the motors, the shouts and gun shots, the screeching of gulls and the rush and splash of water.

The crew, at his insistence — for they had strongly objected — were in an open boat in the midst of the slaughter. Suddenly the craft's movement changed from a wave rhythm to a forced teetering, and the cameraman, who had one eye shut and the other pressed to the finder, cried out to stop jiggling the boat. But no one was; it had been lifted from the water on the back of a dying whale. Then the creature sank, streaming blood.

Everything was awash with blood. Blood surged, spilled, slopped, was flung, gleamed and glittered. It flowed from the shiny black animals fatally gurgling in the shallows, it splashed on small children toddling in the pinkish surf and stabbing the baby whales with sharpened sticks, it sprayed from chunks of warm flesh dogs were tearing loose — and gulls, carrying bits aloft, scattered some drops on the fishermen's wives, who had prepared tea at a small campfire on the hillside, and were sitting there, silently watching the broad red stain spread out to sea.

*

The whale meat was fed to ranch mink; the fishermen being collectively paid by the pound. It was a budding industry the provincial government wished to encourage.

*

Those were their last shots; the end of the assignment. The cast had left two days earlier, and that evening, in the small outport house where they had been taking their meals, the crew had a final dinner together. Robert made a little speech, thanking the men for all they had done. They listened in silence, and then the cameraman, who had not touched his food — he had vomited immediately after the shooting —fixed on Robert a look of such loathing that the director paled, and said nothing more.

*

Still, Robert was taken aback, the next day at the airport, when the others, having deliberately changed to a different flight, parted from him without a word. He watched them go with choked feelings of humiliation, rage, guilt and fear. Then his own flight lifted off, and his relief was overflowing. It was followed by a peculiar sensation: the taste of triumph. He knew he had done a good job, and that successful directors were seldom criticized. He felt he could look forward to compliments, more esteem — perhaps even a raise in pay!

But as the plane droned on his elation subsided, and recalling all that had happened he began to wonder at the effort, the suffering, the risk of life that had gone into those television films, which would merely fill three weeks of the schedule and be forgotten by the fourth. And finally he had to admit that he might have gone to such extremes not because of devotion to his work, or to advance his career, but only to impress Nora, as if she had been there.

*

Robert's home was in an old squat section of Ottawa that clung to the south end of the Governor General's grounds like the bedraggled feathers on the underside of a peacock's tail. He had left it with the usual sense of escape, but as the taxi carried him through the remembered streets he began to feel drawn to what awaited him, and when he stood once more before his house he was surprised by the rapid beating of his heart.

He ran up the steps, eager to embrace all the dear familiar fragments of home.

There was no one in — on a Sunday. He felt sharply annoyed, almost angry; but when he had put down his suitcase and had seen that all in the house was in order, he began to look at the matter more reasonably. *After all,* he thought *she didn't know I was coming.*

Yet he was left with a distinct feeling of disappointment. He went into the bedroom he shared with his wife, opened some drawers, and raised a piece of her underclothing to his lips. He was hoping for a perfumed scent, but it had only a cleanly laundered smell. Then he stretched out on the bed, wondering when he could decently go back to Eldon and the unit.

2

Eldon Arnold had been made a producer a year and a half earlier, when the television unit was formed. By that time TV had already surpassed live audience screenings in popular appeal, but at the National Film Board it was still considered a crass medium, unworthy of serious filmmakers.

None of the senior producers who were sounded out about heading the unit wanted the job, so James MacCurry, the Chief of Production, promptly — and surprisingly — gave it to Eldon.

Eldon had been one of a small coterie of directors who met each week at MacCurry's apartment to drink and play poker. Occasionally, when their burly host was feeling his liquor, he wanted to wrestle, and usually his choice of opponent fell on Eldon. MacCurry, of course, expected to win these contests, and Eldon was careful to oblige him, but with sly defiance the director managed to get in enough throws to make the game enjoyable to them both.

When Eldon's appointment was announced there were strong murmurs of favouritism, but MacCurry ignored them. He was not a bad judge of ability and he expected that Eldon, who had shown some skill in organization, would prove to be a competent producer. Moreover, he wanted to place a man of his own among the producers, because lately some disgruntled ones had gone over his head to the Film Commissioner, and even, once or twice, to members of parliament. However, to assure Eldon's loyalty he took the precaution of making him only an *acting* Executive Producer, whose appointment he could revoke whenever he wished.

Yet despite his cunning there was something about producing films for television that MacCurry failed to foresee. His former dealings with the public had been indirect, through screenings arranged by the Board's distribution division, and always in terms of small audiences, whose complaints could safely be shrugged off. He had never imagined a situation — this bureaucrat spending public funds — in which the public might influence his decisions. But he soon found that an ongoing commitment to fill the screen on a national network meant he had very little control over those doing the job, for in every argument Eldon had only to throw up his hands and shout *No! That'll keep us from finishing on time!* to get, finally, his own way. By skillfully wielding this new power Eldon soon acquired, extorted, MacCurry felt, more freedom than had been given any producer before. And Eldon was not afraid of being fired, because he was quickly becoming a public figure whose removal could raise awkward questions. Eldon was confident the Board would go a long way to avoid that; it had many enemies within the civil service who resented its monopoly of all government film production, and even its right to exist was sometimes questioned in Parliament.

When MacCurry saw what he had done he decided to let Eldon hang himself. He bristled about the licence being taken, but did nothing to prevent it; he took it for granted that an inexperienced producer, *running wild*, would soon stumble badly enough to call his appointment into question.

But Eldon was far more able, and ambitious, than MacCurry had realized. During the critical first months he never once made a serious mistake, and in half a year he was operating an efficient unit whose members behaved as if they belonged to an exclusive club. By the end of the first season he was finishing a film a week — a rate of productivity never before known at the Board. In spite of himself MacCurry was impressed, and because he was genuinely devoted to the Board he began to feel a certain pride in the achievements of the television unit.

Yet the established producers remained hostile. Privately they made faces about Eldon's tact and taste, and at meetings they listened to his opinions with that polite disdain with which comfortable householders regard the work of garbage men: as necessary but rather disgusting.

Eldon wanted to bury them all.

*

So when Robert appeared before him again the producer congratulated him warmly on his island shooting and told him to make his next film *original, different, and an artistic success!*

In any other unit such a demand would have seemed absurd. But the television directors had become accustomed to the unusual, and few of them were old enough to have learnt their limitations. Robert's only outer response was a nod, but he could barely restrain a rush of high feeling, which was further quickened when Eldon whispered *Listen, cock, you do this and there'll be no stopping us!*

Eldon's confidence was compelling; and as well he was attractive, which added to his persuasiveness. His flushed milky skin and close-cut black hair gave an impression of vigorous good health; he would have looked boyish if it was not for the webs of wrinkles in which his small sharp eyes were sunk. His body, which had been muscular, was rounding out from too much tense eating and drinking, but instead of coarsening it was growing sleek, like a rubber doll's. He seemed to thrive on excitement, snorting slightly as he talked and quivering a little, like a jack-in-the-box ready to spring.

*

When he was alone Robert wondered what he could do that would fulfill all of Eldon's expectations. The Film Board, which the government of Canada had created as a propaganda unit during the Second World War, and which had tenuously remained in existence since, had been in operation for more than fifteen years, and films had been made on almost every activity in the country. Yet there was one subject that had never been tried, that of Canadian history. It had been assumed that the sets and costumes would simply be too expensive for the Board. To attempt an historical subject on the standard budget for a television film — which was even smaller than that provided for most films, seemed fantastic, *really mad* . . . and yet what could be better? Particularly, its effect on Nora.

In keeping with the stance he had adopted, Robert had said nothing about her to Eldon. He hadn't seen her, and was doing his best to avoid her. When he heard her laughter through the open door of her office — across the hall from Eldon's, he hurried on, afraid she might come out and catch sight of him. He felt exposed in the bare corridors of the Board; it had been quite another matter to dream of her in the exotic surroundings of the islands.

Nonetheless he wished to show that exciting woman all the excellent qualities he secretly believed he had. Until now he had been limited, but in this new film, which he would both write and direct, he could speak to her in many subtle ways ...

*

That night he lay awake, going over the historical stories he had learnt in his school days. Dramatically, one stood out from all the rest: the tragedy of the opposing French and British commanders who fell in the siege of Quebec, each doomed by circumstances he could not control. Montcalm, middle aged, gallant and compassionate, had been overruled and undermined by the obstinacy of the governor and the thievery of the governor's friends; while Wolfe, at thirty-two the youngest general in the British army, was dying of a fatal illness and desperate to complete his last campaign, which the onset of the Canadian winter was about to bring to a futile end.

On the morning of battle, Wolfe put on a bright red uniform, targeting himself for the French marksmen, and successfully died for glory as his troops were sweeping the field. Montcalm, on the other hand, would have preferred to live, but he had his own sense of the dramatic, which he called *duty and honour*. This devotion to an ideal appealed strongly to Robert; he in his way had often longed to rise above his restrictions and prove himself extraordinary. At times he still indulged in daydreams in which he won out over tremendous obstacles, or, if he saw himself defeated, it was always by unbeatable forces that left him *bloody but unbowed*. Recovering, he would smile at these residues of adolescence, but they continued to abide in his depths, like certain underwater plants that are seldom seen on the surface.

Wolfe too had a side to his character the superficial stories did not disclose — he was warm with his mother but wary of other females; his entire romance seemed to have been with the army. And Robert, now only a few years younger than Wolfe was then,

16

and still far from the first rank, wondered if he ought not to be as single minded. But it was, had always been, too late: he was hopelessly drawn to women. Women were his flowers and fruit, the air he breathed, his oxygen, his keenest interest in living. But all of this generalized yearning was well hidden under a plain faced, unfashionably dressed, rather drab exterior. No heads turned when Robert passed. He was considered talented, but otherwise nondescript. And when some of his intensity escaped and was directed at a woman, without explanation, it often made her uncomfortable. Nonetheless, for this film his audience would be primarily a woman, and as Montcalm liked women, plainly the Frenchman must be his spokesman and the hero of the film.

Montcalm's story was full of intrigue, greed, conceit, folly. Robert wanted to get right at this rich stuff without a lot of explanation, and he soon began to see the film as a series of brief incidents, of verbal clashes mostly, which would reveal the motives of the characters and impel the action. He felt he could cut away all that was not essential and go, with the directness of poetry, right to the core of each situation, which in turn made him realize — and this thought so excited him he sat bolt upright! — that realistic sets would be unnecessary, because it would be more in keeping with the abstract style merely to suggest an ornate chamber by a hanging tapestry, or a military headquarters by a wall map. As for the action of battle, he remembered having seen in the National Archives a number of large engravings depicting various stages of the siege; these graphic tableaux were the news pictures of their day, and he could use them, with their ships and troops and smoking guns, to frame the scenes of live action — telling the story, as it were, through engravings that at significant times came to life.

He went on all night in this way, and by dawn he was drenched in sweat, parched and hungry, but he had in his mind a complete outline of the screenplay.

*

Eldon was delighted. He was especially pleased with the idea of using the engravings, which would keep the cost of the film within a standard budget. And then, in the excitement of the moment, he told Robert he saw the unit going on to ever more ambitious projects, until one day they might leave the Board and form a production company of their own.

It was a breathtaking notion. There had been so little private production in Canada that the Film Board sat like a prosperous walled city on a barren plain; yet its people, while scorning *Hollywood and all that*, could not help feeling that they were only playing at being producers and directors, that the real world of challenge and reward lay somewhere outside. Robert parted from Eldon with the heady conviction that a splendid destiny was opening before him.

He went back to Ottawa the same afternoon, to do historical research — he had to be able to prove his assumptions — and to write the actual script. He had written before, but was grudging about calling himself a writer; directors, he liked to say, were *forced to write* because of the poor quality of scripts. However it was not unusual at the Board, where there were no trade unions to prevent it, for capable persons to combine roles; the term *filmmaker* had been coined to describe such an all-rounder, but gradually it came to mean anyone who did any of the writing, directing, producing, or editing of a film.

*

Sifting through the litter of history stored in the Archives, Robert found a letter by Montcalm to his wife in France. The general had written it in his last days, when, he must have known, there was no longer any hope of sending it through the British blockade:

> The night is dark, our troops are in their tents,
> with clothes on. I in my boots, my horses saddled.
> We wait with impatience and dread. My thoughts

are of home and you. Dearest wife, when will I see you
and my children? When will I see my chateau of Candiac,
my chestnut grove, my oil mill, my mulberry trees?
I would give up all my honours to be with you again.
But the king must be obeyed. Adieu, my dear,
I believe I love you more than ever.

This was sure to affect Nora! But Robert was moved by it himself, and when he compared its clear intensity to the confused dis-
order she roused in him he felt ineffectual and ashamed, as if he,
more than Montcalm, were an unwitting actor in an unfinished
drama.

*

He wrote most of the script sitting on a lawn chair in his back-
yard. Though it was October and there was already a chill in the
ground he was out every day, under sun and cloud, wrapped in a
blanket like a Roman senator, his brow furrowed, his gaze turned
in. His wife did not speak to him when she came home from work.
She called him to the table only when dinner was ready.

This aloofness hid a joyous ferment: his mind was overflowing with ideas. Never had scenes suggested themselves so rapidly,
or words fallen so easily into trenchant speech. Some force within
the work seemed to have control of it; it was *writing itself*, as if the
characters were commanding the author. At times Robert had to
scribble frantically to keep up with his thoughts.

Three weeks after he began it he carried the finished script to
Montreal.

*

He put it on Eldon's desk. Then he shut himself in his own
office downstairs, one of a row of identical cubicles entered from
a bare grey hall. He calculated how long it would take them — Nora
usually read scripts first, then Eldon. He was sure they would do
his right away.

Would Nora see his messages? He had several times stated his feelings, but then, uncertain of what he wanted, had hidden his meaning so skillfully that it could scarcely be discovered. Yet he hungered and hoped.

*

Vague images of lunch goers moved across the ribbed glass of his door, then returned. Robert continued to sit at his desk. The room was still, smelling of dryness. The sky was blue. A fly buzzed behind the sun-glazed blind, stirring dust into the air. There was a gritty grey film on the unread notices and memos stacked in piles on the shelves. Only the floor was clean. Of pale grey vinyl, it shone like a frozen pond. The placid cleaners polished it every night; employees of the Department of Works, they were as detached as if the filmmakers were creatures in a zoo.

Suddenly someone was knocking. Eldon stuck in his head. *Busy?* he said.

Well, uh . . .

Come up when you have a minute Eldon said, his eyes shining. He had the script in his hand. *It's great!* he said.

*

Nora was bending over its pages when Robert — having one by one, his heart racing, counted out sixteen excruciating minutes — finally rapped at Eldon's open door.

She looked up. *You're writing lovely dialogue, Mr. Aronson.*

Robert was stunned to find she was all he remembered, but softer, less sensational.

Oh, uh . . . thank you he stammered, and barely held back *I love you too!*

Her lips parted, then closed to contain a smile.

If Eldon noticed any of this he gave no sign. Taking charge, he said *Montcalm* was to go into production at once, and that Nora was to help with the casting.

20

During the war, when the Film Board was located in Ottawa, it had occupied a crumbling structure that backed onto the high bank of the river, next to the pale immaculate French embassy. It was there, *at the Board* — in that cramped makeshift building that had once been a sawmill, and where the lab shifts kept up a running competition over the number of rats each could kill — that most Canadian filmmakers had learnt their craft. When the war ended and the Board, instead of being disbanded, was assigned a peacetime role, the French ambassador delicately but persistently reminded the government of Canada that it had promised to remove the eyesore when the emergency was over. A decade later the pledge was carried out; the Film Board, with its staff and their families, its equipment and supplies, was moved to Montreal. A special team of architects and engineers had laboured for three years on the new building, which blended perfectly into its surroundings, for it looked just like the drab factories among which it was placed on the Cote de Liesse.

This new headquarters was *a triumph of technology.* It was as solid as a vault, as sterile as a hospital; it inspired a burst of efficiency, and charts and graphs became the latest craze in wall decorations. Uniformed commissionaires were stationed at the entrances, the maintenance men were issued white coats. But the untidy filmmakers soon marred its purity by putting up cartoons and posters, coming and going at all hours, and loitering in the cafeteria, complaining of the terrible food.

Robert and Nora were having coffee there one afternoon about two weeks after they had started working together. It was the first time they had sat down in this way, because Robert had deliberately avoided any chance of intimacy, keeping their meetings brief and to the point — which had done nothing to relieve the tender tension that was always present in them. However, this afternoon was different: they were celebrating having cast the last of the major roles.

Their work had gone well. Robert was sure of the qualities he wanted and Nora had easily, with marvellous speed, arranged for him to audition the likely actors. Robert mutely marvelled at her quickness in everything. She grasped ideas at once, spoke rapidly, in short spurts, as if she hadn't time for ordinary conjunctions; she moved quickly, with grace, usually on high heels, and responded instantly to the stimulation of a joke, words, the feelings of others, smoke, taste, sounds, sunlight, darkness. She seemed always totally aware. She wasn't a bimbo; there were signs of age. Robert guessed she was about thirty, a little older than he. Her pretty face topped a slim but full lithe figure, and with her hair up she could look elegant. But what was most impressive was her warmth, wit, immediacy, lack of any pretension. She was, he felt, utterly charming.

This served well with actors. She often became instant friends with them, or had previously known some, as well as a large number of other performers, musicians, writers and producers whose names carried that aura of fame and success that Robert, who had no experience of it, both envied and felt he ought to despise.

Nora had been at the Board for six months and a good deal had been learnt about her previous and private life by those who made it their business to know such things. But Robert had been away during most of that time — at first on a film celebrating women through sculptures of them, the film from which Eldon had recruited him for the television unit — and since returning from the islands he had been careful not to ask about Nora, for fear of drawing attention to his interest in her. Several times during their meetings he had been tempted to put a question, but then the phone had rung, someone had come along, or such familiarity had seemed to conflict with his pretense of detachment. Now, however, the moment was ideal: there was no one at the nearby tables, and the clatter from the kitchen would prevent their being overheard.

Still, he hesitated. He did not want to be indelicate, or seem to be prying; above all he had a horror of being repulsed. Yet time was passing. Nora had finished her coffee and was on her second cigarette . . . the silence between them was becoming strained. Finally she gave him a small smile and began to get up.

Tell me about yourself! he cried desperately.

Of course she had expected this. That she fascinated him she'd known since their first meeting. And she was still drawn by what she'd seen then, the intense maleness underlying his plain looks, his awkwardness and lack of sophistication. But she felt that for now she'd had enough of men.

The wrenching brutality of the abortion, and then the divorce, with its sordid haggling over support, though not custody — her husband hadn't wanted to be saddled with a young son — had left her more battered than she'd ever been. Withdrawing from that emotional hurly-burly to the relative quiet of the Board, to living — wasn't it symbolic? — on an obscure island, was a time of licking wounds. Moreover, after leaving her husband, carnality had repelled her. There'd earlier been the movie stars who in public behaved like princes of the blood, but in bed were no better than any groping boy. Yet Robert stirred in her something more than physical attraction.

I'm divorced — she said, sitting again. *I live with my son, Joel, who's eleven, and my mother, and a little dog named Jester — we have a house on an island.*

Robert thought *Not the island of Montreal. Perhaps one of the smaller islands, connected by bridges to the mainland.* He was delighted to learn this, but, as usual, frowned.

Why did you come here? he said sternly. *After New York —*

Why? Well, I'm Canadian —

His mouth opened.

She laughed. *I'm from Portage la Prairie.*

Saskatchewan!

Manitoba she corrected. *North of Winnipeg.*

He was shamefaced about not having known that, but frown-ingly concealed it. *Mmn. Yet you were — you could easily have worked in* — he hesitated to say Hollywood — *Los Angeles.*

I've — been there. I was glad to get away from all that.

He wondered what the last phrase covered. She still officially called herself Mrs. Nora Wilson, but that was probably for the boy's sake. Peterson, one of the chinwags had told him, was her maiden name. *Does your mother keep house?*

23

Nora laughed. *Mother? No. I cook and clean when I get home. Lunch and snacks she and Joel manage — more or less. On the less days I'm greeted with 'Mom — not a thing to eat in this house!'*

Robert noted no mention of a father, or any other man. Maybe the coast was clear.

By the way, she said *close friends call me Nia. You can, if you wish.*

Oh — he said. This had to sink in, and they were both silent for a moment. He saw that she was watching him, with a slight smile, waiting for more questions. But his curiosity was now wildly tangled with hope. Then suddenly she jarred him:

What about you?

He became confused, because instantly his marriage seemed to lose all substance. He said *Well . . . uh . . . I'm married. No children.*

She touched her tongue to her teeth the way she did when surprised. *That's funny —* she said. *You don't seem married.*

*

Afterwards Robert was troubled about what he felt had been a close call, a near loss of control. He decided, darkly, to stick to his work. In work their relations were defined. Or rather, he grumbled, they ought to be. For despite her title, Nia's role in the unit was far from clear.

Titles helped little in understanding real functions at the Board. *Executive Producer* did mean someone in charge of a unit, but the term *Producer* implied only that the person was responsible for all aspects of a film, particularly its budget, though that was a burden often assumed by a *Director,* who, strictly speaking, normally directed only the actors and the framing and movement of the camera. To make matters worse, some of the more prominent filmmakers were called *Producer-Director* or *Director-Producer,* while *Produced and Directed by* was a credit everyone wanted. Nia's title of *Assistant Producer,* when it stood for assisting the head of a unit, could mean much or nothing.

No more was apparent in the television unit than that Eldon liked to have his assistant's opinion in matters of taste, and that she often took his place in dealing with actors, writers and other persons outside the Board, especially when persuasion was needed. Inside the Board she carried out various tasks Eldon did not have time for, but which he could not quite leave to a secretary. In all this the uncertainty about Nia's position had so far been of advantage to her, because no one could be sure of whether she was speaking for herself or the producer, or whether her opinions would not in any case sway him. The suspicion that she'd been hired for other than professional reasons — for she had seemed much too beautiful and overqualified — had not altogether died out. Though there was no evidence of anything between her and Eldon, it was hard for men and women alike to understand why there would not be. She and Eldon were often closeted in his office, and they had been on brief trips together.

These circumstances, added to Robert's dread of dishonour, weighed heavily in his thinking. He tried to imagine Nia and himself having only a very friendly *work relationship*, or even an intimate *non-physical friendship*, but all such formulas were so utterly unlike what he was feeling that he gave them up and tried to suppress his feeling altogether. It was like trying to suppress water, to bury a natural spring. It simply came up elsewhere.

*

Two days after the conversation in the cafeteria they were alone in Nia's office, going through a file of performers who might fill the minor roles. The light in the room was subdued; the sounds of the building seemed to have receded. A single window overlooked the gravelled yard where equipment trucks were drawn up. Beyond the chain link fence stretched dry unkempt fields. The nearest houses were a quarter mile away.

Robert was standing at the open top drawer of the cabinet, with Nia beside him. Neither had spoken for several seconds. She moved closer to check a resumé. Now as he raised each photograph, his arm brushed hers. She began holding her breath. She was already in the grip of a nameless excitement. She wanted to embrace him, to hug him, out of fellow feeling, out of — eroticism, she knew, in spite of her resolve, lurked not far behind. Yet there was his marriage. She didn't want to hurt an unknown woman. But her body temperature was rising.

Its warmth soon reached Robert. His mind became muddled; the glossy photos gleamed, meaningless names heaped in his head. He shook it, and trying to concentrate, looked carefully at every face, read each caption, and comprehended nothing.

Nia drew a breath, and was suddenly breathing hard.

He saw a wisp of her hair, and grew aware of her smoky scent; gradually both hair and scent came closer, becoming sharper, stronger. But Nia was standing still, her heart beating. Robert sank towards her, blood draining from his face. Going faint, he, then she, clung to the drawer.

Until gasping *Oh God!* Nia spun away from him, and staggered, shaking, into the hall.

*

The shooting began. In his enthusiasm Eldon had squeezed the production into the studio between two other films that had been booked earlier, so an exact number of scenes had to be completed each day, regardless of the overtime worked. This sort of scheduling usually angered a crew — because, unlike *outsiders*, Film Board employees got no pay for overtime, but only an equal amount of time off later on, yet these crewmen were so intrigued by the unique style of the film that they willingly worked the extra hours. Indeed, an uncommon excitement pervaded the whole production, and it soon spread throughout the Board.

Small crowds were needed for some scenes, and to fill them Robert drew on people from all departments: secretaries, janitors, telephone operators, clerks — whoever could be enticed from his or her job for a few hours was pressed into costume. These *extras*, eager to be seen in their finery, escaped into the halls whenever possible, imbuing the stolid building with a carnival air. The Film Commissioner, going up the stairs to his office, was startled to see a huge Highlander — sword in hand — descending towards him, and when he reached the safety of his anteroom he found his receptionist in the habit of a nun.

With the inevitable delays in shooting, and the holiday spirit with which the employee actors became infected, they were away from their work longer than had been arranged for, and Eldon soon began getting calls from their department heads. He treated these complaints as if each was of the greatest importance, leaving the callers soothed and flattered, and glad to be on good terms with a man who seemed destined for a high place in their small world.

*

Then one day, when Robert was directing a scene in which a crowd falls silent as the wounded Montcalm is led from battle, James MacCurry brought a party of visitors into the studio. Several of them had important connections in Ottawa, and one, to whom MacCurry was paying particular court, was the wife of a cabinet minister. He was explaining the process to her when Robert, ready to rehearse the scene, called for silence. As the studio grew quiet the production chief's voice could still be heard. Robert frowned, but waited. His chair had been put on a wheeled equipment box so that he could see and be seen by everyone on the floor, and now all the cast and crew, and even some of MacCurry's party, were watching him. Again Robert called for silence, and when he had demanded it a third time and MacCurry's voice went on sounding he turned and politely asked him to leave the studio.

It was a mild confrontation, but nonetheless deeply offensive to the senior man. MacCurry left at once, but as soon as he could part from his guests he went straight to Eldon.

Yet that strategist, so cajoling with his equals, stood up firmly to his superior. He reminded MacCurry that it was a director's right to bar from a set anyone who interfered with his work, and told him that he himself never went there, preferring the wise practice of leaving his directors to work as they wished and judging them by the result. MacCurry merely grunted. Perhaps he even enjoyed being lectured to by Eldon, taking it in the spirit of their wrestling matches, which he had come to miss. But the incident in the studio remained painful. MacCurry was a vain man, and he did not forget.

*

Although Eldon was content to watch Robert's work on the screen, he soon saw that Nia was spending a lot of time on the set, and he learnt that she stayed there every night until the shooting was finished. She sat off to the side, out of the way, and said nothing. Robert didn't speak to her — she had no part in this stage of the film, but he was well aware of her presence. When he called out orders his voice had an extra ring to it, and when he made a mistake or changed his mind he cheerfully apologized for the extra trouble caused. He joked with the cast and bought coffee for the crew; he had the insular assurance of a man who knows he is admired.

Each night when the last shot was finished Nia got up and went out before Robert left the set. Then the night guard would call a taxi for her, and by the time she arrived at her island home it was long past midnight. As a result she was tired each day and neglected what she ought to have done for other films being made by the unit.

*

Eldon wondered whether to interfere, but then shrugged. He hadn't expected Nia to remain unattached for long and an alliance with Robert would at least keep her attention tied to the unit. However, he had to smother a pang of jealousy. There'd been a time soon after she began working with him, when at the end of a busy day in Toronto they were relaxing in his hotel room, he lying on the bed and Nia sitting on the edge of it beside him. His delight in getting her for the unit hadn't yet worn off, so he had not tried, before then, to go beyond being courteous and friendly. But when she pulled the pins from her hair and took off the horn-rimmed glasses she usually wore in the office and at meetings, and they had exchanged a silent smile, he got the feeling that he had only to reach out . . .

Nia drew back when he did, but her amused expression showed no offense, and Eldon smugly believed she would yield to his next approach. Then the phone rang. It was his home returning a call he had placed earlier, and in between instructing his wife to send some papers he had left and listening to her account of how their youngest child had to have three stitches in her chin, he coolly decided that an affair with Nia would be too complicated. He had been with an actress the night before. In Montreal he was already spending an evening a week with a woman from the distribution division. His wife no longer believed he worked those nights . . . it was becoming a mess. And as well, getting involved with Nia might interfere with his plans for the unit. So when he had replaced the receiver he sighed and said he was tired.

Nia nodded and got up. *Boss, dear* — she said, bending over him *it's really better this way.* Then she kissed him lightly on the brow, which Eldon found oddly comforting.

*

On the last night in the studio the shooting went on until two in the morning. Nia stayed through it all, watching and waiting.

Then she came over and stood behind some of the actors who had gathered around Robert. *Thanks, everyone* he said. *You were great. It was a pleasure* . . . and together with him they all laughed, knowing he had begged and bullied, shamed and flattered to effect their strong, concise performances. Nia was silent, but she was gazing at him with such intense warmth he felt that between them there was already something understood, some bond partly formed, perhaps fated.

She couldn't have said whether the stumbling block of his marriage had been slowly crumbling all through the production. Perhaps it had. But just then she realized she'd been seduced, released

29

from her resolve. Not merely by the need to fill emptiness, or even mainly by their mutual sexual tension, but overwhelmingly by Robert's talent. Talent had always been her undoing, her chief attraction.

At her side was the actor who had played Wolfe; no sooner had his scenes ended than he had gone to sit with her. They were, it seemed, old friends.

Come out with us for a drink? the civilian Wolfe said.

Robert frowned. The idea of *going out,* to drink, at that hour, shocked him. And in some bar, stripped of his status, he could only appear clumsy beside the suave, worldly Wolfe. *Uh . . . no thanks* he said *I still have to write some notes . . .* and while thinking of how to make that good he managed, with less confusion than he felt, a fairly cordial farewell.

*

In any film the final shots are seldom exciting. Usually, when everything else has been done, there remain some *inserts:* small technical shots that are made without actors. Robert finished these the next day, while the sets for the incoming film were being assembled at the other end of the studio. Then he closed his script, heartily shook hands with the crew, and went upstairs to Eldon's office.

He had every reason to think the film would be a success. Eldon's reports had been glowing; the editor, whose comments were usually caustic, was said to be impressed; and the unit's accountant had calculated that the production was roughly within budget. The engravings still had to be shot, but they could be done later, without pressure, because the film wasn't to be released until the end of the season. So Robert enjoyed the pleasant weariness that follows a sustained effort, and he looked forward to the congratulations he felt certain awaited him.

Eldon wasted no time on them. He had *marvellous news:* the film would be released in less than five weeks!

His original date had been a precaution. Although eager for recognition from his colleagues, Eldon had been unwilling to risk a flop with the public; if the film was a failure, he had reasoned, it would be less noticed at the end of the season. But when he became confident it would be successful he wanted it seen as soon as possible, and by a quick juggling of the schedule had placed it in the peak viewing period.

Robert assumed he was joking. He had told Eldon that the archivists who had charge of the engravings would not let him take them out of the building, nor allow them to be shot where they hung, for fear that the clutter of equipment might pose some danger to other treasured relics. He had arranged to have a room in the Archives set aside for the purpose, but it had been on the firm understanding that it would not be available until some time after New Year's, for during the Christmas holidays large crowds were expected. The holidays were almost upon them, and he could hardly, he now told Eldon, go back to the anxious archivists and ask them to upset their plans because of a television schedule. They were sure to refuse.

Then do something else.

What? Robert cried. *The whole film is styled on using the engravings!*

Ah, cock . . . Eldon said *think of something. You can do it.*

Robert shook his head. *You'll just have to put off the date.*

Sorry Eldon said. *I've already released the publicity.*

*

Eldon left Robert to think it over while he went to MacCurry and pleaded for more studio time. MacCurry was still piqued, but he was not so small-minded as to take it out on the production; besides, he was interested in Robert's film as a prototype that might be used for other subjects. So he phoned the producer of the incoming film *to explain the situation,* which is to say he gave the poor fellow no choice but to offer to delay the start of his own shooting. Robert was still sunk in the numbness that follows shock — dully listening to his own heartbeat — when Eldon returned and told him he had four more days in the studio.

Sadly shaking his head, Robert turned away. But it was partly play acting: the insidious appeal of another challenge was already stirring in him. Yet he was deeply disquieted. This was the first film that had freely allowed him to express his artistry, and he knew he had made of it a consistent, pure work, which could easily be spoilt by a change of style, or by pushing its style to extremes never intended. A realistic battle, a movie battle, would be out of keeping with the rest of the film, and a stylized battle, with real actors, ran the risk of being comic. On the other hand, there was this immediate crisis . . . which only he could overcome. Eldon's eagerness, Nia's probable approval, danced in him; he wanted to be the hero they hoped for.

*

A cold rain was falling when he left the building, but it refreshed him, and he began to feel buoyant as he walked to the neighboring stores to buy food for his supper and the night ahead.

It was almost bedtime before he got to work. Beside his script on the kitchen table lay a thick ruled pad and three sharpened pencils, and beyond them, where he could touch it by reaching out, lay a woman's black velvet choker.

It belonged to the mistress of the Director-Cameraman, then on location, who was letting Robert use his apartment while he was away. *I'll leave you her too!* his host had said with a laugh, and Robert had hoped that the girl, who had lately been living there, would stay and share the place. But out of delicacy, or perhaps pride, she had taken her things and gone elsewhere, leaving only a few dresses, some shoes, and, on a chest of drawers, the soft black choker.

What did Robert want with that strip of fabric? It stood for tenderness, for soft, sensuous notions, for the soothing caresses he would have liked at that trying moment. It was one of those vague symbols, floating like bubbles in his mind, whose airy fantasy could inspire his boldest acts.

*

Eldon met him in the morning and saw at once that Robert had not slept. The director was scowling horribly, his eyes were red within a blue-black pall, but the assured way in which he tossed over his sketches showed Eldon, who was trying not to smile, that the problem was solved. The producer listened impatiently while Robert explained how he could suggest a battle without actually staging one, and then urged him to go ahead.

The film's production manager feverishly ordered more costumes. The Canadian army sent a platoon of soldiers. The navy supplied boats, the city police, horses. The museum lent its entire supply of muskets. And the special effects men brought out all the smoke and explosive devices they had. No one, now, mentioned the costs.

*

When the battle scenes were screened Nia smiled at Robert in open admiration. Eldon pressed his shoulder and talked ebulliently about this *latest experiment* to the group of filmmakers who had come to see it, and all, even those who were grudging, agreed it *would work*. Only Robert was troubled. He knew that the battle shots, though clever, were a craven compromise — neither fully convincing as realism nor abstract enough to contrast with the main parts of the film the way the engravings would have. But it was too late to speak of that, especially in the face of such enthusiasm. He was being plied with flattery; and when the whole party emerged from the theatre Eldon's secretary ran up to Robert with a letter — *It might be important!* she exclaimed — which had just come from The Actors Studio in New York. In reply to his request to attend some classes, it invited him to come for a single one and specified a date early in January. *I can't go* Robert said. *Montcalm...*

But Eldon wouldn't hear of it. *Christ, go!* he said. *Take a week or two. You've earned it!* And he promised Robert that the film would be finished with as much care as if he were present.

Robert looked round to see what Nia thought of this, but Eldon's secretary, Gwendolyn, was talking to her about plans for the Christmas party.

*

It was held in the lab office, where there were beakers for mixing drinks, and a stretch of smooth floor for dancing. Eldon and Nia started it, by jitterbugging, joyously. Everyone else pressed in; Nia, laughing, was swept up by one man after another. Robert waited for a waltz and claimed her, but after a single go-round of bumping and being bumped she whispered *I'll have to teach you to dance.*

He nodded and tightened his hold, and their hearts began beating wildly. But suddenly someone stopped the record, and despite cries of complaint, put on another very loud, fast number. Robert shrugged his regret, and Nia was immediately snatched away.

*

Then Eldon packed his car with his closest people and drove through the snow to his place, stopping at a suburban station where Robert could catch the Ottawa train. Once more, as at the party, there was an exchange of kisses and good wishes, and Robert, feeling bolder, kissed Nia on the mouth.

Watching, Eldon wondered whether he had been wrong about *those two.* Apart from the time Nia had spent in the studio, and this Christmas kiss . . . there had really been nothing, and he liked the feeling that she could still, if he wished, be his. But that brought back her remark after first meeting Robert. The director had just left the office, when:

Wow, has he got it — !

What?

Sex appeal.

Eldon had hooted, for in that vein he thought Robert repressed. The idea was simply absurd.

34

But Nia, tilting her head with an expert air, had said *Take it from me —*

*

Robert stopped in Montreal on his way to New York because he wanted to talk to the composer who would write the music for *Montcalm*. But no one had been assigned; the music department was protesting that it had to have more notice, that everyone was up to their ears, and so on. Robert knew that finally one of them would do the work and do it well, for the composers were serious and capable men. But he was worried about the effect of the new scenes and hoped to modify it by having the music stress his original intention. And because he had to leave that night — his class in New York was to take place the next morning — he decided to write some notes outlining his ideas for the music:

> Don't be misled by soldiers, drums and bugles
> into thinking that this is only a conflict between armies.
> It is first and foremost a conflict between personalities.

The notes went on for four pages; he suggested separate themes for Montcalm and Wolfe, and showed where each should come in, then clash, and finally mingle. He left the notes with Eldon, who promised to give them to the composer.

*

The Actors Studio building, crowded between decaying brownstones in midtown Manhattan, was, fittingly, an old church, long deconsecrated. And Robert, having come disposed to worship, went up its cracked steps more reverently than if he were about to enter Canterbury or Notre Dame.

The lobby was filled with men and women talking, laughing, smoking. Many of the faces were familiar to him from movies. No one even glanced at him. He threaded through to an animated

35

young woman at a desk, waited until she finally turned to him, and showed his letter of invitation. She told him he could go in, and indicated, to one side, a dim, empty corridor.

Down it ran a scuffed track— *The famous path* Robert repeated to himself, with mingled regard and irony *followed by stars of stage and screen.*

The main hall, in what had been the body of the church, was laid out like part of an amphitheatre, with curved rows of plain seats descending in tiers to a low platform that served as a stage. A few scarred flats concealed the corner from which the actors entered. Behind them the rear wall was stripped of plaster and paint, providing a mottled background of grey brick; the wooden floor too was bare and worn to a dull greyness. But what most caught Robert's attention, by its prominence, its arch modesty, its symbolic authority, was a folding white chair, bound in green canvas, which stood in the center of the first row of seats: the traditional director's chair, which he guessed was reserved for Lee Strasberg, teacher and taskmaster of the Studio.

Robert had heard much about him. It was said that Strasberg had come by direct line of succession from the great Stanislavsky; certainly Strasberg had been foremost among the actor-director-teachers who'd gradually established the Russian master's *Method* on the American stage. But Strasberg and others had given it their own intense, American emphasis, and years earlier, in New York, standing behind the last row of the orchestra, the cheapest spot in the house, Robert had seen Marlon Brando as Stanley Kowalski in *A Streetcar Named Desire* when, Robert felt, Stanley's brutal and pathetic cry of *Stella! . . . Stella!* had sounded a death knell for all more affected forms of acting.

Brando had been taught by Stella Adler, another *Method* disciple, but he had also attended the Studio, which was quick to claim him. His success made it known; when Marilyn Munroe began taking classes it became a sensation. Then the media began to connect other stars: Julie Harris, James Dean, Shelley Winters, Paul Newman . . . with each report the list grew longer and more impressive. The Studio was besieged with applications, and not only from actors, for its official president was the renowned director Elia Kazan, and it was rumored that sometimes Tennessee Williams watched from the balcony.

Robert looked up there: this morning it was empty. But the seats below were rapidly filling; there seemed a general rush to quit the lobby. Then, sharp on the stroke of eleven, Strasberg entered: a short, greying man with a broad brow and a fixed, fierce expression. In the hush that followed came the sound of the door being locked, barring anyone late; the Studio, supported by the private donations of theatre people, wasn't beholden to its students.

Strasberg took his chair and read from a prepared card that the first scene would be from Pirandello's *I'm Dreaming, But Am I?*

The house lights dimmed, the stage became lit. The players stirred and spoke. And their acting was a revelation. Even in their silences there was such ardent but controlled feeling, such vivid but restrained intensity, that the man and woman on the stage seemed to rise above ordinary human behaviour, as if they stood for a truth that transcended common reality. To Robert they even appeared at times to glow, for they radiated an emotional force that touched their spellbound observers. He felt he was watching something exalted, ideal ... Indeed he was: it was art.

But not flawless art; Strasberg had a good deal to say about it. He asked the players what they had been trying to achieve, heard them out, listened to comments from the audience, and then criticized both the acting and the judgments made on it. He went straight to the point and spared no one; his wit was biting, often cruel. And he liked hectoring. He launched into a talk about theatre that ranged from the classic Greek to Japanese Noh; it ran on for more than an hour; no one dared interrupt him. The great stars sometimes sighed and hung their heads. However, this infliction — for the seats were hard! — helped them to feel that they were serious persons, perhaps worthy of their fame. To Robert every word was precious; he was taking notes.

The class broke for lunch, then resumed. A pretty blonde woman took a seat to the side, near Robert. She wore a simple skirt and sweater, and was without makeup. Someone stretched back and spoke briefly to her, calling her *Marilyn*. Robert stared: it *was* her, whose face and figure were everywhere on magazines and posters. She caught his gaze and seemed shy; he looked shyly away. But her closeness evoked nuances of Nia, and unsure of whom he was responding to, Robert became aroused. Yet that brought back what he'd heard yesterday, in Montreal, that when they'd all driven on to Eldon's, Nia had partied until dawn, and then had failed to get home until the following afternoon. He wondered now, with dismay, what she had done during that time, and with whom. Fortunately the hall darkened; several different short scenes were given, then the final exchange between husband and wife in the last act of *A Doll's House*.

Robert had read Ibsen's play, and seen it on stage, and had been moved by it before. But experiencing it like this, stripped of sets and costumes, its basic man-woman conflicts laid bare, he was overcome by a sense of the sad grandeur of human hope and sacrifice, and betrayal, and then, in spite of everything, again hope. And now hope rose in him, along with a feeling of his potential power as a dramatist, a power he felt was still bottled up, but which could be released by what he had seen here.

When the class rose he tried to speak to Strasberg. But the little popinjay, surrounded by fawning admirers, had an uncanny knack of turning to someone else before Robert could open his mouth. Satrasberg's eyes darted past the stranger as if he were not there. Smarting, Robert suspected that the teacher knew perfectly well who he was and what he wanted; then he understood that it was because he wanted it so badly that he was being rebuffed.

Abruptly he left the room and planted himself outside the front door. His classmates streamed past him, nattering, nudging one another, hurrying to other appointments. These busy people, with their mingling, vaporous breaths, were quite used to strange characters, and uninterested in the mere oddity of someone standing stiffly in the cold. Robert's toes began to pinch; he was afraid his man might have left by another door. But at last Strasberg appeared.

Sir! Robert cried. *I can stay in New York until the end of next week. For three more classes. May I? Please. . .*

Strasberg brushed by, his terrible scowl forcing Robert aside. But as the teacher went down the steps he flung back, with something like a smile, an emphatic *Two more!*

*

They were marvellous classes, seemingly full of instruction. In the course of them Robert heard that the next class, the one denied him, would fall on Strasberg's birthday, for which the Studio was planning a surprise party. However, even by the end of his last class Robert had learnt some lessons a second time, and felt that for now he had absorbed enough, and could, with confidence, return to Montreal.

*

Stanley Lehn-Langbord, the senior editor of the unit, at once arranged a screening for him of the cut picture interlocked with the finished sound track. *It's great* Stanley said, lightly touching Robert's arm and giving off, as he came close, a pleasant scent of mint and eau-de-Cologne. Such currying attention was assuring, for Stanley was not the sort to waste flattery.

The editor had to dash — Eldon was clamoring for a release print. Left alone, Robert leaned back in the plush comfort of the silent theatre. He was anxious but optimistic. Everything seemed full of promise. In New York, he had submitted an application for membership in the Studio, with a wink from the secretary indicating that it might be welcomed. Then here, minutes before, hurrying past him in the hall, Nia had given him, along with her merry *Good morning!*, a look that was wonderfully warm. And the work that all at the Board already admired was about to unroll before him.

39

The screen lit and trumpets sounded. They were followed by drums, by bugle calls and martial airs. The music had verve and taste . . . but was not what he had imagined. And the film, bewilderingly, became less and less of what he had intended. Instead of having the abstract quality of poetry, it had only a stylish semblance of realism, instead of being a study of personality it had become a kind of pageant. The battle scenes, he saw now, had been fatal. *God!* he thought. *It's a travesty!* He felt utterly crushed, humiliated, gouged out.

In his rage he turned against the composer. Learning who it was from Stanley, he rushed to the music department and found the culprit quietly listening to a tape.

Why did you ignore my notes?

The composer stared at him, his pale eyebrows twitching. *W-what notes?*

Robert ran to Eldon's office.

Why didn't you give the composer my notes?

Eldon took the four pages from a drawer and dropped them on his desk. *There was so little time,* he said *I didn't want to confuse him.*

3

The success of *Montcalm*, for which Eldon was showered with compliments, was followed, after a week or two of lingering glow, by a period of sombre strife. The start of the new fiscal year was approaching, when the production chief held the power of giving or refusing funds, and MacCurry decided it was time to check Eldon's rise. He was proud of the television unit, and pleased with the way its performance had discomfited the older producers, but he had no intention of allowing Eldon to upset the basic balance of power, or letting him make a name for himself that would incur general resentment.

So he simply cut the unit's budget. He did it by cutting the estimates of all units and putting the amount to be saved into what was called a fund for special projects, but he made it clear to Eldon — reminding him that *Montcalm* had gone *way over budget* — that the television unit had little hope of getting any of it.

Eldon kept Robert off routine work, urging him to think of *new ideas* — something sure to be another hit — but as each new idea had to be dropped for lack of funds, or put off until the time Eldon called *when we get rolling again,* Robert soon found himself doing nothing. He spent more time at home, made some repairs, and wondered whether to use this interval to move to Montreal. He was one of the few employees who had not yet moved, and the time was nearly up in which the Board would cover relocation expenses. He mentioned it to Myra, but she was still reluctant. His wife liked her work at the Research Council, and would lose it if she left; marrying Robert had already cost her one career. *No one else will carry on my study,* she said *and I happen to think it's important.* Besides, she helped part time in the Information Office, whose urbane head, a biochemist close to retirement, she was particularly fond of. Montreal seemed to offer only an empty exile. *I know travelling there is no fun for you,* she said stubbornly, holding back tears *but in balance it's less than the price I'd have to pay.* And underlying that, both she and he privately felt that the move, with its new arrangements, would oblige them to confront how little the present ones held. They were no longer lovers, except in occasional fits of yearning, and they now shared no common interests.

Initially, it had been their differences that had drawn them together. Myra's father and grandfather were lawyers, her mother a smartly-coiffed matron always busy with cultural committees, and Myra herself, when she and Robert met, had just come back from Massachusetts with a master's degree in biology. Not a subject her family would have chosen, but they were proud of her scholarly discipline and consistent achievement. Moreover Myra was healthy, pretty, and *a good girl* — altogether a package of high worth on the marriage market. But just that made her feel stifled, and in insolvent Robert, who was struggling to be a filmmaker, she had found someone totally unlike what her parents expected. Both young people were barely twenty-one, it was spring; after a few days' giddy flirtation they secretly went away for a weekend. When, to his surprise, Robert deflowered her, he scrupulously declared they would marry.

Despite their sincerity, the ritual never led to an intimate union; even after seven years, each inwardly lived alone. But there was comfort in the sameness of their polite, evasive patterns; like old friends they chatted amiably and duly shared the daily tasks, their meals, their bed. Typically Robert slept while Myra read by the light of a tiny lamp. These nights, though, it was more often he who was awake. When lying beside his sleeping wife he would evoke, in all her remembered wonder, the alluring woman who was always on his mind.

*

For Nia it was a time of developing despair. Day after day Eldon concerned himself less with scripts and scenes than with the verbal battles he fought with MacCurry. At first he came from these meetings vexed and resentful, and would talk angrily of quitting, but as they went on he got to like them, and he would recount each episode to Nia, telling her what MacCurry had said and what cutting remarks he had made in return. Gradually the two men restored the jousting friendship they had enjoyed earlier, but this time on more equal terms, and it was understood that no serious blow would be dealt provided the game was played within the rules. MacCurry hinted that the television unit might not be squeezed much longer, and Eldon's hopes revived. But Nia had grown weary of these clashes of vanity, and of dealing with the routine details Eldon more and more left to her.

It was now the middle of winter, when it seemed the severe cold would never end. The long taxi rides between her home and the office, on icy roads flanked by grimy snow, and then back again through the early darkness — pierced only by obscure gleams against the frosted windows — made her uneasy and left her dejected. She couldn't afford to be always travelling by taxi, but she could not abide the pressure of suburban train schedules and the push of crowds. She fretted about money and indeed often had none before the next pay cheque was due. At times Gwendolyn had to lend her some with which to make her way home.

She wondered whether coming to the Board had been a mistake. She remembered New York, with its ample income and outward glamour, where friends had been eager to step in and help. However, she had needed the change. She could have looked for a TV network job in Toronto, but living there would have been less quiet, and even more expensive. Her rented house was adequate, its trees and setting by the river, soothing. But problems within were multiplying. Her mother was suffering sinusitis, and making the most of it. Every day she managed to wring guilt from sighing *Dear, I know you must go to work . . .* Joel was unhappy at school, where his easy familiarity with the arts and literate language was resented. Considered by other pupils a big city swell, he was often picked on. Pranks were played with his books; his pencils and eraser scattered. Nia had bought him a new pair of white sneakers for exercise class; they were stolen and discovered a day later in the janitor's storage room, one smeared with soot in a trash can, the other hanging from the shut-off handle of an overhead pipe. These petty persecutions had caused her to see the principal, a fat fellow with little steel rimmed spectacles, who was so taken with her, so flattering and soppy, it made her slightly sick.

And she wasn't at all well. Her shoulders ached and sometimes her back; she attributed it to stress and fatigue. She felt life was beginning to lean on her like an irresistible weight against which her abilities, looks, charm, wit scarcely had the force of feathers. As for Robert, the prospect of him now seemed to have been a sand castle that dark waves had washed away.

*

He began coming to the office only when he had to, because staying overnight meant asking someone to put him up. He had to bear the cost of the fare from Ottawa, and tried to avoid paying for a hotel as well. He was loath to spend money on comforts, and liked to make do with less than others would; rather than indulge in a bus ride he would trudge for blocks through the snowy streets carrying his heavy government briefcase. Sometimes he walked because he had given part of his pocket change to a panhandler — he could never pass one without remorse, but secretly he resented it, and his scant bounty often brought only a sneer. He was still the least paid of the unit's directors — MacCurry was wary of encouraging mavericks — and though Eldon promised to get him a raise as soon as conditions improved, he stuck to his chary habits. Even when Nia borrowed two dollars from him in the cafeteria, refusing to let him buy lunch, he remembered the amount and half hoped she would repay it. However, he followed her with his eyes whenever he could, and nursed her image when apart.

Between them there had come to be a tense apathy. Now that she was busier than ever, and he idle, Robert felt unmanned and even more outclassed. He imagined her home to be a place of fashion and her evenings filled with the attentions of handsome, amusing men. Moreover, she seemed reluctant to encourage him; she seemed to be skirting situations in which they might be alone. Yet sometimes when he paused in what he was saying she would knowingly finish the sentence, and once, from the gloom of an editing room, while showing Stanley the exact point at which to cut a scene, Robert said, with a snap of his fingers, *Now!* and then looking up saw Nia stopped in the hall, staring in at him, as if startled.

They were like beached creatures, waiting for a tide.

*

One morning in March it began snowing heavily, and when the workday ended the city was a fairyland. Snow had settled on branches, wires, chimney tops; it lay along ledges and draped the hoods of blinking traffic lights. It swirled from big trucks and cars churning through drifts — and still it fell, obscuring the badges on the fur hats of policemen and whitening the shoulders of people walking home. Nia was advised to stay at the Board until the roads could be cleared, and Robert, who was there that day, found he had no reason to leave early. When everyone else had gone, Nia said *Do you think we could make it to the corner? — and have a drink —*

Good idea Robert said. *But, uh . . . I don't know if . . .*

Oh, I have money — ! But when she had emptied her purse, and he his wallet, and they had put aside her fare home, there was less than the price of a single round. *I keep them in business* Nia said. *Maybe this once they'll give me credit —*

Well, I don't have to drink. . . . I'd be happy to watch you.

Oh, really — she said, smiling. *That could go to your head —*

It would! he thought, already feeling tipsy, and delighted to have even his silliness teased. He had seldom been so excited. The smell of her cigarette seemed an intensely sensual scent, her nearness tantalizing. He knew this night was heaven sent, that he should recklessly spend, do, go with her wherever it might take them . . . and for seconds wild fancies of escape, flight, sudden fulfilment flashed. But they were soon crushed by the crippling constraint of being married, and by the horrible, cramping necessity of counting cost.

Maybe — they both began.

Nia laughed. *I was going to say,* she went on *maybe there's still somebody in the building I can borrow from —*

Or I can Robert said. *But listen, what about Nigel's? It's where I'm staying.*

Nia's eyes widened. Nigel continually sought her company. To Robert he had confessed that if she'd have him he would marry her in an instant. And Robert knew that Nigel, who was a linguist, was conveniently at some consular reception.

But he lives downtown, doesn't he?

They were silently pondering this problem when there were footsteps in the hall and a man, who had been about to go by, stopped in the doorway. It was the actor who had played Wolfe! He was back at the Board for another job, and had a car, and was driving down, if he could, to keep a dinner date . . .

∗

In Nigel's kitchen, the liquor cupboard was full. *What would you like?* Robert called. *There's some premium rye.*

Rot gut! said Nia. *I'll have scotch if there's any. Or rum if there isn't —*

There was scotch, almost a full bottle. Robert was pouring it when the apartment door opened and Nigel, returning early because of the storm, stomped in heavily, scattering snow. At the sight of Nia he exclaimed *Ah, a royal visit!* He liked to call her *the queen,* saying she ruled his life. In truth she had twice, when he was in trouble, given him advice and restored his confidence. *Glad to see my man is serving* he added.

Nigel White was cute in a way that usually made people smile, sometimes sourly, when they saw him coming. He was short and tended to be plump, but his body sagged as much as it bulged. With his rounded head, sad eyes, and floppy blond hair he was like a mournful clown hugging a core of hysterical mirth; with any prodding his lips would lose their composure and allow irrepressible giggles, which often led to the whole of him shaking with laughter.

Like Nia, he came from Manitoba, from St. Boniface, where his parents still kept a small corner store, and he had learnt his first French from the urchins who'd tormented him in the street. But he had seen in the language a road to a romantic world, and had polished it so well through his university years that he was taken on by the Board's French unit as a writer for English versions. Lately he had also written original scripts, but as yet none had been produced.

∗

I envy you guys Nigel said. For some time they'd been sitting on the faded flowers of his frayed living room rug, with the lights out,

46

sipping scotch. The bottle was nearly empty. *Nia, you're wrong, your unit isn't going to pieces. You're turning out some of the best films being made.*

All those were started months ago Nia said. *Now we don't have a damn thing that's new — I mean in ideas. Dear God, is no one else pained by platitudes? Eldon doesn't seem to be, anymore — It's driving me crazy —*

For some time Robert had been silent, suffering from the gnawing awareness that he'd allowed Nia, and this evening, to escape him, as if she had stepped into everyday muck and become mired with Nigel. And her words were raking his idleness, raising that humiliating wall already keeping him out. Trying to climb it, he said *Yeah, Eldon's distracted. If he'd let me direct . . .*

Then you might make them a little better Nia said. *But not enough. Nobody could, with what we have.* She yielded to the feeling of betrayal. The Board's seeming promise of helping to make exciting films had gone painfully awry. *Anway —* she said listlessly, looking at Robert *he's thinking of something for you. Oops — I shouldn't have mentioned that. Even if it happens — it's weeks away —*

Well, there you go Nigel said. *Things are still happening. Nothing happens with me. I'm being treated like I don't exist. It's this French nationalist thing. They think one of them should be doing my job.* He looked at Nia. *I'd love to be working with you.*

She said nothing. Nigel refilled her glass. He had done it several times without words, as if he and she were a settled couple, at home, entertaining a friend.

It was galling, yet Robert could only blame himself for bringing her here. He should somehow have found money, a romantic place, a flying carpet! But instead . . . Myra was sitting on him. He had earlier slipped into Nigel's study, where the phone was, and called her — it was Friday — to say the weather was keeping him in Montreal. Like it or not, he *was* married, and Nia, he felt, must have misgivings about it. What else could he expect? Considering the magnetic, almost magical way they'd been drawn to each other, an ordinary adulterous affair, as much as he could imagine one, would be unworthy of them both. He wanted something — something sublime, to soar them over the barriers between them.

The night was luminous; a faint light, enough for them to see one another, had been coming through the large old-fashioned windows. Robert turned to stare up at the heavens, as if there he might find the high purpose he was seeking. The snow had stopped; the sky was clearing. A few stars sparkled.

Nigel switched on the kitchen light and began rattling a pan. *Anybody else need ballast?* he called.

Here! Nia cried. *I'll do that — !*

At once they became lively, glad to dispel the sombre mood the talk of work had left. Nia quickly fried some liver and onions, Nigel sliced bread and pickles, Robert laid out the cutlery. At Nia's command they carried the table from the kitchen into the living room and put candles on it. Nigel brought out a new gallon jug of Saint Emillion.

They sat down to supper hungry and a little drunk.

The food might have sobered them but Nigel kept refilling the wine glasses. *I dunno,* he said *what I have to do to get my ideas accepted.*

You could try expressing them truthfully Nia said.

Nigel stared.

Nigel, dear — she said *listen to me. You're Jewish, you're from the prairies — you're trapped in a difficult situation. You care — God knows you care — But none of that shows in your work —*

Nigel, reddening, sat still.

What's your Jewish name? Robert said.

Natan. Nathan the other said miserably.

Nia shot Robert an angry look. His picking on Nigel, particularly when the poor fellow was vulnerable, infuriated her. She understood Robert's work frustration, but indifference to another's feelings was insufferable. Jewish . . . ! That Robert was Jewish she'd at once guessed. Her husband hadn't been, but Jews had been prominent throughout her life in radio, movies, the music business. And as friends. As lovers. It simply wasn't an issue. But she couldn't bear anyone being petty or mean. *You make me so impatient* — she said *all you clever, creative men* — *You know everything* — *except what's important* —

Both saw the sudden blaze in her eyes. It gave a sense of something charged, ominous. It had that same heightened intensity Robert had seen at the Studio.

Don't you know that blaming others is wasting precious time? I'm so sick of people being small and missing the point. People who can't rise above competition — *who destroy everything in their clamouring* — *who waste talent* — *and waste the women who get caught and neglected* —

Her hands were waving; her hair, which had been upswept, was coming down. Under the words of her outburst she was mixing in the abortion, her divorce, betrayal by the Board, all the resistance to restoring her life. She didn't care. She was tipsy. And at the same time reaching for something.

What Nigel said in a low voice *is the point?*

The point? The point is that there's nothing behind all this but the grave, but worms. Our time is so short — *to create* — *to achieve* — *to love. Without art, poetry, love there's nothing. Only emptiness.*

There were tears edging her voice. She could feel that her listeners were unhinged. They had never heard bitterness from her. *You have to be menshen.* She had adopted the Yiddish word. *Not boys. Not conniving, competitive boys. But* — *Oh, what's the use! It only makes me crazy! Real men* — *men who know themselves and are true to that* —*and their women* — *are few and far between. Oh God* — she said shuddering *the world is loaded with boys!*

The two of them were stunned. Robert, sitting across from her, was thunderstruck.

He had watched her hair flowing down, the beautiful half-drunk face with aliveness throbbing from it, and felt that her accusations were at the same time a hymn to joy, to the possibilities of being alive, of living a life of sensitivity and passion beyond anything he had ever known. A real man! And he felt that in all his years before this moment he had been dead, and that out of it he stirred, that she had wakened the poet in him, the dramatist and the man.

What a great woman! he thought.

A strong smell of coffee was coming from the kitchen. Nigel got up and went to take the pot off the stove.

Lowering her eyes, as if to rest and recover, Nia did not see so much as sense Robert's sudden gesture. Almost in tears himself, he wanted to say by it that he *knew,* that in a basic sense he understood all she had implied, and that it mattered more to him than anything else he had ever experienced. He reached out his hand, she met it with hers, and for an exhilarating moment, across the table, they clasped hands.

Nigel came back with the coffee and cups. From the street below came the sound of a car driving by. Nigel went to the windows. Across the small park he could see snowplows moving freely on the avenue, their blinking blue lights sending reassuring signals. He reported that the roads appeared to be open. It had grown late; he said he would drive Nia home.

After coffee he brought her coat, then went to put on his own. Nia's was of white wool, fashionably old-fashioned, with a high collar. Robert helped her on with it, and then facing her, with a hand on each side of the collar he turned it up around her head, and hearing Nigel still wrapping himself in the hall, quickly kissed her. To his surprise she returned the kiss, and the sweet caress of her lips was the most tender touch he'd ever known. Overwhelmed, he could still feel its softness long after she'd left. Collapsing on his cot in Nigel's study, he lay staring into the darkness.

If she wants a real man, he thought *I will be that man!*

4

The next morning he rented an apartment, but cautiously, by the week. It was a tiny ground-floor bachelor at the back of a drab brick walkup, one of a look-alike row that had been hastily thrown up after the war to bury illicit profits and bypass taxes. Robert's single room was a strange brownish pink, with a cramped bathroom on one side of the entrance door and a scruffy kitchen unit on the other. The only window, hung with a dusty venetian blind, looked out on a grimy lane. However, the building was fairly clean, quiet, and away from the usual haunts of Film Board people.

He told his wife he had everywhere used up his welcome and the apartment would be cheaper than a hotel. From home he brought a few chipped dishes and some old cutlery; Myra urged him to take sheets and blankets as well, but he firmly refused, saying they were too bulky for the train. He didn't want to mar the purity of the bed to which he meant to take Nia.

It was a three-quarter continental, lent to him, along with a little table and two mismatched chairs, by the Director-Cameraman who had been kind before; the lady of the velvet choker, finally fed up with her lover's philandering, had departed for good, leaving him with more furniture than he needed. He and Robert moved the four pieces roped to the roof of a Film Board station wagon that was filled with equipment. At Woolworth's Robert picked out a can of paste wax, a bulb for the ceiling light socket, and two small clear glasses. Then he spent half a day choosing the bedding, going from one department store to another, then back, anxiously weighing the prices against what seemed most appealing. At last he bought one foam-rubber pillow, two sets of white sheets and pillowcases, a pale blue blanket, and two thin towels.

*

Over several evenings, standing on the table, he washed the apartment's ceiling and walls, which lightened their colour. Then he washed and began to wax the floor. He had it half done when, without warning, his chance came.

In the cafeteria, Nia was last in the lineup, and he quickly stepped in behind her. The room was assaulted by sunlight, both shining from the sky and shot back from cars parked in rows below. For lunch the choice was reheated shepherd's pie, made worse by fat stains, or gray pork, with what the sign said was raisin sauce. *Looks more like melted grease* Nia whispered.

Let's get out of here he said, and at once she nodded and left. Highly excited, he caught sight of a friendly technician calmly eating, and rushing over through the glare tersely asked for the use of his car. Thinking it an emergency, the fellow tossed him the keys.

*

Robert hadn't driven for more than a year, and with Nia beside him he was tense and flurried. First a wheel climbed the curb as he rounded a corner, then, stealing a glance at her, he almost hit the car stopped ahead, and when the light turned green he stalled — it was standard shift — and had trouble starting. Nia quietly asked if he had a licence. But she said nothing, nor showed any surprise, when he parked in front of the apartment building and told her he had a place there.

It's a cell she said, and sat on the edge of the bed. The sheet was turned back in a precise band across the blanket, which was neatly folded at the corners and tightly tucked in.

It's all I need he replied gruffly, as if it were a woodsman's cabin in the wilderness. *Would you like a martini?* He had heard she did, and had stocked the ingredients. But he'd never mixed one before.

Best I ever tasted. She sipped, saying little. She was wearing a tailored navy blue suit, with a straight skirt and a jacket whose plunging lapels crossed on her bare chest just above the point of cleavage. She finished her drink and he made another mix, to which she silently added more gin.

Robert was becoming giddy. This was the scene he had antici-
pated, but in his rehearsals he'd been glib, grave, dramatic; now
that she was alone before him, within reach, and more beautiful
than ever, he was unhinged. He couldn't compose his lines or find
where to begin. Standing and facing her, his back against the wall,
he swallowed, bit his lip, and finally blurted out *I've been meaning
to speak to you.* She looked at him, waiting. *About the way you're
personal with everyone . . . at work, I mean. It's not professional. It
causes problems.* This wasn't quite what he'd intended. The tone
was petulant, instead of judicious and advising.

Nia was only half listening to this ritual. The alcohol, as it
always did, had eased somewhat the weight of disappointment
with work, worry about her mother's health, her son's well being,
the household bills without end, and worst, being inwardly so
solitary. She was secure in her sense of self, but felt frighteningly
weak against the accumulating weight of her immediate world.
Watching Robert, she saw in him, despite his fumbling, a creativity and vigour that could provide needed strength. Even his naivety
was somewhat touching. *Yes . . .* she said.

*With your looks, and intelligence, and the kind of empathy you
have, which gets to a guy . . .*

Yes . . .

He broke off. Nothing was going as planned. His punch line
had been carefully prepared, and he'd meant to deliver it in a low
and trembling voice, but he really was tight, choked, shaking. He
was starting to sweat. *Take me — I'm — I'm on the verge . . . of . . .
of falling in love with you.*

Yes.

He sat down beside her. Their heat enveloped them. She sank
into it with a sigh. He embraced her and they kissed, their faces
hot. Nia lowered her head to his shoulder.

I'm going to lean on you so hard, she said *you'll be sorry.*

∗

That was all. They'd had to hurry back, because Nia had an appointment with a writer from Toronto. It was after five, and she had already left, when Robert realized he hadn't arranged for her to come again to the apartment. The next morning he slipped into her office. *Tonight?*

She nodded impatiently, as if it were understood.

*

He went ahead by bus; she followed in a taxi. They made a meal of what there was: canned mushroom soup, cheese and crackers, instant coffee. And martinis; this time Nia mixed them. Then they lay on the bed and kissed and talked. It was amazing to Robert, as he held her in his arms, how comfortable he felt, and how naturally Nia understood him, and he her. Often their mouths simply remained joined, allowing, for a long time, the feelings of each to flow into the other. This too, though new to him, seemed entirely natural.

He was thrilled by her shapely body, her soft breasts pressed against him. Each sensation seemed fresh, as if he had never experienced them before. *I feel as if I'm born again* he said.

How old are you — ?

Twenty-eight.

Abruptly she pushed away from him, her eyes darkening. *Then I'm too old for you — I'm almost forty.*

He hid his shock. She looked young. There were a few gray hairs, but he'd supposed, from what Nigel had said, and the fact of her son, that she might be as much as thirty-two or three. Five would have seemed extreme. Yet she was so beautiful, and, he guessed, rich in loves, in friends, in knowledge of the great world. Pulling her close again, he said *Yes* and kissed her.

She paused. *You're always so solemn — I thought you were nearer my age.*

Robert smiled. *I guess in spirit I am. I've always liked being with people older than I am.*

How old's your wife?

54

My age.

Nia lay silent. With his arms around her, his lips occasionally touching her temple, terrified of what she was thinking, Robert was afraid to disturb her. After a while he wondered if she was asleep. But her eyes were partly open.

She was remembering how initially she'd resisted this attraction, how often she had considered what might follow — the difficulties at work, the inroads into her time, the messiness of his being married. But throughout it all she'd thought of them as equals, with freedom of choice; it hadn't once crossed her mind that she was opening herself to the only threat she couldn't do anything about. At last, with a sigh, she stirred. *What time is it?*

Robert looked at his watch. *After one.*

Then I have to go —

Do you? His dismay was real. Desire flared now.

Yes — she said, untangling herself from him. *I didn't make any arrangement about not going. Why didn't you make love to me earlier?*

I didn't feel like it then. It was true; it had been enough just to hold her. He was now fully roused, but secretly not sorry, because, having been unwilling to presume, he was without a condom. And too, he was a bit uneasy about that test, and rather glad to leave it for the weekend, when she promised to come again.

*

On Saturday morning he cleaned the apartment, finished waxing, and carefully polished the dark floor boards. Then for lunch he ate some sardines and crackers, shaved, bathed, and dressed in spotless clothing. And wanting Nia to find him at work, he sat at the table and spread out his Actors Studio notes. Now, at this distance, the written points seemed obvious. It was what he had tried to do before the Studio, without having a name for it. But when another long hour had passed, and then another, and the afternoon was dwindling to dusk, he became increasingly frantic.

What could be keeping her? He was balked by knowing none of the details of her private life. He imagined an accident on the road, and thought wildly of phoning her home, but was afraid her son or mother might answer. He felt in constant danger of exposure, yet was ashamed of his cowardice and invented scenes in which he bravely made the call, declared his love, and rushed to take his place beside her. Then he thought of pretending to be an out-of-town writer who . . . But making any call meant going out of the building to find a pay phone, and Nia might arrive while he was gone. It didn't occur to him to leave a note, or his door unlocked.

Finally, when he'd given up hope, had resigned himself to a life of stern solitude, and had already rehearsed the look and recriminating words he would use when he next saw her, there came, curiously, a soft knock. He flung open the door — and there she was, startlingly beautiful, her arms full of parcels!

Good God, she exclaimed *I thought I'd never get here!*

She placed on the table a pot of flowering hyacinth, whose fragrance was already pervading the room. *Everything — everything delayed me — !* she said, and while she told him of the day's small disasters she took from her wicker basket a foil-wrapped cooked ham, and crisp greens, and oil and limes and a bottle of wine and a whole round fresh bread, and some sweet butter. And she had brought an iron frying pan and a wooden salad bowl, and candle-holders, candles, salt and pepper shakers, and paper napkins. And from the pockets of her coat came two wineglasses, an ash tray, a nutcracker, a handful of chestnuts, and a clump of garlic.

*

He watched her make a salad — of lettuce and parsley, oil and garlic and lime juice, and a little salt and pepper. It was so clean and smooth, melting and delicious, it reminded him of that first, now sacred, kiss at Nigel's. He said *I didn't know salads and kisses could be like this.*

Much can Nia said. She was happy. She'd decided she needed this boy, and . . . perhaps loved him. As she prepared their plates she hummed the opening bars of a popular ballad, then began to sing the words in a sweet, low, slightly husky voice.

Robert was enchanted; his paltry world had been transformed into this state of delightful excitement in which Nia made everything simple, pretty, perfumed, tuneful, and, when she kissed him or tucked a morsel into his mouth, so good tasting. At times, moved by wonder, he tentatively reached out towards her, and was always rewarded by a smiling look that promised something deeper than pleasure.

They lit candles and put out the light. The room, with its warm shadows and scent of hyacinth, had become magical. They ate slowly, satisfyingly. And Robert, intoxicated by joy and wine, reveled in the richness of all Nia had brought him, and in the forms of her lovely body, which, difficult as it was to believe, would soon be his.

She undressed in front of him, unembarrassed. She was superb!

Have you ever he said *thought of modelling brassieres?*

Until recently I never had to wear one. At least not for support.

She had, though, taken one off. And when she slid into bed she modestly covered herself to the waist, and lying back with her hair spread on the pillow, waited for him like an elegant offering.

But when he tried to caress her, she squirmed. *I don't like to be touched* she said. *Just make love to me.*

She had always insisted on that. Each man had been puzzled, but finding her unyielding, had complied.

Oh, why? Robert said.

She shrugged. *It's the way I am. Ever since I was little. I don't mind giving myself — really, I like it. I like to — to give. Please, just do it —*

It was her earliest bad memory. She'd been three. It had also been a Saturday, when her parents were busy at their movie house. The neighbor's son, a shy, doting boy of fourteen, was baby sitting. He'd paused in reading from a children's book to tell her how pretty she was. Then had tentatively laid his hand on her bare knee. And slowly, his face blushing from increasing excitement, his fingertips felt up along her inner thigh. They were finally pressing on her panties when she'd said *Don't* — and he at once desisted. But since then any fondling instantly evoked those creeping fingers, and an involuntary small shudder of disgust. *Darling,* she said now *please, just do it.*

However, Robert hesitated. Propped on his elbow, his arm across her, with his hand still near her hip, where her twisting had thrown it off, he waited for his thoughts to settle. It seemed incredible that this woman — whom he'd dreamt of for months — was now here in his arms, completely nude, yet encased in a kind of invisible armour that rejected, humiliated, even threatened him. He knew there was a lot he was guilty of, but he felt that however base he might otherwise be, his touch was pure and came from what was best and most wholesome in him. If he yielded, it would be fatal self-betrayal. It would, with her, forever unman him.

Dearest, Nia said *I want to be made love to. It's only the touching I don't like.*

You will he said, and deliberately moved his hand onto her belly, then up to her breasts.

She stiffened in anger, but he went on caressing, and then cradling and kissing her. Although afraid he would lose her, he steadily continued.

Nia had never encountered such stubbornness, nor so tender a touch. Her first impulse had been to get up and leave, but Robert's hand had an authority — like, she thought, his directing — that she was reluctant to disrupt.

Finally, at first imperceptibly, her tautness lessened. When he had all but given up hope, she sighed and let go. And when he raised himself to enter her she started to tremble.

But then he broke off and began fumbling under the mattress.

What is it — ?

I have something . . .

No! she cried. *If we have to use something — I will use it!*

But nothing was used that night.

*

Their joining surprised them. It was oddly familiar, mellower, and much, much more passionate than either had thought possible. Wildly passionate, in both sound and movement.

Afterward, when they were sweetly draining, Nia said *I swear I was on the ceiling— Did I make a lot of noise?*

Some. Fearful of others hearing, Robert had stopped her mouth with his.

She took his hand. *That — like that — I swear — never happened before.*

Nor to me. But you were . . . wow . . .

A woman doesn't age that way she said.

*

Nia had told her mother she was going to country friends for the weekend. She and Robert had the Sunday before them, and it was bright with sunshine and fresh-fallen snow.

It's gorgeous! she cried.

Robert, carried away, said *Well . . . why don't we go out!*

But what with breakfast and bathing, caresses, kisses, dawdling and dressing, it was three o'clock before they took a cab to the foot of the mountain. Robert secretly fretted about the roundabout route the driver seemed to be taking, but this first taxi ride with Nia gave him such a cavalier feeling that he freely added a dime to the ten-percent tip.

The air was snow scented, balmy; the sun sailed gaily in the blue western sky. The path to the summit was full of lively people walking in both directions. Colourfully dressed children, their parkas and tuques sporting tassels and pompoms, were sledding and rolling on the sparkling slopes. Nia took Robert's arm. They passed an old gentleman leaning on a cane who smiled at her and inclined his head; then a group of boys rapidly approaching parted ranks and made way for them, though some of the boys stared and even looked back.

Everyone sees how beautiful she is Robert thought, and proudly pressed her closer.

Nia was used to being looked at. Often, over the years, people she encountered had asked if she wasn't this or that movie star. She might have been — her screen tests had been admired — but for her husband's jealous insistence that she leave public life to him.

She had on lipstick but no other makeup. Her bare skin could still stand up to the sharp winter sun, but she knew that her face, so long unblemished, was starting to wear. A slight puffiness was developing under her eyes, laugh lines were extending, little hollows were forming at the corners of her nose. These signs of aging, as yet unnoticeable to others, she greeted with calm regret, like visitors coming to stay who were expected but might have delayed their arrival a little longer.

*

The ascent grew steep; they had to stop twice to let Nia catch her breath, but when they reached the lookout she said *God, it was worth it* — Below them the spires of the city shimmered in a golden haze rising from the sun-warmed roofs, and the wide flat river, gleaming greyly in the distance, lay curved against the low bank of purplish smoke hanging over the southern shore. She thought of all those people, living more or less normal lives, sheltered in their protective houses. And suddenly she felt unprotected, vulnerable, in danger of emotional violence. *Darling,* she cried, seizing Robert's arm *let's go home!*

But considering the time, she parted from him at the first taxi stand and took a cab to her own home instead.

*

They settled into a pleasant routine. Once or twice each week Nia left the Board ahead of Robert and had dinner ready by the time he arrived at the apartment. They dined simply and superbly, by candlelight, with flowers on the table; and then, half smiling, politely, without haste, they would undress . . . and come together in a tender, quivering, fervent embrace.

Afterwards they were talkative, and their conversation seemed to reach its most interesting point just when Nia had to get up and return to her island.

She had told her mother and son she was very busy those nights, and they understood that she was reserving them for some other part of her life. But when Robert pressed her for a second weekend, she said *I can't. Those are my family days — I have to be there for them.* So on weekends he too usually went home, to Ottawa.

*

For the first few hours there he would inwardly still be in the small pink room, talking and eating and making love with Nia. But the immediacy of a cracked window pane, a dripping tap, or tiles that had come off the bathroom wall would gradually bring him to the reality around him. By suppertime on Saturday, when he had finished the repairs, and had showered, and had lounged in the wing chair looking at the local paper, he was once more back with his wife. She would have ready a meal of lamb stew, or baked fish, or another of his favourite dishes, and she'd try to make herself equally appealing, because increasingly she was becoming uneasy about his weeks away. However long he'd been away before, there'd always been only her and their home to return to, and then they'd resumed, with little sense of interruption, and with the assurance of continuing in them together, their familiar, equable, if make-do, roles. But the apartment seemed to have given him a life from which she was wholly excluded. Once, when she suggested coming to Montreal for a performance of *Don Juan* by the Theatre du Nouvéâu Monde, and staying overnight, he said *No! It's just a work pad. I have papers all over the place. I don't want things disturbed!* It hurt, but she felt she had brought this about by her refusal to move. Later, in bed, when she stroked his back, though he remained rigid for a while, he then slowly turned to her.

But on Sunday morning after breakfast Robert would open his briefcase and bury himself in a script until it was time to take a streetcar to the station and board the Montreal train.

He now had the assignment Nia had alluded to at Nigel's. It had originated with the Commissioner's Planning Committee, and MacCurry had referred it to Eldon, who'd declared, without much opposition, that Robert was the best person to carry it out. An experiment, it consisted of filming a story with both an English and a French cast, using the same lighting and camera setups for each. The idea was to end up with two original films, rather than an original in one language and a version in the other. The Committee would then evaluate their quality and cost as compared to the usual practice.

MacCurry had a particular interest. Instead of calling on Nigel, or one of the few other bilingual writers at the Board, he had compelled Eldon, by way of agreeing to some concession the producer wanted, to commission the scripts from an outside drinking buddy whom MacCurry had taken to seeing in lieu of losing Eldon from his weekly gathering. But the resulting screenplays, though sincere, and in no obvious way objectionable, and which Eldon, with a little prodding, had accepted, were, unfortunately, rather pedestrian. The production chief was worried that the failure of this project, in which he was dealing directly with the Commissioner, would open him to a charge of patronage. Eldon, for his part, had avoided responsibility by giving Robert, and letting it be known that he had, a completely free hand in everything to do with both films.

*

By late April the films were in rehearsal, and one night Robert left the studio feeling not only satisfied, but amused. He had made changes to the scripts, yet the basic story, of a countryman corrupted by the city, remained a sentimental urban-evil drama, and though the English cast was performing it earnestly, the French actors were treating it as something no sensible person would take seriously. They were playing it more like a Molière farce than a

Thomas Hardy tragedy. The Committee, Robert knew, would be surprised that despite the same scenes and dialogue the two films were quite different, but he believed that each, reflecting its cultural bias, worked best in its own way. And would show, better than anything anyone could say, how inherently absurd the whole theory was.

He walked leisurely to the bus stop. The air was mild, and the breeze, blowing from the west, towards the refineries, seemed to carry the smell of moist earth and fresh shoots. The sun had just set, leaving an afterglow of pink and gold, and a single star, and then a second one, was twinkling in the luminous sky. And all this beauty suffused into the body, breasts, mouth and eyes of Nia, who was awaiting him.

*

The meal she served was exquisite: pan-browned, aged and chopped steak lightly garnished with garlic and bacon, tender new potatoes, carrots and asparagus, and some of her great, simple salad. Then cheese and grapes, and to go with it all, a bottle of rich, clear red Burgundy. Robert insisted on paying for the food, but Nia invariably spent much more than she confessed to. He couldn't imagine a more womanly woman, or a better mistress.

After dinner they moved, as always, to the bed. They were lying languidly when Nia said *Darling* — *Why do you never call me that?*
What?
Darling. Or anything like it —
Well, I'm not much given to fancy phrases . . . But such cloddish denial was too much even for him. Embarrassed, he stole a glance at her. Luckily, she was looking away.
You may not love me now — she said *but you will one day* —
Just because I don't say I love you doesn't mean that I don't.
Yes it does.
He was silent, annoyed with her for creating an issue when everything had been going so well. He wished she'd calm down

and just let them be as they were. Yet he had to admit that from the time she was his, he'd resisted further commitment. But what a change: *she* was asking him for love!

He moved closer and gently embraced her. *What does it matter* he said *whether or not I love you, if you love me . . .*

She tore herself from his arms. *No, I know that knife —* she cried. *I don't want it — !* Then she sat up and wept uncontrollably.

He was astonished at the force of her feeling. But it irritated him. Why was she making such a drama of it. Besides, he was anxious about the sound of her sobbing. *Nia, sh-h-h* he said. *It'll be all right . . .*

No — she gasped. *I've done it again! I've made another horrible mistake —* And she clutched at the futility of her life, in which almost every time she had given herself, like an unconditional gift, it had been squandered.

You haven't. Anyway, look, it's not your fault. I fell for you . . .

She shot him a sharp sideways glance. *What makes you think —* she said *any of it was your idea —*

That was unfair, he felt. It saddened, flattered, and angered him. It was as if all he had felt for her, about her, was suddenly without worth. He got to his knees and confronted her. *Nia,* he said sternly *look at me . . .* She stayed as she was. *Nia,* he said. *Please . . . Please look at me.*

She raised her face, and in her tear stained eyes he saw only his own treason.

Damn it! he thought. *What does she want of me?*

Then he remembered she had wanted a real man.

*

Nia huddled in the corner of the car, her high collar up around her head. She was cold. Before seeing a cruising cab they'd had to walk several blocks in the late night, she with only thin pumps on the icy pavement. And the tearful time that led up to their leaving the apartment had been chilling too. She was wet eyed, remembering other women twisting on the blade of being unloved, with

64

the indifferent male completely in control. Never, she had vowed, would that happen to her. Always before, at the first hint she had swiftly cut her bonds and fled. Yet, with Robert, she'd stayed. Held by shock and hurt, and the insidious hope that something could be saved. And he had all the while grovelled, pleaded, cajoled, weakening her with a mawkish wooing of words, touches, squeezes, hugs. And even when feeling that knife already plunged into her, feeling anger and contempt, she'd felt strangely tied and — God help her — ruefully loving. *But such a child!* she said, half aloud.

Eh? the driver said.

Sorry. I was talking to myself.

He nodded. They both reverted to silence. The bleak darkness stretched ahead.

*

Walking back, Robert felt the reproach in Nia's wan smile when he'd pressed her hands on parting. How idiotically he'd behaved! But anything was better than the humiliation of losing her. And why his reluctance to love? He'd been so possessed, impassioned, inspired by her. *Maybe* . . . he thought, but all maybes were mere evasion, and he knew it. No, he realized, love would mean accepting Nia as a person, instead of merely adoring her as an admired object: glamorous woman, queen, beloved — something one could walk away from. *I'll really have to grow up* he said softly, aloud.

It was a fine phrase and he turned it over in his mind as he went to bed, trying to think of how he could become worthier of her. But the bed was still warm and the sheets gave off her fragrance; his healthy body was soon lulled and he slipped from wakefulness in mid thought.

5

The onrush of spring had its usual heady effects. Eldon saw a chance to increase at one stroke his power, independence and income. He called a meeting of his directors and told them it was time to act.

The meeting was held in secret, on a Sunday, in the living room of a director who'd recently remarried. His new young wife had left coffee and cake for the guests, and urged on by her anxious husband, had gone to visit her mother. Robert was relieved, then disturbed, to see that Nia wasn't present; nor had she been invited.

The windows were open and the inspiriting sun shone in on the assembled men. There were seven of them, apart from Eldon, and in the work of the Board each had achieved some distinction. They thought of themselves as a select group, whose opinions carried intrinsic weight.

Eldon spoke darkly of their *deplorable situation.* Despite some easing of budget restraints the unit hadn't regained its former portion of the Board's total production budget, and there'd been no increases in salary. He said he'd twice asked for a raise for Robert — *who's still getting zilch,* only to be told it would have to wait. And meanwhile raises were being given in other units!

They've become used to us splitting our guts Eldon said. *Now they take us for granted.*

He well knew nothing could rile his directors more. They were all veterans of hard productions. Each of them had often willingly worked all night, or missed meals, or carried on when ill, and they expected these sufferings to be remembered and esteemed. The figures they cut, the excitement they stirred, were as important to them as what they were paid — more, they liked to think, for they frequently muttered that if it came to money, they could *always go to Hollywood.*

Eldon outlined his plan. As a group, with him as their spokesman, they would tell MacCurry they must have more money for the unit and higher salaries for themselves. If he failed to come through, they would resign. Eldon would resign first, then each of the others. Faced with that, the Board would have to concede, because it could not have its television production come to a halt in mid season.

Their nervous host, who'd been waiting to refill the cake plate, raised his hand. *But what if the brass see it as a precedent?*

Yeah said another. *A bad one.*

Bingo! said Eldon. *They're bound to. Then we form a private company and contract with them.*

God damn! Really?

Sure Eldon replied. *Same work, more money, and much more independence.*

Robert had at first wondered whether he could escape what was coming on the ground that his current films had put him outside the unit, but it was too flimsy a pretext. He still formally answered to Eldon and the producer would certainly resent it. However, when the plan was revealed, its stunning simplicity awed him. He'd seen that exceptional advances in life were seldom the result of patient effort, but rather of a sort of lightning luck, and he suddenly felt all the frustrations of his position, and began to hope that this bold move might be a breakthrough.

Eldon was immediately nominated, seconded, and acclaimed president of the new company.

Now, cocks, we keep this all very, very close said the producer-president. *We keep it, strictly, to ourselves.*

What about Nia? This came from their eldest; he had once worked on a classic film in England, albeit as a junior technician, and the glory of that still clung to him. Robert, who had been anxiously awaiting it, was pleased that another had asked the question.

She's a problem Eldon replied. *She's not really one of us, and I don't know how much we can count on her. But anyway, as a company, we can always hire her.*

The eldest nodded. *Well*, he said, looking around to include each of the others *for my money . . . All in all, it feels right.*

＊

Eldon took care with his approach to MacCurry. He knew that if he went in person he would get a warm reception, with the usual banter and cursing, but MacCurry might fail to realize that the threat was serious, and the affair could degenerate into a brawl between them. Instead he set out his demands in a letter whose tone could not be mistaken, and a day later he continued the attack with what he pretended was a casual dropping-in.

MacCurry sat still while Eldon repeated what in substance had already been said in the letter. *I'll think it over* MacCurry finally let out, and then paused, forcing a silence that pressed Eldon to get up and go. But Eldon, who'd often dismissed others in that way, could not quite believe, or accept, such untypical coldness.

Mac . . . he began warmly, but the hostile glance he got only deepened his discomfort.

In truth, MacCurry was hurt. He regarded his battles with Eldon as the roughhousing of friends, comrades in a common cause. He had assumed that however keenly they fought, their ultimate objective was always what was best for the Board. He saw through Eldon's hints of what might follow a refusal of more money, and he felt it went beyond the rules of their game, was insidious, and smacked of sedition.

Deeply disturbed, Eldon got to his feet. MacCurry stood too, and for a moment they stared at each other with a sense of having lost something that could never be regained.

Eldon knew he ought to leave without saying more, but he couldn't bear such a stark end to all the crude affection he was used to from his chief. He fought down his distress, and was about to turn away when abruptly it overcame him. *Mac, we'd appreciate quick acceptance of these terms. We don't want any break in the work.*

MacCurry's stare turned scornful, and the silence became ear-splitting. Eldon flushed hotly and threw in *If I don't have agreement by the end of the week, then — by Christ — I'll quit!*

The production chief merely nodded.

When Eldon was returning to his office he saw Gwendolyn coming out of Nia's. The secretary had typed the letter to Mac-Curry and had promised to keep it secret, but she was enchanted with Nia and felt it scarcely amiss to have whispered the news to her. Eldon snorted angrily, but there was no point in berating Gwendolyn; she cheerfully spared no effort and was necessary, and otherwise loyal. Nor was he worried about Nia stabbing him in the back. It was rather what she might say to his face that had kept him from telling her his plans.

*

Nothing, however, restrained her with Robert.

It's childish! she exploded. *And stupid! Sheer megalomania — You'd think Eldon would have more sense — ! And for you — when you've just started directing again — it would be the worst possible thing. Darling, I hope you're not involved in this dangerous nonsense!*

This did nothing to lighten Robert's misgivings, which had been preying on him. His hopes for the future had soon evaporated, leaving him acutely uncomfortable about the tactics and the secrecy; perhaps it was too close to what was happening in his personal life. He believed it would be better for them to go as a group and have a heart-to-heart with MacCurry, but he dared not voice a differing opinion, any more than did the other directors.

*

If Eldon hadn't foolishly committed his next move he might have been able to manoeuvre, but when the week passed with no word from MacCurry, he had to submit a written resignation, and he told the directors to begin doing the same. When MacCurry got the second and third letters the dimensions of the plot became evident to him, and he went to the Commissioner, who called a meeting of the chiefs of all divisions.

The problem was new to them. Always before, when someone had resigned in a huff, or as a ploy for more money, they'd been able either to let the person go or make some compromise to keep him — or her, because once it had been a woman all admired. But the mutiny of virtually an entire unit, particularly the one best known to the public, could not long escape the notice of the government, and might even become an issue in the press and in parliament. And that could lead to an inquiry which, for political reasons, might not stop at the conduct of those who had started the trouble. Yet, on the other hand, any yielding to the money conditions could open the Board to more such blackmail.

Everyone had a different opinion as to what should be done, and when the meeting had gone on for four hours, when all had exhausted their wisdom and wit, and were worn out from discussion, choking on smoke, and awash with coffee, they felt that on the whole they'd made a satisfactory effort. Their final decision was that MacCurry would keep them daily advised. It didn't much trouble them that they'd neither adopted a policy nor decided on how to proceed; their instinctive reaction to doubt was to do nothing. Therefore the resignations continued to draw no response, while both sides waited with growing apprehension.

*

Heedless as Eldon might have been, he was now beginning to see weaknesses in his position that had been plain before but to which he'd impetuously shut his eyes. The unit had in production enough films, which others could complete, to fill all but the last few weeks of the season; if the series were broken off then, it would hardly cause much of a stir. Moreover, the start of the next season was almost five months away — time enough to replace all the mutineers and still get some sort of programmes on the air. He had little doubt that if the Board were given a straight choice between yielding to his demands and accepting poorer quality it would certainly choose the latter. So he looked for a way to establish that what was at issue was a principle that couldn't be evaded simply by changing staff.

Robert, as the youngest of the directors, the newest, and engaged on the special project, was to be the last to resign, and Eldon decided to use his resignation to emphasize the question of principle.

*

What principle? Nia retorted when Robert told her about it. He'd finally brought himself to speak openly about *the strike* — for everyone else had spoken to her already, including Eldon, who wanted to know if she had heard anything from MacCurry.

The principle Robert answered *is the future of the unit. What's the point of killing ourselves if every time we do something outstanding we get our budget cut!*

For a moment she was silent. She felt that fundamentally he was being very foolish, but not insincere, and it was his sincerity that was frightening.

*

MacCurry looked up blandly when Robert was shown into his office. *Hi-ya Rob* he said. *What's up?*

Robert gave him his letter and MacCurry took it with faint surprise. He had earlier expected Robert's letter to follow the others, but when a longer time passed after the seventh than between any of the previous ones, he'd begun to hope that Robert had kept clear of the strike. MacCurry hadn't forgiven the insult in the studio, but he had a grudging respect for Robert's integrity, and had thought that he'd reward his loyalty with the long delayed raise in pay.

Therefore he was disappointed to read the familiar opening sentence, but when he came to the statement of principle, he smiled.

Principle? he said, echoing Nia.

Inwardly sinking, Robert explained it.

Balls! said MacCurry.

So long as the production chief had thought he was faced with a united and determined revolt he'd been eager to consult his colleagues, because he was by nature a bully, who needed to be sure he was on the stronger side. But when he saw what he had to deal with he acted swiftly and on his own. He summoned Eldon and said no to all his demands, including one for more negotiation. He accepted the producer's resignation and gave the directors a week in which to withdraw theirs. The mutiny collapsed at once. The oldest director was the first to submit, telling the others, with the same gravity with which he'd blessed the affair, that *You can't fight the front office.* All but Robert scrambled to follow. Each man believed himself less guilty than the rest, and tried to excuse his own part in the conspiracy. MacCurry listened to their pleas with irony, and told them to get on with their work. He was satisfied that they wouldn't trouble him again.

Now he was left with only Eldon and Robert. For Eldon he was devising a special penalty, but he was uncertain of what to do about Robert, who hadn't yet withdrawn his resignation.

*

It was several days before Robert fully grasped that what seemed to have happened had actually taken place — that the tragicomedy of the strike and the company had fallen apart, that the other players had deserted their roles and slunk off pretending to have been only members of the audience. He had of course known and understood the events, but emotionally he was bewildered by them. They seemed unreal, like in some distorted dream. He was in flustered suspense, unsure of how it might affect his job, or his relations with Nia.

When he had sufficiently collected himself he tried to override it all. *Look,* he said to Eldon *why can't we go on with the company? You be president and make the arrangements, and I'll do the actual work. When we need more people we can pick whom we want from the Board. Every one will be glad to work with us, even Nia.*

Cock, it's a nice idea, but it wouldn't be fair to you. No, you'd better look out for yourself. And don't worry about me.

There was no need to worry about Eldon. The next day he meekly accepted a freelance contract, renewable every three months, to go on doing his same job, but with a big boost in pay. MacCurry wanted Eldon helpless, but not crushed.

*

During this time Robert scarcely saw Nia. Her mother was sick with the flu, and Nia left right after work. Then the older woman's condition worsened; she suffered laryngitis and chest pains; pneumonia was thought possible, and for several days Nia stayed home.

In between her mother's almost constant needs Nia wearily reflected on her reduced state. In Los Angeles, when Joel was small, they'd had a live-in maid, and in New York, one that came each weekday. For illnesses they could then afford a nurse or home-care person; rarely did Nora Peterson miss any engagements. Now she didn't leave in the morning until there was food for lunch and Joel safely off to school. That meant she never arrived at the Board until at least 9.30, sometimes closer to 10. Few of the producers or directors kept regular hours, but she always felt guilty about being late, and would walk in briskly, as if preoccupied with something on which she'd already been at work. This petty pretense was stressful too. Such introspection inevitably brought her to Robert. Impatient, annoyed as she was with him, she longed for the comfort of his arms.

*

Night after night he sat alone in the apartment, feeling robbed of the balm of her body and the aid of her advice. He even tormented himself by wondering where she really was. He was still afraid to ring her, terrified of what might happen if her mother found out; he imagined the old woman as a huge fierce crow who'd swoop down on them with flapping wings. Nonetheless he blamed Nia for the silence, as if it was her fault that he would not, and she could not, phone.

He hadn't yet told Myra about the strike or his resignation. It seemed to him that for the time being it concerned only Nia.

*

Humbled as Eldon had been by MacCurry, he was imperious in the unit. He ordered everyone to work harder to make up for the time lost, he stripped cartoons from the bulletin board and put up a chart listing the directors and their next assignments — with a blank after Robert's name, and in Gwendolyn's hearing he openly cursed Nia for never being around when he needed her. For a moment or two he even angrily toyed with the idea of asking for a temporary replacement, but decided that would be going too far. MacCurry, he knew, was fond of Nia.

Gwendolyn secretly phoned her daily, often several times a day, to tell her *the latest*. She reported every detail, every nuance, every conjecture of her own; her relish of events was incomplete until she'd poured everything into Nia's ear. And Nia's mother, straining to hear her daughter's few responses, would groan pitiably from the next room, trying to hold her own against the inroads of that other drama.

By weekend the old woman felt better, and her demands grew as her voice returned. She wanted her mustard plaster changed, she wanted tea with milk and toast and then without toast and with lemon; she wanted her other slippers, a warmer robe, then the window opened. And of course she wanted to know who had been on the phone, or at the door, or walking by on the road. Nia was now almost glad to exhaust herself in these tiresome tasks; they kept her from thinking of what was happening at the office.

*

Halfway down the hall from Eldon's door, Robert had been daily working on the French-English films, running footage roughly assembled by an assistant and marking the cuts for the other to make. The director edited deftly, intuitively, essentially matching the scenes in his mind; it was absorbing work and allowed him to remain semi-hidden in the darkened cutting room. No one had dared ask him what he was doing there when he was supposed to be on strike.

But on Monday morning Gwendolyn came to say that Mac-Curry wanted to see him.

*

The production chief wasn't unfriendly. But he pointed out that the week of grace had passed. *Well,* he said *what's with you?*

Robert had no reply. He wanted only to have everything back as it was, but to say that aloud might make him seem even more of a fool than he felt.

I have to know, MacCurry said *whether you're staying or going.*

The *going* stung. *Going!* — it opened a black abyss, from which Robert drew back in dismay. Not once during the excitement of the strike or his solitary brooding had it occurred to him that he might actually be cut off from the Board — outcast, alien. *Well . . .* he offered after a while *I'd like to finish my films.*

Yeah. How are they?

Okay. Not bad.

This was highly reassuring to MacCurry. *How far along are you?*

Robert took it as a test of his ability. His single-minded work during the past week had put him well ahead of schedule. *They're rough cut. Fine cut really. They might just need one or two small changes.*

This meant Eldon, anyone, could supervise the music and add the titles. MacCurry relaxed; the enemy was now disarmed, wide open. He meant to relieve, if possible even to eradicate, the sore he had carried since *Montcalm*. Regarding Robert with mild scorn, MacCurry said softly *Are you withdrawing your resignation?*

Robert longed to say *Yes . . .* to have the whole nightmare vanish. But as he hesitated, the effects of surrender flooded in. *Bloody but unbowed* came to him, and he felt that if he went whole out of MacCurry's office it would be a humiliation he'd have to live with forever.

I can't he said.

I see. MacCurry did not see at all. He'd intended to savage Robert, not lose him entirely. *Well, if that's the way you want it. Are you interested in a freelance contract?*

What? Oh . . . Yes, sure . . . It was sudden flooding light after darkness!

We could make it for three months, or even six, depending on the terms.

What . . . would they be?

Well, salary. MacCurry drew his dagger. Then, with satisfaction, struck: *Three-quarters of your monthly salary for three months — per month, that is. Two-thirds for six. Or, I'll cut you for the six.*

Cut me?

With cards. If you draw the high card, it's the same deal for six months.

But either way I'd be getting even less than I am now?

MacCurry succeeded in restraining a smile.

Incredulous, Robert cried *I thought freelancers got more. . . !*

Ordinarily they do. But you can't expect to have your own way and be rewarded for it too. The production chief silently rejoiced in the accidental rhyme; he felt he'd put it rather well.

*

Robert became a stranger as he walked the halls looking for Nia. He no longer had a right to this floor, and might soon be barred from it. And the busy people passing him seemed not to notice or care. He was a pebble lifted from a stream: the waters had immediately closed over the spot.

He found her in the cafeteria, having coffee with Nigel. She'd returned to a mountain of work, but having heard from

Gwendolyn that Robert was with MacCurry, her anxiety had impelled her to leave everything and desperately make merry.

She was laughing at something Nigel had said when Robert approached, but her eyes immediately fastened on his, and were at once stricken.

Hi, Nigel said *comment ça va?*

Right out of here. I just quit.

Really? Nigel said, his astonishment quickly becoming camp. *You couldn't kiss ass?*

Get paid off at the end of the week, and that's it.

Well . . . what's next? New York? Hollywood? But God, Rob, it won't be the same here, without you. No indeed, Nigel felt; Robert's place in the unit would now be open, and he would no longer be around to interrupt a tête-à-tête with Nia.

*

For the next few nights Nia avoided the apartment. At first she said she still had to nurse her mother, then she had to go to the dentist, and then her son's school was having a bake sale for which she had to make cranberry bread. Finally, on Friday, when she heard Robert had arranged to return the furniture the next morning, she arrived late, looking sombre.

Neither had shopped; they ate what remained. Nia left most of her food but finished the gin — the vermouth was already gone — and smoked one cigarette after another. No flowers adorned the table. The spent blooms of the hyacinth had been plucked and the withering leaves drooped over the rim of the pot. The candle stubs melted down; one flame went out and the other began to char the wooden holder. When the overhead bulb proved too harsh Robert turned it off and put on the one in the bathroom. Its pale light came through the doorway. Steam from their coffee made vague shadows that moved across their faces and into the background.

I had to Robert said.

It's probably the stupidest thing you've ever done — You need the credits of straight TV directing. However much a boy wonder you

77

were at the Board, in the outside world you aren't that well known — you're hardly known at all. You're going to have to prove yourself again.

I will.

But it won't be easy. And I guess I'll always needle you about it.

The *always* gave him hope. He'd been thinking about Nigel's mention of going to the States; the idea had become appealing.

New York? Nia said. *Well — maybe. I could certainly use some new clothes —*

We could make it a holiday. Or even . . . even more he added, inwardly damning his dishonesty; but then, because he wanted to, beginning to half believe what he had implied.

For a few seconds Nia was silent. Then she looked at him. *Since that first time we made love — I haven't had a period.*

Robert panicked; but his terror at once mingled with pride.

It may be nothing — she continued. *I'm not always regular now.*

But if you are . . . What then?

She shrugged. *Another expensive abortion —*

His relief was riddled with fear: where would he get the money? Yet that was soon replaced by sadness. He wanted to hold her, to let his conflicted feelings flow into hers, and took her hand. *Let's move to the bed. . .*

Not yet.

It'll be our last time in it.

I suppose there'll be other beds she said flatly, then paused.

Robert was afraid to push.

I'll tell you about one in a minute — But she fell silent, and seemed distant. *The first time I saw midtown Manhattan* she finally went on *it looked to me like a giant stage set. All those shining towers — and the gilded swank of Fifth Avenue — with the opulent window displays — the perfume sprayed into the street. It never entirely lost that glamour, even when we lived there.*

When was that?

She tensely shook her head, refusing to let facts intrude. *One day I went to lunch at The Pierre. I looked good — I had on a lovely yellow silk with a looped neckline — and I liked the girl I was with — she was fun and we laughed a lot. I was eight weeks pregnant. And after lunch — walking over to the theatre where the band was rehearsing — I saw in an antique store — in the window, all these old clocks — all showing the same, correct time — and it was just the time Joel would be arriving home from school — hungry and full of incredible energy — and mother would toast the snack I'd prepared — melted cheese on whole wheat with tomato and roasted garlic, which he loves — And for just a moment I had that rare feeling of everything being okay — of all things in their right places — and then I went into the theatre and when Buddy saw me he stopped the rehearsal — stopped in mid number — and pointing his baton at me, said snidely 'Gentlemen, my loving wife and implacable critic'.*

Despite his own anxiety, his insecure need to hold her, Robert couldn't help feeling her pain.

It was the first time in public like that she went on. *The band laughed uncomfortably — I smiled — and sat down — for their sake — but I was hurt — God was I hurt. Poor Buddy, he was always jealous, and always on the make — always eager for compliments, opportunities, women — And I was cramping his style — Too many people — were drawn to me, instead of him.*

They were both silent for a while, encircled by shadows.

Where was the bed you. . . ?

Nia hesitated. It was something she'd never before spoken of. Nor was her trust in Robert total. But she felt a need to disillusion him, perhaps to clout him with facts. *In our expensive apartment on East 66th. The doctor had used a gooseneck lamp we'd had on a desk — then he took it away and the room got dark — but I could still see the blood smears on the sheet. He'd been down on his knees by the bed — he'd wanted to do it on the dining room table, but mother was near hysterics and wouldn't stay out of there —and then after he'd left — mother had by now collapsed in her room — Buddy arrived — and lit a cigar — said he couldn't stand the smell of the disinfectant — and he was pacing impatiently at the foot of the bed — stepping around the basin covered with a spotted towel*

— *and then he said, annoyed* — '*Why is this here? What is it?*' — *and I said 'Our second child.'*

There were tears in her voice. Robert took out a tissue.

I'm not crying she said. I didn't cry even then. Buddy said 'Oh. Well — *I love you. I'll always love you.' Then he left, probably to avoid having to clean up any of it* — *and I lay there and thought 'He wanted this because he doesn't want me. Why didn't I see it sooner?'* She sighed, then said *I did, of course* — *but denied it* — *too much invested. A week later* — *I sued for divorce, then* — *a few months afterwards* — *when I felt well enough* — *mother and Joel and I came back to Canada.*

Does Joel see him?

No — *Buddy can't be bothered. And I don't want Joel to be like him* — *I don't want him to have those values.*

Do you hear from Buddy?

His accountant in LA sends a cheque every four months. Occasionally on time. It's overdue now. If it comes — *I can go to New York.*

6

It was again Friday when Robert left the 34th Street Y. He'd been staying there, in a tiny rectangle, for two dollars a night. Anxious to arrive in style, he took a cab to the residential hotel. He'd found it after a frantic day of searching, when it seemed that every apartment for rent was either too showy and high-priced or was strewn with cracking plaster and crawling with roaches.

This building had a sedate and genteel air. A green canopy led to the entrance, a doorman in green uniform swung open the imposing glass door. Robert gave him a dollar, hoping to buy courtesy for the week with Nia. The lobby was small, deeply carpeted, dim even by day; a shaded amber lamp made the little front desk seem intimate and warm. Beyond it, in a high-ceilinged room, dinner was being served. The guests were elderly, as was the staff; there was an unhurried familiarity among them, as if they had grown old together. The place looked clean, well brushed, with the grime of age confined to cracks and corners.

The apartment was on the eighth floor, facing the street. Through the two tall windows Robert could see at an angle across Riverside Drive to the blue Hudson. Nearer there was a grassy strip where people were sitting on a stone parapet. Some had reflectors of tinfoil under their chins, garnering from the setting sun the last of its splendid rays, which lit Robert's face and the chintzy drapes and armchairs, bringing out the rich browns and oranges in the rug and bed and cushion covers. The bathroom, by contrast, was all white tile. The kitchen, also separate, had white appliances and a shining double sink.

Robert washed the dishes and knives, forks and spoons, two of each, and the aluminum pot and iron frying pan he had got on sale at Macy's. And then he carefully unwrapped the clear glass vase he'd bought at Woolworth's.

Several flower stands dotted the district, which kept him busy comparing possible bouquets and costs. Even after he'd gone back to the first stand, and had chosen Shasta daisies and a few blue iris, he still hesitated, because ... the flowers would last longer if he got them after Nia came. This penny-pinching shamed him, but he felt he had to be prudent now so as to be grand — reasonably grand, when they were together. *Some nights we'll have dinner in the dining room* he thought. *Oh, just let her come!*

*

He woke with the pleasant feeling that he belonged there. Staring sleepily at the Audubon print on the wall, the varnished mahogany desk, the glass-topped coffee table with the waiting vase, it seemed to him that these impassive objects cheerfully sensed how much in harmony he felt with them. And the sandstone building across the street, already brightened by morning sunlight, looked approving too. Its squat windows, gleaming with a dewy blueness touched by gold, reflected an unclouded sky. A fresh breeze stirred the edges of the open drapes, and the hum of traffic from Riverside Drive sounded like the tuning up of a vast orchestra bent on giving expression to his joy.

He stretched comfortably and pictured the room as it would be with Nia in it. There would be — as well as flowers — wine and food and laughter, and there would be love. He thought of her at her best, her constant delight in being alive, which often intoxicated his senses. And in only a few hours!

The reminder of time made him uneasy; he scrambled out of bed and went down to breakfast at a corner snack bar. It was his first food since the previous morning and he finished every morsel of its forty-cent special.

Then, nude in his bathroom, Robert studied himself in the full length mirror. His body was still shapely; he hoped Nia would find it pleasing, as if she'd never seen it before. There was actual anxiety in this: his every romantic impulse would be realized in this honeymoon week. He wanted it all to be perfect. True, to get here he'd told Myra he needed further study at the Studio before starting his freelance career, and said that the money he'd withdrawn was for expenses owed in Montreal — but all such lies and connivance would now be behind him.

He shaved with a new blade, and then shaved again, until his face was smooth in all directions, showered until his skin glowed, and carefully combed back his wet hair into a casual, rather bohemian, upsweep. With only two attempts he made a perfect knot in his tie, and after struggling repeatedly with a breast-pocket handkerchief — folded square it looked too severe, flared out, too debonair — he succeeded in stuffing it in so that only the tip showed, striking a chic balance, he thought, between having no handkerchief and making too much of one. Then a final polishing of his shoes, a last washing of his hands, and crying *Oh God, the time!* he ran to the subway.

And rushed headlong down the steps, sure it was the express he heard roaring in. It was a local; the express screeched to a halt a few minutes later. Robert hurried aboard, tensely ticked off the stations, and arrived at Grand Central almost a half hour early.

He waited outside the gate at the end of the track on which the overnight train from Montreal was due, imagining how the people gathering around him would stare at Nia, wondering who the stunner was, and how surprised they'd be when she came lovingly into his arms. And as he stood there, in his unseasonable grey felt suit, which was old, becoming a bit baggy, and a bad fit, and in his worn black shoes, on which the shine couldn't hide the thick loops of thread with which the soles had been resewn, he felt he was the most favoured of men, absolutely fated to succeed. And there came to him a vision of the new life Nia and he would begin here, a life free from all that was petty and mean, and that would grow into the great life of creativity and vivid feeling she wanted and deserved. And none of this seemed pretentious or absurd, because had he been told before he met her that at this moment he would be in New York awaiting a beautiful woman who was herself great, and who loved him, it would have seemed much more fantastic . . .

He was recalled from this reverie by the rumble of the approaching train.

The crowd stirred, people craned forward, stretching their necks. Robert's excitement reached a pitch when passengers began coming into the station and throwing themselves on those expecting them. Person after person came, then small crowds, then a dwindling stream, then singly, each making it more likely that the next would be Nia. *She was late getting up* Robert thought, amused. Or held back collecting her things . . . Or for some other silly reason he could twit her about.

But then there was a gap, and no one else came.

Oh no, he thought good naturedly. *Something's happened . . . maybe her suitcase has fallen apart. Now she'll be all contrite, with lots of excuses.* Yet he was slightly annoyed, because she'd be distracted by whatever had delayed her, and that would spoil the pure joy of their meeting. However, anything . . . if only she'd appear.

He was now alone in front of the gate, and could see no one between him and the train. He looked around, and seeming unobserved, bolted into the train shed, where he stopped short, blinking at its cavernous gloom. Before him reared the huge bulk of the sighing engine, from whose oily flanks wisps of steam were rising. The dark cars behind formed an unbroken line. Alongside it the concrete platform was empty, except for a single stout conductor approaching.

Sir, Robert said, stopping him *are all the passengers off?*

Yes. They've been off for five minutes.

You're sure there's no one left? I'm expecting someone.

Yes. Yes, I'm sure. The conductor smiled, compressing all his chins, as if counting on his smile to end this.

Do you mind if I look?

Well, do! the other muttered, and hurried away, indignantly jiggling his ticket case.

Robert entered the first car. It was a coach, unoccupied. He went swiftly through to another coach, then another, all of them empty and still. The next car was in deep shadow, and he recognized it as a sleeper. *Ah, now I'm getting warm . . .* he thought. But there was no one in it either. He went on into another that was totally black, the curtains still up on its berths, and he touched each as he felt his way down the aisle. *Nia. . . !* he called. *Nia!* There was no answer: not even an echo.

Beside himself, he went on and on, looking into berths, compartments, even toilets. *Where can she be?* he thought. *She must be here somewhere, she must be!* But then he opened the last car door and there was nothing more, only a metal tailgate drawn across the doorway. And beyond that the endless track stretching back through the sunlit city.

*

Nia's suitcases, still packed, stood in her closet. The wildly flowered wallpaper, which had come with the house, gave her no rest, but her eyes were already hurting from shutting it out. She rose from bed and went slowly downstairs, her hand sliding on the railing. The smooth wood felt supportive. Though it was not yet noon she went to the bureau and poured a stiff scotch. Then sat in the armchair and sipped, while her fingers pressed the cool compress to her cheek. The pain, from neck to mouth, was severe. She sighed heavily. The damn dentist was at a conference, and she hadn't the mental energy to search for another. When he returned, the tooth would probably have to come out. She felt she was falling apart, that the props of her life were crumbling. At least, thankfully, the house was quiet; her mother, complaining of leg aches, was lying down in her room. The phone rang.

It was Robert. Fearful, angry at having been made a fool of, he was phoning from a paybooth in the station. *Where are you?* he cried stupidly.

Didn't you get my wire? I sent it to the Y —

He hadn't let her know he'd left there, or where he was going.

A tooth inflamed she said. *I'm in a lot of pain —*

Robert could scarcely credit a tooth. It was too little for such a disaster! He wanted her damaged, deformed, dying! He wanted sympathy for the terrible loss of all he'd expected. He told her about the lovely apartment.

I'm very ill Nia said. *I can't think about it —*

The operator rasped *Deposit another quarter, please . . .*

But Robert, though he had one, refused to prolong this. *All right* he said. *Okay. Good-bye!*

*

When he next phoned her, twenty-four hours later, he was alone in Stanley Lehn-Langbord's apartment. He felt grim and revengeful, yet the thought that she was so much closer, almost within reach — damn, if distance were all that separated them he could walk to her island! — flooded him with an unexpected tenderness. The phone kept ringing at Nia's end. He was ready, as he watched through the wide window the scattered spills of soft sunlight moving on the mountain, to forgive her anything.

Nia answered tersely. *Yes. Yes, I'm a little better. But this is my family day — I have to make dinner. Maybe — I'll see —*

It left Robert in a rage. Her power over him was intolerable! He was always waiting for her, always at her mercy. His self-pity roused him to such fury that he wanted to knock her down, twist her hair, make her writhe . . . but then the image, the feeling of her writhing under him, as she sometimes did, led to voluptuous yearning. This was calming, allowing him to succumb to his accumulated fatigue.

*

Yesterday, following his misfortune at the station, he'd been unusually lucky. The hotel had given him back sixty of the seventy dollars he'd paid in advance, and he had been able to return to Macy's the things he had got there. The vase was in his bag, but at least he hadn't bought flowers!

Then, driven by disappointment and anger, spurning further classes at the Studio, wanting to strike back with some dramatic *Damn the expense!* gesture, he'd gone straight to the airport, intent on taking the first plane to Montreal. But prudence prevailed, and he waited for the Night Owl, the cheapest air service available, which operated with old Constellations in the small dark hours.

His flight landed at three, in a downpour. By the time the airport bus arrived at the Mount Royal Hotel it was almost four, though not yet light. Whom could he impose on at that hour? Only Nigel. But when he phoned there was no answer. He no longer had a key to Nigel's, and he felt, wrathfully, that all doors in this sleeping city were closed to him. The very one he ought to have been able to go to — Nia's, was beyond even imagining. Then who else could he call? *Stanley. . . !* Yes — but it was too early to wake Stanley.

Robert stared, scowling, at the creeping hands of the hotel's large clock. When he had read and reread all the posters in the dim lobby, and had inspected the windows of all the darkened shops on the lower level, and had gone back often enough to harass those obstinate hands, he finally succeeded in getting the shorter one to move to five, the longer to twelve. After that he stood outside and watched the occasional police car go by. The rain had stopped; some pallid sky peered back through rifts in the clouds. At six a restaurant across the street put on its lights. He bought a chocolate bar and ate a quarter of it every fifteen minutes. At last it was seven.

Stanley sounded sleepy but when he heard who it was he became cheerful and said it was time he got up. There was a week-end film seminar at a resort in the Laurentians. Nigel was there, and he was going for the day; indeed he was being picked up soon. He was without a car, he explained; Jean-Michel, the dominant, manly young musician he lived with, had got word that his father was down with a wrenched back, and taking Stanley's sleek Kar-mann Ghia had sped home to the farm near Trois Rivieres to help plant the potatoes.

*

When Robert got there, Stanley was waiting with fresh coffee. Robert gulped his gratefully. Sitting in one of the neo-Chippendale chairs, he felt rumpled and grubby. Stanley reclined in the other. His round relaxed face was shaded against the hazy light seeping through the sheer curtains, which were flanked on either side by graceful sweeps of damask drapery. Backlit, his curly blond hair gleamed lightly from pomade, and when he raised his cup to sip, holding it carefully away from his silk shirt with all but his two small fingers, the jeweled cuff links glinted in response.

This dandy was one of several Englishmen who'd been invited to the Board during a decline in the British film industry. Out of work in their own country, like Scottish crofters forced off the land, they had come to Canada with the condescension of visiting lords, but finding easy sinecures, every one had stayed. Stanley was thirty-nine; clever and skilled, an editor or director as opportunity allowed, he worked in the unit with an air of calm infallibility. When Eldon's opinion clashed with his own he yielded with the aplomb of a prince indulging a peasant. Only to Robert did he sometimes defer. Without openly admitting it, he deeply respected the younger man's skill.

When Stanley left, Robert ate the rest of the breakfast his host had prepared, stared at his bristled face in the mirror, shaved, showered, and out of curiosity chose one of the many bottles of scent and dabbed a drop behind each ear. Then he crossed the sitting area to the broad double bed, stretched out on the shot purple spread, covered himself with a loose blanket, and slept.

*

The phone call had been made to Nia after he woke. She'd replaced the receiver with a trembling hand and had sunk into the high wing chair, a refuge from the one-hundred and fourteen cartoon strips of *Peanuts* with which Joel had covered the living room floor. *I won't go — !* she said under her breath.

What? said Joel, but getting no reply, he nudged Jester out of the way and returned to arranging his strips into stories. The dog, a silky Spaniel he'd raised from a puppy, and who was only four years younger, put his head on his paws and squinted at *Peanuts* through slit eyes. The phone rang again; Joel jumped up and ran to answer it. *Yes, she is* he said reluctantly. It was Eldon, in whom he had no interest.

The producer irritably asked if Nia would be at the office tomorrow to meet with the network manager.

Yes, sir she said. *Dear God, Eldon, you know I cancelled my leave!* But he was scarcely mollified. Because of her tooth she'd been away on Friday — when she had planned to take her travel cases to the commissionaire's cubicle and go right from work to the New York train — and Eldon was anyway still annoyed about her having requested a week of holidays so soon after she'd stayed home with her mother.

And now the old woman was calling *Nia-a . . .* in that nagging, demanding tone that instantly drove her mad! But she got up wearily and went upstairs — saying to herself, as her name kept being called *Wilma, Wilma, shut up!* — to see what her mother wanted.

Yesterday, when Nia's face was still inflamed and she had needed cold compresses, her mother had made a heroic effort, but had left the kitchen for her daughter to clean. There were still mashed potatoes in the mixmaster, pots and plates in the sink, droppings smeared on the floor. And the outside weather too had not much improved. Despite glimmers of sunshine, dark clouds lingered.

Nia came down to the kitchen intending to start the dishes, but instead sat back on one of the wooden chairs and lit a cigarette. Events, mixed with her private anxieties, were pressing heavily, and beneath that weight everyone was tearing pieces from her. Not Joel — Joely she didn't mind, and at least with him there was the compensation of sweetness and love. But her mother, Eldon, Robert — it was too much. Her lover now had no job, they had no place to meet, and he was married. That distressing quagmire she'd so far sidestepped, but it was still there.

Damn you! she heard Joel shout as he kicked at Jester with a stockinged foot, striking well short of the scurrying dog, who had just scrambled a section of the *Peanuts* strips. And in the same outraged tone, but half smiling, because he was about to mimic his mother, he called after the spaniel *Have you no story sense!*

Nia laughed, and that momentarily lifted her gloom. But with a rush it returned, and she thought *I can't handle it all. I haven't the time, energy, or money.* Her earlier image of a swamp recurred, but now spread throughout her life — she was only managing, she felt, to keep her head above its surface. The unsparing demands of passion could pull it down.

*

Two hours later Robert dialed Nia's number once more. He felt nervous — with each call the odds of disaster increased, but he was determined not to be robbed of her again.

I have to make dinner — she answered. *I don't know. When I can* —

He hung up with an exasperated sigh. The sun had moved around, in a now sometimes blue sky, and was shining on the western face of the mountain; but only a pale reflection penetrated the room's shadows. He refused to switch on a lamp; it would seem too much like defeat. *She must come* he thought. *Damn it, she must!*

*

She arrived after four, in a bad temper, but carrying an armful of white lilacs. Robert was immediately intimidated by her mood, and awed by her beauty. She was wearing a white sheath dress and in the subdued light her flushed skin was a rosy tan. Her face showed only a slight swelling.

How are you? he said gently. *Does it still hurt?*

She shook that off as too trivial. *I think it blew up — because I didn't really want to go —*

His world shattered: it was the collapse of all order. He felt like hitting her!

She opened her purse. *I was going to send you a note — I wrote one — and called a cab — but then I started to edit — which is my curse — and ended by tearing it up. So I came — and scribbled on the way. Here —* And she thrust at him a small piece of folded paper. He took it to the window, and read:

> It's no longer just no place
> and the telephone and everything else
> that comes between us — there's something
> very wrong with us now. I don't want
> to analyze it — I don't want to discuss it.
> I just want it to be over — this — us — now.

His heart leapt. *Over*! Yes — suddenly released from these torments...! But at once his pride and will hardened, and he wanted her desperately — her body, her love. *I'm sorry*... he started to say, and then stopped, because there would be too much to explain, and too little possibility that any of it would make sense.

I'm not blaming you she said. *But don't you see — this isn't working. We can't go on hiding in corners. New York would've been nice, and I meant to go — but really, I couldn't afford it — Buddy's cheque was torn to pieces, eaten up — just devoured by a thousand bills — and when that was over — there were still debts. And I can't be away so much from my mother and son — I have obligations to them just as you have to your career — and your family.* She looked straight at him. *I won't — I can't call you in Ottawa — I don't want to hear the woman's voice on the phone. And that's always there — though we haven't talked about my dishonesty in that frame. And then — there's your health — which is incredible — and your energy — when I'm so often tired and ill.* Her eyes filled with tears. *I don't know how much time I have left and I don't want to spend it in turmoil — darling, I don't —*

Robert was struck by her pain, and her sense of danger — which frightened him, though he soon began thinking it theatrical, because it seemed to him, as he stared at her beautiful, sad face, that the moment was beginning to loom larger than life, that it was becoming art.

Then she began to sob, and her sobbing returned them to the ordinary. She rummaged in her purse for a handkerchief, found none, and Robert brought a box of tissues from the bathroom. He waited patiently for her crying to allow an approach, and when she sank into the chair Stanley had sat in, and bent her head, he placed a gentle kiss on the clean part in her hair.

One kiss inspired another; soon he was on his knees kissing her hands, face, neck. Deliberately, with craft, he roused her desire. The sobs stopped, she grew warm; he could feel her heart beating and gladly encouraged his to beat strongly too. But throughout it all she said not a word. It was only when he was about to follow her into bed that she asked him to get a towel to shield the mauve sheet. Relief . . . relief . . . balm for heated feelings and loins. Now, Robert felt, all was restored.

*

So he was surprised when Nia, still silent, got dressed and said, finally, that she was going back to her family. *And* she added *this will have to be good-bye.*

Really? Robert said. But he was sated for the moment, and instinctively knew his only strength was in staying aloof. Slipping on his trousers, he entered willfully into the ritual pathos of parting. He went to where she stood, took her in his arms, held her close, and let her go.

Nia walked to the door, put her hand on the knob, and then stopped and hesitated. In that moment, with his seed still damp within her, she felt overwhelmingly that she was doing the only sensible thing, to bring order to her responsibility to her child, her mother, her work. To war against her insane romanticism. And yet there was an acute sense of loss, as if while everything about her was careening into bitter destruction she was leaving behind the one bit of sweetness she had been able to cling to. The many men she could still have, that she knew she could, at will, with her almost effortless rascally charm, were simply, in anticipation, another depressing burden. This boy moved her.

She came back and kissed him. Only their mouths met — in a long lingering kiss, with rising, filling excitement, from which she broke with an ebbing sigh.

I don't understand that at all she whispered, then turned and left without looking back.

*

Robert tried to be sad, and told himself it really was all over. But the golden light on the mountain seemed to belie it. The sky was now completely clear, promising fair weather ahead. He sighed, but only enjoyed the sensation in his chest. He stretched his muscles and felt that they were supple and strong and capable of anything. Then his eye caught the clock — he had to be getting home! Quickly he straightened the apartment, ran to catch a street bus that was pulling away, and leapt aboard the Ottawa train when it was already moving.

The parlour-car passengers who saw this stunt stared at him as he passed; he took it for praise, and blithely went on to the coach.

At ease in a window seat, he set about composing a touching farewell letter to send on arrival. He considered it carefully, smiling when a good idea struck him, and then deliberately wrote it on the back of the note Nia had handed him:

> On the train
>
> I left that dim scented room feeling full of affection for you. The lilacs, when I put them in water, in a vase that was to have been ours in New York, were still fresh and I thought . . . was it only such a short time ago? From my window I see green fields and stately trees. I know the fields must turn brown, and the trees shrivel to bare branches, and that in time, in time, all will be green and fruitful again. I know it . . . but now what good does it do to know. . .
>
> I've thought about what you said and it seems justified to me. Only it doesn't make any difference. Yet this is an ending. Nothing follows. Unless. . . but who can know about that?
>
> Robert

He did know, all too well, that his last words owed much to the closing lines of *A Doll's House*, but thought it unlikely Nia would detect the source.

*

When she had read his letter Nia sat for a long time over it; then she picked up a pencil and added, under the signature:

> I love you, Robert.

Part Two

7

When Robert returned from Montreal, Myra set out to rewin her husband. *Thank you for consulting me!* she cried on hearing he'd resigned, and for an hour she went around with downcast eyes and a hurt air, while inwardly rejoicing at the prospect of having him imprisoned at home. In truth, she was unconcerned about their welfare; her salary was enough for them to scrape by on, and she half believed Robert when he said that before long he'd be doing better than ever. However, she soon saw it was bravado: he was not the same. He seemed oddly detached, adrift, and for the first time, vulnerable. Myra blamed the shock of change, and was grateful for it. She found his new instability strongly appealing — certainly he still drew her more than any other man.

She began to dress with care. She bought a perfume called Désir, and feeling that her shoulder-length page-boy was uninspired, went to a private hairdresser on Rue La Joie for a completely new cut. It was clipped, upturned, decidedly chic. Robert gaped and had to admit it made her attractive — *Even prettier!* was the way he reversed what had carelessly come close to being disparaging.

Myra was elated. During the next few days when she came from work she went straight to Robert and kissed him. Then in bed she snuggled so playfully against his back that partly out of politeness, and because she was desirable, he turned and took her in his arms.

But this only made him strongly remember love making with Nia, its sensations and smells. How could something that seemed so right be wrong?

Myra said *It's even better now. But I've always loved it.* He was surprised, and wondered where that had been during the intervening years. Although, except to serve himself, he'd done little to encourage it. *Remember . . .* Myra went on *in the park, just before we were married, it was almost daybreak and we had to be quick.* She giggled. *You were great.*

Robert recalled acting as if he adored her, and that it had been an effort. But in a sense he had hungered for her availability, her warmth, her skin. However, by the time their licence became legal, neither was left with much actual ardour. Yet Robert felt he had to keep his word, and Myra was determined to defy her family. So without pressure — no one knew they'd gone off together — and without telling anyone about the wedding except three friends of Robert's — as teenagers they'd acted in his first shoestring film — who now held the canopy, and were behaving as if this were another comic scene: one had to hold two of the poles, and the canopy kept drooping over the couple's eyes, in the modest home of an obliging cantor Myra took a deep breath and her vows, and Robert, repeating the binding words, told himself that whatever was wrong they'd have plenty of time to make right.

But a week later he was hired by the Board, where he'd applied long before meeting Myra, and was required to report at once to Ottawa. While she, in Toronto, being the protégée of a powerful professor, became the youngest lecturer the university had ever had.

Apart, they needed nothing from each other, until Robert, feeling barred from other women, wanted his wife in his bed. Badgered, Myra declined reappointment to a second year, suffered the regrets and headshaking of her parents and colleagues, and one rainy spring day, alone, afraid that the best was already behind her, she took the train to — to — *Oblivion!* she told herself, and then sobbed quietly in her seat.

She and Robert had both been mute, remembering. Now Myra said *Have you sent all your résumés?*

Yeah. Mailed the last today. Fifty-six. I was getting cross-eyed. My fingertips still hurt.

Wouldn't it have been better to have them printed?

No. Too expensive.

That was a constant, from the start. When Myra came off the train Robert led her to the two tiny rooms he'd just rented, brightened with a bottle of wine and buttercups picked in the yard. She too had nothing; her lecturer's pittance had barely covered carfare, personal items and staff coffee. She'd gone on living with her parents, but had taken no money from them, and had even offered to pay for Robert's collect calls, which they plainly resented. That first year he roomed with an old couple near the Rideau Canal; the man, though crippled, was a shoemaker, and the humble place reeked of leather, glue and polish. The only phone was in the shop, which had been the living-dining room and was next to the kitchen. Always overheard, constrained to a kind of code, Robert had nonetheless managed to convey his need. And indeed, when they were once more in bed, Myra too was glad, and hoped they could build, somehow, a satisfying life.

She began by working hard on her thesis, which was all that remained to be done for her doctorate. But as Robert was away all day she became lonely and listless, and would sit at her desk — a wide board clamped to the window sill — blindly staring out at the dull back lane and sadly longing for her lecture room. By Christmas she was colossally bored, and thought of running away, but then her periods stopped. In this emergency, quickly confirmed, her father relented and lent them money for a down payment, Robert asked for and received a small raise, and they bought a ramshackle bungalow near the Board.

Every evening and on weekends Robert worked on it. For months they lived among shavings and plaster dust, but by the time Myra was counting the days he had applied the last of the paint. One night she was holding the ladder for him as he hung a wall clock in the kitchen above the open doorway to the cellar. The stairs were behind her, she stepped back too far and took a tumble. When he helped her up she tried to laugh, but it hurt too much, and she had to lie down. A few minutes later she began to bleed.

Twice afterwards she miscarried in the first months, and the loss of those babies tied them in much the same way children might have.

*

The only response to Robert's résumés was an ad for a two-day screenwriting course at Saratoga Springs for ninety dollars, plus accommodation. That came from New York. From Hollywood, nothing. Nia had been right: outside the Board his name and the titles of films he had credits for were unknown. His television films had been more widely seen, and had resulted in favourable reviews, but he now wondered whether anyone but critics had watched them. Because even Toronto, from where they were broadcast, was silent. Live TV dramas were staged there, but only the crudest kind of news coverage was filmed. Besides, he was realizing, producers didn't take on unseen talent. *Ottawa* he sighed to Myra *must seem as remote as the moon.*

Which sharply reminded him that platitudes caused Nia pain. He thought about her all the time, and spoke to her in his thoughts. Often she replaced Myra in his arms. Yet it was his wife's body that warmed and satisfied him, it was his wife who cooked and cleaned the house, it was her work sustaining them, and it was she with whom he now talked and laughed. Nia was in his blood, but Myra was all around him, an attractive, intelligent and cheerful presence whose pain — and it was, he knew, deep and pervading and without cure, gave him pause. He could not help but feel for what might have been.

*

One day a government cheque came for almost a thousand dollars in pension pay. He'd forgotten that a small portion of his salary had regularly been deducted, and partly matched, and with his employment ended the total had been sent. He wondered whether to tell Myra about it, but then decided, guiltily, to put it into a private account. It was needed, he pretended to himself, for the trips he should be taking to see producers. But he kept putting that off. And though he thought and talked of writing a play — about a headstrong woman like Hedda Gabler or Anna Karenina — he could not settle on a plot, and days passed without his doing anything. Because all the while he was inwardly certain that his exile from Montreal would soon end, that his obsession with Nia must yield something more.

*

His absence was giving that lady some much needed peace. She was patching the holes the past months had worn in her family life, and almost all her evenings were now spent at home. She held lively parleys with Joel about his school work and his bedtime and *Peanuts* — they decided she was *Lucy* and he was *Charlie Brown* — or at other times she read current novels, played cards with her mother, and even, occasionally, took Jester for a walk. She'd become regular in her habits and was driving to and from the Board with a lab technician who'd moved to an old farmhouse a few miles beyond her; she paid for his gas and sometimes he brought her a few fresh eggs or a little homemade white cheese, for in a hut behind their house his wife kept a dozen chickens and two long-eared goats. With the money saved Nia bought summer clothes for Joel — who was outgrowing everything he had — and, as a birthday present for her mother, an upright piano. She got a *marvellous* buy, with only a small amount down and the rest in thirty-six monthly instalments.

Wilma was delighted with the piano and played without stopping for more than an hour. Then the next day she touched the keys and was lost in reverie, smiling as she remembered watching the screen, in their family owned movie house, called the *Aurora*, for a hand lifting a cream pie— at which she'd break into a rollicking caprice — or for the clasped fingers that cued a lovers' serenade. After that she dusted the instrument a few times, then seldom went near it again.

Their living room boasted a fireplace and on cool evenings Nia would light a fire. It cast a cheerful light on their faces as they leisurely watched TV. Wearing a warm robe, with a cigarette in her fingers and a drink in her hand, gently dulled by nicotine, alcohol and the banality on the screen, she'd experience moments of mindless contentment in which the world outside her became a soft buzzing blur that was unthreatening and didn't oblige her to stir. At night she slept without desire and almost without dreams, like someone recovering from exhaustion.

In the office, however, she was more conscious of Robert. His flair was missing. Scripts and rushes lacked his vitality, his sure sense of visual storytelling. But there was no way of bringing him back. The directors behaved as if he'd never existed, and Eldon didn't like to be reminded of him.

*

Yet in the large carpeted office downstairs MacCurry was thinking of Robert. He had expected him to come crawling before this, and was surprised at his obstinacy. The pleasure of revenge had passed, and the production chief now regretted the loss of someone who had at least stood up to him.

MacCurry was like a cat without a mouse. Within the Board all defiance of him had disappeared, so awed was everyone by the decisive way he had crushed the strike. Eldon seldom argued with him, and the Commissioner deferred to his judgment even in matters beyond production. MacCurry was sinking into a torpor of boredom. Now he sighed wearily when his secretary brought him the day's routine business he had formerly dispatched like warming-up exercises. The summer holidays would soon start and he wondered whether to take any; there was nowhere he wanted to go. After work he went to his silent apartment and lay on the bed, thinking of women with whom he could start an affair, but the tempting ones involved too much trouble, and those he could summon with a phone call failed to arouse him enough to lift the receiver. His weekly poker sessions had been stopped at the time of the strike and never resumed. For the next few months so many of the players would be on location that there was no point in starting again before fall.

What a shitty life . . . MacCurry murmured, as he dozed off.

✳

A day later Martin Clee came to him complaining that all the staff writers were busy, and he'd have to use an outside one for the new air force film. There was no real reason for Clee to confer with the production chief; he was simply eager to be noticed.

At once MacCurry said *Get Aronson.*

Clee opened his mouth to protest — he'd hoped to give the job to a young writer whose wife was very pretty — but MacCurry's sweet smile allowed no denial.

Martin Clee was the Board's producer of films for the armed forces. He was a little man, barely five-foot-five; he'd come to the Board straight from high school, thanks to an uncle who drove one of the equipment trucks. Beginning humbly as a splicing boy, he'd devoted himself with such zeal that eventually he was made a sound cutter, then an editor, then film librarian, and finally one of the four lab supervisors— which placed him, he proudly maintained, *in management.* He even overcame an early stammer that used to occur when he was under the brow of some bigwig. After he married he had no trouble with his words, except, rarely, in moments of extreme stress. When he was made a producer he felt he had reached the acme of his ambition.

But the service officers he dealt with, resplendent in their glittering buttons and gold bands, excited him. He was dazzled by their innate assumption of power, their stylized manners, their good-natured cynicism; they were even a little frightening, they seemed to be giants at play. By agreeing to everything he got on well. They said he was not bad for *a film sort*, and once commended him in a liaison letter. All this was transfiguring; his stance straightened, his walk quickened, he developed an abruptness of speech, he grew a small moustache, smoked a pipe, and began looking at other women. On his mantelpiece he kept a worn swagger stick a colonel had given him; sometimes when he talked to his wife he casually tucked it under his arm.

*

Exactly parallel to the broad blotter pad on his desk, Clee placed a letter opener, so it pointed straight at Robert. *I'll expect an outline in three weeks* he said.

You'll have it.

It will also have to satisfy the air force.

Robert reddened slightly; his stomach tightened. When the phone call had come, and while the Film Board operator was slipping in a personal *Hi!* before making the connection — she'd been one of his extras in *Montcalm* — his mind had raced, excitedly wondering who . . . Eldon — MacCurry — or even . . . and his heart had raced too. It was Clee. Clee! He'd hardly ever spoken to him.

Mac thought you might be free Clee had said sourly, all but indicating his bias. And now the little man was fingering his ascot . . . an ascot! and defiantly waiting for him to speak.

Of course.

Well, you know, your experience hasn't been in this field . . .

So?

So I just want you to understand, Clee said *that if the outline isn't right I'll have to get someone else.*

Robert stared at him in genuine wonder. No one had ever spoken to him like that. That it should come from this nonentity was truly revealing . . . Clee was in and he was out. As he went on gazing at Clee, Robert began almost to feel sorry for his small size and funny little moustache. He even stifled an impulse to reach over and pat him on the head.

Despite the poignancy of being once more in this place, close to Nia, he was disheartened when he went upstairs to look for her. She wasn't in her office. Nor was she in Eldon's outer one. Gwendolyn was alone there, the telephone to her ear, turned towards the row of filing cabinets under the windows.

In the hall, Robert hesitated. He could think of no credible excuse for crossing the threshold.

Suddenly Eldon's door opened and Nia came out. Robert backed away, out of sight, as furtive and excited as a small boy. When he peeked in again Nia was bent over Gwendolyn's desk, making notes on some papers, a lit cigarette in her other hand. She had on a dress of cream silk; her hair was swept back into a chignon and held in place by short combs. She looked familiar but impersonal, like an actress he recognized from pictures.

Gwendolyn put down the phone and Nia said something to her, whereupon the secretary took her dictation pad and went into Eldon's office. Nia sat down at the desk to finish what she was writing. Robert entered silently and stood before her. She looked up; their eyes met.

Neither was visibly moved. Both had instantly clamped down on their feelings. They regarded each other warily. Seconds passed. Then Robert said *Uh . . . Clee called. A service script . . .*

Oh — Her voice was even, professional.

Uh . . . How are you? It sounded totally trite.

Fine. And you?

He nodded. They fell silent again; there seemed to be nothing to say. But as they remained locked in each other's gaze a fine tingling began in Robert's fingertips, which, racing upward, overran his brain. And Nia felt all her self-control sliding away. In total stillness Robert heard the thunderous beatings of his heart and hers. Nia's mouth opened, there was a glint of metal among her teeth. This hint that she was real drove Robert wild.

I'll be . . . he whispered *in the small theatre.* He had noticed, on coming in, that it was empty.

He waited just inside the door. This was where his high hopes for *Montcalm* had turned to shame and rage. Though his fire now had more to do with lust than art, he was pleased that this same dark place might be about to witness a true triumph. Tensely he listened to the muffled sounds and voices of people in the hall. They died to quiet, and out of it, faintly at first, came the quickening tap of trim heels, stopping suddenly as she pushed against the padded panels. Then she was silhouetted, until with two swift steps she flung herself into his arms.

When she could pull her mouth away she said *We can't stay here! Come Friday — I'll arrange something. Give me half an hour. When you leave look in your pigeonhole —*

It was there: a small envelope in the second square box of the black honeycomb that hung on the wall outside the unit office. Originally it had been inside, but the directors tended to tear open their mail at once, which led to litter and lounging, and Eldon, in one of his sweeps, had it moved out. It still, after six weeks, had Robert's name on it. He reread Nia's message in the taxi taking him to the train. It merely said:

Friday, 6.30, in front of —

and gave an address that seemed to him near the middle of Mount Royal, not much more than about a mile from the Board.

8

At five minutes to seven she still wasn't there. Last night Robert had told Myra he'd have to go down for a meeting, that some Air Force people he had to see would be in Montreal only the next day, and if he missed the five o'clock train he'd likely stay over. Now, as instructed, he was standing in front of a stretched apartment row. It was a cheerless length of red brick set in black mortar, which had been built down as well as up, for it appeared to be sinking into the ground. The bottom layer of units were already buried to their window sills. A cab came. It was Nia, flustered, with a large bag of groceries and liquor, and a key.

Afraid of being seen with her on the street or in the lobby, Robert followed without stopping to read the name above the mail slot.

Ah . . . he said when he learnt whose place it was, for that person had long puzzled him. She was a good-looking woman with a senior position in the Board's distribution division. She dressed smartly, answered intelligently, and laughed when told something amusing. Moreover nothing shocked her, the opinion in the cutting rooms was that she was *super*. But her mocking manner kept men at a distance. There was no hint of romance of any kind, or sex, and she called herself 'Miss' with no suggestion that she'd ever been married. Occasionally, as now, she'd be in New York for a weekend, but then it would turn out that she'd merely been shopping.

Later, when Nia, who was bathing, asked him to look in the large double closet for a robe she could wear, Robert was amazed at its array of colorful coats and dresses, shoes, purses and scarves. It seemed heaped with frilly riches, like some female treasure trove. But the rest of the apartment was gloomy. Stuffed with ill-matched heirlooms — including a heavy dining table and eight stiff chairs — it had the funereal air of an auctioneer's warehouse; the activities of its occupant took up little more space than a path through a forest. There was one toothbrush in the holder, one cup and saucer beside the teapot, and only one lamp arranged for reading. The woman Robert knew seemed confined to the closet.

Two photographs in hinged wooden frames stood on the bedroom bureau. One showed the full face of a girl whose open gaze looked warm and gentle and altogether innocent; it was with surprise that Robert recognized it as a picture of their absent hostess.

The other was of a young man in naval uniform. Taken outside on a lawn, it showed him standing with his thumbs hooked in his pockets, smiling the way someone does who is both pleased and embarrassed.

Yes Nia said when Robert asked her. *She's never gotten over it.*

The small shake of his head masked a shudder; he'd glimpsed the terrible tyranny of love. Then at once he was pulling Nia against the banked pillows on the bed.

Hey! she protested. *What's with the horseplay?*

He needed to feel that she was tangibly there. *Why do I like you so much?*

Because — she said, letting the robe slip open *I have good legs!*

*

Beyond the bedroom, deep in the forest of furniture, the tall grandfather clock groaned, chimed, and after what sounded like a wheezy gasp, solemnly struck.

Nia sighed. She'd woken soon after coupling. Robert too was awake, an arm around her, his hand cradling her breast. She'd been thinking of how evenly her life had gone on without him, despite the low hollow ache of his absence. And then how in no time they were comfortably close, their bodies sweetly pressed together. There was more to this, she reflected, than romantic excitement, or even fleshy yearning. It had to do with the feel of skin, with smell, with the warm fleece of Robert's hair.

The clock struck again.

It tolls for thee . . . Robert said.

Yes . . . it reminds me of the Peace Tower. My wedding night. After all my affairs.

Was Buddy . . . ?

Yes — briefly. He'd been in the orchestra that played for a radio show I sang in, with two other girls. But he was soon in uniform — an army band — he did trombone and sometimes drums — he was a good drummer, actually —

And you stayed together. . . ?

No. He wanted to marry me — that's why I broke it off. I laughed in his face. However, he went overseas and got caught in the London blitz. Shrapnel ruined his arm — he was in hospital for months — and started to write to me. The letters kept coming — written with his left hand — in this painful scrawl — bunches of them — he must have worked on them every day — and songs — he ruled the staff lines on that thin airmail paper. They were derivative — and the lyrics sentimental — silly, really — but still, so many — sent over three years.

She was silent.

And then. . . ? Robert said.

The war ended in Europe and he was discharged — and finagled a flight back. He'd taken up conducting — he and some players formed a group —

Didn't he come to you?

Oh — right away. That was the trouble. There was that eager young man — with his scarred right arm — and there were all those letters. And he kept it up. Showered me with telegrams, phone calls, flowers, gifts — telling me a hundred times a day he loved me. I said to him 'Look — we don't really know each other.' What I didn't say was that he might not be good enough — but I didn't want to see myself as some kind of cruel snob. And he went on insisting that he'd loved me from even before the affair — that he'd always love me — Steadily I got sucked in. Then he said the war hadn't killed him but this would. That was talk, of course, but I couldn't quite bring myself to hurt him so much.* She hesitated, then added *Besides — he had talent and drive — everything was starting up again after the war — it was exciting.*

This happened in Toronto?

She nodded.

Then how'd you end up in Ottawa?

There was a booking agent —Buddy had missed him in Toronto — and he wanted me to go with him — to make a honeymoon of it.

109

He was in such a hurry — we were married at city hall and went straight to the train — and then to our room in the Chateau Laurier — and the instant the bellboy was gone he wanted me in bed — and I wouldn't. I felt trapped. I thought ' I might spend the rest of my life with this man but first I want to catch my breath'.

And you didn't. . . ?

No. Not then. After a while he went to sleep, worn out, and I sat up in an armchair — unwilling to let him have as his wife what I'd freely given him before. That's when I heard the Peace Tower — through the night — ringing the hours.

She fell silent. Robert too. He was keenly jealous but also pleased, almost proud, as if she'd been saving herself for him. After a moment Nia added *By dawn I was cold and tired — and resigned. And I crept in beside Buddy. That's how my marriage began —*

Well, it didn't last.

No, but it was my marriage.

9

The air force outline was child's play. In Ottawa, Robert went to Defense Headquarters, an austere building he'd always before passed with awe and unease. On the inside it turned out to be a hive of offices as drab and featureless as the Film Board's. There he called on the key people, listened to their *concepts*, all derived from other films, and then arranged these notions in logical order.

However, he added his own ending. The film was meant to impress on pilots, with more impact than a lecture, the need to know their aircraft, so that if systems failed they might still be able to bring it down. Robert's climax had a lone flyer losing almost all his instruments in a storm, and in zero visibility fighting panic and fear as he thinks his way through the crisis. There was to be no narration; the audience would hear only sound effects and the pilot's thoughts.

When he saw that sequence Clee wanted to object, but he had already been told, by a senior officer to whom Robert had mused about it, that it was a good idea, and the producer, unable to find anything else unconventional, had to be content with changing some simple words into service jargon.

Robert had eagerly looked forward to being in Montreal. He was still buoyed by the night in the sunken apartment, but capriciously, perversely — in fact afraid to risk a letter or phone call — he hadn't let Nia know he was coming. He'd hoped, imagined, that they would arrange something delightful on the spur of the moment. But she was fully committed. She was going to lunch with Eldon and a novelist who was now one of their most important writers, and afterwards taking her son to a doctor; the boy was going to summer camp for a week and had to have a required medical. Moreover, there was no place she and Robert could be alone. The novelist was waiting in her office and a new person had moved into Robert's. The theatres were in use, the cafeteria was crowded; there wasn't even an empty cutting room. Finally they retreated to the front steps of the building, where they stood uncomfortably in the sunlight, blinded by the strong glare.

Oh, this is too much! Nia cried. *We really must go away for a few days —*

Robert readily agreed, seeing no possibility of it.

*

That evening the heat in Ottawa was oppressive. The roads were like radiators, and near naked children, too sweaty to sleep, were poking holes in the softened asphalt. Robert walked from the streetcar. Famished, he had eaten nothing all day. This allowed him to pocket his taxi and meal allowances, poor pickings, but many at the Board resorted to them. Myra was sitting on the front steps cooling herself with a bamboo fan. She had on only a light silk kimono he'd once bought cheaply from a cameraman who'd brought back several from Japan. She looked charming, and in the light from the living room her brown eyes were bright.

Mother called she said. *They've rented a cottage in the Adirondacks for the rest of the season, and they'd like us to come.*

Frowning, Robert said *Can you go?*

At the end of the month I can, when Allison comes back.

Allison. . . ? Oh, your lab assistant.

Yes. Think of it, two weeks on a lake. And there's a boat. We haven't been in a boat for years.

Robert didn't reply.

You don't want to go Myra said.

No, I'd like to. But I can't. The script . . . But that shouldn't stop you. The change will do you good.

I'll miss you. So will mom and dad.

Yeah. They'll be heartbroken.

After he had supper they went into the bedroom, which a small electric fan had kept airy, and when Myra let the kimono slip from her shoulders she seemed as fresh and pretty as any of its printed flowers.

Nonetheless, the next morning, as soon as his wife was safely at work, he placed a careful call to the Board, counting on Clee to be out — he'd heard him say so — and then asking, in a exasperated tone, to be connected to Mrs. Wilson. When Nia came on he quickly told her he could go anytime after the end of the month.

10

They fled. Robert drove fast, gripping the wheel, his chin taut and outthrust. He'd already been highly tense by the time Nia, in a taxi, almost two hours late, finally turned into the supermarket parking lot where he'd been waiting with a rented car. It was

Friday afternoon — another fateful Friday! — and the place was a favourite with Film Board people. Nia too was terribly rattled. Eldon had prevented her planned noon slip away by demanding cast lists he could easily have asked for sooner. *I'm not going to shop!* she said. *Let's just get out of here —*

✳

They had almost crossed Bordeaux, and could see the bridge to Ile Jesus, when Nia told him to stop. He had fifty dollars for food; she took twenty and came back from a little liquor store with a bag of bottles and, to his silent surprise, no money left over. It was worse in the large Dominion store on the mainland. Robert trailed her, pushing the cart and mentally trying to add up the prices, but at the check-out, not looking at him, Nia impatiently opened her purse, and it both pleased and troubled him to let her pay.

Their disquiet was carried to the car. They were still pursued by a sense of danger, and were nervous and mute as more miles sped by. But by now they were on an open and largely empty highway, far from anything that might prevent their getting away. Robert glanced over.

Nia was staring straight ahead. Her mouth was shut tight, trying to contain her anger. The difficulties at home, when she repeatedly had to go over items with her mother, who was being deliberately obtuse, and the hassles at the office, all fuelled her irritation with Robert. *Really!* she thought. *What am I doing here with such a child!* Which had nothing to do with his age. Yet it did — because hers was moving on. She felt the unfairness of it, and sat silent in a welter of rage, distress, and self pity.

Yet, on both sides, purple vetch and golden trefoil fringed the rolling hayfields. The fields were cropped and resurging, already green. Here and there black-and-white cattle lay in the shade of shining pines. Scattered water holes flashed in the sun.

Robert was keenly regretting having revealed his anxieties and money grubbing. He wanted on this trip to seem strong, caring, confident.

Why are we stopping? Nia said.

For answer he took her in his arms and pressed open lips to hers, drawing her in like a deep breath. Nia's resentments melted. The kiss was sustained until they became unsettled by the sound of an oncoming car.

Well — she said *that was just in time* — *!*

And he knew she meant more than the passing motorist.

Oh! Nia soon said. *I have to tell you about Gwen* — It was a fishing shack owned by Gwendolyn's husband they were going to. *She came down with me to the cab, and she said* — *you know how big and moist her eyes get* — '*Whoever he is, I hope you'll be fantastically happy* — '

And?

I said to her '*You should be the one going* — '

Gwendolyn Lavois, nee Ellis, had grown up on an eastern Ontario farm that had gone from father to son for six generations. She had never questioned her existence or doubted God's goodness. In the office she kept a set of the three monkeys that see, hear and speak no evil. She'd married a French-Canadian telephone technician whom she met when he was at the Board doing some repairs. And when her relatives muttered *He's French? And Catholic?* she'd smilingly said *What's wrong with that?* And when the parish priest came to remind the new couple, who had married *derriere le sachristie,* about raising their children in the father's faith, she said *Why not? At least 'till they have their own ideas.* Her good humour carried her like a light skiff over those perilous waters; by refusing to look down she avoided seeing what lay below.

The small ways in which the secretary shared in Nia's life expanded her own, making it seem much more exciting. Her husband sensed it, and was jealous. He'd removed the cook stove from the shack, saying it needed fixing, then had kept finding reasons why he couldn't take Nia there. Gwendolyn had driven her up one evening after work, to show her the route.

*

A steeple appeared, then the small town around it.

Did you bring a stove? Nia said.

Yes. It's in the trunk. It was a new Coleman camp outfit, whose cost still rankled.

Well, you get gas and matches for it — I'll pick up what else we need.

Resigned, Robert then rejoined her and carried the parcels. Watching her thoughtfully choose foods as diverse as chick peas and Polish sausage, minute steak and cantaloupe, he saw that she planned her intricate menus in her mind, just as a chess player thinks out moves. It increased his respect and made him uneasy. When they were under way again he said *Here*... and handed over his thirty dollars.

It's all right —

No, it's what it's for. Nia put the bills on the dashboard. But the breeze threatened to blow them off. She sighed and placed them in her purse.

*

The road became a rutted track brooding under long shadows. It left the conifer forest, wound through scrub land, skirted a marshy basin and all at once entered a mixed stand of white and yellow birches, where the car slowly bumped over rock outcroppings and fallen branches.

The last gleams of sunlight were slipping from the small glade when they reached it; in a moment the light was blue, the air a heavy mix of summer scents.

Nia said *We're here* — and went up to the shack. It was a plain, square box of fir plywood. Four cedar posts, from which bark was peeling, held it off the ground, and a shaky step, made of a short board laid across concrete blocks, led to the only door. Behind the door stood an old icebox, painted white; this left a kitchen space so small that anyone sitting at the narrow table had to get up to let another go by. Nia lit an oil lamp: a single bedroom, its floor almost entirely taken up by a metal bedspring, led off the kitchen, and separated from it by a partition was a small empty room that held only a spattered card table and two rolled-up mattresses hanging by wires. Through the kitchen windows they could see the glimmer of the lake, and when they went out again they heard the quiet lapping of water.

Nia wanted to use the outhouse. A relic, dragged there from some derelict place, it humbly faced the entrance of the shack. Its door, fallen from the rusted hinges, served as a dry walkway over the leaf mold. There was no paper. Robert brought a roll from the car, and discreetly turned away. But a minute later, when he was coming back with their block of bought ice and his hand axe, he stopped, lifted his head and stared.

Hey, don't look here — ! She called.

He laughed. *Right now I feel I want to be close to you, even in that.* Just then he felt that toilet functions were also part of the poetry of that lovely body. Still smiling, he went on before she could respond. But what he'd said was true, and it troubled him.

*

In the morning, when Robert heard Nia stir, he brought her a cup of hot coffee. While she sipped it he sat beside her on the bed and tacked to the wall a small shelf with a candle holder, made from slabs of wood he'd split from a log, using his hand axe. When she got up there was warm water for her to wash with, and before she had breakfast ready he'd firmed the front step. The night before he had immediately dealt with the icebox, skillfully chipping the block of ice to size. He had fitted every sliver into place, and then neatly packed all the perishables into the lower compartment. And he had quickly set up the stove, while airing the larger mattress on a stripped pole he'd wedged between the forks of two trees.

Nia said *I've never had anyone who could do such things —*

Well . . . he said evasively *I've used that axe for quite a while. Bought it when I was a kid, with money from snow shovelling. Five cents a driveway . . . and some were pretty long.*

He was avoiding her wonder, her regard, because earlier, when he had quietly risen from Nia's side and had begun to put the day in order, he'd been happier than he could ever recall. Carrying water up from the lake, doing things for her comfort, looking in on her as she slept, he had felt an intense sympathy for her, an urge to shelter her. He was afraid of what had been happening in those few hours, afraid of becoming rooted, not to this place, but to the powerful tenderness that being here together stirred in him.

For Nia there was something elemental in Robert's services, as if he and she were alone in the world. It had an Adam and Eve quality that seemed to erase their difficulties. She felt softened and close. *My period's started —*

Really, from . . . ?

Yes. It's the longest I've ever gone without one. And there's not much — it should be over soon.

He suspected her flow was because of being here, and though the news freed him, it also caused fresh anxiety. *Do you think you're still fertile?*

Oh, I think so — As long as I'm ovulating —

He nodded, barely.

I'll go on using the cream.

It was a contraceptive cream, which he'd come to like. The smell, vaguely perfumed, was pleasant, and with it she was delightfully, doubly lubricated.

*

Her food was delicious. She'd brought her iron frying pan and a bag of spices, and was as deft in the tiny kitchen, cooking on the camp stove, as he with his axe. He wondered where she had acquired such skill.

I like to cook — she declared. *I've been doing it ever since I was a youngster. And sometimes I'm a party person — I like to cook for people to eat.* In the same way she liked to give herself. She made generous snacks and cool drinks of gin, bringing them to where

Robert was working — he was always working, always finding things to do.

A large basswood tree had fallen at the edge of the lake. Balanced by the earth mass torn up at its base, the long trunk was only half submerged. It was broad enough to walk or sit on, and as the shady hillside offered no suitable place to stretch out, Robert had decided to make of the tree a dock on which Nia could sunbathe. He was trimming off the branches when she came down, carefully carrying a small tray, but almost tripping over roots and rocks.

Oh, sorry, he said *I'll make a path.*

In a little while, when he was clearing the crown of the tree, he glanced toward the shack and saw Nia struggling up the steep slope. At once he scrambled over and took the pail of water from her. *Hey! You're not supposed to carry heavy things.*

I know, she said, smiling *but just now I feel I can —*

They should have been happy. But happiness was welling up their fears.

*

In the afternoon Nia was sitting on the front step, smoking, drinking her third or fourth gin-and-lime. She was painting her nails a jaunty red, and pensively gazing out at the lake. Stirred by the sun, a slight breeze was rippling the water towards the farther shore across an expanse of quivering brilliance, as if countless firework sprinklers were bobbing on the tiny waves. Beyond it the glare softened, and the wooded hills rose palely against the hot white sky. Nearby the tree trunks were deeply shaded, almost black, while below, bent over his path, in which he was digging dirt steps, Robert was all but obscured by underbrush.

She was dismayed by his display of energy, by the obvious disquiet driving it. That it should happen on their first day magnified the mounting threat inherent in his mood. The morning's tenderness was gone. She now felt more than ever mismatched. *I can't turn back the clock —* she thought.

Robert's feelings were completely confused. Presently he put down the piece of shale he had used and started walking away from the shack. The farther he went the better he felt, and then, becoming released from his conflicts, and boyishly daring, he began to circle the lake. But after a mile or more he saw that the bay he was going round gave on to another, and that on to one more; those hidden inlets made the whole thing much larger than it looked. Besides, he was beginning to worry about having left Nia alone, and turned back.

The afternoon was slanting through the trees. The tawny forest floor smelled comfortingly of dryness and damp, growth and decay — cycles in balance, he felt, while he, torn, was inwardly so tangled. The relief of his escape from Nia was now rapidly changing to anxiety. He struggled up a height of land, and when he could see her still sitting on the step, he felt flooded by the warm sunshine. Suddenly he seemed strong, able to carry all before him, and he hurried over to her.

*

At supper — they'd agreed that while they were here they would speak of *breakfast, lunch and supper,* which seemed fresher and more country than *dinner* — Robert peered at her over his wineglass and said hesitantly *You have a few more grey hairs...*

Well, it's going that way.

It's your drinking. The alcohol...

Her shrug cut him off. He backed away, then went around. *You don't rinse or anything?*

No — what comes will come. It's sad when women try to cover aging. It was as she'd feared. But pretense about her person was futile. And she resented having to defend it. *Moreover,* she added evenly *I don't like pastes and powders.*

He noticed the tiny lines forming between her nose and lips. *Well, you don't need them* he said a trifle too heartily. *You've got lovely skin.* It sounded patronizing, though he hadn't meant it to. *Still that gorgeous figure... and marvellous breasts.* He silently rebuked his unwonted formality: ordinarily he'd have said *great boobs. You're* ... he went on, trying to lighten his tone *very beautiful.*

She took a drag on her cigarette, and breathed out a sigh.

*

When she had washed the dishes Nia dressed in a sheer white blouse and brightly-striped cotton skirt. She put on thin white sandals held by narrow thongs, then let her hair loose and gathered it at the nape of the neck with a black ribbon. Against the chill of the evening she hung a light black sweater around her shoulders. And after applying a lipstick, the colour of the spirited red of her nails, she went out to join Robert, who was leaning against the bar on which he had aired the mattress. Even he, in vague acknowledgment of Saturday night, had changed into clean khaki trousers and shirt.

The sun had set, leaving a rosy orange sky behind the dark screen of foliage between them and the lake. Robert said *You know* ... and took her into his arms. *Being here brings things down to basics. Really, our differences don't matter. And your age doesn't matter.* He had meant it as a fundamental truth, but the moment it was out he knew it was terribly wrong.

Well, thank you! Nia cried, pushing away from him. And she burst into furious, fierce weeping. Robert reached out a comforting hand but she drew back, glaring at him through glittering eyes, flooded with tears. *You're a coward* — she cried. *It's incredible how shut up in yourself you are. You won't commit to anything! You can't really get close to anybody —*

To any — body he thought, trying to dismiss her decrial, and grimly enjoying the word play, continued silently *I got close to yours.*

— You're so damn frightened of losing control!

Nonetheless he quailed. Each accusation cut with an edge of truth.

I on the other hand plunge on! she sobbed. *Long ago the fear of being hurt took second place with me. God, my husband — and all my lovers were younger than me! But not one has been such a child as you!*

Her outburst about lovers was almost literally true. Because of her facial bone structure, trim, lithe figure and especially her spontaneous manner, she had always seemed younger to others.

But what startled and frightened Robert more than her words was the bitterness and contempt in them, the kind of primordial female rage. As well, he'd been instantly jealous of those other men. Though wounded, he stood his ground like an ox with his back to a storm, because he perceived that she was also taking out on him anger over the fading of her beauty, and other fears and burdens for which he wasn't responsible. His resistance gathered round what he felt was unfair, and staring at her from under frowning brows he thrust back the whole attack. *It's all crap!* he thought.

She'd stopped shouting, but was still brokenly crying. He began to hope the worst was over when abruptly she raised her head. *Maybe no one's big enough to give himself completely — probably people just aren't capable of it. The hope that makes me go on trusting — in the end hurts only me. Only me.*

This, he thought, was rhetorical self-pity. Yet he felt wounded by it, as if he were suffering on her behalf. But before he could say anything soothing she turned and stumbled into the shack. There she threw herself onto the bed, keening and biting her hands. He followed, amazed at the immensity of her grief. For a while he stood at the foot of the mattress, sadly watching, then, feeling thoroughly sorry, he stretched out beside her and, as much as he dared, started gently stroking her back.

Beyond the windows the dusk deepened; inside it was already dark. Nia lay facing the wall, and had long been silent. An hour or more passed. Robert went on slowly brushing her hair and neck with his lips. Gradually the warmth of her body, the softness of her skin, the gentle contours of her figure, the essence of her living, breathing, tender presence encompassed him, and he felt it was infinitely precious. It was as if some kind fate had generously placed her beside him, as if she was a wondrous gift that had been inexplicably conferred on him. It seemed to him that this moment held what was more important than anything else, and that he must devote his life to this feeling. All his qualifications dissolved. He put his mouth to her ear and whispered *Nia, I love you.*

*

The next day was extraordinary for its detail. The vivid blue flame of the gas stove, the rich smell of coffee, the sweet cantaloupe juice, their touch on each other's skin, even the click of his spoon against Robert's teeth — at which they both laughed — all struck them as singular and exquisite.

When the light faded they stood once more by the crossbar, watching the rising rim of the moon. Nia leaned back against Robert, his arms were around her, her head rested on his shoulder. The breeze slackened; songs of birds died away. There was a moment of stillness. Then from the depths of the woods they heard six clear, sad notes.

Nia recognized the song and gave it words: *I — could — cry — sal-ty — tears —*

Instantly the phrase was repeated.

Darling — Nia cried *it's a love bird — a wonderful crazy love bird!* The actual sounds hadn't gone beyond those six notes, yet in her mind she heard reverberations of all the love songs she had ever sung, or cared about. It was like a swelling chorus that floated her dreamily through the rest of the evening.

*

The following morning they were wakened by a scratching above them. Looking up, they saw a small brown mouse peeking over the top of the partition. It regarded them soberly, then twitched its whiskers, sat up, and began washing its face with its feet.

*See —*Nia whispered *he's not afraid.*

Maybe he's a love mouse Robert said.

They swam, Nia read, Robert finished the path. They exchanged glances that were gleams of pleasure; they had a sense of something settled, of peace after a long struggle. At supper Nia took only a glass of wine, and refused a brandy. Robert noticed she wasn't smoking.

I'm happy she said. *I don't want to dull it.*

When it grew dark they took a blanket and went down to the dock. Sitting on the broad trunk, arms around each other, their free hands clasped, they looked out at the water, a layer of molten light, and at the surrounding hills, which seemed bathed in silver. The round moon was so bright it almost obscured the stars. Robert could distinctly see the shadow of Nia's lashes on her cheek.

Listen — she said, and freed her talking hand. *The summer Joel and I were at Martha's Vineyard — when the divorce was being processed — mother had gone to her relatives in Woodstock — we had a beautiful studio house on the lagoon —*

Your own?

No, no! Rented, of course — anyway, in it there was a curving staircase from the upper balcony bedrooms down to the large two-storeyed studio room — the man who had helped the owners build the house was called Broni something — and very brawny he was — anyway he built this beautiful staircase — it has a name — something like Dancing Stairs — Francis will remember —

Francis? Though he guessed she meant Francis Findlay, a music critic who was widely read and admired. A consummate musician, Findlay had failed to achieve his own standards as a pianist and at nineteen had given up the concert stage; he now lived in Manhattan and wrote for a prominent journal. Nia said she'd known him *forever,* and that he was *very dear,* and *family.* Then going on with her story she told of the unexpected arrival, that summer, of two other friends, and Robert certainly knew who they were — the man and his wife both acted, often together, and always in starring roles.

*One day I was looking up the back lane —*Nia continued *and saw him on the crutches — and she behind him — he'd just had a horrible hip operation — but they were on holiday — having driven over— and had reservations at the village hotel. He took one look at our beautiful place and said 'Nia, we have to stay here — please let us.' I was delighted but worried, because the only available beds were two cots in the studio main room that were daytime couches — but they wanted to stay — and they stayed —*

Robert interrupted again, this time to kiss her: he was becoming uneasy about this lustrous past, from which he was wholly excluded. Nia gave herself to the kiss, but when their lips parted she went on at once. *Joely and I had the master balcony room overlooking the main room — Francis was ensconced in his hideaway in the basement — and at night they had the cots pulled together in the studio — one about three inches higher than the other. One morning I was awake very early — and I decided to sneak down the winding stairs to the kitchen for coffee. I got halfway down and glanced over at them — on their uncomfortable cots — and they were holding hands.*

Robert said nothing; he was wary of finer feelings in her successful friends. Nia sensed it and hesitated, but his arm tightened around her. After a moment, in a low voice, she said *So I sat down on the steps and looked — and said to myself, solemnly and to remember — 'I will never marry again — or love again — until I can do that. I've never done that or felt that — and until I do it won't matter'.*

Robert wanted to take her hand, but was afraid it might seem too maudlin. Then he did take it, pressing slightly.

Funny — Nia said *the next day on our lagoon beach — separately — he and she both told me they were unhappy and confused — and thought they should divorce. So I told them separately about the dancer's steps — and the hand holding. I'm not saying that their deal is a good one — or even an honest one — but I'll never forget how important those hands holding tight were and are to me.*

124

Now she too remained silent. Robert sighed. The story had moved him, but he couldn't help wondering whether either Findlay or the actor, or both, had been her lovers. *Well. . . ?* he said.

Well now at last I have that.

Intoxicated with pleasure and pride, he groaned *Oh God, I love you. . . !*

*

Now that he loved her, as he knew he'd never loved anyone before, Robert felt that all he was belonged by right to Nia. He was ready to give her — if only he could simply hand it over — all his manly strength and talent, and certainly his every possession, and wanted to tell her that, but was held back by that other self in which Myra shared. How he would resolve this he didn't know. His shadowy memory of Myra was the only blemish in these days of bliss.

It seemed to the lovers they were completely alone in a world of clean water and balmy air, sparkling sunshine and velvety nights. They'd seen no other person, and only once had the distant sound of an outboard motor, coming from some hidden, far reach of the lake, momentarily reminded them of a wider existence. *We'll have lunch by the beach!* Nia said.

Below the shack and towards their tree dock the hillside plunged steeply into the water, but in the other direction it flattened around a minuscule bay, a low curved inlet into which eddying ripples had deposited a thin ribbon of sand. Succulent grasses and wildflowers grew there. Robert carried down the folded card table and rested it on four small rocks. Nia, following with the food and wine, moved the table over against a graceful clump of blue flag, which then looked as though placed there to decorate it.

Below its covering of leaves and tiny debris the ground was damp, so Robert brought the smaller mattress, a squashed, worn-down pallet more like a thick mat, and they sat on it while slowly relishing their meal. The sky's warmth, mingled with a slight breeze off the water, was softly caressing. *I'm not leaving* — Nia said.

She smoothed oil on her exposed skin, then laughed and took off her clothes. He did the same, and they anointed each other from head to toe and sank back, their oiled bodies side by side. Soon all that delicious, encompassing warmth became desire. He raised himself and looked into her knowing eyes.

She nodded. *I'm all right now* —

They coupled in full sunlight. Nia, with her moist hair framing her face and flowing beneath them, and her fingers among the small plants on either side of the mat, felt as if she was of the earth. She shut her eyes. Robert was almost incidental, his movements warm water, breeze and sun. As if the elements were making love to her. She'd never felt more fulfilled. Just at the climax she opened her eyes and said *I've got the best of it* — *'cause I can see the sky* —

This is sublime Robert thought. *Life can't be better than this.*

*

The following days seemed almost as good, and on the final one they were sad, and often stopped to look at the small sights that had become dear to them, and which, though they said *until the next time*, they knew they were unlikely to see again. During their trip back that mood of tender rue lasted through the late afternoon and evening, when for long periods Nia sat close to Robert and rested her head on his shoulder.

But at the bridge to her island all the old difficulties arose. She asked Robert to stop short of it, saying she would walk over. They could see her house: all the windows were lit, either because she was expected or because the old woman and boy, alone all week, had put on the lights to keep up their courage. Robert got out and gave Nia her suitcases; she murmured lovingly when she kissed him, but he felt her mind was already on her family. He watched her walk across, holding a suitcase in each hand, like a porter. It struck him as monstrous — he wanted to run and take the load from her, but . . . couldn't imagine facing her mother.

11

Myra returned with a tanned face and two fresh pickerel, which her father had caught and packed in dry ice.

Where were you? she said. *I phoned you twice the first week, when we went to town, just to say how much I missed you.*

Well, in the mornings I've been going for walks, while it's still cool. And in the evening I've been at the movies.

The last, at least, was partly true. Back in Ottawa, during his wife's second week away, he'd gone almost every night to the neighbourhood movie house, or to one within walking distance. Their third-and-fourth-run features, which he actually did analyze, had helped keep his mind off Nia.

*

Now that he'd affirmed his love, to carry on as before with his wife seemed too great a betrayal of both women. And he found a way, within the frame of his home and marriage, to withdraw into a separate space.

In the basement, next to a tiny toilet with a miniature sink and stand-up shower, there was a clean little room roughly lined with varnished pine boards, where the previous owner had built model ships. Its former workbench was a wide shelf that could be used as a desk, and Robert moved in his typewriter, a small lamp, a thin rag rug, a wooden chair and a folding cot, which when opened fitted from wall to wall. He said he needed this study in order *to think,* and after the first few nights, when he pretended to work late and fall asleep, Myra asked whether he meant to eat there too.

Look . . . I don't want to offend you, but I simply need solitude.

For an air force script?

No! I'm thinking of other things . . .

Indeed, he was taken up with announcing the change to Nia. He wrote, intimating that this was the beginning of a separation from Myra, but carefully avoiding anything that could be construed as commitment. Even the loving words with which he closed, when he reviewed them, seemed to imply that he was liable, and he rewrote the last page. Moreover, he was afraid that the letter, to Nia at the Board, but without a sender's name or address, might go astray. Yet despite this fitfulness he expected Nia to read a good deal into what he'd said, and he anxiously awaited her response.

When it slid through the mail slot he pounced like a hawk on its prey, imagining that Myra, who was at work, might just then, for some completely unexpected reason, return home suddenly. But all his concern was wasted: Nia's letter, in its thick Film Board envelope, bearing the Canadian coat of arms, and with *TV Unit, N. Wilson* neatly typed in the corner, looked like any of the official letters he still occasionally got from the Board.

He trembled, and was dismayed:

> Darling, do you recall a lunch we had at the lake? That crazy salad to use up the Polish sausage — and we drank the bottle of wine — I'm bad at sequences but that was a building day for you, I think — now don't say what day wasn't —

Having expected a rush of gratitude and hope, he could scarcely believe she'd begun with vapid memories. And on the day she referred to they'd made love in the sun — he thought she might have remembered that!

> Anyway, I shopped on the way home at the Dominion store on Lucerne, and I saw a can of chick peas (part of our salad) — and until then I was just finding food as they say — and suddenly it was all wonderful again — I went mad and bought the chick peas and Polish sausage —and steaks for tonight's dinner and to look pretty on a plate until we eat them — a pineapple, an eggplant, limes for white rum — my new drink — bananas, and — it's never happened before— nectarines — Joel and I ate one as

soon as I got home — they are heaven — have you ever
eaten one?

All this trivia, in which he was hardly mentioned, was distinctly
vexing. Though he admired her means of writing directly to him,
he couldn't help blaming her for his abrupt disappointment. He
had a sudden sour feeling that she would always dash his hopes.
Frowning, he read on:

> Funny, I haven't really wanted to cook or eat since we
> were away. I had forgotten that I'm really a big baby — and
> that all I had to do was pretend — and the pretending
> though childish is comforting.

He skipped impatiently through a paragraph about having
supper with some wine and then coffee and going to bed, though
he reread with pleasure its closing sentence: *I miss you and love
you.* Then:

> Couldn't you have a flower or something in your small
> room. Plant a seed please — a lemon seed, or a grapefruit
> seed — an old coffee can will do. They grow very pretty —
> there isn't any life in that sepia, orange and yellow room.

And that was all! No mention of his fidelity, of the sacrifices he
was making. Robert sat for a long time with the letter in his hand,
pondering the caprice, the perfidy of women.

*

Nia had skirted the main issue because she was unsure of just
what Robert thought it was. His letter, which had come to her
desk in a plain business envelope, was completely unclear. True, he
seemed to have taken a step — but towards what? Legally and finan-
cially they couldn't be together, and even if that changed, there
would still be her family, age, and ... After her childhood illnesses

she'd had health and energy for everything, but now, increasingly, she felt tired. And only a week back at the office had brought on a miserable summer cold. She'd penned her letter with a damp tissue in the other hand.

*

Robert read and reread Nia's letter. It was his beloved's handwriting, and he kissed the pages. Believing he could almost detect her perfume, he was ready to forgive them both, to fling aside everything else, if only he could have her in his arms again. Her words evoked her tender flesh and being, almost as if he could feel her body and spirit. Yet he wondered that a beautiful, professional, accomplished and widely experienced woman could, within herself, harbour such simplistic, even childlike, feelings.

*

Without her presence to sustain it, the gentleness he'd felt evaporated like morning mist, leaving a smouldering lust. Everything fed it. The sight of every female reminded him of her, and one evening when he was out walking — he could no longer sit in the house — the sweet fragrance of white nicotiana so recalled Nia's contraceptive cream that it drove him in a frenzy to his cot.

*

However, he could find no excuse for going to Montreal. He couldn't tell Myra he was going to the Board and meet Nia instead; that, he now felt, would be too mean, too vile a betrayal. And one too easily exposed. And though he had all the *gen* — an RAF term for general information he'd heard from Clee, which Robert liked to repeat with mild contempt — needed to complete the script, and he could have done that in a few days, he knew the producer would be suspicious of such speed. To satisfy him he had to drag it out another three weeks. The Air Force wanted to fly him to their base at Trenton, but he kept putting that off, fearing he might miss a chance to be with Nia.

It was a hot end-of-August night. He lay nude under a single sheet imagining, by way of a surrogate, the unseen mother superior in Cape Breton. But soon surfeited with carnal fraud, he began to think of Myra on the floor above. The house was quiet, and the glow of a quarter moon, diffused by thin cloud, faintly illuminated the rooms. She blinked in confusion at his touch, but silently moved over when he slid into bed. In a whisper, he asked her to take off her nightgown. She got up, went quickly to the bathroom, rinsed her mouth and came back bare, shutting the door behind her. They embraced without words, and Robert, feeling guilty, made love to his wife.

After lying with her a little while he twisted away.

You're not going? she cried.

Yeah, I think. . .

No! I'm not a whore you can use as you like! I don't know what you think you're doing, but — and she burst into tears.

He felt wretched; and though resolved, he sincerely used her pet name. *My, I'm sorry . . . I have to be alone.*

You bastard! she cried. *You goddamn bastard!* Shaken, furious, she beat at him with her fists.

Her blows, which fell on his arms and chest, were delivered with force, but their meaning was much more painful — neither had ever struck the other before. *My, I'm really sorry . . .* he said, and went out, leaving her quietly weeping.

The next night was again warm; the windows and all internal doors were open. Robert was wakened by a wraith-like figure beside his cot, and in an instant Myra let her gown fall in a sheer white mound around her feet. *Okay, you bum* she said. *I'm coming in.* She climbed on top of him, and he, not ungratefully, embraced her.

Then after the long weekend she suddenly returned in the middle of the afternoon, skittered down the basement stairs, and still in her tailored suit sat herself in her husband's lap and abruptly seduced him.

When they untangled he said *How is it you're here?*

131

I'm on my way from a meeting at the Bureau of Mines. But I have another back at the lab. She giggled as she swept up her clothes and glanced at her watch. *I've got to fly —*

And that remark led Robert, as he lay there musing after his wife had left, to consult Clee about the psychology of the last script sequence.

*

The producer was puzzled but pleased. He listened gravely, nodding his head and muttering *Hmm* and *yeah . . .* and *you may have something there.* He was flattered. It was the first time he had been sought out by one of the *artistic types,* and he began to think he might become a moulder of talent.

For Robert the ruse was ideal. Clee had immediately agreed they should meet, and had raised no objection to his travelling to Montreal for the evening, so they could *start fresh* in the morning. Robert had phoned Nia; when he arrived at his hotel she was already waiting, holding a large soft handbag and sitting near the elevators on one of the grey pseudo-leather settees. From the desk he had a moment to observe her. She looked stately, like a movie star expecting her chauffeur, or her agent. When he passed her Robert repeated the room number in her hearing, as if verifying it with the bellboy, and in a few minutes, after the other had gone, Nia was at his door.

Even as they kissed he sensed that she wasn't the woman he'd been obsessed with. She was less sensual, more poised and self-contained. He too had to pretend the intimacy he'd felt at the shack. It was as if the posturing persons who had exchanged letters were interposed between them. But for the business at hand Nia knew just what to do. She took from her bag a bottle of white rum and two limes, and hid in the bathroom when the room-service waiter brought soda and ice.

Drinking, talking and fondling brought the lovers close again. After they had been intimate, Nia sent Robert for food, and from a French restaurant a few blocks away he returned with hot roast chicken and big broiled mushrooms flecked with fennel, all of which they ate with their fingers. In the morning they took a taxi to the Board. Robert got out and walked the last few blocks, and they met in the cafeteria as if by chance, sharing a table for breakfast. Robert, refreshed and alert, was studying the script in Clee's outer office by the time the producer came in.

In this way they were able to rendezvous twice more, free, for Robert, of the restraint of costs. Though Clee had bargained hard about the price of the script — in keeping with the Board's belief that freelancers' fees were always suspect — expenses, for outsiders and staff alike, were treated as a matter of course. Robert's collect phone calls, taxi and train fares, hotel and meal allowances were paid without question. The only drawback was Myra.

*

Why do you have to go overnight? she said. *What's wrong with the early morning train?*

That's what's wrong with it — it's too early. And all the commuters are rushing to catch it. This way I have time to collect my thoughts.

Well, you can think about me before you leave she said on the third occasion. It was a Sunday, and she began to unbutton his shirt. He had to oblige her, but though she was normally moist, even apt to run, this time she was strangely dry, and Robert went to Nia chafed and sore where it mattered most.

*

However, for Nia these trysts were nurturing. She'd come to crave Robert's caresses. Lately, when coupling, he'd begun to lock a leg around one of hers, leaving his hands free, and his continuous kissing and fondling of her breasts, arms, face and hair, while he slowly brought her to climax, was a bountiful, voluptuous bath. Later, lying beside him, she had moments of mindless contentment.

133

Yet she felt stifled by the furtiveness of these meetings, and enjoyed her scope between them. Most of the Board's production people had long lost their awe of her; increasing familiarity had resulted in friends. She had more dinner invitations than she could in conscience accept. Moreover, she sometimes met after work with several Jewish authors who were sharp and very funny. With them she would drink, talk and laugh until the wee hours. This conviviality was vital. Wit and laughter had been a large part of her life. With her lover she seldom laughed now.

After the third of their hotel nights, when Robert was sitting with Clee the following morning, and felt he'd extracted all possible delay from the flyer's thought process, he sighed and said *Well, have we done it?*

Yep. I think we've brought home the bacon. And now, the producer added almost paternally *it's time you went to Trenton. Then you can tidy the whole thing up.*

*

At the base he was treated with regard. Escorted by officers, wherever he went men sprang to attention; one, thinking him in civvies, even saluted. Robert was tempted to take himself seriously; he narrowed his eyes and scrutinized the new fighter as if he knew what he was seeing. Then he was separately shown its jet engine. Mounted on a pedestal, gleaming like a piece of Brancusi sculpture, it did inspire sober respect. Its stout ring of combustion chambers, finely formed of stainless steel the colour of pale gold, bespoke its power and precision; and on a small aluminum plate, like an artist's initials, was the double-R insignia of its maker. A tall, handsome man with wide bands on his epaulets, close-cropped greying hair and a tanned, serious face — a movie-star officer — said to him *We have in this an almost perfect machine. If only there wasn't the human factor. . .*

*

134

A day later, in Ottawa, as Robert was coming from Defense Headquarters and trying to cross Confederation Square, popularly called *Confusion Square*, he heard behind him a voice calling *Rachmiel —!* He turned round: it was Nigel. The latter was in town to research a film on parliament. But they could scarcely hear over the traffic; besides, the encounter seemed to call for some festivity. The Chateau Laurier was a few steps away. They descended to its *Snake Pit*. Neither was at ease in a tavern, but they clinked their glasses of beer in the tradition of Fitzgerald and Hemingway and tried to behave like hard-drinking writers.

Fourteen years earlier, high over their heads, Nia had endured her wedding night huddled in a red armchair.

Nu, how's service life? Nigel said.

A farce. A boy's game! Robert exclaimed. *They'd prefer tin soldiers. They don't want any 'human factor'.* The fumes of alcohol, the dim light, the enclosed booth, all fed his bravado. He went on mauling the military, ending with *I don't know whether to laugh or cry!*

*

On the Friday, in the Film Board cafeteria, Nigel saw Clee eating alone, and asked if he could join him. This hadn't ever happened before; the producer had always been ignored by the *egghead hoity-toity*. But ah, now that he had Aronson . . . Indeed, Nigel mentioned running into Robert, and by way of telling an amusing story, related all that Robert had said.

Clee's sudden dismay was too much for him; he excused himself and went off to nurse the pain in the privacy of his office. He felt he was the victim of a bluff, that he had been made the butt of a sly, cruel, and snobbish joke.

Nigel too lost his appetite. Apart from their rivalry he was rather fond of Robert, and pleased about having earlier helped him with a place to stay, but he was envious of the other's apparent freedom and success. He had hoped, of course, to replace Robert in the television unit, but Eldon had pointedly kept putting him off. And the proposed film about parliament, aimed at placating the government, was merely insipid PR. Nigel was becoming the Board's odd-job man. He knew he should be independently writing stories or plays, but he lacked the courage to plunge into blank spaces. He admired romantics who aimed beyond their abilities, but he was too worldly wise, in his quiet way, to risk the comfort he had. So he clung to his misery while holding it in contempt, and that it had caused him to target his friend made him feel, for a few seconds, slightly sick.

*

When Robert phoned to say the script was finished he was startled by Clee's coldness. The producer told him not to come down but to send it by special delivery, and wait for his comments. They came by return mail, scrawled in the margins: *scene too thin, wrong emphasis, relevance not clear,* and about the last sequence *doesn't work.* Robert was flabbergasted, and immediately phoned.

There's nothing wrong with this script he said.

That's your opinion Clee replied. *I think it needs a complete rewrite.*

Jesus Christ . . . I'm not doing any rewrite!

Then I'm not paying for it.

Stunned, Robert mumbled *We'll see* and hung up. When he had sufficiently recovered, he called MacCurry.

After a silent pause the production chief said *All right, we'll sort it out. I can see you . . . three-fifteen tomorrow. That'll let you get the train back.*

MacCurry knew the schedules. But it would leave no time for Nia. *How about the morning after?*

Can't do. I'm in Toronto. Then I'm tied up for at least two weeks.

*

Robert got to the Board by city buses at ten minutes past three. He'd dithered too long to call Nia, and when he phoned from the Montreal station some strange voice said she was out and might not be back until the next day. This series of setbacks rattled him; he reverted to cautious thrift and walked for a while before definitely deciding to pocket the cost of a cab.

He dashed to the Director of Production's office. Clee, red faced and rigid, was standing by the secretary's desk. They were shown in at once.

I don't know what's eating him. It's a perfectly professional script Robert said, handing the marked-up copy to MacCurry.

It's not! The whole tone is wrong Clee exclaimed. *I think we'll have to get someone else. Right from the start, if you recall, I had doubts about his f-f-fitness f-f-for this kind of thing.*

MacCurry stared. He hadn't expected such stress, and wisely wanted to gain time. *I'll have it read by a third party.*

Who? Suspicious, Robert felt the bureaucracy was being stacked against him.

Nora Wilson.

MacCurry didn't mean to be cunning. It was Nia's job to evaluate scripts for the television unit and now and then he asked her opinion about other work. He knew nothing of her tie to Robert. Had he known, he would have been astonished.

No . . . Robert said. *What has she to do with it?* He was afraid it might lead to some disclosure.

I've had enough of this! cried Clee. *Let's just call it quits. He's been paid f-f-for the outline.*

Clee's fury was forcing MacCurry to act. He had no doubt that Robert was right about the script, but in this extremity he wasn't going to sacrifice a producer. And he reflected, a little sourly, that once again talent had proved to be trouble. *You'll be paid in full* he said to Robert. *Good-bye.*

Robert caught his eye and understood that from now on the NFB would be completely closed to him.

*

In the Board's main hall some people were already heading out, wearing preoccupied expressions, as if they were hurrying to

137

important engagements, though half of them, everyone knew, could be found, if necessary, in the nearby taverns. Robert went upstairs, passing Eldon's outer door; a young woman he didn't know was dusting the three monkeys with the brush end of a type-writer eraser. Nia's office was open too; he stepped into her tiny anteroom and stopped in the inner doorway — she was at her desk!

Oh! she said.

They both smiled. Robert could feel his face refusing to erase its flush, and Nia immediately registered it.

What's happened?

Who's that new girl? he said evasively, jerking his head towards the hall.

Gwen's on holiday —

Where were you?

She gazed at him with rising impatience, but held it. *With the director of the Nouvêâu Monde. They've proposed a series —*

Of plays?

Films of plays. Now, what's going on?

He told her, ending with a whispered *Hope we can do something tonight.*

Her distress deepened. *It's mother's birthday. She and Joel are coming here — we're taking her to dinner.*

They were both mute, momentarily in despair.

Where are you going? Nia said.

Back to Ottawa, I guess.

And then — ?

I d'know. Something will turn up.

Yes. You and Micawber —

*

He came home tired, hungry and discouraged. Myra was in the kitchen, reading a magazine. She hadn't set the table.

I wasn't sure when you'd be here she said, getting up. *I'll put on supper. Oh, there was a phone call, a Hugh Car . . . Car something. He left a local number.*

It was a downtown hotel; they connected him to the room. *Hugh!* Robert said, elated.

Hi Hugh said. *I've been waiting for you. Have you eaten?*

Ten minutes later Robert was in a taxi, squandering the fare he'd saved hours ago. When it drew up at the Chinese restaurant, which Hugh had selected from those he had proposed, his friend was being bowed in.

When they were seated the builder waved aside the menu and ordered a sumptuous variety of dishes. *Sorry your wife couldn't come* he said.

She had something she wanted to do. Actually he had managed to make Myra feel unwelcome. And she, in no mood to put up with her husband when he was excited and flustered, or to run the risk of being bored by some man she'd never met, had, with hurt dignity, declined.

Why are you here? Robert said. Hugh was a boyhood friend, who had lived on an adjoining street.

Hugh said *I came to look at property. It has possibilities, and I might be interested, if I had someone to manage the project.* He tucked a corner of the large linen napkin into his collar. He was wearing an open-necked sports shirt. Robert had dressed in a suit and tie. Their soup came, and the table was being spread with colourful foods. *And you,* Hugh said *what are you doing now?*

Robert confessed that, at the moment, nothing.

Then how would you like to manage my project?

Me? What do I know about building?

You manage your films. Indeed, at the Board, people had called a well-organized production *Aronized,* while those who'd resented the director's tight control retorted with *baronized.*

How do you know that? Robert said.

I thought of you and checked you out. I also heard about the strike and your leaving, and figured you might be ready for something new. Especially when it pays a lot better than what you've been used to.

Robert thought of Nia, and couldn't combine her with construction. He shook his head.

Wait Hugh said. *Don't worry about lack of experience. I know at first you'd have to depend on the foremen, but you'd learn fast. Your chief value would be that I could trust you.*

You don't have . . . reliable people?

They steal. Everybody steals. The workmen build their own houses with what they carry away. You can't stop it all, it's part of the business. But I'd like to keep it within bounds.

Oh, I don't know if. . .

Look, I'm prepared to invest a project in your education, because by the second one you'd be saving me money. You have the basic ability, and it can be applied to anything.

It was Hugh's creed, which he believed he had proved. At age ten he'd taken apart a faulty pocket watch, made it work, and concluded that it wasn't worth doing. His father, a watchmaker, had eked out a meagre existence replacing wristbands and crystals, fixing cheap alarm clocks and repairing what the big stores sent him when their own staffs were busy. Occasionally, from the single showcase in his tiny shop, Mr. Carson sold a timepiece or locket, but mostly Robert remembered him bent over his workbench, his greying hair combed thinly across a bony skull, and the wrinkles on one side of his face converging, like the threads of a cobweb, at the eye that gripped his jeweller's lens.

The old man — he'd always seemed old to Robert — had lived, along with Hugh, a firstborn sickly sister, and their short, sturdy mother, in four dark crowded rooms at the top of a staircase hidden behind the curtained doorway at the back of his shop. Whenever *H and R* came in from the street —they were inseparable in those days — Mr. Carson would look up from his dials and springs and say *Nu, what's new in the world?* and whatever they answered he would twist it round to the plight of the poor, the evils of government, the still-far-off joys of perfect freedom. Often he'd also throw in the martyrdom of Sacco and Vanzetti, who had died, he would remind them, *for all mankind.* Anarchy and utopia were linked in his mind like sunlight and flowers, and the deep wheezing sighs that accompanied his sermons stressed his yearning to set society straight. The boys would listen and nod, sometimes sneaking a smiling look at each other. When they could escape they'd race up the stairs to the drafty back porch that was Hugh's private den.

It was enclosed with only old canvas and sheet board, but when Hugh was in university he insulated it, and with a piece of plywood for a drafting table and an old wooden filing cabinet it became his first office. He put himself through school by working each summer in housing construction; when he graduated as an engineer he borrowed money, bought some lots, built houses, sold them at a small profit, and bought more lots . . . Shrewd and forceful, he was soon building duplexes and triplexes that he rented rather than sold. Then he went on to six, nine, fifteen-storey apartment buildings. By the time Robert had been at the Board for almost three years, and along with Myra was straining each night to patch up their shabby bungalow, Hugh's net worth was close to a million dollars. And his successes had multiplied many times since.

I'll tell you what, Robert said *I'll manage your project if you'll back me in a film.*

Well . . . it's something to think about Hugh said affably. *I don't really care about this Ottawa deal* he added. *I looked into it only because I thought it might be something to start you on, if you wanted to work for me. But I see it's not your thing.* Then he signalled for the check and took from his pocket a thick wad of paper money held by a metal clip. He had to peel back the hundreds to get at bills small enough with which to pay for the meal.

*

Leaving Hugh, an idea occurred to Robert that so excited him that, thinking about it, he walked the seven miles back to Myra. She was still awake when he got home. He sat on the edge of the bed. *Listen,* he said *I have to go to Toronto. After today there's nothing for me at the Board.*

Are they paying for the script?

Yes.

Congratulations. She offered to shake, and though he understood her hurt irony, he took the hand held out.

Oh, you're cold! she exclaimed. *Come in* — and she threw back the covers.

No. I want to explain. I have to find work.

We can manage.

No we can't! I'm not living on your salary.

She stared steadily for a moment. *How long will you be gone?*

Oh . . . long as it takes, I guess. I just don't know.

Do you want to stay at mother's? There's my room.

No, I don't want to bother them. They seemed to him hostile spies, who might find out about Nia. It was abhorrent to think of sleeping in a space permeated by Myra's diplomas and pictures. Her parents, deploring their daughter's marriage, had hung the room with every relic and souvenir. *I'll go in the morning* he said, standing.

12

Straight on, it looked like a red brick pillar supporting, seemingly, the sky. But as the narrow face stretched back it became a rectangular slab, with apartment balconies on both its long sides. Existing trees, Robert could see, had been preserved wherever possible, and others had been planted on the site, along with evergreen shrubs and grass, giving the building the appearance of resting on a ruffled base.

He went into the vestibule, rang the penthouse, and hearing the intercom answered, tried to explain. The substantial brass door unlocked with an oiled click. In seconds he had crossed the small lobby and was rising swiftly in the elevator. It opened onto a marble landing leading to a polished mahogany door with no number or name. He knocked; it swung back to reveal a spectacular smiling vision of pale pink, gold, and some kind of shimmering, translucent blue-green.

The girl smiled, showing clean white, perfectly-even teeth. She was exceedingly pretty. Her sleek black hair fell almost to her waist, and her face was like a pale rosebud, with green eyes, a pert nose, a pink mouth. She said *I know who you are. Hugh told me. Come in.*

She stepped aside to let him swing in his suitcase, allowing her blouse to open. He couldn't help noticing, knowing she meant him to, the firm round breasts set up by the tight low bodice.

He placed his bag and briefcase discreetly beside the door and followed her into the living room, where he was struck by another astonishing sight: huge windows that let in the afternoon sun and displayed a wide panoramic view of the lake — an immense blue plane spreading to an infinite horizon.

Wow!

Yes the girl said. *It thrills me too. Every day it's different.* She smiled again. *And I like knowing that over there is New York. My name is Sally,* she said, shaking hands.

Are you here often?

Oh, I live here now. My husband found out about Hugh — by the way, he had something he had to do, Hugh did, but he'll be back real soon — and the bastard, my husband I mean, threw me out. Her face grew sad, and the green eyes greyed. *The worst is that he kept my children. And one isn't even his.*

Children! Robert cried. *You look much too young.*

Yes she said, and shrugged. *My husband adopted her, though. She's from my second marriage.* She glanced around vacantly, as if looking for help that couldn't be had, then slowly sat down on the leather sofa beside which they'd been standing. Robert did too. *He's my third husband* she now went on. *And I was never mean to him. But he's being mean, very mean — he won't let me see the children.* Her dark mascaraed lashes narrowed, the slits glazed with moisture. *My children love me!* she cried in a rending tone. And tears spilled and ran down her cheeks.

It was, Robert thought, tragic theatre, but at that moment, moving. She was entrancing. He felt a giddy tenderness.

Oh, said Sally, suddenly becoming cheerful *would you like some tea?*

No, I'm fine, thank you.

We'll have tea when Hugh comes. Tell me about your plans. Where are you staying?

I don't know . . . He glanced apologetically towards his suitcase. *I came straight from the station.* He had phoned Hugh, who had told him to drop in.

I've thought of a film Sally said. *Even a title. 'Sisters In The Skin'. It would be about how to keep your skin nice. I know the magazines are full of that, but I've never seen it as a film. It would go great at coffee klatches.*

Well, you could star Robert said. *Yours is flawless.*

No! I have a little scar. Look . . . She leaned forward, turning her face to him, a fingertip to the hollow of her cheek. There was a tiny, almost imperceptible, dent. *My first husband did that. Hit me with a riding crop. With a metal tip.*

You have freckles too . . .

She blushed, or perhaps it was an instrument of charm. *Yes . . . pale ones. I'm really a blonde. But this is black month.* She giggled. *Actually, I've been black for three months. You know, sometimes I feel I'm my hair, and I just have to change . . .*

Hugh came in. *Ah, hi Rob* he said warmly, and took the place Sally left. Hugh was handsome. Not overly tall, but square-shouldered, solid, muscled. In university he'd done some boxing, and he still moved on the balls of his feet, with something of a dancer's spring. But his most arresting feature were the thick brows that met over the strong straight nose, below which the lips were full, sensual, moist.

When Sally returned with a tray Robert saw that she'd gathered her long black hair and tied it with a scarf of the same transparent turquoise that made up her loose outer outfit. She was, in a sense, dressed from slim neck to shapely ankles, but all that securely covered her was rather like a gilded bathing suit. She settled beside Hugh, gracefully balancing a cup in one hand and lightly caressing his thigh with the slender, tapered fingers of the other. Robert had the feeling that she could sit there totally nude in exactly the same relaxed way, and would be, if anything, even more lovely.

He had told Hugh, while Sally was gone, what it was he had wanted to see him about. It was Eldon's notion of a production company, but with Hugh as president. And supplying the start up funds. *I can handle the filmmaking* Robert said now. *What's most needed is a good producer. You could do it, Hugh* he concluded. *There's no one I'd sooner work with, or for.*

Hugh breathed a shallow sigh, and through it raced many thoughts. He'd learnt to think fast. The fierce building barons he played poker with brooked no fumbling. From them he'd acquired a taste for gambling, cigars, and the services of whores they hired to pleasure them between rounds. But the values his father had nurtured, though he'd discarded them as briskly as his boyhood name of *Hymie*, secretly nagged. In the business world he was a bold dynamic figure, but privately he had periods of doubt, and knew that the conflicts in his nature remained unresolved.

To satisfy his more sensitive side he'd been quietly assembling an impressive library of the best known philosophical classics. At times, after looking into a work like *Siddhartha,* he would muse about selling most of his properties and retiring from business, but he always emerged from such bouts of brooding with more gusto than ever, reminding himself that he enjoyed planning big buildings, liked commanding armies of construction workers, and took a vain pleasure in the compliance of bankers and the piling up of profits. Yet . . . even in the midst of those activities he'd ask himself why he bothered. Young as he was — only two years older than Robert — he already had enough wealth to last well beyond his lifetime, and no one he cared to leave it to. His parents were aging and had all they needed; indeed, they decried whatever more he tried to do for them. His sister was dead. Her death, which had been a relief from no longer having to watch her struggle, had left him inwardly impassive about life generally.

Still, a movie company, such as Robert proposed, could be refreshing, and might lead to a role in the arts. As a gamble it was merely an amusing reversal of what he'd suggested in Ottawa. The engineer, builder, possible film mogul flipped a mental coin, and shrugged. *Okay . . .* he said. *But we'll need distribution. No point in putting up houses or apartments unless there are buyers and tenants for them. Can a full length movie recover its costs in Canada?*

I . . . think so. The Film Board did a study last year. But it'll be a long time before they do anything about it.

What's in the study?

I don't know. I never saw the file.

Well, get it. If we can recover costs here, we'll make our profit in the States and elsewhere.

But I don't know if I can . . . Robert began. *That file is confidential.*

That woman you know — Robert had mentioned Nia as a possible recruit — *she's there, right? Have her get it.*

The study, Robert knew, had been handed on to Eldon, and was probably somewhere in his office. But asking Nia for it . . . *Can't we just talk to some distributors ourselves?*

Yes. But I'd like to know what the Film Board found out. And if they're not acting on it, I want to know why.

Robert thought better than to argue. *I'll try* he said.

Sally had been listening with interest. Now she leaned against her lover. *Darling . . . Robert doesn't have a place to stay.*

Well, stay here, of course. Hugh's hard tone at once became benign. *There are two extra rooms.* Sally poked him and he laughed. *One. She uses the other to dress in.*

*

When she got Robert's excited phone call, Nia was completely nonplussed. First, that he was in Toronto, second that he seemed

146

to be charging at windmills. She was at her desk, at work, amid a furious sea of activity, and couldn't think, let alone talk. Tersely, as if he were a stranger, she asked for his address, then thanked him and said good-bye.

Her letter came the next day, by special delivery:

The office 3 P.M.

This morning — I could have shouted — <u>Can't</u> you tell when I'm <u>not</u> <u>alone</u> — Stan was sitting here and everything you were saying is so very important to me. All day — in between the usual craziness that goes on in this frenetic place— I've been thinking about us and work — and your friend who will maybe supply money — and then I thought about you and work — and I started from the opening frame of Montcalm — then back to your sculpture film which was really about the women — then another turn to the three maritime shows last year — and there is one very big exciting thing in all of them — something that very few people can do — lots of directors quite good can handle a film technically and also a reasonably sensitive interpretation from professional actors — but you my darling Robbie (remember our tim'rous beastie) made real people real in all those films —and this is very very rare. If you do make some films (now please don't get immediately No it won't work, it might) I d like to look for ordinary people to cast in all the minor roles. Of course I'll be with you.

me — Nia.

It was the best she could do. She, who well knew the convoluted ways in which movie deals were put together, the trade offs, the lying, the empty promises, felt herself sink at the prospect. That two unwashed babes like the builder and Robert were about to blunder into that labyrinth was both laughable and pathetic. The whole thing could become a nightmare. She'd do best to break away. But to what? Loneliness and despair. Moreover, basically she was to blame. If she hadn't kept responding to Robert, none of this would have happened. Maybe by some chance, a movie might work. His instincts were, she knew, essentially dramatic. Though at the Board his films had been called *documentaries,* they were all really dramas in realistic guise. That's what had set him apart. He should be making features. Torn this way and that, Nia remained uneasily neutral.

*

Robert's room in the penthouse, though small, provided all he needed, including a desk and telephone. The larger space next door, in which Sally dressed, had, like the still larger bedroom she shared with Hugh, its own full-piece bathroom. When she emerged from it, rarely before midmorning, she was bathed and groomed, and in breathless haste to *head downtown,* where, it seemed, urgent appointments with hairdressers and others awaited. She told Robert that ordinarily she came back only in time to meet Hugh, but had been returning early to be with him, their *special visitor.* The day before she'd brought packages of prepared food, which she'd spooned out for the three of them at the dining-room table. Today she was empty handed, but with her hair in an elaborate beehive, and she had on a soft wine-red woollen suit, and shoes of the same colour. The outfit was complemented by a demure ivory cameo. *We're going out to dinner* she said. *A new place. Italiano. Quite swish. You'll like it.*

I'm sure to. But I feel awkward about being a free loader. You'll have to let me take you and Hugh out.

Oh, pooh! He can afford it. And he has to eat. If I leave him alone he forgets, or he opens a can of sauerkraut and has it on a piece of bread. If I didn't push him, even going out would mean eating only Chinese. It's good for me that you're here. He doesn't mind if it's for you. You go back a long way with him, don't you?

Well . . . we were closer as kids. We were in the same grade. Once in the same class.

But aren't you younger?

I skipped twice.

Ah, smart.

No. In the Depression years they weren't building new schools. If classes were too crowded the top one or two kids were simply moved on.

But weren't you smaller?

Yeah. Until I shot up and filled out as a teenager, I thought I was puny.

Well, you're not now, are you? she said, coquettishly appraising him.

No. And *No!* he said to himself. *It's too dangerous.*

*

I spoke to several distributors in New York Hugh announced at dinner that night. *They all say pretty much the same thing. That nothing good has ever come out of Canada.*

Robert flushed. *That's not true...*

They mean in American showbiz terms Hugh said placidly. *When I go to New York I'll explore it more with them. Is that file coming?*

I'm working on it Robert said. Afraid of her reaction, he hadn't yet asked Nia.

*

Her life was very busy, and solitary. After the frantic hours at the office she had to shop for food, cook, serve, wash dishes, do laundry, mend, phone the plumber to fix leaky taps, worry about whether there was water in the well, take things to the dry cleaner and attend, always, to the emotional and physical wants of her mother and son. Joel, fortunately, was a sturdy, sensitive and charming boy, but he had his moments of rage and fear, of shouts and hot tears, which he needed to share, just like jokes and laughter. His mother's wit, reasoning, warmth and sweetness shaped the world in which he thrived. These days Nia gave herself wholly

149

to work and home, and was at the same time inwardly alone. She tried not to think of Robert, and thought of him all the time. His absence was a void all her activity failed to fill.

*

At close to noon on Sunday, Hugh, still stifling yawns, joined Sally and Robert in the dining room for brunch. Sally had set out bread, anchovies, ham and cheese, and scrambled some eggs. She was wearing a simple but pretty print dress; the grand upsweep had subsided, over two days, into a pony tail. She also had the dye washed out of her hair. It was now blond, close to her natural colour.

Sally, Robert remarked *you're a daily fashion show.*

Well, I brought a few things.

A few! Hugh said. *We had to send a moving van for them.*

They were of no use to my husband Sally said to Robert. *But you know what that bastard did? He took the children away for the afternoon, and even the nanny and maid, like I was contagious or something. And if that wasn't hurtful and insulting enough, when we were leaving a guy comes to change the locks. Imagine! I could have had the movers clean out the whole house, but he knew I'd take only my clothes. Why did he have to be so cruel?*

Robert nodded sympathetically. Hugh went on eating as if he hadn't heard.

Oh well, said Sally in one of her lightning shifts of mood *why worry about people who need to bear grudges? It's too nice a day.* It was indeed a splendid day, with warm air, the sky a pale clear blue, and sunlight flooding the windows.

But Robert was ill at ease. He still hadn't asked for the Film Board file. Plainly, at this stage, he was uselessly imposing on his generous host. And he decided, as he forked pieces of egg from his plate, that he would express his thanks and leave for Ottawa on the afternoon train.

But suddenly Sally said *You know what I'd like? To go to the country. Hugh, honey, don't you find it gets heavy, being in here all*

150

the time? As if they were prisoners in a cage she glanced with mild distaste into the spacious living room. The furniture there, all custom made to Hugh's design, was of rosewood, black leather and pink marble. The rugs, lamp shades and paintings ran to reds, browns and blacks. *Oh, I miss my garden* she said with a sigh, and Hugh aimed a covert wink at Robert, for she had seldom gone into it, except to show it to visitors. *You know,* she said wistfully, and apparently without irony *I'm really a country girl.*

Then she looked from Robert to Hugh, to see whether either would challenge her. Supreme, she said *Hughie, darling, why don't we get a place in the country?*

Get what?

A cottage . . . or something like that. It'll be fun. We can have picnics. Come on, we only sit around every Sunday. It'll do you good to get out in the fresh air.

Oh, God . . . said Hugh.

But Sally went to him, and kneeling by his chair put her arms around his neck and kissed him slowly, sensually, on the mouth. Then she pulled back a little, letting him focus on her lovely, open-lipped, pleading look.

That face . . . he said to Robert *it's like a gift you have to repay.*

Damn right! said Sally, getting up. And she brought him the newspaper. *There must be places advertised.* She pushed away dishes and spread the paper in front of him. And bending over his shoulder, lightly followed, with her forefinger's flawlessly-shaped and polished nail, Hugh's supposed perusal of the ads. *There!* Sally said, pointing. *That seems perfect. 'Rustic retreat . . .' We can be there in an hour. Oh, darling, let's go. Now –*

*

They drove into hills that gradually rose higher. Behind them the city trees were still green, but here there were widespread spatterings of colour, and sudden startling splashes of yellow and red. Hugh's car, a heavy gleaming Thunderbird, was also red, a fire-engine red. Perhaps feeling it was roomier, or better suited, he'd taken it rather than the silver Jaguar in which he usually drove with Sally. She was beside him in the front; Robert, too intrigued by this outing to miss it, was behind her, occasionally shifting his gaze from the broken pageantry of small fields and woods to the sheen of her pale gold hair.

Past the open gate they descended a dark leafy tunnel. On both sides the forest disappeared into dense shadow, while interlacing boughs screened the brightness overhead. Suddenly, to Robert's right, there was break in the foliage, a peep hole, through which he caught sight of sparkling water below, surrounding — so it seemed — a sun-splashed log cabin. Then again blackness, broken only by brief streaks of mottled light, bark, boughs, evergreen needles and cedar sprays, until the road, levelling as it turned, emerged from the trees into a little grassy meadow divided by a clear winding stream.

Hugh stopped at a low bridge of rough planks loosely laid across a single span of logs. The water running under it was splashing down an old concrete sluice set in a high earthen dam. Beyond the bridge, against the far slope of the valley, stood a pioneer house of dark square-hewn timbers chinked with whitened mortar, and facing it, where the ground was fairly level, stretched a neat furrowed garden. At its far end a woman in a long dress was slowly hoeing.

Into this pristine scene the blinding automobile brazenly intruded. Robert, followed by Hugh and then Sally, got out and moved away from it. The woman leaned on her hoe, waiting for them. Over the grey flannel gown she wore a man's faded denim jacket, and on her head a bleached blue cotton cap with furred earflaps. Closer, she wasn't as old as she'd looked. Her short greying hair framed a bright tanned face with sun-cracked girlish lips, and her eyes were impishly alight, like those of a child playfully dressed.

Hugh asked about the cottage for rent. It was the log cabin Robert had glimpsed, and the woman led them to it along a path that went around the old house.

From a distance the cabin appeared to be sitting on the edge of the wide pond formed by the dam, or *weir* as the woman called it, but when they came to it they saw that only its screened front porch was attached to the shore — the rest of the building seemed suspended like a diving board over a pool. Yet the thing was strongly built of cedar logs cut from large trees, had spacious windows on the sides, and across the far end of it, above the pond, a broad balcony.

Hugh peered under this curious structure and saw that the basic cabin, which was square, rested securely on concrete columns. Of its two extensions, the screened porch and the balcony, only the balcony was not underpinned. But it was held by the strong base logs that ran back into the earth bank.

The screened porch had a kitchen area at one end and a closet containing a chemical toilet at the other. The main room was cheerful, with windows on all sides, its varnished orangey logs contrasting with the darker brown floor. It held an old box stove, an old but working counter-top electric fridge, a simple sideboard, and a hardwood table and chairs. Two small bedrooms, one containing a cot and the other a doubtful double bed, were walled off with the same narrow dark boards used for the floor. Beside the back door, slats nailed across studs rose to a little loft where two small windows gave sweeping views of the pond. Only Robert climbed up there. When he rejoined Hugh and Sally they were peering over the railing of the balcony. The water there was too deep to see bottom.

It's creepy Sally said.

Yeah, Hugh said *the whole place is kind of spooky.*

No! Robert exclaimed. *It's wonderful!* He turned to Sally. *You wanted country. Nothing could be more so than this. If it wasn't for the electricity we could be back a hundred years.*

Back then, Hugh said *nobody would have built anything so impractical.*

Yes they would, because there have always been romantics. This place is utterly romantic. It was made for love!

153

Really? said Sally, newly intrigued. *Well, it is kind of quaint. Hughie . . .*

What? Do you want it?

Maybe . . . For a little while. Could we please?

Hugh went out to speak to the woman. She had hoped to rent by the year, but settled for a month.

*

Darling, you must come! You have to! cried Robert. *It's terribly important. I can't tell you how important it is!*

Then I shouldn't ask — Nia said.

Oh, it's a place. I have the most marvellous place for us to be. Come, come for as long as you can, please!

I don't know — But her face was alight from the sheer energy that flashed through the phone. Never had she heard Robert so excited, and she was free to respond: at the moment there was no one in her office. *Wait* — *Stanley is taking a crew to Toronto in three weeks* — *it's his first time directing for us* — *Eldon said something about my going to help him. Maybe I could come a few days earlier* —

It can't be later! I won't have the place after that.

Nia said to leave it with her. They exchanged passionate assurances, airy hugs, erotic hints, and Robert hung up. He had decided, fearfully, to put off asking her about the file until he could do it in person, but otherwise he was fired with purpose. In his mind the log cabin combined the shack at the lake with the apartment they'd failed to enjoy in New York.

But three weeks seemed an infinite time. In the interim he'd have to find other work. Hugh, after a moment's hesitation — reflecting that his friend did deflect some of Sally's whims, and also discreetly absented himself whenever the atmosphere became carnal — kindly agreed to his staying on. If anything, Hugh had observed, Robert's presence elsewhere in the penthouse seemed to whet the young woman's passion.

Robert made a conscience call to his wife, telling her he'd be away at least another month. That done, he felt ready to run to New York, to hurl himself at Hollywood. But thinking of the cost soon collapsed these high-flown fancies. What remained was to make an impression on the Canadian Broadcasting Corporation.

13

Only two television networks operated in Canada, an English and a French one, and both belonged to the CBC. Created by parliament, financed mainly from the federal treasury, the Corporation both regulated broadcasting and was itself the industry's largest programmer of radio and television. In the name of the public it owned stations in major cities across the country, and was affiliated with many more private ones. Through its influence on viewers and listeners, it had become a national arbiter of culture and taste. And because the Corporation was by far the industry's biggest buyer of goods and services, and offered the widest audience for advertising, it was virtually imperial. Suppliers and advertisers, writers and performers, and even the Film Board awaited its pleasure.

Toronto was *the Corp's* main production centre. For a few days Robert made the rounds of offices. No one wanted to see him. He left his name with countless secretaries; when asked if he had a résumé, he said he'd already sent one. None of them remembered it, or seemed to care. Finally he boldly decided to hold a screening. He went to the Board's distribution office in the city, and was grateful to find there people he had never met but who still regarded him with reverence. They provided him with 16mm prints of his films — CBC television had spurned the professional movie size — and with their help he obtained, in the broadcast building, the use of a small room and a portable projector. Everyone was invited. Through inter-office mail, notices went to all producers, and in person Robert pinned one on every bulletin board.

Hugh and Sally came, and a few seats were filled by idle technicians. Finally, when the last film, *Montcalm*, was halfway through, a loud group of people passing the open doorway fell silent only when the erect man in their midst returned to it and fixed his eyes on the screen. He was Vincent Adams, the Executive-Producer of drama, who controlled several hours a week of prime time. *Who wrote this?* Adams said regally.

When Robert stood and replied *I did*, the producer, after an indifferent nod, strode on.

Robert's disappointment was doubled, a day later, when Hugh told him that for some time business matters would delay him from going to New York, where he intended asking distributors whether they'd invest in a Canadian feature. Hugh was comfortable dealing in concepts. The plans, i.e., the script, could come later. And as well, Sally, who insisted on being taken along, said she had to study fashion magazines before flying off for serious shopping.

Robert felt that pieces of all he'd hoped for were falling from his hands. His sole mainstay was the promise of Nia at the cabin.

*

But to her he was becoming a cherished notion. Whether she truly loved Robert, or mainly the idea of him, he was the vital man in her life, and his absence was a void underlying all her daily doings. Even when arguing with Joel, in the half serious, half humorous way they bickered, which usually ended with shouts or laughter, she secretly wished her lover could hear and see it, could somehow know of it.

*

Hugh and Sally went to the cabin on the weekend. She'd bought a wicker basket complete with plates and cutlery, and filled it with fine foods in cans and containers, to which she added brioches and croissants, red and white wines, and, as a concession to Hugh, a few fresh bagels. He had given her one of the newly-introduced credit cards, and she used it with discretion, seldom exceeding a monthly total of more than he'd willingly pay.

They returned feeling grubby, tired and bored. *That bed . . . damn near killed us* Hugh said, and Sally added that it had also been cold. She put the leftover tins into the kitchen cupboards and shoved the basket far back into a deep closet where suitcases were stored. Therefore it wasn't surprising that when Robert asked if he could use the cabin during the last week of the rental, Hugh said *You might as well.*

And then, as Robert's spirits were rising on a swell of ardent expectation, there came from Nia something unexpected, but confirming:

> At home, my crazy rose bedroom — not really mine —
> but I'm here. The kind of missing I have for you — I want
> and miss you here and now — just being you — getting
> ready for bed— talking quietly about nothing or anything
> or something — suddenly looking amused. Now
> something you don't do as much as you used to. There
> used to be a time after we'd made love — mainly in the
> apartment days — when you drifted into a work thought
> — you don't do that now — you stay with us. I didn't ever
> mind your doing that, you know, so please when it happens
> again (and I'm sure it will) don't be inhibited. What am I
> saying? This would not be your kind of problem.

Robert paused, thinking that she knew him intimately, yet hardly at all. And that it was just as well.

> I will love you all my life for that evening. The evening
> I was so exhausted and spent from my weeping and
> being — I felt as though I had had a very high fever and

was just coming out of it — you were so wonderful and loving and kind — I've never felt that before and no one has ever been that gentle with me. I guess you that evening and the next morning mean more to me than anything in my life except having my son. Except that having a baby is a big giving thing, and that night and morning was a taking love. I've never accepted or been given all that before.

I miss you in my office — in the cafeteria — in a taxi — in the dusk — in the early morning — on a slightly cloudy rainy day — on a late sunny afternoon. I want to be with you for the rest of my life — to talk to listen — you know "they" were right "for richer or poorer". If you were here I could talk — or you could talk but I don't want to write anymore. I just want to lie here and think about you — and be peaceful and loving. Good-night my dear Robert.

This mixture of affection, idealization and near make-believe both troubled and elated him. He wanted to embrace the paper.

*

The overnight train was on time. When Nia woke, some windows were already uncovered and there was movement in the aisle; the car smelled of fabrics and perfume and polish. She washed and dressed slowly, unwilling to dislodge the tranquility gradually gained through the night. As a result she was among the last passengers to enter the station.

Robert had grown uneasy. The details were so like that morning in New York. But when Nia appeared — walking forward with her slightly swaying motion, like a wave flowing smoothly from one crest to another — and was more strikingly beautiful than even in his memories, he recklessly swung himself over the restraining rope, ran to meet her, and relieved, proud and eager, hugged and kissed her in front of everyone.

*

Why don't you ever fly? he said as they were driving to Hugh's building. *Is it the money?*

She shook her head. *Those machines are much too heavy to be up in the air —*

The one defect threatening their day was that Hugh and Sally had slyly decided to go to the cabin. Hugh said he'd left a cap, and when Robert pointed out he could bring it Sally said she would anyway enjoy the ride. By then they knew he wouldn't be alone, and were curious to see his companion.

Robert had rented a car near the station, and had to stop for his bag, sheets and blankets. He urged Nia to come up to the penthouse, but she bluntly refused. *I don't* she said *want to meet Hugh by way of his bed.*

*

For hours they lay side by side near a murmuring stream. From time to time a fly fisherman in long waders went by, but he would either avert his eyes or exchange with them a small smile of contentment. It was a serene Sunday afternoon; fluffy white clouds floated in the blue sky, birds sang, there was a sweet scent of cedar. The roast chicken and wine Nia had brought from home were ideal fare. The food, the gentle sounds, the dappled light made them drowsy; they dozed languidly for a while and woke to marvel again at how many of their love meetings had been sunlit.

The soft yellows of the hillsides, even the low red sumacs lining the winding sandy road were beginning to fade when they drove slowly up towards the gate. Nia was holding Robert's hand. Their mutual desire, unfulfilled for so long, had gradually given way to this soft and tender mood. *Surely to God they've gone by now* Robert was thinking.

All at once the gleaming Thunderbird came streaking around a curve. Both cars swerved, passed safely, and stopped some sixty feet apart. The men got out and met in the middle. Sally was looking back, straining to see Nia, but the older woman kept staring straight ahead.

Everything's in order there Hugh said, as he casually walked Robert back up the road. *Mrs. Carey left ahead of us, with her daughter, a kid about thirteen. They also have a place in the city, and they'll be there all week. Oh, hello* he said to Nia, in his most charming manner. *I'm Hugh.*

Nora — she said, and they shook hands through the open window.

Smiling, Hugh studied her, made some trivial remarks, and then said *Well, Sally's in a hurry, so I guess I'd better get going . . .* His final smile to Nia, when he left, was both suggestive and complicit.

It disturbed Robert, but he couldn't now allow that to clash. Getting in again, he said *That's the great Carson. If you realize all he's done, he's really something.*

Yes — Nia said. *He's a little boy.*

No.

Darling, he's a pitiful little boy —

Robert was surprised, but felt that what Nia might be missing was that Hugh was a very formidable boy.

*

He stopped the car beside the break in the foliage. Nia looked down and saw the blue water and the brown cabin perched over it, and gasped. *Darling!* she cried. *It's the dream department* —

They drove down to the small wooden bridge and across the swift stream rushing away from the water falling in a glistening wall from the high sluice of the weir, and Robert carefully steered the car around the log house and right up to the cabin.

Nia walked slowly through to the balcony and stood at the railing. Fish were jumping, spreading silent rings across the twilit pond. A frog croaked, and back in the woods a bird began its evening song.

Darling, it is a dream.

Yes Robert said, and held her tightly; for he suddenly felt, as he had at the shack, that oneness with a woman and a place.

All right — she said *that front part, where the kitchen is, we'll call the kitchen, and this I want to call the porch.* Then she took to the bedrooms. *They're so small and dark — darling, do we have to sleep in that enclosed space — ?*

Let me see . . . He found that the partitions were held only by corner braces. In a cigar box on the sideboard, among other odds and ends, there was an old fork with a square-ended handle thin enough to fit the slot of a screw, and the screws, though long, were not tight. He soon had the wooden sections stacked in the corner where the cot was, and it folded up against them. The main cabin room was now completely open.

It's getting cold Nia said. *Maybe we'd better push the bed closer to the stove.* They did that too, though it threatened to fall apart. It had old oaken head-and-foot boards, side rails that were shakily connected, and legs that for some reason had been sawn off a little at the front end, making the mattress slope downwards.

There was dry split hardwood stacked in the kitchen and Robert soon had a fire going. Then he brought in the groceries they had bought at a farmer's market and put them on the counter. Nia, taking out a pot and dishes from under it, disturbed a mouse.

Look — she called *it's running under the firewood.* Robert picked up a piece. *Oh, don't hurt it — !*

I wouldn't dare! he said, taking the wood to the stove.

After an hour of sleep they woke up feverish. Robert had built up such a blaze that the cabin was torrid. It took ten minutes of fanning with a blanket through all the open doors and windows before the warmth was bearable again. Laughing, they made love once more and fell asleep clinging to the mattress.

*

After breakfast Nia found a tiny purple violet still blooming, as if it had hidden under sheltering branches while two seasons passed overhead. It was in a shaded glade near the cabin, where water entered the pond from an inlet fed by a single brook that splashed over a foot-high waterfall after flowing freely, almost giddily, down a rocky slope and through small beds of shining watercress.

On this golden morning, with the leaves crisp underfoot and a faint smell of wood smoke in the air, with the taste of toasted rolls and coffee and the sight of their own *colours* fluttering on the line — last night's bed sheet, which had damply taken on rainbow hues from the cheap flowered ticking of the mattress — Robert and Nia felt joined in a snug sensuality from which all the less-satisfying world was securely shut out.

For the moment she was no longer desperately compelled by countless demands, and he wasn't merely a younger, unemployed, impractical misfit. All divisions had disappeared. They were woman and man, lovingly alone in their perfect, private realm.

They lunched on the bright bank of the pond, beginning with a drink of gin flavoured by wild mint Robert had found beside a spring near the stream. The sun was warm, the shimmering air saturated with the mellow shades and smells of autumn. Nia felt tipsy, Robert too; they undressed each other and ardently tumbled off their blanket onto the grass. Suddenly she shrieked: a bare foot had dipped into a little cold soup left in her bowl.

*

The sky, by daybreak, had become overcast. Soon it was thinly spitting. As the cabin was dusty, the floor dirty, they decided to stay in and clean house. Nia wiped about with a damp cloth; Robert, on his knees, did the scrubbing. He stopped and stretched his back while watching her. Then said *Whatever you're doing, you're always elegant.*

Me? Well, yes — that's the impression. But, darling, I'm a girl from Portage la Prairie — my elegance is a surprise to me. Funny, last week — when I was rushing around the Board getting ready to come here — I met — in the hall — MacCurry — and he did a kind of swaying imitation of me. He said ' You always just glide along looking so composed and sure of yourself.' I was actually terrified that he — or Eldon — or something was going to keep me from getting away.

She smiled. *But — there've been times when I really have felt elegant. Like washing my hair in the lake in Quebec, and yesterday — when we walked up through the woods and came out on that sunlit summit — and we could see looking down here the cabin and pond — and off in the distance the tree covered hills — with the combed-hair replanted sections — just then — with the sun and the sky and all that spread out below us — I felt elegant.*

Robert wrung out his cloth over the pail, but then sat back again on his heels, still watching her.

I guess there've been other times over the years she went on. *Times when I've been strong within myself. Not strong aggressively — but — oh, moments when I've been most alive, I guess.*

Were those solitary moments? Or shared with someone?

Nia said, gently *Darling, there were a lot of someones, and with most of them I didn't feel elegant at all.*

Tell me about the other ones.

She paused, sorry she'd spoken of it. He had resumed scrubbing, stubbornly. It was evident from the set of his mouth that he'd allow no change of subject. *Well,* she said *there was —* and she told him about a poet whose words made her think of butterflies alighting softly on the page. *He was a good friend. That's when I was still trying to be faithful to Buddy —*

Where was that, New York?

No — before. In L. A.

You mean Hollywood?

She nodded.

Did that poet make a living?

Not with his poetry. He was an actor.

Robert could picture him, spry and sophisticated, and exceptionally good-looking. *A star?*

Does it matter? He's dead now —

There was distress in her voice. Robert sensed behind it a rising rage, and knew he should let this subside. But he was racked by jealousy. *Oh . . . what happened?*

He intervened in a street fight. They beat him — with bats and chains. He choked in his own blood —

She blinked back tears. He'd been so sweet, the actor poet, at least to her, sustaining her whenever Buddy, stung by setbacks, was being particularly nasty. *Why do you stay with him?* the other had said, and he'd offered, often, to take her away, to take her in, along with her mother and child. But she hadn't been ready to leave her baby's father. And her friend, for all his immediate devotion, had a tendency to imitate the selflessness of his screen characters. Unfortunately, he was infected with the vanity-centred courage that ultimately killed him.

Robert had remained mute and glum. He perceived from Nia's pain that she had loved, and still loved, the poet hero — perhaps, probably, she was lying about not having slept with him. And, maddeningly, death had made him inviolable. *Then what about* he demanded *all those other guys . . . all your lovers?*

Her face darkened, alarming him. But she drew in a sharp breath, something between an intake and a sigh, and controlling herself, turned away to wipe the window ledges.

Well? Robert said.

She swung around and stared at him.

He looked back in defiance, his heart fearfully beating.

I think we should drop this she said evenly.

No. Tell me.

Nia lowered her lids. But pride rebelled. She wasn't going to be bullied into silence or lying. And there welled up not just men she'd been to bed with, but the countless encounters when an open-mouthed smile, or the gleam of an eye, had conveyed instant love. It had always happened at parties, in offices, on the street — wherever men had met her look, her person. She was loved for her vivid spirit. In those unsullied moments, which usually hadn't gone further, which, indeed, usually had nowhere to go, she'd given joy. Looking back on her life, she had given a great deal of joy. She regretted some instances, when another woman had been hurt, but none was she ashamed of. If Robert loved her, he must love her as she is. Resuming her cleaning, she began, in a low resigned voice, to relate her history with men, those, before him, with whom she'd been intimate. She omitted only her husband. The incidents ranged from Winnipeg and Toronto to Acapulco, from Hollywood to New York. She tried to keep her tone cool, but inevitably there crept into it traces of warmth and nostalgia.

Robert was bewildered. That her sweet body, which he'd last sampled only hours ago, had been trampled by such an army of intruders, was . . . unbelievable. He, who'd briefly known only one woman before being married, all but collapsed under that load of lovers. Wanting to wipe out the mass of them, he said weakly *I wish I'd met you earlier, ten or more years ago.*

No! cried Nia. *You wouldn't have liked me then!* Those were the times of nightly parties, of drinking, smoking, and sex even on pool sides. Robert in Hollywood! What a horrid clash of cultures that would have been —

Yet the image, pointing up his unworldliness, mixed with the churning up of that past, depressed her. She looked beyond him, as he was still sitting back on his heels, holding the scrub brush, and tried to recover the charm of yesterday, but failed. Nothing lasted, especially love.

*

Lunch was bleak beneath Robert's forced assurances that they were lucky to have each other, to be here in this beautiful place. Nia was silent, but afterwards said she needed a phone — she had to call a friend about staying there the night they'd get back to the city, the night before she moved to a hotel to begin her work with Stanley.

They drove down the sandy road and turned onto the broad gravel one. It was about seven miles to the nearest town. It had been raining on and off; the winding valley was wet, grey, misty. The ragged sky hung low. Nia was wrapped in a brown corduroy coat, worn with the sleeves empty, like a cloak. Around its collar

165

was draped a long woollen green and orange scarf, its ends trailing across her lap to the floor.

What's Stanley shooting? Robert said. Plainly, Stanley, not Nigel, had taken his place in the unit.

Staff —

What staff?

She hesitated, and then said *The Staff of Life.*

My Staff of Life? he cried. It was one of the outlines he'd written when Eldon was urging him to think of new ideas, then putting them aside. It was an original idea and entirely his; he had even written almost all the dialogue. This was unbelievable! *Who finished it?*

Stanley — and I helped. And Eldon helped.

Robert wanted to cry *How could you, how could they?* — but he knew, and instead said angrily *I hope all the humour isn't lost!*

Look — she said. *You weren't there, and the script was. We needed another show.*

But you could have told me. You didn't have to go on without me!

You know I did she said quietly. *It was my job. I tried to keep as much of you as I could —*

*

There was a call box on the town's main corner. Nia stood in it with the door open. The streets were quiet, with little traffic. Robert waited nearby, leaning against a brick wall, hoping the locals wouldn't connect him to her. She looked absurd, bundled up in that hooded coat, and not at all lovely. He heard her say *No — he has a place.* When she finished phoning she told him, with none of the usual relief, that all was well at her house, and that in Toronto she'd be staying the night with her friend Betty.

Nia wished she were there already, away from Robert's envious spite. And from her pathetic attempts at happiness. With Betty she'd be back in her former, familiar social sphere, in which, if it was all facade, there were at least no false expectations. And then she'd resume work, essential now to support her mother and son, and as a dulling sop for inner dreariness. *How bitter* she thought *everything becomes —*

But she sent Robert to the liquor store with a list, while forcing herself through the required grocery shopping.

*

Returning to the cabin, she kept her hood up. She sat against the window, as far from him as she could.

I'm sorry Robert said finally. *All that talk this morning. It's a little hard for me to take.*

I shouldn't have told you.

No, you had to. I'll get used to it. Which should also apply, he realized, to Stanley directing his film, but that still rankled. He reached for her hand. *Please sit close to me.* She moved over into the centre of the seat. He tried to draw her against him, but she shook her head.

I'm barely floating she said. *Don't pull me under.*

When they had carried in their purchases she made herself a drink and left the bottle and a glass for him. He saw them when he brought in some dry kindling from the open woodshed of the old house. She'd never done that before, nor was she anywhere in sight. He found her sitting on a log, under a clump of cedars by the shore, facing the pond. The water was a pitted sheet. A spiky drizzle was dropping from the darkening sky. Nia's face, bent over her drink, was hidden under the brown hood.

Come inside he said quietly. *I'll make a fire.*

I'm all right. I just want to be alone.

But that was what he feared most. *Why?*

I'm thinking.

He tried to sound gentle. *What about?*

Well, if you must know — I was thinking about my son.

Oh . . . he said, as if concerned. *What about Joel?* And he did care: the boy was his one, perhaps only, unbeatable rival.

I don't especially want to talk about it. Well — I will she said. *I should be there with him. I shouldn't be gallivanting around like*

167

this. I should be settled down — married to some nice man who can take care of us.

Like St. Augustine. Phil August was a slow white-haired fellow who worked in the Film Board lab.

She smiled mirthlessly. *Yes — but with money.*

*

Softened by alcohol and candles, supper was neutral. They sat kitty-cornered, as always. Robert took Nia's hand and again talked about how happy they were. Indeed, in the grip of the wet night their glimmering circle of light seemed warm. But what with the steady rain, the darkness, their pent-up tension, neither was in a mood to do the day's dishes. They stacked them and got ready for bed.

Nia put on a nightgown.

Why . . . ? Robert said. *Come on, take it off.*

I'm cold.

The fire was softly hissing, the cabin already too warm.

Nia, sweet . . . He embraced and kissed her. Her body remained stiff. Only her mouth, out of habit, limply responded to his. Then he slowly pulled up her nightgown and began stroking her breasts.

I don't feel like it tonight she said.

Why? Don't you feel well?

Oh, I feel all right. I just don't feel like it, that's all.

But he was trying frantically to stimulate her.

Please — leave me alone. I just want to sleep.

Robert stopped and lay quiet. Then he withdrew his arms and sat up on the side of the bed. After a moment he sighed and went to damp down the fire.

Nia glanced at his nude body, lean and hard in the faint flicker from the stove's mica window, and defensively shut her eyes. But his bounding footfalls startled her — suddenly he was back on the edge of the bed.

Nia . . . he said shrilly *Nia, it's me, Robert. You know, Robert!* Then, with less roughness *What's the matter? What's happened to us?*

I don't know. I just know that right now I don't want to have anything to do with you.

Robert felt feverish, and skewered by a sword of ice. The dim body on the bed, huddled away from him, seemed to have changed into something hostile, macabre, nightmarish. *God,* he thought *what am I doing here, with this woman?*

But from pride he sat a while longer, in silence, before getting up and putting on his trousers and shoes. Outside, the rain was lighter, calming to his skin; he scarcely felt the cold. He breathed deeply a number of times, then went in and dried himself with a towel. Quietly he approached the bed again. *Nia, can't we talk it over? If there's something wrong surely we can straighten it out.*

She began to cry. *I don't think it's anything we can straighten out by talking.*

But I love you. We love each other. Doesn't that mean anything?

It doesn't mean anything now.

He sat down heavily and took her by the shoulder. *Let's make love. You'll feel better after making love. . .*

Let go! Nia cried, striking his arm and knocking it away. *You're making me hate you — !*

Robert drew back in dismay. He'd been driven, he felt, beyond endurance. He had to escape from this wounding, horrible woman. But he couldn't abandon her just as she was. Nor could he bear the thought of starting another day with her. Then it came to him, how he could end it all tonight and wake tomorrow as if it'd never been. *Well,* he declared *I guess there's no use hanging around here.* Standing, he said *Come on, let's get straightened up and leave.*

Now? At night — ?

Why not? What's the point of staying?

She hesitated, and then, as if crushed by his conviction, timidly said *All right.*

Robert dressed rapidly. His mind was instantly compiling the tasks — pull back the bed when Nia is out of it, restore the partitions, pack their suitcases, put out the fire — all a matter of minutes. Then a final check of the porch, the main cabin, the kitchen —

the kitchen! He spun around. *The dishes! The damn dishes! We'll have to wash them before we go.* The hold-up would be humiliating, but there was no help for it. *I'll do them!* he said angrily, and went out there.

But something was wrong with the overhead light; it kept going out. He'd meant to look at it, before all the trouble began. He lit two candles. Their beams streamed softly into the main cabin and across the bed.

Nia heard him filling the kettle and a stock pot. They usually preheated water on the stove; the old electric burner was painfully slow. The cabin seemed cool, the night forbidding. She sat up and pulled a blanket across her back. Robert came in and stood uncertainly by the door.

The damn dishes are going to delay us he said, sighing.

What time is it?

He studied his watch. *After midnight. At this rate we won't get away until two, or three.*

Deprived of drama, their plight became embarrassing. Robert thought of leaving the dishes and coming back to deal with them another day, but now the idea of returning without Nia was intolerable. He raised his eyes, she too; then both glanced away. But Nia, wrapped in her blanket, had looked beautiful. And vulnerable. She was, he knew, helpless against his plan, but it was losing the pleasure of vengeance. Abruptly he felt weary. *If only we didn't have to do them . . .* he muttered.

Under this impasse, Nia's despair, regret, anger drained away. She had a feeling of futility. She was, for the moment, still tied to Robert. *Well,* she said *I guess someone has to.*

He had started to step into the kitchen when he suddenly turned, giving her no time to prepare for the arch note that leapt into his voice *Say, what about that mouse?*

That's not fair! Nia gasped, doubled over with exploding gaiety. *No! No — it's not fair —* she cried *to do a thing like that!*

Robert rushed to her. She threw her arms around him and covered his face with kisses. Shocked delight appeared in it.

Oh, darling! Nia said. *What would we do without our mice?*

14

Bursting with excitement, Betty Bobchenko scarcely paused to be introduced before announcing *Francis is in town! He arrived on the q.t., and he's coming to dinner tonight. Shall I ask anyone else? No, it's too late — it'll be just us.*

Robert was holding Nia's suitcase and smaller case, having carried them up the stairs to Betty's flat. He followed the women in from the landing, wondering whether *us* included him, when Nia whispered *You'd better go and dress. And bring some wine.*

He drove to the penthouse, feeling pushed. The liquor stores had already closed, and he could not now return the car until very late or in the morning, though that was of less concern, because he'd anyway have to pay the rental for this day. Hugh and Sally were out, giving him scope for distress.

Francis Findlay . . . In Nia's circle an aristocrat of the highest rank. Compared to Findlay, he'd be, could only be, *unknown, ungainly . . . unemployed.* And then there was the immediate, impossible problem of what to wear. Apart from shoes, socks, and a pair of grey pressed pants, the only clean clothes he had left were an old, short sleeved, white summer shirt, lacking its neck button, and a gray V-necked sweater. A perfectly ludicrous schoolboy look! He hadn't dressed like that for fifteen years. But, grimly, he decided on it. *Let it say* he thought *whatever I'm not, I am young and strong and Nia is mine!*

She at once discerned what he'd done, but no one else appeared to notice. Betty, in a purple frock that nicely displayed her auburn curls and ample bosom, pecked him on the cheek for the two bottles he'd brought from Hugh's stock, and Findlay warmly shook his hand. Francis was tall, with long arms and legs and a friendly face, and soon proved gracious and witty. But both he and Betty, Robert saw and was impressed by, affectionately deferred to Nia. She and Robert were seated side-by-side. Across from them were the serving dishes, while their hostess was at one end of the table and Francis at the other. Nia held her fork in her left hand, Robert had his in his right; between them, under the table, their adjacent fingers fondly entwined.

Nia had no need to flaunt a conquest. These old friends had seen others in Robert's place. They were her age, had known her most of her life, and knew from her manner that she wasn't being frivolous. Indeed, the last cabin hours with her young lover had been especially sweet. Physically, he was the most satisfying man ever. But she was inwardly anxious. Whenever she and Betty and Francis spoke of past events, and people with whom they were intimately familiar, Robert was left out. He was half a generation behind.

Francis, Betty said *did you come for the concert?* Under the name of Betty Bobs she locally reviewed music and movies. *I'm not a 'critic',* she was forever saying *not like Francis Findlay. I only say what, where, and when.*

No, Francis replied *I'm here for my mother's semi-annual solo. I listen carefully to her complaints. The motif never varies: if I don't come more often, one day it will be too late. I daresay that's true. But in the meantime we have tea.*

How is she? Nia said.

Dying, of course. As she's been for twenty years. Otherwise hale and well, thank you.

For all his fame, Findlay was humble at heart, nothing having erased his feeling of being a failed performer, of having had to forsake what he had most wanted to do. Moreover, he knew of Robert from the whale-hunting film, which at the time Nia had alerted him to watch for. He had told her it was definitely the best of its kind. He and Robert got on fairly well. Indeed, when finally Findlay got up to go, the younger man rose too, ready to accompany him.

Hey, you can't leave yet — Nia cried, and when Betty was in the kitchen, leaving them alone, she sat in his lap and said *Let's smooch.*

Like kids Robert said, kissing her.

Exactly. It goes with your little-boy outfit. Darling, you really don't need to prove that kind of thing. At first sight it had annoyed her, and still troubled her somewhat. Also she felt uneasy about having come to Toronto to help with what was really Robert's work, but which would now be done by another.

*

On registering at her hotel Nia enquired about Stanley. He was booked to arrive, and she had barely time to bathe and dress when he phoned from a room on the floor below. Then he came up with some single-malt scotch. Their reunion was merry; Nia had to push him out to convince him she really had other plans for dinner. She was expecting Robert.

He came in scowling and disgruntled. He was smarting from the ironic sneer with which, he felt, the desk clerk had finally given him Nia's room number. The astute clerk, faced with Robert's pretense of stern professionalism, had taken him for a tacky character actor, probably looking for a part, and had wondered whether to alert Mrs. Wilson. Then, as Robert was waiting for the elevator, he'd seen Stanley, his erstwhile editor now busily climbing his back, sashaying into the dining room. And before all that there'd been the shocking price of replacing Hugh's wine. Flopping down on the sofa, he said *I don't feel like going out.*

Okay — Nia replied slowly. Sitting again at the dressing table, she resumed pinning back her hair *I'll have something sent up.* She was wearing high heels and the black dress in which he'd first seen her in Eldon's office. They had planned, by dining out, to celebrate last night's emergence from furtiveness.

Room service came with flowers and a bowl of fruit that the manager, eager for Film Board business, had added as a gesture of welcome. The quiche and salad were charged to Nia, but Robert peevishly felt he'd paid for his part by the humiliation of hiding while the waiter wheeled in the order. Despite Nia having told him there was no reason he shouldn't remain.

Her small suite came with a kitchenette, which she'd already stocked with instant coffee and a bottle of brandy. By the time they were sipping those it was difficult to talk. Having to skirt around Robert's resentments, they'd run out of topics.

Tomorrow I'm going to be very busy — Nia said. *We've only two days until the crew arrives* — *then once they start shooting I have to get back to Montreal. You can't imagine* — *it was incredible* — *the fuss Eldon made about my taking time off* — *when even with the cabin days I still have some statutory leave* —

She was interrupted, in her uneasy small talk, by three soft double raps at the door. Opened, it revealed Stanley offering a dozen florid roses and a fistful of Javanese cigarettes. *Oh no* — Nia exclaimed, taking the bouquet *we're becoming a funeral parlour!* And indeed, on seeing Robert, Stanley turned deathly pale.

I thought you'd be back from dinner he said to Nia. *I thought we'd . . .* He began blushing. Then he stared at Robert, who had risen. *Hi. Are you here about . . . the script?*

No Robert said scornfully.

Oh . . . Rivalry mingled with Stanley's fear, deepening his flush. Advancing behind Nia, he planted his feet firmly.

Robert's ridicule was fast changing to impatient rage. He was now seriously scowling.

Well — said Nia, sitting down and lighting one of Stanley's cigarettes. *What an original plot* — *which boy gets girl?*

It's not funny Stanley said. *I'd like to see you alone.*

No, Robert said, taking him strongly by the arm *you'd better see me alone.* And before Nia could intervene, he pushed her hapless suitor into the hall.

They went down to Stanley's room. Stanley entered first, into the short hall, then turned like a quarry at bay. Blood was beating in his temples, his lips quivered, he began to shudder. Robert's physical presence filled the small space between them, Robert's strength overwhelmed him without a blow. Tender vibrations spread through Stanley's fright.

Robert could sense this, but it was all too complex. And in the past, Stanley had, after all, mostly been helpful. Something of that collaborative spirit returned. *Stan . . .* he said *what is this? She's a woman. . .*

But I love her! Stanley cried with a vehemence that startled them both. And both, with the instinct of dramatists, paused for the beat they would have allowed in editing.

Well, she doesn't love you Robert said steadily. *She loves me.*

And Stanley, staring into Robert's blue eyes, became uncertain about just who he loved.

*

When Robert rejoined Nia the wheeled table was gone and the flowers stood in glass vases not unlike the one he'd left with the lilacs in Stanley's apartment in Montreal. Meanwhile Nia had been nonplussed by the editor's behaviour. That he truly liked her, she knew. Virtually every man who encountered her liked her; most were drawn to her. Even Eldon's tyranny was partly punishment for the adroit way she avoided his sometimes hardly-veiled advances. He wanted the conquest basically because it was no longer available to him. But Stanley, though he'd always been warm and caring, responsive to her every mood, had been such a quiet queen. She had assumed his sexuality was quite settled. Yet, as she knew from experience, people were capable of surprising quirks. *How is he?* she said. *I hope he can work tomorrow.*

Oh sure. He's a pro. You know what he ended up telling me about? The Bentley limousine he once had at his service for a 'fortnight' in London. I think he wants you the way he'd like that Bentley again.

Oh — she called from the other room, where she was drawing back the bedcover *at least I'm not a tin lizzie. Are you coming to bed?*

Here? But . . . won't the desk clerk. . . ?

They change at eleven. Anyway, it doesn't matter.

When he gathered her into his arms she said *My period's started.*

Again? he said, smiling. Then, cavalierly, he added *does it matter?*

I don't mind if you don't.

Later he pointed to some smudges on the sheet.

Well, it's good clean blood — she said.

Rinsing it from himself, it stained red the water in the white bathroom sink. And Robert felt there had been something basic in the mingling of his seed and Nia's blood. Myra had always been fastidious.

*

The suite was stuffy and warm. Drugged from the fumes of brandy and flowers, and the exhausting ups and downs of the last days and nights, they slept late. The phone woke them. It was the novelist Nia and Eldon had lunched with the time Robert had taken the air force outline to Clee. He was calling to confirm that she'd be at his house for dinner. *How could I forget that* — she exclaimed, all instant enthusiasm and charm *I've been thinking of nothing else!* Then, just as intent and hard pressed, she leapt out of bed and hurried to the shower, calling back *No time for breakfast — make yourself coffee if you like* —

Disgruntled, Robert dressed and sat down on the sofa. He felt Nia was flying off like a bird taking wing, returning to a glittering realm of personalities and affairs while he remained mud bound and forgotten in the shadows. She swept in, looking rushed but splendid in the same dress and shoes she'd worn the night before, and went straight to the phone. *Nothing else to put on?* he said snidely.

Won't have time to change — she replied over her shoulder, beginning to dial.

It riled Robert that she was going to the novelist in a dress symbolically *his*. It was as if another, or others, were already, again, romantically preying on her, pushing him aside. He said *He's a fraud, you know . . .*

Alarmed by his tone, she cut off her call. *Who?*

Your dinner host. He pretends that his life's in literature, that he's doing you a favour by writing a script, so you pay him more than anybody else. But in fact he's a failed writer. Nobody buys or reads his novels. He makes all his money from the Board.

And where did you make your money?

I don't lie about it.

Her eyes dealt mild contempt. *Darling, your whole current life is a lie —*

Shamed anger rose in Robert. It was true that he claimed principles he failed to live by, talked about filmmaking he no longer did, pretended to belong with Nia while he betrayed his wife. Instead of accusing him of this and more, Nia held him in a sad gaze and said *Why do you still carry that briefcase?*

W-what? But that too he instantly understood and guiltily conceded: he still went everywhere with the heavy bag stamped *Government of Canada.*

Yet at that moment it seemed the slim prop on which his whole being tottered. *Ah-h-h* he snarled, standing *what does it matter! Don't get so damn worked up!*

Nia sat up straight, cheeks suddenly blazing and tears sparkling on her lashes — how beautiful she looked! and Robert, in his desperate wretchedness, abruptly felt that if everything crashed it would also bring her down, and with her that whole other world — of scripts, crews, busy phone calls, and cozy meals with novelists — from which he was now excluded.

Scowling, he added heavily *Do try to control yourself.*

This loutish decrial of her worth exploded Nia. She snatched off a high-heeled shoe and half stood, brandishing it. *Ooh —* she cried *I'll throw this at you —* !

Robert, fearful of physical violence because of the fury it roused in him, and sheltering behind the boy-scout notion that one should never strike a woman, was surprised and hurt that despite his browbeating, Nia, like Myra, would resort to blows.

Come on, he said *act your age!*

It was the ultimate thrust. Nia collapsed and began to cry. Tears coursed down her constricted face and into her mouth, choking her sobs. She threw herself onto the sofa like some doomed thing and between stifled moans muttered *I can't do this. I haven't the strength for it. Please go — leave —*

Chastened by success, Robert stood uncertainly, then tried to touch her.

Go on — get out — ! she cried.

Nia . . .

Just go — Get the hell out! And she gave vent to a fresh flood of weeping.

*

Down below, on the main floor, Stanley was finishing a leisurely breakfast. He lifted from his lap the smooth linen napkin and let it fall in arrowhead folds beside his gold-rimmed bread plate. Quite recovered from the excitement of the night before, he was thinking of what he could get Nia to do for him this day and the next.

His relations with her, he expected, would be better than ever, now that they shared the secret of Robert. A notion of the three of them amorously allied brought a sudden smile to his lips. He knew this was mischievous make-believe, but it was intriguing. And it pleased him that he'd even briefly desired a woman, and that he'd continue to be close to her, a woman who could stir so many men.

*

The morning air, when Robert emerged from the hotel's revolving door, was cool, but fouled by car exhaust, diesel fumes, and chimney smoke that low cloud deflected onto the street. He walked without purpose, obsessed by the fact of his life being a lie . . . A bristled face loomed near his; the man was holding out a hand. After blankly considering this, Robert said, honestly, *Sorry, I've no change* and the other impatiently jerked away. More faces surged by, and a woman, not young, with a fur piece round her neck, blocking him, said *Where you goin', sweetheart?*

And he, stepping around her, innocently replied *To the corner...*
and only then dimly realized he'd been solicited. There seemed no
refuge from the real world.

*

Nia lay drenched in tears and damp misery. Strewn around her
was the chaos of her existence.

Outside her door, holding a warm paper bag, Robert carefully turned the handle. Nothing gave. He knocked. There was no
response. *Nia...* he said. *It's me.* He tried tapping with his fingernails, then kicked lightly. *Please... it's Robert. Nia, please...*

There was the sound of the elevator stopping. *The desk clerk!*
he thought wildly, and was about to panic, when suddenly the latch
clicked from within.

At first he didn't see her, so quickly had she regained the sofa.
When he did, he hesitated, then slowly put down his purchase on
the other side of the room. Nia lay under the brown bedspread,
which had been dragged across the floor. Her hair was dishevelled,
her face darkened and streaked with half-dried tears. She looked
pinched, rigid, remote.

From the bag he took two capped cartons, and a large woman's
comb in the blue colour Nia liked. Earlier she'd been unable to find
hers. He said softly *Here's coffee.*

I have a terrible headache. Give me a 222, please.

He looked round for the pills.

In my purse.

The warm scent rising from that jumble of small things evoked
his Nia more than the crumpled creature on the sofa. But when
she raised herself to sip water, when the cover slid from her shoulder, leaving it bare except for the slim black strap of her slip — he
saw that in the midst of her agony she'd hung up her dress — the
warm desire her flesh always kindled, his fervent hunger for all
she was, shudderingly came over him, and he knew that any life
without her would be unendurably empty and cold.

179

15

Swaying on his coach seat, Robert dozed fitfully until an un-friendly dawn flared through the car windows and forced him, blinking, awake. He thought of Nia as he'd left her on the sofa. Then of Sally, who'd offered to drive him to the bus depot, and on the way fender-bent the Jaguar into the rump of a streetcar, dis-lodging the tram's power pole, so that they had to stay to speak to an inspector and then get hold of Hugh for the insurance stuff. By then, of course, there was only the overnight train.

Through the long lonely evening he'd waited in the blaring sta-tion, near banks of empty phone booths, unable to call Nia, even to ask how she was feeling, because it was now clear that words alone would no longer do.

In Ottawa the passengers spilled into the Square, where people were crisscrossing towards the grey government buildings. Robert veered sharply away. Carrying his bags he walked the five blocks to a former saddle and harness shop. It no longer displayed a life-sized white plaster horse in full regalia, but was still renowned for its strong, dependable leather goods. Their day's first customer, they gladly sold him an identical briefcase and packaged the Board's official one. He addressed the parcel to Gwendolyn's attention and mailed it on his way home.

*

The fridge was virtually empty. There was a little leftover soup, but he put it back, in case Myra, when she came from work, wanted it for her supper; he felt he could not now take what was hers. Yet his stomach was squeezed. In the past thirty-six hours he'd consumed only part of a roll of mints and, at the railway station, a thin liverwurst sandwich and a glass of water. Earlier in the after-noon, when he would have welcomed some food, Sally hadn't offered any. But — *aha!* — in the bread box he now found some shriveled slices of rye, which he wet first before toasting, as Nia had shown him how to do at the shack. He downed them with a can of salmon and descended to his cot, to think of what he would say to his wife. He woke to the sound of her key.

Robert?

He sprang up, meeting Myra on the stairs — the fatal stairs.

Oh, she called *you've been gone so long I thought maybe it was a stranger.* Their positions were too awkward to come close, but she leaned down and kissed his shut lips. *It is a stranger!* she said. *What's going on?*

Actually, he was embarrassed about the bad taste in his mouth, and hadn't meant to hurt her, but it served to start him.

I don't think this, you and I, is working anymore he said, borrowing from Nia. *I'm not getting anywhere as things are. I want to cut loose.*

What does that mean? You're never here anyway.

But I'm held by the idea of here.

They had sunk onto the hard kitchen chairs, at opposite ends of the table. He was carefully keeping his distance, while uncomfortably wishing he could brush his teeth. His wife stared at him in silence. He was shocked by how suddenly familiar she was — how minutely he knew her skin, her smell, her small breasts. He could feel the smooth undulations of her body down to the curly dark hair and below. He had — once — held this pretty woman in his hand.

We've been through rough times before she said. *Are you sure this isn't another of your whims?*

It's not he said submissively. He couldn't afford to feel offended. *I've thought about it for weeks . . . years.* Which was hardly true, but truth, he felt, had too many strands to be easily assembled.

She breathed deeply, bitterly, once, in and out. Distress rushed to fill the space. *You want to part, then — is that it?*

Yeah. I guess that's it.

*

I can get you a divorce said the robust lawyer they had agreed to see. *A legal separation, in my opinion, is a waste of time — like trying to save last year's snow.* He paused for their praise of his humour, and when it only seemed to make them more sternly sad he added, as if among connoisseurs *That's from Babel, 'Tales Of Odessa', good writer, great writer, have him in my library. Now then* — Myra had met the lawyer once when he had acted for the government in a patent grievance involving the Council. He was considered cultured, this cardsharp of corporate law, this well-known doer of deals. Along with his glossy dyed hair, silvered at the temples, the tanned sheen on the balding forehead, cheeks a plump expense-account pink, striped undertaker's suit with bunched hankie in the sleeve, and striking gold signet ring, he had a blithe air of disdain for anyone dumb enough to disagree with him.

Husband and wife — they had never been more conscious of it, looked narrowly at each other. The week while they had waited for this appointment had seemed merely to intensify the state that had existed since summer, except that they had been more than usually polite. Robert had tiptoed around Myra's pained coldness, and she, behind her curt behaviour, had been glad to have him home, preferring it to an empty house. But confronted by this formal ending of all the years for which there was so little to show, they could not escape feeling that their marriage had been a massive failure, a debacle that seemed to dwarf every previous calamity. Robert could see dismay welling darkly through his wife.

Whatever you decide, the lawyer went on, confident of their concurrence *there are the assets to divide. Your house . . . no liabilities, I take it, no mortgages?* They shook their heads. *Any other real estate, investments, cash?*

We have a joint account Myra said. *There's over five thousand in it.*

Well, whatever settlement you make, and I recommend fifty-fifty as by far the most fair, unless one of you can raise additional funds, neither will have enough to buy the other out. So we'll sell the house, and —

Robert's fierce frown cracked like lightning across the desk.

Something you're not following, Mr. Aronson?

Robert felt keenly guilty of gross deceit, of destroying their life together, of having caused Myra much innocent suffering, but all his being rebelled against now adding meanness. The talk of finances sickened him. However he might scrape and skimp on his own behalf he was not going to have his freedom besmirched by dollar signs.

I'm not taking anything he said. *All there is, is for Myra.*

Her mouth pursed in shocked protest. The lawyer compressed his lips to keep from smiling.

And what's more, Robert went on *I want to give her a weekly or monthly sum, to make sure she has enough in case she's ever in need.*

The lawyer assumed his most judicious expression. *Do you have that kind of money?*

No. But I will have. Just put it in the papers. Say . . . he thought for a second or two *six-hundred a month.* It was slightly more than his salary had been, but he felt he owed her no less.

That's insane the lawyer said.

And Myra immediately and vehemently agreed. She wanted no support, she said, but Robert just as strongly insisted, and it was only when he looked at her with what she felt was love, and said *Please, My* . . . that she haltingly consented to half.

Well, if you must do this, the lawyer said *then I suggest it be done in stages. Start with a smaller sum, to give yourself time to adjust.*

Fine, said Robert in full flight *I like the idea of stages. Let's start with a separation agreement.*

And nothing would move him from that, nor from the promise to pay Myra three-hundred dollars a month.

*

On their way home from the law office they sat together on the long wooden bench that stretched bleakly along one side of the streetcar. It was an ancient car, one of the last of its kind still in service, and made a fearful creaking and squealing as it went around corners. Moreover they were whispering, to keep other passengers outside the shell of their tense seclusion. Seldom had they felt as inseparable. They had scaled an impossible mountain and were now, as it were hand in hand, sliding down the other side. *He said* Myra giggled tearfully *that as long as you paid me I had to stay chaste. I know how to make you stop.*

I won't stand in your way Robert replied with a fond grin. *But I'll always look after you, My.* And he meant it. He felt empowered to create great productions, to make lots of money. The erotic brotherliness he felt for her, at that moment, was boundless.

She started to cry. Large limpid tears spilled silently. Robert said *Sh-h-h, it'll be all right.* He put his arm around her, letting his fingers rest lightly on her hip. At their stop he helped her down. On the sidewalk she began to sob openly.

It's all my fault she moaned. *If I hadn't lost our babies . . .*

No, My . . . Sh-h-h . . .

But she wailed, leaning, letting him hold her. Her suffering stabbed him, and perhaps stung his pride.

It's not like that he said. *There's another woman. . .*

Instantly she stepped back, the blinding light of insight flooding from her startled eyes. The tears stopped at once. He never saw her cry again.

16

Robert returned to his room in the penthouse with all he had taken from Ottawa: a suitcase packed with his best clothes, a heavy duffel bag holding the rest, his hand axe, the Coleman stove he had bought for the shack, in its still-clean cardboard box — he had kept it hidden from Myra in a narrow space under the roof — the small, spindly grapefruit plant he had grown from seed, as instructed by Nia, which his wife had watered, and his new briefcase stuffed with papers, among which was his copy of the Separation Agreement.

They had gone separately to sign it. On their reaching home from the streetcar and the revelation on the sidewalk, Myra had made a phone call, frantically thrown into an old carpetbag a few of her things, and fled to Allison's, leaving him alone. It took two days for the papers to be ready. The house echoed loudly of Myra's photo portrait, books, perfume. And pulsing within had been the problem of what to tell Nia.

In dreams, waking and sleeping, he had wanted to shout *I'm free! I'm really free!* and to spread before his beloved a shining future, but he realized that in the real world he might have made some matters worse. He debated whether to phone or write, and unable to decide on either, he had at last, just before boarding the Toronto-bound bus, mailed to Montreal a short note merely stating that he had legally separated and would again be staying with Hugh, who, he hoped, would soon have a film under way.

Almost by return he had this reply:

> Home, in bed
>
> That pond, it has become a drug — a prop — a crutch — I've been trying to figure why the pond? — Please know — nothing — lagoons, lakes seas or ponds could be complete for me without us — but why of all those waters — the pond? I think because it is so wonderfully living — in the evening when we first saw it — the fish constantly creating circles — then the moon twice — then the moving mist — and then all of this spilling over the weir — to the incredibly long-ago spring with the cress and the mint. Do you suppose that mint has a wild magic — I've never in my life been giddy on one drink — but we both were so loverly loaded —and I'm actually laughing now — I put my foot in the soup — it's the only answer — that mint is bewitched. I'm becoming quite impatient with Hugh — maybe he's a big pooh-bah in

building — but a producer? You know what we need? Old operator Eldon — the three of us would be in New York by now — or we need me with a little money and some new clothes and I'd have been in New York by now. It seems to boil down to the same horrible god-damned thing — MONEY!! and crazily enough not all that much. But then I wouldn't trust Old Eldon across a small street.

Back to the pond — I keep thinking of those cerise and white spiky berries in the woods — they top my flamboyant double petunias — every time — and those burrs and their insistence on living — perhaps that's it — the domestic flowers have to be petted and fed RX 15 or whatever — and then there in that forest glade was a small violet still operating and being a violet out of season. I love them.

That cabin room — it too has a living quality. I'd like it to be that late night again — after we'd made up — with you asleep and me sitting looking at the night mist on the pond and the little aggressive stove going — that was wonderful — that mattress is murder — it would be fun to lie up in the little loft. Now there's a big late autumn wind blowing.

Wind makes me lonely — I guess or rather I know — it goes back to the winds of a prairie town — forever blowing — dust in the summer — and snow in the winter — Ooh the wind in the window is cold — I wish you were here to keep me warm.

That was difficult for you in Ottawa — well now it's over, and you have to go on.

I'm sleepy — Goodnight my darling Robbie —

Nia

Against all reason, Robert was disappointed that Nia had not done what he had failed to do — assert the way ahead.

*

Did you make your call? Sally said the next day, and in reply to his puzzled frown *I put the message in the dial, on your desk.* He went back there and found that the cleaning woman, who'd come in his absence, had neatly filed it under the phone. It was the CBC number, and a local, which connected him with a secretary.

Yes, she said *can you come in this afternoon? Mr. Adams would like to see you.*

*

You're supposed to be good . . . Adams said, peering mockingly over his half specs *probably you're not. Everybody who comes in here wants me to believe they're God's gift.* Robert had said nothing, nor was he going to respond to this goading. The producer tilted his chin higher, examining him blurredly through the little lenses, which had slid to the end of his long nose. Then sniffed in distaste. *Well,* he said finally *I want a one-hour television script on a historical subject. Something back a hundred years or more. It has to involve Britain, Canada and the USA, or whatever their status was at the time. One-thousand dollars. Think you can handle it?*

I can try.

Good Adams said. *I like confidence. See my secretary about the contract.* And to conclude this performance he furrowed his cheeks into a thin smile, pushed up his glasses and turned back to the papers on his desk.

*

When Hugh heard about the assignment he told Robert there was a vacant bachelor apartment four floors below.

But I . . . won't be able to pay the rent.

That's all right, we'll accrue it. You'll pay when you can.

Robert was abashed, but he could hardly fault Hugh's kindness and hospitality, and he understood that his long presence in the penthouse must have incommoded the lovers. Indeed, they had enjoyed some freedom during his absence. Sally had once more been able to go about seductively half dressed, and Hugh, who knew she was no more capable of fidelity than a snake of flying, and who felt there was no point in prolonging enticement, was released from the slight unease of having a possible rival underfoot.

The apartment is empty, he said to Robert *but you'll soon fix yourself up.*

Yeah . . . of course. And speaking of fixing, I'm sorry about the Jaguar.

It wasn't your fault. And it's as good as new. Anyway, the insurance increase was chalked up to Sally's business expense.

Sally is a business expense?

Hugh's grin widened. *Sure. She's my consultant on apartment design.*

And if he listened to me, Sally said *his units wouldn't be so damn dull.*

Stunned by his own naivety, Robert recoiled from the crassness of charging a love life to the public purse, but recalling that he had done partly the same thing, in a minuscule way, with his three hotel nights in Montreal, he admired Hugh's prodigious cunning.

Do you think Sally said soothingly *it was your screening that got you the script job?*

Oh, I suppose so. It must have.

*

But only after a staggering, roundabout course. There had been a reception in Ottawa for the visiting British Prime Minister, to which the Chairman of the CBC had considered himself lucky to be invited, and taking care not to spill his drink while he nervously sidled up to the great man, who was at that moment chatting with the American ambassador, the Chairman succeeded in getting himself introduced. *Do you fellows do any history dramas?* the Prime Minister said. *Our BBC's been staging some splendid stuff.* The Chairman, beaming from every pore, immediately assured the two luminaries that the CBC happened to have in the works a widespread drama that actually linked their three countries. Then, sobered by dread, he had rushed back to his office, phoned Adams, and told him to get going, *at the double*, on such a subject.

Adams, however, disliked being dictated to, and did not relish inflicting on any of his favourite writers a task that was bound to be boring and would probably result in something he would not care to produce. It needed someone with sufficient credentials to satisfy the Chairman that the project was not being thrown away, but to whom the producer had no obligations that might later prove troublesome. It was then that he heard that Francis Findlay was in town.

Behind his humorous mannerisms, Adam's hauteur hid a genuine contempt for his co-workers, and, with few exceptions, for people generally. But like most Canadians he had an inherent regard for those of his countrymen who had *made it* elsewhere. He had been quick to seek out the critic, whom he had known for years, and the evening after the dinner at Betty Bobchenko's, just when Nia and Robert had been confronted by Stanley, Adams had been in the bar of Findlay's hotel, sitting, in a sense, at his feet.

Met an interesting writer-director last night Findlay said. *He used to be at the Film Board. Name of Aronson.*

Can't say . . . no, haven't heard of him.

I believe he had a screening at the Corp.

Oh . . . Adams now vaguely remembered the small empty screening room and the scene that had momentarily roused his interest. The next day his secretary traced the event back to the Board's distribution office, where she was given Hugh's telephone number.

*

The apartment to which Robert was sent was an empty square space in which, on one side, had been inserted, like oversized closets, a small windowless bathroom and a tiny kitchen. But it had the same kind of plate-glass southern exposure that was striking about the penthouse, though on a smaller scale. And it had no balcony.

Every second unit, which was somewhat larger, had one. The whole building had been designed for professional singles and couples, though over time a few babies and toddlers had crept in. The hostile deep-red halls and high lobby sculptures discouraged children.

Robert borrowed a folding cot and a few dishes from Betty Bobchenko, transporting them in the Thunderbird, which Hugh lent him. And the janitor, on his boss's say so, brought up some odds and ends left by previous tenants. When the furnishings were in place — the cot, a three-shelf bookcase of bare boards, a battered radio with a broken brown cabinet but which still played, a scarred wooden table and a pair of tubular metal chairs with torn padding, Sally came down with a split of champagne. Hugh was at work somewhere. Angry afternoon clouds filled the large sky, smothering the sun. Sally sipped from one of the water tumblers into which they had poured the sparkling wine.

I could live like this she said.

You?

I'm not such a fool as you think. Yes, if I could write or paint or compose music, I would gladly live like this. It would be a small price to pay for the privilege of creating something larger than myself. But I wasn't given any of those talents. Only . . . this face.

And figure . . .

Yes, she said with a smile *it's part of the package.*

*

The glimpse into herself Sally had given him tugged temptingly for the next two days, while he waited for his phone to be installed. It seemed more revealing than if she had stripped, and just as stimulating. But Robert knew that for him it ran terrible risks. He transformed its excitement into desire for Nia, and the moment the technician left he made a person-to-person call.

Exciting stuff . . . he announced, and told her about the new place, the CBC script, and that Sally and Hugh were at last in New York.

That's terrific — ! she said, but she couldn't talk. Gwendolyn was with her; they were going over a schedule for which Eldon was screaming. *I'll try to call you tonight —* she said. When she did, it was only to say that things at home were also impossible. *You can probably hear the racket downstairs — Joel's dribbling a basketball, mother is going at him — and Jester is running in circles. I'm sorry — I'll write —*

★

Her letter arrived by special delivery:

Almost asleep
9.20 P.M.

Right now everyone is going to bed — poor mother, ill again and unhappy, trying very hard, but it must be frightening. I really must soon try to figure out something for all that — it is driving me mad — and it isn't good for her either. I hope when I am seventy-six I'll have something to lean on in myself — I think I will I've been trying for years for some kind of personal strength — and yet look how I fall apart with love for you.

Saturday, shopping in the village — I missed you so much I imagined how a widow might feel — this has been so since the minute you walked out the door in the hotel —after our last turmoil — but thank god the thread of our love held. Great heaven how fabulously lucky. I've been burrowing — sighing — nudging searching — sometimes yelling for this my entire life — and here it is. We've come such a long way in a few months. I'll never throw a shoe at you again — that's not true I just might — if you forget that thread. And as well I am filled with hope — perhaps it's only because of the phone call — with your news — that I couldn't respond to again (Gwen in my office) and I had so much I wanted to say and to tell you — will there ever be time to tell you —

191

Robert was inflamed, but at the same time left with the nagging suspicion that this supposed love was taking on a life of its own. Yet in the arid confines of his wretched little room Nia's letter seemed to light the white walls with a glow infinitely warmer and more precious than could be had from all the riches and fleshy pleasures of the penthouse.

*

He was summoned there for breakfast. Hugh had returned from New York the night before.

I met with the distributor, he said *the one that had indicated some interest. We talked for a long time, and I told them what a terrific director you were, that you could do as good a job as is done anywhere. They took that under advisement. They want a first class theatrical product, naturally.*

They'll get it! Robert said.

Anyway, Hugh replied *they're now willing to read a script. If they like it, and the rest of it checks out, they might put up a quarter to half the cost.*

Really . . .

If the New York people will go for as much as half, and you defer half . . . Christ, you can practically make it for nothing.

Defer? Robert said.

You pay each person and supplier half their salary, or price, whatever you can negotiate, with the provision that they get the other half when the film goes. It's done all the time Hugh said, smiling.

Robert hadn't known that, but did not doubt it.

We'll presell, of course. We'll probably have to bank the sales agreements, but I can arrange that.

Robert was highly excited and just slightly confused; none of this seemed to have much to do with filmmaking. But it was why he needed Hugh.

Do you have the Film Board file? his producer said.

Uh . . . not yet.

Hugh stared at him with a touch of irritation. *Well, get it. Then we can go ahead.*

*

He could not phone, for fear that a switchboard operator might overhear. Instead he wrote Nia a long reasoned letter full of optimism, about working together, and about their future. He pledged his continuing love, but also made it seem, without quite saying so, that only that single file stood in the way of all they hoped for. He ended with 'I've come to the point where I can no longer put up with purposes which are intrinsically mediocre. What I want is to try for only the finest possible result. I'm prepared to fail, but only at that. Are you willing to take a chance on that?'

The office
Your long and wonderful letter just arrived. (And now you are putting your name on the envelopes!!!). Almost always and often without even being aware of it we give each other love and comfort — you are a wonderful loving man and person — and to answer your question — I'd take a chance on you anywhere anytime doing anything — and I'd even take a chance on you being what the boys call a success, and that's the toughest — I mean — it's the toughest to have and to keep — your own self at the same time. Hell you've seen and heard that theme a million times — but I believe if it happened to you — you could do it — keep your own wonderful loving person. My I do love you my darling Robert.

Home now
Oh dear — it ended up a crazy day — I don't care much for Tuesdays. I feel lousy — physically I mean. I have sinus — and also a terrible exhaustion. Mother, as I told you, is not well again — and when I think of the long winter with illness I swing back to thinking one day at a time. I needed

those days with you so badly — I need quite a few days with you and then I eat properly and sleep properly and relax. Also time away with you gives me or reminds me of my convictions — I used to need to be alone to find strength — but now I need you — not exactly you — us. Wrote a few pages of "things" about how I feel re the file — none of it readable — too many interruptions.

now much later

Got to sleep about 10.30 —Then I woke again at 4.30 wide awake — had a glass of milk a cigarette and stared into space. One of the things I stared into this morning about was anger at myself. Angry because I felt so lousy and you seem so wonderful and energetic — and I suddenly felt I'd been selfish — good god I've been tired before and felt sick before, I'm just being spoiled by you (thank you sir) So — at 4.30 I felt all that goodness for you and was very happy and nearly content. Now it is almost time to get up, but I am first going back to bed for even a few minutes so I can sleep with you — I love sleeping with you. Will you please hold me close I am brimming with love for you —

He melted and wanted only to shelter and comfort her — and he was furious with her self-willed stubbornness about the file. Still, he had to be certain of his own position before he pressed her further. The way it had been explained, their producer would have virtually all the control, with no commitment.

Having phoned the penthouse, he said *Hugh, can I assume that if we get the needed info, and it looks okay, you'll supply money for a script?*

Robby, please just get the file.

He wrote again, hoping to rouse Nia's enthusiasm, knowing that would be more effective than pressure. Her reply came three days later.

It's funny all day every day I have things to tell you —
just things. The incredible sadness of railway stations.
Last night coming home (I've been taking the train every
day — my old ride is on night shift — and no money for
taxis — have become a regular suburbanite) I walked to
the newsstand looked at magazines but didn't see — and
suddenly my arm was clutched by a woman in black, a
familiar face, and "Madam — you remember me, from the
cafeteria." It was one of the staff — French fiftyish and eyes
brimming — she saw me across the station and had to tell
her grief — her sister had died of cancer and her brother
of a heart attack two days later. By the time I got on the
train I was shattered.

Other things — I wanted you to see the round night sky
of the island while walking from the station. Took me back
to the incredible feeling of the unusual mixture of love and
admiration and excitement of you in the twilight light of
the cutting room in front of a moviola saying with a finger
snap "Now" — like the old feeling cue of a radio booth.

About the file, I have had (as usual) too many long
thoughts — I think that's what puts me off dealing with
it — I collect all these thoughts and their offsprings and
then their offsprings and it's a ruddy novel and there isn't
time — so I'll leave all those and only hint — for instance
why meddle with what the Board did —.

Oh I have so much to talk about — and I'm impatient
with the pen or this pencil — I must get my typewriter
fixed and the typing will be horrible but I can go better.

This time he phoned, which cost him more in anxiety than expense. But his bank account was down to less than two-hundred
dollars, though, thankfully, he didn't yet have to pay Myra. The
suave lawyer, injecting what he considered a modicum of common
sense, had deliberately drawn the agreement so that there would

be no payments for the first six months. Both signees had been surprised, but neither had said anything. Myra because it all seemed anyway somewhat unreal, and Robert, who had already by then fallen to earth, out of relief. For which, nonetheless, he felt rather ashamed.

Now, feeling that there was a crisis, he put the case succinctly and strongly. *Nothing can be done without money. Hugh's a businessman. He won't budge. Please, it completely depends on . . .*

*

That evening, after Gwendolyn had left and the outer office was empty, Nia went to the locked filing cabinet, to which she had a key. There was light under Eldon's door, he was working late; she hoped he would not hear. But the metallic roll of the drawer made a grating sound, and in seconds, Eldon, his little eyes glittering, was at her side.

What are you looking for?

It was such a classic case of being caught red handed that she laughed aloud. Eldon smiled, with tight lips. Unwilling to lie, she told him. He took out the file and gave it to her, then relocked the cabinet. *I'd love to make a feature* he said. *But the problem is always political. Mac and the Commissioner aren't sure we have a mandate for pure entertainment. You know, parliament . . . It's all in there. Let me know what you think* he added as he went back into his office, shutting the door. Eldon had smelled something, and was ready to exploit it. But Nia went home torn apart.

> The island
> Tuesday night
> Here is the material. Also my old typewriter with
> absolutely every leter on the rrrrrrrrrrrllllllllllll
> rrrrrrrrrrrrrr eeeeeee rrrrrrrrrr ddddddddddd sssss
> wwwwwwwwwwww aaaaaaa wwwww qqqqqq rrrrr tttttt
> ffffffff vvv ggggggg ccc eeeee No. . . . I've been testing, only
> the "e" is now sticking this turns out to be one of the most

important vowels. I am going to stick with it though, it may save me from my introspection, which has been quite wild for the last little while.

I wish I could remember my exact words in my last renouncing of us, because basically I'm sure they were the same. They had to do with your young years and a career and energy, and I said I just couldn't go through it, and my darling I don't think I can. I feel we are just too late. I work all day, I deal with and make every decision for a twelve (or nearly) year old boy and a seventy-six year old woman, I'm hopeless with money, I hate the whole god damned thing, I don't want to decide whether to send this file or not, and yet as soon as I typed that I did decide, I'm not sending it, it is confidential and very wrong of me, and at this moment I feel hopeless and as though I might crack into hundreds of small bits, I almost wish I would, and then someone would have to pick me up, even if only to clean up the mess of Nia in bits. I also know that of course I won't break apart, that I'll have a hideous lonely and impossible night, and then go drearily on, but there is no future for us, for you yes, but not for us, and frankly I don't give a damn about mine.

I had to give up the balky typewriter — and you'll have to make do with my scrawl — because I want to talk without coping. About the work — I'd love to work with you and Hugh — but I can't feel all the operation leaning on me — I'm too tired darling — I'm excessively tired — almost to the point of wanting to cry and scream — I don't know why this should be so — in New York I seemed to have plenty of energy — but of course we had help there — anyway here I am in a strange city — a small island — with unfamiliar people — is this for me for the rest of my life? Day after day worrying about money about bringing up a boy — about mother dying in the middle of the day alone and Joel having to cope — please don't say — "That's life" — I know it is and I'm tired of the pressures — of being strong.

There I just had to call you and thank heaven the line was busy — this would only be a burden to you — and you can't do anything about it anyway. My darling Robert — I can't inflict this on you and I know we can't just stop — but we can try.

I want to go to sleep and never never wake up — but first I want to cry until I'm unconscious then someone else can look after the bills and Buddy can look after my Joel and mother can live it out and I'll be asleep — without dreams.

Now I've had a bitter cry — I love you my darling, very much, thank heaven your phone was busy — this would have been so upsetting. Now I've stopped (and it only took a few minutes) to find out what I'm so troubled about — and it turns out to be of all things — money — and when I go back to where the trouble begins it turns out that I should move — closer to the Board — and that means a new school for Joel, a search for another place to live, and that means more decisions and arrangements and things to cope with at home — and then the new business things interrupted and it all seemed to depend on what I could do — and then our ridiculous and sometimes tragic separation and then the new career beginning for you — and then the dishonesty of the file — and then with the file the manoeuvering of Eldon — and then Joel's winter clothes and mine — and again the money problem — and always underneath all this the self-pity of being alone — and it all builds and builds — and then I cried — quite hard and tasted the tears and from there on it's obvious. I heard that crazy wonderful love bird — "I could cry salty tears" — and I went back to that night I left you —for how long was it on the bed crying — and you were with me — and you whispered in my ear — "Nia — I love you." And now I've done it all by myself — with you far away — that bird and that night saved it.

Now I know just what I'll do — I'll reread your letters and have a rum and milk and keep on writing — just wait one minute love, I'll be right back (Do you feel all this in Toronto — you must)

I'm reading the letters out of sequence. They are painfully comforting. I've just reread this one I'm writing — I write only the surface — how frustrating — in these pages in this time only a little over an hour I've gone through a turbulent hell — but this letter looks and feels quite sane and I can only depend on you knowing me with love, to know what I'm saying — it must be wonderful to write well — and you do my love — so very well — you also build wondrous docks — and steps — and I love you — and where is that mouse? — and I love you.

me again — Nia.

When Robert had read all this he sat bent over the pages, eyes blurred, his chest heaving with an effort to breathe, his whole being rocked by horror, relief, regret over the loss of the file, an aching tenderness, and guilt. He made and received very few phone calls, and remembered why his line was busy that night — he had been flirting with Betty Bobchenko. It had been social seduction, in the name of their mutual friend, and had resulted in his going there the next day for dinner.

*

Betty had fleshy shoulders and breasts, a round, inviting face, and the creamy warm skin artists commonly confer on milkmaids. She had, despite her weight, a waist, and the effect of her full forms, hourglass shape, and small, pretty hands and feet was captivating, particularly when she was helping to fill the hollow of his craving for Nia. With Betty there were no barriers. He could speak freely, ask her anything, and though she remained firmly silent on the subject of Nia's former alliances, she was generous with other tidbits. He learnt from her that Nia had once been part of a singing trio, but had to abandon that when she married Buddy, and could have had a career in movies, but again there had been her husband's objections. Robert delighted in hearing about these triumphs. They confirmed that his love was indeed beautiful, a regal person, adored by all, and not the crushed woman on the couch he had last seen, or the broken writer of the later letters.

Also with Betty he could talk boastfully about himself, about the books on American history he was reading, about the ambitious script he hoped to finish in a month or two — empty, pretentious, almost desperate talk he had never needed before. Indeed, the kind at which he used to sneer, and of which he would have been too ashamed to spout in front of Nia.

17

You're gorgeous MacCurry said.
Mac — I'm getting older.
You're still gorgeous MacCurry said softly, his eyes shining. *Christ, you know that. Everybody tells you you're beautiful, don't they?*

Blustering November sunshine tore from the first rent in the clouds and flung itself into the office, further confusing her. MacCurry smiled. He had put off this meeting with Nia until late afternoon, when the forecast had called for clearing. She had been fearful from before lunch, when he had phoned and asked her to come down at four-thirty. He took a chair near hers.

Is that a new suit?

No one at the Board had ever seen it on him before. It was of an odd red-green and dark blue material, in broad bands, stripes and counter bands. *Oh,* he said *I noticed it in a shop window the last time I was in London. They were featuring tartans. I was curious and went in. I hadn't known the MacCurrys could claim a tartan. This is it.* Nia smiled slightly, searching for something kind to say. *I know,* he went on *it seemed silly when I got it back here, and I hung it away. Until today.*

He had a small blue aster in his buttonhole. A brown vase of the cordial flowers, in mixed colours, stood on the pale oak cabinet beside Nia. Their subtle, earthy scent surrounded her. MacCurry twisted round and picked up a pair of rimless spectacles from the desk behind him; the bright light from the large windows bounced off the corner of one of the lenses when he put them on. Outside the clouds were recoiling, sent sprawling by the conquering sun. Wearing the glasses seldom seen by anyone but his secretary, MacCurry smiled benignly.

You're wondering why I wanted to speak to you.

Yes, Nia said, with forced charm *wondering what I've done wrong.*

MacCurry smiled warmly, enjoying that idea's absurdity, and what he chose to acknowledge as her wit. *Look,* he said, with his more characteristic bluntness *I could do the romantic thing, wine and dine you. But, we're both grown up.* He paused, and then said earnestly, *Nora, I'm getting lonely. My life until now's been pretty much the Board. And for fun, well, there's been cards with the guys, women when I wanted them, you know, the bachelor life. But it isn't enough any more.* He paused, and then with a show of shyness said *If some of this sounds rehearsed it's because I've been thinking of it for weeks. I haven't slept well for a month. I want . . .*

Someone you can talk to — Nia eluded, and then immediately said *I'm sorry. I don't mean to be flippant. It's just that — I'm a bit surprised. You want someone to — share with.*

Yeah, share my life with. It wouldn't be a bad life. I have money. Quite a lot that was left to me, more than enough for a big house, if you'd like that, and all that goes with it. And I get a good salary, and then later I'll be getting a pension, a pretty good one. I've been here almost seventeen years he said with pride. *Began as little better than a gofer. And you could go on working, if you wanted to. Or not. We'd have plenty either way.*

But — what — ?

To marry me, of course. I know your mother and son come with it, and that's okay. I think we could be happy.

Oh Mac, there are so many —

No, there aren't. Not like you. Not with your brains and person-ality, and charm, and looks. Not a lot. And I don't happen to know any other.

I think I'm older than you.

Yeah, I know. It's just a little over two years, less than my mother was older than my father. Big deal. Nobody would know it to look at us. And anyway, I'll be old long before you. C'mon, what's to stand in the way? Don't you like me?

Of course I like you she said, starting to cry.

Maybe I haven't put it well . . . I watch you, and I can see through your clothes. Up here he said, touching his forehead. *This dress you have on, it's as if it wasn't there. Just you in the necklace and earrings. This has been happening gradually. Probably began, unconsciously, long ago. But now I dream about you too. They're almost wet dreams, like when I was a kid. I want you, Nor, I really want you. But I don't want it to be cheap. Or just a roll. Marry me, please.*

Mac, Mac, Mac — She was weeping now, shaking from the struggle to contain her sobs. He opened a drawer in the cabinet and offered a box of tissues. *Thank you —*

You want time to think about it ?

She shook her head, a tiny almost intangible shake that quiv-ered the room and sent a distinct tremor though him. She stood up and stepped to the doorway. He followed and took her hand.

Nora, he said humbly, and the misery in his voice was unmistakable *I'm not shopping.*

Oh, Mac — she cried, and reaching up to his shoulders laid her shaking head against his chest.

He did not attempt to hold her. She broke from the embrace and turned sharply away, blindly striking her forearm against the door jamb. It was a brisk hit and made a dull hard sound.

Are you hurt? he said swiftly, chivalrously.

No, it's nothing — She bit back the pain, indeed used it to help dry her eyes and compose her face so as not to betray either to his secretary, whom they could hear typing in the outer office. *Bye now* — she whispered as she went out.

In the empty stairwell she burst into a long shuddering sob. The Film Board, she felt, had suddenly become threateningly unsafe.

As she opened the door at the top of the stairs she met a smiling Stanley, lounging in the hall. He had seen her coat and scarf in her office and was waiting to ask her to dinner. It was a horrible, head-spinning idea, yet at that moment she wanted a drink more than anything. They went downtown and she laughed a great deal.

*

When she got home a blessed silence hung in the house. Joel and her mother were both asleep, and Jester, after vigorously wagging his tail, soon returned to his padded bed. It was late, but she quietly placed a call to Robert. The operator could barely catch the words, and asked her to please speak up. Robert answered sleepily. She said she just wanted to hear his voice.

He was thrilled and told her she sounded chipper. *I wish you were here* he said. *Or I there. I want you now . . . this minute!* He went on to say that only the immediate mattered, that there was now no pleasure in talking about memories. He thought it better not to mention Betty, and Nia was completely silent about Mac-Curry. Robert said he would soon be finished his research. Their words, even the muttered endearments as they hung up, seemed lacking. It had been all too little, and she took to her pen.

                                        After phone call.

Yes — I guess now I am chipper — although the word chipper reminds me of a very ambitious but sweet baby chick — a children's book we once had. I don't feel like a sweet naive baby chick — but I do feel sure again — of what really matters. You say the pleasure of talking about memories has gone — now only impatience. I don't think that's true all the time. I know sometimes I feel that impatience almost with a violence — but other times it makes me happy to talk to you in a letter.

I love you more deeply every minute that goes by. That's the one clear, simple thing I cling to. God knows I try for it — simplicity — to everyone I say "keep it simple" — it's practically my personal motto— but except for my loving you, everything is so damn complicated. That's why it helps even to talk to you in my mind. Last Saturday — coming from the little store over the bridge — I stopped at the roadside farmer's stand — and "Oh look, Rob — how beautiful" — the lettuce and green peppers, cucumbers and rose tomatoes all wet from the rainy morning. The farmer wrapped them all in a large newspaper bundle — for 60¢ and I walked back — still with a sense of you — feeling much better and with what seems necessary for me — a kind of there — that's better kind of feeling. And I feel that now, my darling — I feel that I have what really matters.

For some time Nia's letters had been becoming literature, about a love that had become a fantasy.

18

Robert handed Adams an outline of the historical script. It dealt with the war of 1812, and had British ships, sailing from Canadian ports, invading the Potomac and landing the troops who defeated the Americans at the Battle of Bladensburg. Then the British occupy Washington and burn its public buildings in retaliation for the Americans' burning of York — now the city in which Adams was perusing the outline. *We would have seen the smoke and flames from here* Robert said. *Actually, we'd probably be on fire.*

How are you gonna burn Washington? said Adams, amused. *Are you going to torch Studio One?*

We show only the flicker on their faces. That we do with lights. For the actual burning we can intercut an outdoor night shot of a model.

You had any experience with models?

No. But I'm sure I could build one good enough to burn.

Adams, who had no wish to produce this screenplay, any such play, was nonetheless impressed by Robert's pluck. He approved the outline, which at once released to the writer a third of the contract price. And when Robert returned to the apartment there was another reward waiting.

The island. Saturday night.

Well alright — if you're going to leave me to pine — I guess I'll just have to pine then —

I wonder how Washington is? (or whatever you're calling that CBC thing)

How is Nia? Well — her arm is nearly better — it was black below the elbow from a dispute I had with a doorway — for two weeks I've had to wear long sleeves — and last night I (Nia) sat up straight in bed from 2 a.m. until six — couldn't breathe — all tight in the chest and I might say terrified — but now after all day in bed I feel much better. I can breathe — and that's handy.

Oh, hell I hate writing — I want to talk to you and soon I must — darling can't we get together somewhere at least once before Christmas — it's going to be such a long winter.

Things I'm not afraid of —
Bats
snakes
Being hungry or poor (Impossible!)
Mice — (oh that sweet one)
frogs — toads — reptiles in general
people (not quite true — some I'm afraid of)
the dark — the light —
sickness (for myself)
death (startled by it and angry but not the real fear —)
I am afraid of
Heights
Escalators (same as Heights)
Hurricanes & tidal waves
Thunderstorms in strange places
Not enough air — (that covers under-water and small
     closed-in places)
Something happening to you — and
     "   "   to Joel.

Eldon waited two weeks for some word from Nia, then one day asked her right out what she was doing with the file.

Nothing. I thought maybe I could — but had to realize I don't have enough time — or energy. I put the file back she added truthfully *without even opening it.*

Eldon snorted and quivered, which was more and more his usual state of subsurface rage, and strode off secretly blaming Nia for having frustrated his ambitions. He then told Gwendolyn that her idol sometimes did things under false pretenses. Shocked, the secretary flared up in defense, ardently appealing to others in the unit, with the result that it became clear to everyone — some had already seen Eldon angry with her — that Nia had altogether lost favour.

> Wednesday night 1.10 a.m.
>
> So it's Thursday morning really.
>
> I have just gotten home — I've had dinner and a movie (Will Success Spoil Rock Hunter) with Bill Ireland from Toronto — yes, you'll say my favored novelist, but I paid my own way — and a friend of his. What would I do if I didn't know you were there? Well I suppose I'd just _do_. Roll around in the night and find some half-assed solution — As you can tell it's a down day — Reasons? — Little and big ones piled higher — the main one futility of my job — first early morning anger — heard via Gwendolyn that Eldon said he needs a program director — part of my job — then Bill tells me he ran into Mac and the Commissioner and Mrs. at dinner last night — joined them — and Mac said program director to be attached to his office. And if that's what they do, who will it be? — you can bet some close friend of Mac's. Then home — personal problems nagging but not impossible. Joel with a strange rash on his face — mother not well — but both asleep — the well nearly dry so trouble with the water pipes last few days.
>
> So those are some of the reasons — a day of people being inadequate, or frightened or stupid and perhaps a reflection of myself being all those things too. Anyway thank God you are there — wherever you are.
>
> Now terribly sleepy — but a little relieved by writing down even this much — Oh darling I want out of this mess here — I'm so bad at playing Eldon's kind of game — and I'm angry at people who can only accept a game. Please give me enough wisdom to go through the winter. Oh to hell — I'm too tired to do anything except love and want you.

The office Thursday A.M.

I have Joel with me — I'm taking him to the doctor his face is murderous looks like poison ivy or something — it spreads while I look at him.

No letter today that always makes me sad although it shouldn't because it means you are working.

I'm getting very restless — the job I mean.

This is a dreary little letter — but I need to talk to you.

N

The next day there was a letter from Robert, apologizing for his silence while he had finished the outline, and pontificating about his screenplay. And that same afternoon, through the inter-office mail, there arrived a letter from MacCurry formally offering her the position of programme director, with a nominal increase in salary. For a function, she knew, which was not needed, was basically unreal, and would daily bring her close to him. She also knew she could inflate it, make it seem much more important, and obtain for it a real raise in pay. She asked for the weekend to think it over, and of course the production chief graciously assented.

Saturday

I woke up at eight this morning — went downstairs — had a drink of milk and a cigarette, went back to bed and slept like dead until one o'clock — Joel wakened me with a cup of coffee — I'm sure I could have slept all day. Then I got up cooked a brunch breakfast — washed my hair — washed dishes — had a cool bath — trouble now with the hot water tank, but plumber doesn't come — a very irritable and hopeless day — Mother half sick, Joel's face clearing but he isn't allowed out so he is full of incredible energy and his own small boy impatience — raining on and off all day — but suddenly too warm and muggy for the cheer of a fireplace. For the last few hours I've had that "there's-no-way-out" feeling — that "this-is-the-way-it-is

Nora Wilson" you know, the Classic situation — the invalid mother old and now sick — the son to be considered and responsible for — the job getting to be only a job — I can smell disaster and hopelessness and being forever trapped — Do people rise above this day by day if they do it must be with lots of money — that dreary old money. I've thought how over-rated, how foolish — who cares about money.

Gee I guess I was very very wrong. What in Christ's name am I going to do other than go slowly nuts — Okay darling — this is not good — you'll get this letter on Tuesday just exactly what you don't need at that point — and I must remember you once said in a letter something about our separate messes and that having each other or the strength from each other might give us strength for the messes —

To be honest one of the things, or rather the underlying thing — is that my irritation with my job, the fear of the home situation — all rest on one thing — they mount to a screaming depression because I'm afraid they will keep me from you. If it wasn't for the inevitable us I would be coping in quite another way — I would be making the job the program director. I think, I know, I could probably make it useful. I would be coping at home with plans ahead — small, insignificant plans but now I can't — because you or our "thread" or the essence or whatever, are so much there that at times like this unhappy lost day it seems almost relentless — thank God. You see my darling Robert <u>this</u> has never never happened to me before — and I know it's what I was afraid of when I used to renounce us, afraid of something big and deep and there.

My God — I can't stand this any longer! — I must phone —

She did. Robert was working on his script. *Darling — ?* she whispered fiercely.

Her turmoil pierced him. *Nia? What is it?*

Oh, that's better — I just had to hear you —

What's upsetting you so? Into his anxiety leapt a violent lust; on the line her voice swelled into a virtual body, breasts, a beating heart. *Where are you? Oh God, why aren't you with me?*

I'd love to be with you. This is crazy — do you think we could meet — even for a few hours?

Well, I could come there, or you here . . .

Could you? I do so need to see you —

I could, but . . . what if you came here? Hugh's away and has left me a car.

I — ? Let's see — I guess I could still make the night train. But it would be so rushed — I'd have to come back tomorrow — Can't you come here?

Where would I stay?

It seemed a conclusive argument.

Half submerged, her life becoming unravelled, Nia clung to her supporting buoy, the idea of their great love.

On the train to You

I am extremely cosmic — I have a sore throat — but
I'm oh so cosmic. I'm thinking a thousand things — and
all progressive — but the mind going much too fast for
this government pen — for the immediate thoughts —
they've been piling up (the thoughts) even during the
frantic rush to make it on time — (Gee the train is so
rocky!) and finally I've dug out this scruffy paper — in the
piling up — orderly one after the other — I've arrived at
you — in that if I'm Program Director then I can propose
special ideas — or projects, as they say in the office — and
maybe one could be a little series — a mini-series — of
three or four films — written and directed by you — we'll
be sneaky and choose the subjects even if we have to label

them history or some such — I think Mac might go for it
— unless you're already sick of history — Anyway — we'll
talk — Oh my darling — there will never be enough time
to talk to you. I have so much to say — I really have — and
I'm absolutely loaded with ideas — and do you know the
energy is coming back — for real — I tell you I am so cosmic — More later, I'll just be simple and save this big talk
— anyway very soon — just a few hours — and I'll see you!

When she arrived he took her across the bustling street. In
one of the sidewalk windows of the big hotel, near where he had
parked, some art was displayed, including a drawing of the head
of a girl, by the painter Varley.

Who does that look like?

Me — ! she said.

It momentarily lifted their mood, which had again sunk at the
start from the surprise of finding in the flesh not quite the person
each, in their own craving, had imagined. Nia was pinched from
the pain in her throat, bleary from lack of sleep, and had red feverish blotches on her face and neck. Of Robert she said *You look
leaner and more — oh, brittle — than I remember. Haven't you been
eating?*

*Not a lot. And sleeping less. Last night, thinking of you coming, I
was too excited to sleep.*

He put her small bag on the back seat of the car, and proudly
pointed out that the Thunderbird had not been ticketed, though
a lesser model likely would have been. Nia sighed, and was silent
as he drove along the lakeshore, trying to take a scenic route, nor
did she say anything when the entrance to the Exhibition was
blocked, and they were obliged to turn onto a drab industrial
road, or when he blundered in the dim caverns of the parking
space under the building and had to backtrack to Hugh's spots.
But at the door of the penthouse she balked.

This can't be your apartment —

No, mine isn't nearly as comfortable . . .

Oh, really —! she said, and returned to the elevator.

But it was stark, worse even than the bare *cell* he had first led her to. *Gee, you're high up —* she said uneasily *but this window I like.* She stood in front of it, staring out at the dreary clouds, then down at the wet roads below. The warmer air mass that had yesterday moved on to Montreal had drawn behind it a messy mixture of sleet and sudden squalls of snow, and the ground was covered with yellowish slush. From the thighs up Nia's figure was dark against the great expanse of sullen sky yielding only to the distant water. It framed her as she slowly swung round and surveyed the room.

Do you have to live like this?

He was startled, hearing Sally's words inverted, and hastened to escape them. *Well, Hugh said I could use his place today. They're in New York again. His lady wanted to return some of the stuff she'd bought last time. Shopping, after all, is serious business.* But he could not long evade what Nia meant, and tensely settled on the cot. She came and sat too, facing him. Even with the white walls, the light was leaden.

Okay he said. *It's like this. When I left my wife . . . I left her everything. But I had to.*

Nia regarded him steadily.

I couldn't do it any other way. It seemed insufficient. Lamely he added *I should have told you earlier. . . Don't worry, I'll make it up.*

She touched her tongue to her teeth, then a deep sigh tore out.

He took her hands and pressed them.

People usually divide up — she said.

He hung his head.

Yet the enormity of what he had done to her, to them, suddenly came crashing in. His body bent under it as their future shattered around them. But from those ruins rose that audacious, foolish courage — he looked up with a hungry smile and leaned forward to kiss her.

His sheer, mad recklessness became virulent, infectious. Nia spread her hands. *Oh my God — oh to hell!* she mumbled against his mouth as he drew her down on the cot.

*

They made love almost continually. The sheet was soon damp; their smell permeated the small room. They were without pain; all their problems were plowed into flesh.

Just before twilight the clouds lifted, parted, and swiftly dispersed. The lovers got up for relief and food. Nia drank glass after glass of white wine. Skimping, Robert had bought no scotch. When they returned to the cot the stars were out. She thought one was moving.

It can't be Robert said. *Not enough for you to notice.* To prove it he sighted a line to the star, using a corner of the cot and a cross he made with her lipstick on the window. But when he checked again the shining dot had moved!

He hurried to the penthouse for Hugh's big binoculars; through their powerful lenses the object appeared to vary in brightness, but it certainly was moving.

It's the Sputnik! Nia cried. For a week the newspapers had been reporting that Earth's first satellite was being seen again. Nia held the binoculars tightly, utterly fascinated. *I'm just crazy about that thing up there — I could give myself to it —* And she lay back with her arms held out to the sky, as if inviting the ravages of a god. *I would love for it to take charge of me —*

Instead Robert came down; and they went on, trying not to think, until it was time to drive her, sore and exhausted, to the train.

All day nothing had been said about the thousand progressive thoughts; nor did she show him that letter.

*

In the morning, rather than going straight to the Board, as she had intended, Nia went home and reported in sick. She had a runny nose, a cough, and was afraid of it becoming flu. MacCurry told her to *take it easy*, that her decision could wait until she returned. But Eldon, savagely riled that his idea of programme director, and perhaps Nia too, were being snatched from him, curtly informed her, when she got back, that her office was needed for sound editing, and that she would be moved, that same morning, to a small room previously used for storage.

During her two days of total bed rest, helped by hot lemonade with honey, chicken soup, and a bottle of brandy, Nia had time to reflect, and as writing was a release from the swarm of her thoughts, and she had already broken the pattern of sending Robert all her letters, she slipped easily into setting out what he was unlikely ever to see:

> Darling — I love you for your intense, uncompromising character — what you did, for the woman you were married to — that was, I suppose, right in itself — but that you didn't give us equal value makes me feel — I can't help feeling — violated. If we hadn't met — but now I can't just forget you. I try shutting my eyes, to make myself bare and black — but you don't go away. It's like the fourteen-year-old, our neighbour's son — who sometimes would baby-sit me. I've never forgotten him either —

Eldon's blow, on top of all the others, made her oblivious. The cares of the unit, MacCurry's concerns, even her lingering sickness subsided. Nothing was as pressing as the urgent love drama playing in her mind. Sitting at her desk, amid the bags and boxes into which she had hastily dumped the contents of her drawers, shutting out the steps and voices beyond her door, she slowly, luxuriously, wrote to Robert:

> The office. Wed. A.M.
> Last night the strangest thing happened — really strange — about 1 A.M. Joel tottered into my room to say he

couldn't sleep — I started to wake up to tell him to get in the other bed — and then it was so real to me I don't know whether I said anything out loud — but you had obviously been sleeping with me, and I reached for you and actually thought my god he's fallen out of bed and then I leaned over to look on the floor, I turned on the light and I could still feel where you had been in the bed — Joely settled down in the other bed and I settled in mine only I don't remember you coming back. I cannot tell you how incredibly real it was — because I was awake — we seemed to have been sleeping spoon fashion — me clinging to your back. Are you sure you weren't there? Now the small men are coming in to move me across the hall —

Bye love
me

The mail boy came as the men were carrying out her belongings, and she gave him the letter to Robert. And it was Robert to whom she made the first phone call from her dismal hole off the hall.

Darling — things have become very bad — I've been put in a different place — remember where stuff was stored behind Eldon's office? No daylight here — no air — one dim window a worm could hardly get through, and too high up for me to see from — a typist's desk — only thing that would fit in — dusty shelves — dirty walls, scum green — I feel like I'm drowning —

He cried *That's unbelievable!*

Wait — surely no one really expects me to stay here, and I won't. Darling, Mac has offered me Programme Director, which I'd do from his office. I don't think I have any choice —

Stunned silence burst between them. Robert had feared there was another reason for losing her, for her escaping, as she had, even while he wallowed in her. He felt that their rapture, for which he had sacrificed everything, was being strangled by MacCurry's heavy hand.

I don't want you with him! he cried. *Oh my love, I want you here — with me!*

Nia's mouth dropped farther open. An insane daydream swept her. Eyes and lips flashed with heady hope.

But I'd need work — and a house —

I'll get them! Leave that to me!

He was off again, charging into the heavens, almost ready to leap from the window rather than wait for the swift elevator to take him to the street.

*

Nora Wilson? From the Film Board? Adams was instantly rapt. He removed the half glasses with his thumb and forefinger and stuck the tip of the earpiece between his teeth. *Yes. Tell her yes. Tell her to get in touch with me.*

The faithful Betty helped him find a house. *I don't know why I'm doing this . . . When she comes back I'll be eclipsed again.*

Robert fraternally squeezed her fingers, fellow victims of the same compelling charm.

It was a small neat house, two storeys, with a false Georgian front and an orderly fenced-in garden. The rent was a bit high, but there was a subway station nearby, and Betty decided Nia could manage by saving on taxis. It was also Betty who paid the deposit and phoned her to come and see the place. With her prior right in friendship, and authority in domestic matters, she was amiably taking over.

Robert was glad to let her. The question of costs had rudely brought him to ground, and he told himself, and Betty, that he had better get on with the script. He was afraid further involvement in the move would require money he simply didn't have. He believed Nia when she cried poor, but it seemed to him that her background, her beauty and style suggested such an affluent life that she would somehow have enough.

*

She stayed with Betty when she came to see the house, which she rented. In the morning Robert persuaded her, *even for an hour,* which is all she insisted she had, to let him take her, by taxi, to the apartment. But she soon got up from the cot.

Well, what did you expect — she said. *Now I have to shower again — I have to see Hal — I have a thousand things to look after —*
Hal?

Adams — it's his nickname — I've always known him as Hal —
Ah . . . the alacrity with which the producer had hired her! It hit Robert hard, making him even more needy.

Not now — she said, pushing past him to the bathroom, leaving his spurned arms sinking to his sides. Then afterwards, as she was quickly dressing, she said *I'm fine, thank you —*
What?

When I was here a week ago I was developing a terrible cold. I'm a lot better. Good of you to ask —

Oh, sorry . . . But you look great. And indeed, fired with purpose, driven by desperation, she had a florid, peach-skin glow.

You didn't get it? My cold —
He shook his head.

You never get anything. It must be nice to be so healthy —
He could feel her withdrawing, sliding ever faster away, as if on skids. Suddenly he clasped her around the waist, pulling her belly tight to his, her breasts to his chest, as if to make their forms flow together.

She pushed him away. *No — I have to go —*

Oh, Nia . . . he muttered as she turned from him and threw on her coat. *I need you!*

Abruptly she stopped and stared at him, her eyes fierce. *I have a son* — she cried. *I don't want another!*

*

She regretted, in the taxi to Adam's office, that she had turned her wrath on Robert, but ever since he had triggered this total upheaval he had increasingly got in the way. She was being led, pushed,

217

dragged by the ideal of love — she who had been so independent, was now completely subject to and inseparable from it — and he, with his troubles and demands, was becoming another major difficulty.

Panicky, she remembered to compose herself. From her purse she took a small mirror and checked her appearance. Incredibly, she still resembled the woman Adams and the rest of her society would expect: good-looking, reasonably well dressed, worldly wise, with a readiness for humour — she supposed she could still laugh, and tried an experimental smile — professionally smart, capable and confident. That was the image she would have to present.

She felt, all in all, that she was being whirled about in a giant mixmaster, and might fly apart from the strain. There was reason to fear: her health was precarious and her energy near its breaking point; she hoped she could hold on long enough to resettle her family — whose stress, whose innocent punishment, was piercing her — and to find again some basic balance within herself. For everyone's sake she simply had to survive all this, and the only part of it that could be sacrificed was her lover.

19

Whatever motive others ascribed to Nia's sudden decision to move — Eldon, defeat — MacCurry, for which he blamed Eldon, hurt and humiliation — her mother, madness — Stanley alone understood that it might have something to do with Robert. But he could detect no taint of that in her. Though her entire sojourn in Montreal was ostensibly a failure, and the job she was going to, as a script reader, one of much lower status, at, to start with, less salary, and she was leaving behind and might be losing forever many who loved and admired her, she behaved with blithe unconcern about the whole thing, like a performer who had completed a gig and it was simply time to go. And though Robert could not entirely be cut out of the move, and her habit of writing to him still gave her comfort, she now imparted nothing beyond the immediate news.

> I have an endless list — Telephone co — movers — the move will cost $445 — eek, there goes my annuity. Then on the list — letters to write — to Buddy — to friends saying no Christmas presents — other things — what now seems like hundreds — but if I list and cross off — it isn't so bad. Stanley and Jean-Michel have sublet — so dates from one house to the other are working out.

With the coming of snow Stanley's young lover, whose father had finally recovered when the work was done, returned to the city, looking crisp and tanned. Stanley was aroused at first sight, and at once they resumed their life as a steady couple. But he continued to be deeply affectionate towards Nia, and when he learnt that she could not legally cancel her lease he offered to take it over, calmly lying about his own being up. The switch cost him several hundred dollars, but he kept that to himself, and instead told everyone he had got a bargain.

*

When Robert delivered the second stage of his script, the long room where the readers and editors worked was aswirl with the drama department's office party. The deal desks held plates of cake, cookies, and small crustless sandwiches in squares and sliced coils. On a bookcase stood a punch bowl in a nest of silver tinsel, along with an assortment of bottles. A few baubles hung from a tree some wag had formed from wooden rulers taped together and stuck between bookends, and a bunch of mistletoe, swaying in the warm waves rising from below, was suspended by a red

219

string from a fluorescent ceiling fixture. People were chattering, laughing, smoking, occasionally kissing. Robert knew no one, except, at the far end, Adams, who was smiling and sipping from a paper cup. The producer told him to leave the package on his secretary's side table. Robert eyed the food and drink, and was hungrier still for friendliness, but no one asked him to stay. Going down the stairs, away from the convivial sounds, he saw that a thread of tinsel was caught on his trousers. He crumpled the thin foil and dropped it among the litter of cigarette butts crowding the sand-filled stand just inside the drab entrance.

Alone . . . haunted him as he made his way home, paralleling the despair rising from his sense of having perhaps already lost Nia. There was no one in his building to whom he could turn; Hugh and Sally had flown to Aspen for a few days of skiing, and to all the other residents, on whose doors wreaths were beginning to appear, he was a complete stranger. By evening he was in turmoil, agitated fears whirling in his mind, and by midnight, when he had worn himself out pacing, and the room was reeling, he collapsed at the table and reached for a pen.

His scribbling was illegible, but allowed a freer flow of thought. 'What have these grovelling words to do with the torrent raging through me, oh love, there are no words, except maybe in an unknown language, for what I want to say. I would call you now but would wake you with my voice insane or perfectly normal which would be more screaming insane still. My head is aching and I want to smash it but I won't do that, always there is some rat—'

He had meant to write 'rational control' but had just then stabbed himself in the face with the pen. When washed, it was only a small cut near the mouth, and not serious, but lined with blue like a tattoo. Then his thoughts rushed on. 'In the near year we've been together, the year of almost continual disappointments for you, and the accumulating fatigue and health troubles that have resulted from them, and still a year in which you've continued to give, to others and certainly to me. And what have I given you? You must have been desperately lonely and unhappy to accept it — conditional love, childishness, petty fears. What do I want from you now? I don't know, just to hold you have you love you oh darling darling darling if you go away from me I'll die that way. If you were with me and unfaithful to me I would die too in a different way. We could never be close close flesh close again. I won't ever be a sophisticate. Oh my love my love my love, I must try to make some sense.'

'I still want so many things, but they are different things. I want you to be happy, protected, sheltered from the troubles that eat at you and drag you down. Oh love, you are wonderful, truly wonderful, you are a divine person, you are alive in the secret recesses where life is. You need things I cannot give you, not yet, but before when you tried to leave me to get them the fear of loss of love drove you back. I was satisfied then, but I care too much now to hold you with that. Love, you've always somehow known what you had to do. Love, do it. If it means you have to go, then go. But— oh god, how can I say this without making it sound maudlin. I'm trying to describe a projected feeling and instead I'm filling with sensory things, wanting to hold you, kiss you, love you. Oh darling, darling love, oh god, are you there?'

It was half-conscious cribbing from Nia's expressions.

'Wait, I think I can say it now — I care enough to see you go, to love you while you're away, and to love you just as much when you return, and to go on loving you even if you never do.'

*

These words, like Montcalm's to his wife, were not sent. The usual stumbling block of the swollen holiday mail made it impossible for a letter to get there in time.

*

Robert was untouched by the festivity that increased during the two weeks before Christmas. The few events that penetrated his small sphere were specific and precise. A cheque from the CBC came without comment for the exact amount of the contract price for stage two of the script, and when he phoned, Adams' secretary, speaking for the producer, told him to proceed with the polish. And a brief impersonal note arrived from Nia.

> Mother will go by air the morning of the 26th, with the key to Betty's — will you please tell Betty — and that I'm so god-damned rushed I can't write — and too poor to phone. Ask her to tell her super, please. The movers will load and leave on Dec. 27th. The next day they will deliver in Toronto. Joel and I and Jester will leave after the movers.

Nia's little family ate their Christmas dinner on paper plates, in the midst of bare furniture and partly-packed boxes. They were having steamed pudding when Robert, spurred by grim resolve, made his fourth-ever phone call to their home. Joel answered and indifferently handed the instrument to his mother. Robert wanted to rent a car in which to bring them to Toronto.

Oh no! Nia said. *It's much too slippery to drive* —

The weather had turned warm again; rain had washed away the snow and roads were wet or ice-glazed. It started teeming when the movers left Nia's house. They had come hours late and by the time she could clean up, the last train had gone. Frantic, she phoned the cabby who had formerly taxied her to the office, and he, old and tired though he was, out of affection, and for the money, drove her, the heavy-eyed Joel, and Jester to Toronto. Only the dog slept. Several times, peering tightly through the cold black downpour, the driver muttered *Madame, what can we do? It is God's will.*

*

The next afternoon Robert phoned information and was immediately given Nia's new number. The businesslike Betty had pre-ordered the service. He called and offered to help arrange the house. Nia told him the movers had just arrived and would be a couple of hours unloading, that her mother was still at Betty's and she and Joel were wiped. When the beds were set up they would need sleep.

Robert called again the next morning, and was once more refused. *No, thank you* — Nia said *we can manage. I don't want you to come as a complete personal surprise to my family. Look* — she added *I'm not doing anything for New Year's — I'm too tired to go anywhere. We'll have a quiet supper here. Come for coffee.*

It rather hurt Robert that he was not included for the meal but he put great store in being scheduled for New Year's eve, which was meant, he felt sure, to herald their new, open, hopefully orderly life.

Who's coming? Nia's mother said.

Is it somebody new? Joel asked.

Nia was unwilling to disturb them. *It's just someone I knew at the Board.*

*

Robert was met at the door by Nia's mother, who took the bouquet he had brought. She was a little taller and thinner than her daughter, with no evident resemblance, and all her sternness was in the way she held herself. The lined face was more foolish than frightening. Joel, however, was Nia — her eyes, nose, mobile mouth, the same supple body. Robert immediately felt himself filling with fondness. But neither showed the least interest in him. They, even the boy, had seen such a lot of men. They were polite, bored, and before long, saying *Happy New Year*, went up to bed. At last, in the normal, neat, tasteful living room, with the part-paid-for piano and Robert's flowers on the card-cluttered mantel, the lovers were alone.

Nia felt that her life was falling apart. Her world had shrunk to her last energy, and to her appearance — her damned appearance — on which the rest depended. She had nothing more.

When he moved to embrace her, she began to cry. She was three-thousand dollars in debt.

It was a jolting shock that depressed the moment, but Robert flashed passionately into inspired flight. *I'll borrow it! From my*

223

friends! Everyone he had ever known leapt into his mind. *We'll repay it a little at a time...*

I can't — Nia said. *I can't go on with you. I really haven't the strength.*

He stared at her blankly, unbelieving. He had written those dramatic sentences hardly believing that they might come true.

Darling, there's no more left. I can't see you any more —

But... you're just overtired.

No — it's much more than that. It's a matter of life and death —

It seemed so fantastic he almost smiled. Then he had that recurring sense of theatre. Then he saw, to his horror, that she meant it.

Part Three

20

At first Robert did not believe the silence around him. He wrote to old friends, asking for money, telling them only that he urgently needed three-thousand dollars and would repay it when he could. He went to the small gallery in whose window he and Nia had seen the drawing of the girl with the teasing smile who looked like her; the print was gone, but he kept going back until they had another copy for him. Then he repotted the grapefruit plant and tended it carefully on the windowsill. But when three weeks had gone by, and then four, he began to understand that this was more serious than he had imagined.

He felt Nia had pressed his pride into a hardened core that could be reduced no further. He was coming to think of her as an adversary with whom he was locked in a tender love-hate combat.

Yet how he missed her! He repeated her name, continually called up her image, and tantalized himself with memories of her body. He had a squeezed-out tube of her contraceptive cream he had taken from the bathroom wastebasket after her last visit, and the smell of it would start him shuddering in an agonizing fit. He could not work, though Adams had given him, as an afterthought, a second assignment: the adaptation for TV of a book of humorous sketches for which the drama department had long ago acquired the rights, then later lost interest in. The producer had paid him for the historical script, but had said nothing more about it;

indeed all he could talk about was plans for a special programme to mark the opening of a coast-to-coast microwave service. Actually, the need for Robert's 1812 screenplay had quietly passed. A rumour had gone round that the Chairman was becoming very intimate with a certain university, and would probably leave to become its president, while the British Prime Minister was fully taken up with the crisis brought on by the resignation of his Chancellor of the Exchequer. As for the American ambassador, he was a former businessman who had little concern for anything beyond trade.

*

Nia tried not to think of Robert. He had been discarded like excess baggage she could no longer carry. Her life was full with the demands of the new job, her mother's endless health problems, and getting Joel settled in a new school. It was with relief that she donned a nightgown, and lay down with only the task of sleep, without having physically to indulge anyone. And she knew she was not well. That the strain of the move, all that had led up to it, and worries about money, were bringing on a deep-seated ill feeling. Yet living betrayed her. She found herself, at odd moments, thinking of Robert's abilities. But that was the past. Gone.

*

Soon Robert could not sleep. Late into the night he roamed the slushy streets, his toes pinched by frost; when snow fell it melted in his hair and ran in uneven rivulets down his cold unshaven cheeks. Hugh took to avoiding him. The builder considered it insanely romantic to carry on so over a woman, and at the same time he felt that such dramatics were essentially self-centred, unfeeling, and insulting to Nia. He even wondered whether she might now be open to his approach; it amused him to think of bedding her while Robert was theatrically lamenting her loss. However, at the moment, though Sally had begun to pall a bit, he was too involved to do more than daydream about another woman. Sally's husband had named him co-defendant in the divorce action, and Hugh, though he considered it hopeless, had promised to support her in a bid for custody of the children. Moreover, for her birthday he had given her some shares in a new project. Hugh expected she would get little, if anything, from her husband, and he wanted her to have a nest egg against the time, which now seemed to him certain, when he and she would part. He had never maintained an affair for more than a year or two, and knew it was foolhardy to start forming business ties with Sally, but this lapse in prudence made him feel a better person.

Robert, with money from the script, and his advance on signing the new contract, paid the rent. Hugh took the cheque but told him after this to give it to the janitor or send it to the office. The slap of that Robert suffered in silence; it seemed only another part of what he had to endure. But as it meant he would no longer have access to the penthouse or the Thunderbird, he casually went out and bought a car. It was a used Chev coupe, grey, with light-blue seats. He chose it, after walking up and down the lot, solely on the basis of how he imagined Nia would look in it beside him. The salesman congratulated him. The car, he said, was a trade-in that had been owned by a commuter who had kept it in good condition, and was going cheaply only because of its high mileage. Robert parked the thing in the underground space allotted to his apartment, then struck it from his mind. He had no present use for it.

*

Despite his beloved's complete withdrawal, it was not until Robert dropped in on Betty, late one Sunday afternoon, that he began to understand that Nia might never come back. Betty met him with her usual glad expression, listened carefully to all that he said, but she offered no news about her friend. While he was there the phone rang, and he quickly guessed, from Betty's eager laughter and demure denials — he gathered she was being thanked for a

229

book she had sent — that it was Nia she was talking to. Yet afterwards Betty did not mention the call. It was as if Nia no longer existed. Or rather, Robert grasped, that she did not exist for him.

Dismal forebodings weighed him down. It was an early dark, icy evening; the deserted streets echoed his weary footfalls. He watched his shadow moving forward on the frigid pavement, shrinking at each street light, furtively reforming and creeping out again, and he saw in it the sort of life he would have: thin and repetitious and condemned to meaningless unending work. He imagined he was on a solitary treadmill that would stop only when it dropped him in his grave. He felt enormously sorry for himself. The more pathos he could wring from his projections the less he felt the shame, the horrible pain, of being unwanted.

By the time he neared his building he was thoroughly chilled and relieved to see the lights of the lobby. Inside, a hulking man in a black coat and suit was sitting in one of the formal corner chairs, completely filling it, his clergy shirt open against the thick florid neck. Seeing Robert, the man sprang up. There was — it came with a start — something familiar about him. It was Father Jovian!

Where've you been? the priest bellowed. *I've been waiting for hours!*

What are you doing here? Robert replied, laughing.

Co-op conference. I've been here since Friday. But man, what a time I had finding you! I phoned the Film Board when we were going through Montreal, and they said you were gone, maybe in Toronto. So I phoned them here and they gave me a number, but then there was no answer until this afternoon, when the guy said you were living in this place. And then you didn't answer! And I'm leaving tomorrow morning. So I've been waiting. How are you? You look like hell.

I'm all right. Just surprised to see you. Come on in.

They went up. The priest walked into the small room and said *Man, you're in the wrong calling. You should be in some monastery. No, you'd be too austere even for them. What's with this?*

Oh, it's a long story. Father, do you want a drink?

Sure. Whatever you've got. There was a third of a bottle of vodka; Robert had been allowing himself an occasional sip, sometimes in hot milk, when he came in after one of his nightly rovings. The priest poured out a half tumbler and drank it down. *So that's vodka?* he said. *Tastes like weak 'shine. Man, I'm starved. Is there anything to eat?*

They hurried over to a corner cafe, Father Jovian striding ahead. Robert struggled to keep up, but the priest's energy, like a boost from a stronger battery, was beginning to revive him. They arrived as the proprietor was turning the door sign to closed. However, he was Italian, and when he heard that the *Father* was from out of town, and hungry, he became accommodating. *If you don' mind spaghetti, an you don' mind we clean up around you . . .*

Spaghetti will be great! the priest said. *Please, just make it hot and bring plenty.*

*

And in minutes two heaped and steaming plates were brought to their booth. The pasta was generously covered with a thick meat sauce, all that had been in the pot.

So, man, said Jovian, his mouth full *what's the story?*

Where did you get this man stuff? Robert said. *You didn't used to talk like that.*

Oh! the priest laughed. *At the conference. We got guys from all over. One was from Carolina, and he kept saying 'man'. I like it. Man! It has a social, earthy sound.*

Jovian's buoyant good nature, his evident interest, his remoteness from the events, and an intense need for fellow feeling all encouraged Robert to talk. He told the priest everything, about Nia, about Myra, about all it had brought him to.

The Father's big face, flushed from food, knotted in concern. *It's extreme* he said. *Extremes are not good.*

The worst of it . . . Robert began, but thinking that would be unfitting, he retreated behind an attack. *Isn't your discipline extreme?*

The church? It's an ant heap of disciplines! And like different ants we pull this way and that. But I do what I think best. He smiled slyly. *I can't be fired, you know, except by the boss.*

Your bishop?

No! The big boss. My appointment was by papal bull.

Robert stared. That this burly priest, based in an obscure, backwater village, had by his character and dedication won such regard sharply deepened his respect, and trust.

Jovian chewed pasta like a gravel crusher, swallowed, and then whipped a napkin open and wiped his mouth. *You started to say that the worst. . .*

Well, if you'll forgive me, Father. It's the physical craving. I can block it out when I'm awake, but if I fall asleep . . .

I know said the priest with a sigh.

You do? But Jovian seemed not to be joking. *Really?*

When I was young. Before I was ordained. But you don't forget. You know, sometimes even the old lady who comes in to clean looks good.

And you, Robert thought *have that young superior in the house below . . .* He suddenly saw the depth of Jovian's restraint, and felt again, much more strongly, the unspoken intimacy that had brought them close in Cape Breton.

What about your wife? the priest said. *Do you speak to her? Hear from her?*

I had a letter last week. She's sold the house and has bought an apartment. She needs me to sign the sale papers.

So, have you phoned her . . . or written?

No. I'll write.

Why not go.

To Myra?

Father Jovian sought Robert's eyes and held them steadily. *What else have you got?*

21

Driving to Ottawa, he tried not to imagine Nia beside him. After a while he became absorbed in the snow-covered fields, the dark woods, the sun-sparkled flakes. There were occasional sprinklings of them, like glitter scattered in the air, but not enough to accumulate on the frost-dried road. The car was warm, but he had to stop often for gas and oil, and once, for water. After Madoç he asked a country mechanic to check it. The man hoisted it up, and holding a trouble light, scanned the underside. *You're leaking at both ends* he said. *And you've got an oil leak too.*

It seemed all right when I bought it.

Hah! The gas tank was maybe plugged with chewing gum, and there's still some putty at the base of the rad. Probably they put 50 oil in the pan.

A heavy oil?

That's right. When it heated up it started to run.

Robert asked what it would take to fix all this.

About four hours. All the oil leak needs is a gasket, but it's a bitch of a job. That whole pan has to come away. The radiator I got to take out and solder, and the gas tank has to come off and be welded. He was a small man with a lively face, an Irish name, and a lot of little laugh lines at his eyes and mouth.

Robert said *I'm going another hundred miles or so. Will they hold out until I return?*

I wouldn' worry about it. It'll cost you a bit more in gas and oil, that's all. The radiator . . . He walked through to the adjoining snack bar, came back with a pepper shaker, and shook some grains into the filler neck. *There —* he said, with a sweep of his arm at the bare fields surrounding the station *you're outa town!* Then he charged only for a quart of oil, part of which he had used to top up the pan, and the rest, after plugging the spout hole in the can, he gave to Robert.

I hear she's a wonderful woman Myra said.

Yes. Robert was surprised, then realized he should not have been. Of course she would have inquired. *But not mine* he added. *We're not together.*

Oh? Myra gathered from the kitchen table the papers he had signed as joint owner of the house, and put them back in the long brown envelope. Then placed it under her purse.

She had said nothing about giving him any part of the sale price. He did not expect it, but he would have liked to have been able to refuse. Looking at her, seeing how pretty she was, Robert thought *She's still my wife* . . . and wondered what she would do if he suggested they go into the bedroom. To be inside her, to feel her smooth skin against his, to sleep . . . seemed to him, at this moment, what he had most ever wanted. But only for the instant of the thought, because he remembered that Nia had been, was yet, what he most wanted. It spoiled, somewhat, his desire for Myra, but Nia was a distant, painful dream, perhaps, likely, never again to become tangible, while his wife he could touch by stretching across the table.

She did not, however, look quite open to being touched. She seemed taut, compressed. There was a vertical crease between her drawn eyebrows.

Am I making you nervous? he said.

No. But she remained brittle, then tensely turned to the kettle. *Do you want anything?*

No. Yes. My . . . maybe I've made a mistake. How would you feel . . . about getting together again?

She suddenly blew up. *You bastard!* she shrieked. *How would I feel? You bastard, bastard! Have you ever understood how I felt about anything? You've never listened to me, you've never wanted to know what I thought, or what my feelings were. You're the most self-centred, selfish man I've ever known!* She began to cry, with tears of rage. *How would I feel! He asks me how I would feel . . . You have to be out of your mind!*

234

Except that the blows were of words, it was, Robert felt, like the time she had beat at him with her fists.

22

Letters with cheques came from his friends. He sent them back, saying he no longer needed the money. Now that his solitude was a settled matter, he began consciously serving what seemed his life sentence. He didn't blame Nia, but could hardly help being aware of how cruelly life had changed through knowing her. And the most harrowing thing about it was that now, with no evident barrier between them, she was more out of reach than she had been when secrecy and distance stood in their way. These past months she had existed for him only as an idea. Not once had he wondered whether she was well or ill, happy or sad, with others or alone. And even now he felt that if he never saw Nia again he had to go on resisting her, because it was as if she had pushed him over a cliff, and he, just managing to cling to its crumbling edge, was grimly forced to hang on.

He began to work. The skits occupied him. They were meant to be funny, but in scripting he made them much funnier, drawing on a well of humour strangely underlying his gloom. Each bit of comedy became vastly diverting. At times, caught up in his levity, he even laughed aloud — thunderously disturbing the stillness.

He sent the first scripts to Adams by mail. He had no wish to go to a building in which, somewhere, Nia might be working. This was less a conscious decision than an instinctive feeling that he must not allow mere chance to influence their fate. Or possibly he simply lacked the courage to face again the fact of her defiance, or worse, indifference. Three days later he had a letter from the Senior Editor saying that he *loved* the scripts, and urging him to write the rest.

Mail was low-priced, and in the city was delivered overnight. It seemed to Robert he could operate entirely from where he was. Except for walking to the corner letterbox, and occasionally another block to a small groceteria, there was no real need for him to leave the apartment. As it was to be his burrow, he improved it a little. He had the print of the girl's head framed, and hung it over the bookcase; he bought a nicer blanket with which to cover the cot, and a yard-long hooked rug, in a floral pattern, to go on the floor where he placed his feet. He bought slippers, a set of four wineglasses — the unit price, he figured out, was less than for a single one, and even a clear flower vase, but he stopped short of putting anything in it. The grapefruit plant he had watered so resolutely had yellowed, withered and died.

His world had become his apartment, its immediate district, the distant CBC, and like a remote planet, Betty Bobchenko.

He made his meals from dried soups and canned fish; for dessert he would munch an apple, and as a special treat sometimes allowed himself a thin square of chocolate, a few peanuts, a cooking fig or a date. These were his sensual pleasures. More and more they took on an erotic cast. Apart from his work, in which his mind was alert and inventive, and which he enjoyed while it lasted, he was no longer dejected nor terribly sad, only apathetic and dull. He remembered Nia saying in one of her letters that she had imagined how a widow might feel, and he thought of himself as a widower, doubly bereaved. The past was closed, the future would perhaps never open.

His parents were in Red Deer, Alberta, from where he had come. His mother had been pregnant with him when they had moved there from a brief stay in Winnipeg. He was uncertain whether that slight brush with destiny — as an embryo he had passed not a great distance from where Nia was growing up — was something to be pleased about, or only another sardonic twist of fate.

Once in a while he phoned his parents, but said only that he was working. They hadn't liked his breakup with Myra, and generally despaired of him.

236

It was a blossom-scented evening in spring when Hugh decided to go to the builders' monthly card game. He hadn't been there since Sally had come to live with him. She was still more or less satisfying, but he was feeling a little stuffed, like a man who has eaten too well and wants something to stimulate his lumbering digestion. *I have to go* he told her. *They cut deals there. I've been out of touch.* But Sally knew what they did at those stag nights, and no sooner had Hugh safely left the penthouse than she quickly showered, dressed, and was downstairs, tapping on Robert's door.

She filled that dim little space with subtle excitement. The click of her heels on the bare parquet floor, the faint tinkle of her bracelets, the glimmering sheen of her cascading hair, her costly evasive perfume all fell like a sudden sweet shower on Robert's starved senses. And the play of her braless breasts, sinuously moving beneath the clinging silk blouse, took, for a few seconds, his breath away. *What?* he said clumsily. *What did you say?*

That the air is enchanting. She had gone to the open window. *Such a special time.* She came and put her hands on his shoulders, then lifted her lovely face to his. *How are you?*

Her closeness was excruciating. Standing stock still, a foot away from her, he was aware of her lithe form down the entire length of his body. And he trembled from the gentle touch of her fingertips, which moved now to both sides of his chin. *Come . . .* she said, and dropping her hands took one of his and drew him to the cot. *Tell me about it.* She sat beside him for a moment; then eased off her shoes, smoothly lifted her legs and stretched out. Robert continued to sit gripping the edge of the mattress.

Would you like to lie down? Sally said. *Would that help?*

He stayed as he was for a long moment, looking at the floor, then shook his head. He had almost forgotten what he was holding out for, or why, but knew he must not sully it.

*

Later, in the penthouse, as Sally sat at the kitchen table and poured herself a cup of chamomile tea, she began to ponder her fruitless excursion. She took off her silver bangles and let them fall in circles beside her cup, then she reached to the nape of her neck and swung her hair out from behind her back, which was still aching slightly from that uncomfortable cot. She was a little annoyed with Robert, not so much owing to his reserve, though that saddened her, for she knew he was otherwise intense and passionate, and fully aware of her charms, but because his lack of response had, before long, become boring. She was much more annoyed, furious really, with *that woman*, for having reduced him to such a pitiful state. And she was angriest of all at Hugh. She sighed, and thought of her children, and thought, with mixed feelings, of the life she had lost.

*

Robert was surrounded by a silence more dense than before. He had finished the skits and been paid for them, and had received from the same Senior Editor another effusive letter, to which Adams had appended, with his initials, the postscript *Good stuff!* No new work was offered him, and he sought none; for the moment he had enough money for his needs. There was still another month before he had to start sending any to Myra. If necessary he would accrue those payments, as he had at first with his rent.

23

One afternoon in April the telephone rang, and the ring — a rare sound — startled Robert. He waited, thinking the ringing must be a mistake, but it went on. Then he cautiously approached the bookcase, where the phone was, and picked up the receiver.
Hello.

At the other end a quiet voice said *Hello.*

He did not recognize the female voice and said *Yes?*

Hello, she said *how are you?*

He felt a sudden stab of fear, almost of dread. It was too hard to believe. *Nia,* he said *is that you?*

Yes, it's me.

She said she was calling because she had heard from Hugh, who had phoned her at the office. He'd said he was still exploring the idea of the film company. He was flirting, and she had refused his overtures, but was left contemplating the emptiness of her life. She knew that an approach to Robert on her part would also be flirting, but thought she could do it tentatively, cautiously. *However, before this goes any further,* she said *I think you and I should talk.*

Robert agreed, of course. He would have agreed to anything. They arranged for lunch at his apartment the next day.

*

In the morning Robert bought gin, vermouth, olives, butter, eggs, parsley, lemons, cheese, grapes, and the most expensive instant coffee. He also bought some fresh daffodils and placed them in the vase under the framed drawing. He had yesterday, after Nia's call, rushed about putting everything in the apartment in order, and now he made a last-minute check, and was satisfied that though it had been scrubbed and dusted, and all the linen freshly laundered, it looked casual, as if her coming was hardly unusual. Then he drove to the leased building that housed the drama department. The coupe ran without leaks. The little man had repaired them on Robert's way back from Ottawa.

At the appointed time Nia came out and got into the car without comment. She looked just as he had imagined she would. She looked, really, slightly fuller than he remembered, and rather tired, with more gray streaks in her hair. But just as beautiful, and he could barely contain his desire. Yet he wondered whether it was truly her he desired, or only to triumph over her.

When they arrived she glanced at the drawing, but still said nothing. She sat in a chair near the cot and didn't protest when he kissed the top of her head. She even reacted with a pleasurable twitch when he kissed *the little place*, as they had called it, between her neck and shoulder. But she said calmly *I came to see if we could possibly work together, and obviously we can't, because this happens.*

Then she ate her scrambled eggs and said she had to go back to the office, where she was expected. And she went into the bathroom to straighten up.

Robert felt completely defeated. It seemed that after all the turmoil and loneliness nothing was left. Nothing had flowed between them. It had surged in him, and perhaps had spilled over a little onto Nia, but nothing more. Desolate, he stood at the table with his back to the big window. Everything was now blank, drained, totally hollow.

Yet not. There were small signs and sounds. Two plates, a crumpled napkin touched with lipstick, her purse on the bookcase, the flushing toilet and then the running of water as she washed her hands. She was speaking as she opened the door, telling him something about a movie her department was making, the first time on film, and absorbed in what she was saying she crossed to him and put her arms around his neck, as she had normally done in the old days. It was partly unconscious custom, and partly an outflow of warmth tinged with tentative affection.

He immediately put his around her, and nodded, and answered, as if it were one of their random, long-ago talks.

Suddenly Nia stopped and drew back. *Oh* — she said, trying to free her arms *all these bad habits!*

But Robert held her tightly, and quickly kissed her lips. Then, with their faces close, their mouths met again, and this time stayed together. And he drank in the sweetness of her. Such sensations came flooding! — beginning with that starting kiss at Nigel's. Now, holding his breath, he knew nothing of conquest, but only humble gratitude for all the filling sweet beauty flowing into him.

Irrepressible tears were welling. He purposely put his cheek to hers. She felt the wetness.

Oh darling! she whispered, and broke away a little.

Thank God he breathed. *Thank God you're back!*

Nia turned from him and went into the bathroom again. A moment later the door opened narrowly and she stood behind it. Her suspended slip was against her breasts, but otherwise she was naked.

A tremulous thrill rose in Robert, along with fear that if he assumed, or disturbed this dream . . . *Nia,* he said, *you have to go back to the office . . .*

I can't go just yet she said, and dropping the slip she moved swiftly into his arms.

*

Driving her home — there had finally been no time to return to the office — Robert said *Were you faithful. . . ?*

Of course.

So was I he said stoutly, oblivious of the proposal he had made Myra.

Besides, Nia said *I was very ill. You didn't once inquire about me.*

I . . . didn't know. And he added *I guess that condemns me.*

I nearly died —

He had a clear pang of guilt, and glanced at her, appalled. At once the enormousness of his self-absorption, his egotism, his — meanness, struck him. At that moment he attributed nothing of their separation to her.

I had pneumonia. If it hadn't been for Joel — *begging me not to go* — *darling, at times the pain was so terrible I thought* — *I've had enough* —

Robert once more held his breath, but from horror. They were nearing her house as the story ended. Robert brought the car to a stop at the curb under some overhanging maples, then cut the ignition and turned to her, shaking his head in despair. While death had yawned he had been, unknowingly, totally indifferent. It struck him as frightening, incredible. With an effort he lowered his feelings. *But, at home . . . how did you manage?*

Oh, friends. Francis made me a loan. Betty, some others, brought in food — helped in the house — looked after the arrangements. Hal sent scripts as an excuse to continue my salary.

*

Nia retired early that evening, to review and revel in the day's events. She was still frail, and knew that even the time with Robert had strained her, but she felt encouragingly relaxed. Before going to bed she had sponged only, leaving a bath for morning, because she wanted to retain all of Robert that was in her. The possibility of pregnancy — they had certainly not stopped for any precaution — seemed too unlikely, even too trivial, to be concerned about. She had to admit that in a remote way she had hoped for this all along. Even in the worst week of the crisis, when she had been slipping in and out of consciousness, Robert had somehow *been there*, on the edge of discernment. Sometimes she had been angry with him for not actually being there, and then had been keenly disconcerted. At more lucid times, she had been dismayed that he hadn't phoned, or written, or even sought to know about her. But she wondered now whether their reunion would have happened if Hugh had not called. She knew that the break with Robert, though it had been absolutely essential for her, could very easily have gone beyond repair.

*

Two days later she was with Adams, watching rushes of that first drama the department was producing on film. Adams had seen them before, and had been disturbed enough to ask Nia to sit in with him. The acting was satisfactory, but something about the shots was not, he sensed, as it should be.

242

It's not film — Nia said. *It's just not filmic. Look at the way they're framed* — *all three-quarter or head-and-shoulders. And they're not going to cut* — *the movements don't match. And, Hal* — *the lighting is all from the top down, like from a TV grid* — *and the outdoor stuff is flat.*

Well, Adams said sadly *the director is very experienced.*

In radio. But he doesn't understand film. Hal — *you can't use this* —

No. I suppose we should have had these people trained first he said irritably. *But he was so dying to do it. And the crew has certainly shot lots of film.*

For news —

Nia felt she had said enough. They were both silent, then Adams sighed and said *Shit ... What am I going to do?*

Well — *there's a very good director right here in town doing nothing. You've had him writing scripts* —

24

Robert plunged into the production like a fish flung back. The resentment with which he was met — most of the cast and crew had long known and liked the director he replaced — soon dissipated when all realized how well this new one knew his work. Moreover, he was sensitive and tactful. He treated the previous effort as a base to build on, and rather than issue orders he gave helpful hints, sometimes whispering into the ears of actors and suggesting framing and lighting effects to the crew. Silently, he incorporated all he had learnt. Then one day he brought to an outdoor location some rolls of tinfoil, thumbtacks, and a sheet of plywood cut into parts, and quickly made of each part a reflector, which gave more light than the crew's strongest lamps. The next day he brought silk and showed how to soften the glare. Everyone began to work with a feeling of discovery, and the results were much better than even Adams had originally hoped for.

He immediately promoted Nia to the newly-created post of Producer of Filmed Projects, and set in motion another production for Robert.

Gossip about the hotshot new director soon led to producers in other departments suddenly discovering that they too had ideas for filmed programmes. And Robert also became an object of interest to women, especially single ones; beckoning smiles greeted him on every side. To all this his response, in polite manner and speech, was that he was simply too busy. Although the half-baked idea of a production company had been abandoned — Hugh was no longer interested, having been approached by a theatre group to become its patron, perhaps its president, which he felt was a more agreeable way to get into the arts — Robert was fully taken up with work for Adams. And his private hours were devoted to Nia.

When, that is, they could be. For secrecy was once more a factor. Because of Nia's new job it seemed important not to be personally linked, and she said flatly that until their future was settled, she did not want her family confronted with it. So they came together on occasional evenings, or for something special.

*

On Robert's birthday, Nia met him in mid afternoon and had him drive to the large liquor store under the railroad bridge. There they were served by an elderly, dour, myopic little man, crooked as a crab, who scowled at the order slip and returned to the counter muttering about the bottles. But when he had placed the champagne and two porter in front of Nia he looked up and said *I didn't think there was anyone left who knew about this.*

And Nia, alight, leaned forward with her nose close to his. *And I can cook too — !*

A bright smile of joy erupted on the wrinkled face, and there blazed between them an instant bond.

To go with their tall tumblers of *black velvet*, Nia made a superb soufflé. It was a luscious nectar of eggs and air laced with subtle hints of cheese and herbs, and its pale melting goodness contrasted with the dark drink. It was set off by a softly-glistening green salad. It seemed to Robert the finest — no, one of the finest, meals she had ever served. And Nia, looking beautiful — they were sitting kitty-cornered and lightly holding hands — had brought from home glazed place mats with pictures of wildflowers, and a silver centerpiece now holding a small cluster of fresh flowers. The sun, though growing rosy, was still strong, and casting a languorous light across the transformed table. Surely no birthday had ever been more blest. And yet . . . their lives lacked a base.

You know what we need . . . Robert said. *A house. An aerie in the sky isn't . . . uh . . . firm enough.*

He hoped Nia might be ready to suggest hers, but instead she said *It's positively scary — apart from the view.*

Robert looked out there, at the lake. From a ship lost in the haze of the horizon there trailed a long feathery plume, and where the vapour dissolved in the blue sky it seemed to be forming into a train of small white clouds, each gilded on its underside by the descending sun. His thoughts drifted. He conceived a place of their own, something out of the way, discreet, at ground level, with a lovely garden . . . he could almost touch it, but could not quite bring it into focus.

Nia watched with amused fascination his brow furrowing, all his features straining towards the central knot of thought, and she slightly shook her head at that terrible intensity. Then all at once his face was swept by a glad smile. *I've got it!* Robert cried. *The cabin!*

*

He drove there without phoning first. He did not have the number, doubted that Hugh still had it, and anyway did not want him and Sally to know that he was going. Nor did he mind that he might be disappointed; he was eager just to see the place again.

It was drizzling when he left the city, but gradually the sky lightened, a soft radiance seeped through, and the dark road faded to a mottled grey fractured by cracks and potholes. Brown fields, newly seeded, stretched in contoured lines across the rolling hills. When the car climbed higher, the open spaces gave way to rocks, clumps of bushes, upthrown woods. This was the watershed. From here the rivers ran both south, to the big lake behind him, and north, to where he was heading.

Obscurely happy, tensely anxious, his heart beginning to beat, he drove up the sandy road, through the open gate, and down the forest tunnel to the valley.

Nothing had changed! But it was sound that struck Robert when he got out of the car. The deep hiss of cascading water, the tinkling of the crystalline stream, a soft sighing of breezes from the hills, and bird calls — the little valley resounded with them — all mingled into a rising...falling...rising song. And there, across the pond, was the magic cabin.

No one was in sight. No car stood beside the house; the garden was tilled but bare. A rake, and a shovel with a broken handle, which were resting against a small overturned rowboat, seemed to have rusted where they lay. But as he approached the log house Robert could detect wood smoke; then he saw a ginger cat scurry from the stoop. The solid plank door stood fully open. Only a screen door blocked the entrance.. He knocked and said *Mrs. Carey?*

C'mon in a male voice replied.

Robert opened the door. He could smell coffee and cigarette smoke. It took a few seconds for his eyes to adjust to the deep shade. Then across the room he made out a long thin man reclining in a worn loafer chair between a potbellied stove and a baroque round table.

Take a seat the man said. *Don't take it away,* he added with a chuckle *just sit on it*. Then swivelling in his own chair — one of those turning, tilting contraptions that lifts the sitter's legs from the floor — he took an enamelled coffee pot from the iron stove and filled two green glass mugs. On the table stood some teaspoons in a clean jam jar, a bowl of sugar, and a punctured tin of milk. The milk had left white rings on the dark mahogany. The table, with its carved rim and cabriole legs, contrasted oddly with the mortar-chinked logs behind it.

Mr. Carey?

The man said *I don't aspire to Mister. Call me Steve.*

Robert explained who he was. And trying to keep his tone casual, he asked if the cabin was available.

I guess so Carey said. *But you'll have to speak to my wife about that.* It was unclear whether he meant the cabin was hers, or merely that he left all such matters to her.

While I'm here . . . may I see it?

Sure.

And abruptly he stood up. Until then Robert had wondered if the thin man was an invalid, but there was nothing infirm about his movements as he strode to the door and took a small key from a nail. And in the light from the doorway it was evident that under his thick plaid shirt and heavy work trousers Carey was sinewy and muscular. He had a high forehead, close curly hair, a strong aquiline nose. All in all he was a handsome man.

He handed over the key. *You know where it is.*

Robert hesitated. He felt he should tell him about Nia, but was not quite sure how to put it. He glanced up. The lean man was looking down at him with a friendly, mildly-curious expression. Even in his stockinged feet he stood half a head higher than his guest. *Mr. Carey . . . Steve, there's something you should know . . . If I have the cabin I won't be coming here alone. There will be . . . a woman with me.*

As soon as he had said *a woman* Robert felt it was a betrayal — clumsy, unreal, made even tawdrier by the chance rhyme. *A woman* could mean any cheap . . . could mean Sally. How could that convey Nia's vivacity, intelligence and tenderness? But when he met Carey's gaze he saw in it a generosity that made him ashamed.

I'm glad, Carey said, neither smiling nor solemn, but with a simplicity Robert thought he would long remember *that you have someone.*

Looking into his eyes, Robert felt he would always love this man.

*

Only the tops of tall structures were still sunlit when Robert got back to the apartment. He picked up the phone to impart his exciting news, when there was a muffled knock at the door.

Hugh stood there, a dark flush, almost like a mask, surrounding his eyes. *My father died* he said. *Will you come with me?*

*

The silver Jaguar moved through streets strange to Robert. The district was flat, quiet, fastidiously new. In the distance, rising like buttes from a plain, stood a group of dun-coloured buildings; closer, they could be seen to be sixplexes, as alike as casts from a mould. Hugh owned them all. He brought the car to a stop at the entrance to one, between the signs that said no parking. In the hallway a woman whispered to Hugh that his mother had been taken to her sister's. Robert followed him up the carpeted stairs. Except for the softer footing, and their slower pace, and the twenty years that had elapsed, they might have been climbing the steps at the back of Mr. Carson's shop.

The dead man lay face up on a gold velvet sofa, his bony hands on his chest, the fingers still clawed from holding the newspaper he had been reading when he was stricken. Hugh picked it up: it was the *Friye Arbeter Shtimeh* — Free Workers Voice — an anarchist weekly, printed in Yiddish. As long as Hugh could remember it had come from New York to their home. Robert wondered what special injustice had rankled the old man at the end. But the corpse gave no clue. The features were a little contorted, the mouth open; the unblinking eyes stared straight at the ceiling.

Hugh tried to close the eyelids, but they slid open again, unnerving him. His gaze wandered across the monogrammed shantung shirt, in robin's egg blue, Sally's choice, which had cost him fifteen dollars, and the faded tan trousers, frayed at the cuffs, which his mother had bought for less than three. Then he noticed with annoyance a hole in the toe of one of his father's socks, through which a bit of the blackened nail was showing. Through the open doorway of an adjoining room Robert could see a corner of Mr. Carson's old work bench, but without its usual clutter of tools.

The two friends stood for a few minutes, faces drawn. They felt a vague kinship in being there together, and alive. It bewildered Robert that what had been so familiar was no more. It made a dark rent in his awareness, through which, strain as he would, he could see nothing.

When they entered the aunt's house someone handed them black skullcaps. In the front room a small group of relatives was gathered around Hugh's uncle, who was quietly crying and stirring his tea. In the kitchen a man was arguing on the phone with a member of the family's burial society. Next to him a neighbour, wearing a white cardigan over her beaded blue dress, was slicing a large angel-food cake. Hugh was pushed towards the bedroom where his mother was communing with her intimates, and there another uncle began showing him a transliteration into English of the prayer for the dead. No one paid attention to Robert. It was assumed that he too knew his role.

He stood apart, afraid of making some blunder, stiffened by the emotion around him. But Yiddish was being spoken; he could not help responding to certain tones, sighs, shrugs. When he opened himself to it, he began to notice that these men and women were busy rather than sad, that far from venerating death they were insisting on life, and obstinately restoring their ties across the sudden tear Mr. Carson's heart attack had made in them. Gradually his fear of the void was replaced by a sense of being strong and whole. *It wasn't me!* he thought, and he wanted to get out into the air, to run and jump — he wanted, desperately, to make love to Nia.

He called her from a booth, and while the phone was ringing he remembered with joy that he also had the cabin to tell her about.

Her mother said she was not home yet. He hung up in dismay. *Where the hell* he sighed to himself *is she?*

*

She was with Adams. The producer had asked her out for a drink, and then suggested they go to his place.

It was the second floor of a converted house in an old, sedate, fashionable part of the city. Built with high standards and cheap labour, the house had thick walls, spacious rooms, lofty ceilings and a general air of convenience and comfort. It had been left to Adams by his mother; he leased the lower floor to a university professor and the attic to a Hungarian refugee lady who painted miniatures and made filigree brooches and rings. His own quarters combined modern furnishings with a period setting. In the living room a large abstract painting hung over the fireplace, Mexican rugs and sheepskins lay on the polished wood floor. On a glass and chrome coffee table in front of the flickering fire sat a terra cotta figure — a prop left from a stage show — of Kuan Yin, the Chinese goddess of mercy. There was a dark scorch on the ledge in front of her crossed legs where one night, long ago, Adams' young wife had burned some incense in a half-serious appeal.

The producer brought Nia another glass of scotch, and then with his own sat back in his favourite armchair and smiled at her with approval.

Years earlier, Adams had entered radio as an actor, and had once played the part of the Prince of Wales in *Henry IV* with such conquering confidence that everyone went on calling him *Prince Hal,* and the name, gradually losing its title, had stuck, at least among those who had known him then. He had gone from acting into production, and had produced on radio the first show for which Buddy had entirely composed and conducted the music. In those days radio was done live, with the orchestra in the same studio as the actors, and Nia, who had come with Buddy to the broadcast, had with Adams' permission watched from the control room. Her nearness had deeply affected the young producer. Nia's beautiful face, her gorgeous body, her eagerness and warmth, the potent charm he could continually feel had so excited him that he barely got through the hour. When he watched her leave on Buddy's arm he knew she had made on him an impression against which he would afterwards measure all women. It was a pitiless yardstick. When he married, his poor wife felt that whatever she did she could not possibly please him — her unknown crime consisting in not being Nia. After two dreadful years she ran off with his best friend, and since then Adams had been without a wife or a tolerable friend.

He had never expected to see Nia again. But he had followed her moves, to Hollywood and New York, and then, having heard that she was divorced and in Montreal, something like hope briefly flared in him. However he was by then too advanced in age, too set in his ways, too pessimistic to do more than add to the dream a vague possibility. But when fate dropped her, as it were, into his lap, he was inwardly astonished and excited.

I see he said, indicating a magazine article *Buddy's married again.*

Yes — Nia replied. *I hope he'll be happier this time.*

His fourth?

Third — I think.

Department store heiress, isn't she? Lots of money?

I don't know, Hal. Like you, I just read about it. You know, every new flower looks fresher.

He's a fool. God, if I had you ... Nia, why not now? Why don't we run away?

Nia laughed. *Because we're not the running away kind —*

All right, so we'll go quietly. Two weeks, three . . . I'll take you to Bermuda, the south of France, Switzerland . . . anywhere. That, he thought, could lead to marriage. *Why not?*

For one thing, I have a job I need and don't want to lose — and it doesn't yet entitle me to holidays. For another, I have a son in school.

School will be out in a month. And the holidays I'll take care of. I'll phone Ottawa and tell them you've been working all hours and unpaid weekends.

No, Hal — I'm embarrassed enough about the salary you continued —

Well, too bad. He gave her his patrician stare. *It's done. Honey bun, you're stuck with three weeks of holidays.*

25

On the following Saturday, both Nia and Robert were silent as they neared the cabin. When they entered the valley they saw the Careys at the end of the garden, gathering a cartload of firewood from a fallen tree that had been sawn into short lengths. Robert returned their wave. He had talked with Mrs. Carey by phone and had agreed to discuss the rent when he came out.

Nia took a deep breath before she opened the cabin door and stepped into the kitchen. *Oh darling,* she exclaimed *it's all the same* — And when she went through to the main room she saw her blue washcloth hanging by the stove —*I want to leave something of us* she had said — and the half-burnt red candles in the wax-dribbled wine bottles, and the wild flowers, dry but erect, still in their vases as she had left them. Robert had slyly kept all this from her. *My God —* she said *is it possible no one's been here?*

No one has. It's been waiting for us.

It was meant. Incredible —

But a moment later she was impatiently ordering her nest. *Move the cot onto the porch. But that old bed — it has to go. Its mattress we'll keep, but put it on the floor. No — on something — so we'll have some air under us. We must have air under us, mustn't we, my darling —*

You're aloft already Robert said. When he had the partitions apart he saw that the smallest section would do nicely. With the mattress centred on it, about a foot of board was left on both sides, providing handy ledges. Then they made their new bed, and Nia placed beside it a bouquet of the lily of the valley and blue columbine she had found near the cabin, and Robert held her close, and it all felt like home. *We're really beginning a new life here* . . . and just as he thought it he began, inexplicably, to feel that he was being tugged along by the old one.

The approach of Mrs. Carey dispelled this notion; he hurried to settle with her. Her sweet, childlike face, heated from lifting the firewood, was as rosy as an apple. She was panting slightly, and moistened her open lips with a pink tongue. She hesitated, smiling a little, and then asked Robert what he wanted to pay.

Surprised, he said jokingly, because he had brought it as a deposit *Oh . . . a hundred dollars.*

Okay, a hundred per quarter. You can pay me four times a year.

It was much less than he had expected. She had charged Hugh sixty dollars for the month.

As he gave his landlady the money Robert noticed that under her light blouse her breasts were round and full, and that her tight slacks revealed the firm lines of her hips and legs. But he was instantly ashamed of the pleasure this gave him. *Oh, the old bed* . . . he said awkwardly, and growing flustered, he explained that there were several things, including the sloping bed frame, and the spring, which Nia didn't want in the cabin.

Put them in our woodshed.

Thanks. Thanks, for everything, Mrs. Carey.

My name is Martha she said, blushing.

He must have blushed too, for Nia greeted him with a wry smile, which made him feel guiltier still. *But why?* he thought. *It was nothing . . .*

*

They awoke to sunlight dancing overhead, reflected onto the roof beams from the rippling water. The day passed slowly, and each part of it, like a film sequence that *worked*, seemed just right.

When they made love that afternoon, in a hollow on the hillside above the cabin, where they had spread a blanket and were screened by a dense, low-lying tree, Robert reflected that whatever their feelings, the lovemaking was always good in itself.

Later they debated whether to have supper; as they would have to leave soon afterwards. Neither wanted to bother with a lot of cooking and dishes. *What about fish?* Robert said. *Maybe I can catch some!*

He went to the log house to ask if they had a rod he could borrow. Steve brought him one, while smilingly declaiming *And God prepared a great fish to swallow up Jonah!*

Robert ignored the slight mockery. He felt the tall man meant it kindly, that he had a private pool of humour he kept stirring for his own amusement. *Be cheery, my lad* Carey went on in singsong. *Let your heart never fail, while the bold harpooner is striking the whale!*

That's me, for sure Robert said. *Have you ever been whaling?*

No, but I'm a Newfie Steve replied, laughing. *I was a whale of a fisherman!*

Really! What kind of fish . . . cod?

No, soul. Only soul!

He had been born, this abstruse wit, in a dreary little outport on the north-east coast of Newfoundland. It had a narrow, rocky bay, a few boats, and about a dozen small wooden houses surrounded by flakes of salted, drying cod. One November, when he was about four, his father was caught in a squall; then his mother began to spit blood. The boy was raised by an ailing great aunt who knitted caps and mitts for a living. She had no time or strength for him. He grew up *half wild*, prankish, lonely — but clever, and nimble with his tongue. He could get around others by making them laugh. *I'd love to fish!* he would say *but I can't afford it!* And indeed he could see nothing in fishing but poverty and toil, and cold, particularly cold, which he hated. But there seemed no escape from his barren existence.

Then came a Sunday when he glimpsed one. The Methodist circuit preacher took up a penny collection to help a distant bible college, and a day later Steven Michael Carey arrived at the minister's home church. He stayed to sweep up, stoke the fire, run errands; and at eighteen, after four or five appeals to mainland congregations and an Ontario college, he was finally called there as a charity student. It was charity: the church, having merged with the Presbyterians, had a surfeit of preachers.

*

The fish were eager to bite. Robert caught two trout one after the other, and put them in a brimming pail, where they swam about flashing their red spots and cream bellies. Nia said *They're exquisite!* After that they had to let them go.

So they went without supper, but it gave Robert a peculiar thrill to see Nia hanging up the clothes she was leaving, and storing the left-over liquor and tinned food for the next time they came. It was wonderful, closing the cabin on their own things, taking away only what had to be cleaned. Their soiled bed sheets made up the bulk of that. They fell to Robert, for Nia could hardly take them home to her mother.

*

She told the old woman she would be working every weekend with her friend the novelist, to help him with a long drama he was writing. His wife, Nia said, would pick her up every Friday at the office. She would stay with them through Sunday — the country house they had taken for the summer was too far for daily commuting — and then one of them would bring her home. It was a plausible-enough lie, no more likely to be tested than other fictions she had used. Mother and daughter had long understood that the essentials were satisfied when decorum was preserved and food provided, and when Wilma knew where Nia could be reached.

Nia arranged with her friends to sustain her story if her mother phoned, and each Sunday she had Robert stop at a phone booth from which she checked with them to see if there had been any trouble. Wilma called only once, early one morning, complaining that some of the electricity had gone off, and the novelist — who said Nia was sleeping — was able to tell Joel how to replace the blown fuse.

*

Driving to the cabin again, Robert asked Nia how she liked the car. *Oh — nice* she said. *You knew about blue — didn't you. And it's one more possession.*

One more?

We have the girl with the teasing smile.

When they arrived Robert presented her with another — this one for the cabin. He had secretly splurged on a new pair of binoculars. Nia used them for hours, watching birds. But as well she installed a mirror, a wash basin, and a towel bar in the toilet closet, and began to sew curtains for the low windows in the loft. And near the clump of cedars Robert built a little dock with a ladder down which they could lower themselves into the cool water. Then they decided to ask the Careys to tea.

They came when the sun had withdrawn to the hills, leaving in the valley a shaded, early summer hush. Everyone settled on the porch, around the makeshift table Robert had made by nailing a broad piece of board to a short round of tree stump. *Well,* he said, speaking to Carey *your wife tells me you're a minister.*

256

Used to be Steve said, laughing.

Is that how the two of you met?

No! they both said.

Well, sort of. It was at bible camp Martha added.

Highly amused, Steve said *She grew up with her own pony and chauffeur.*

— *He was the family's chauffeur* Martha demurred.

Her parents Steve went on, laughing heartily *sent her for bible study hoping it would tame her. She came back with me! Penniless me!*

And were they ever mad Martha said.

But they resigned themselves?

After a while they did. I think she added, blushing *they were afraid I might be capable of worse.*

Oh? What . . . denomination were you?

United Church first Steve said. *Then I became a Baptist.*

Just like that?

Well, Steve said, grinning widely *the Baptists were mounting a mission to Haiti, and that's where I wanted to go.*

And they accepted you?

My father, Martha said *paid for most of it.*

And you went, and made converts?

We were there nearly three years Martha said. *The people, especially the children . . . were they ever sweet. But . . .* she looked to her husband for confirmation *I don't think we made any converts.*

Carey could hardly contain his hilarity. *Martha was doing some practical nursing. She took a course before joining me there. And I was preaching to the ladies.*

Why just the ladies?

Well, the men couldn't be bothered, but the women liked it. They were happy and free. Oh, free. Oh, God, free! He slapped his thigh. *There was one girl . . . I had ridden to the coast and gone to a hotel. The room wasn't ready so they sent her to make it up. She gave me the eye, and then dawdled so long I finally said 'Look, I'm sweaty and horsey and I'm going to take a bath while you finish.' When I got back she was still there. I said 'What do you want?' And she smiled and* said 'All!' That was some all! That's when I learned that all is best!

While he revelled in mirth, Steve managed to glance directly at Nia, to make sure she got the message. She certainly did, along with observing that above the fine wrinkles in his face his dark brown hair was dyed. Martha, who was bravely trying to smile, looked like an abashed, greying child. Sitting next to her, Nia said *Have some more tea. . .*

Robert too was embarrassed for Martha, yet he felt it best to continue the conversation. *But you're not a missionary now?* he said to Steve.

No. I was defrocked!

Why? Not because of the ladies. . . ?

No . . . Mainly they called me on the carpet because of no converts. I had to come home and face a Council of Pastors. I had fun with them for a while, but then they hammered me with their ultimate nail.

Robert waited, then said *Which was?*

Do you believe in the supremacy and divinity of Jesus Christ.

And?

I said that like doctors who don't necessarily take the medicine they help people with, we shouldn't have to believe our own myths. What does it matter, if it makes others feel good? And I'm still doing that, under a different label. Psychological counselling. Suddenly he smiled and said *Anyway, what's in a name? Would Nora be less beautiful by any other?*

Would you be less of a bigmouth? she retorted, to Steve's increased delight. *You're certainly no Shakespeare — and I'm years and pounds from Juliet. So let's just drop it, shall we?*

*

The next morning Nia had a headache. *I'd say it was listening to Steve — if I hadn't had two already this week. One was so bad I wondered whether I'd be able to work —*

It might be your eyes Robert said. *When did you last have them tested?*

258

Oh — not for years.

Maybe you need glasses. Or different ones. Anyway, you might as well go to the best man in the city. And, proud of knowing whom to recommend, he named an eminent doctor. *Call him tomorrow!*

Yes sir Nia said.

*

The specialist looked inside her eyes, checked her sight, dilated her pupils, even measured the flow of her tears. In the end, finding nothing, he advised Nia to get more rest.

*

When she phoned Robert later that day she said *I have a surprise —*

Something's wrong with your eyes?

No — my sight is fine. Here — someone wants to speak to you.

A feminine voice, sounding excited, said *Hello Robert . . .*

It was familiar. *Gwendolyn?*

Indeed, and not alone. But the two women would say no more. Nia told him to meet them where Gwen was staying. It was a small hotel. At the door of her room he heard a baby crying.

She had a two-month-old child, and had left her husband. *I overheard his sisters talking about me,* she complained a*nd finally realized, Jesus, I could hardly believe it, you know, but had to, that from the moment we married, his whole family, every one of them, was waiting for it to end. And you know I did everything they expected of me, and more!* She had hung a crucifix in the kitchen, had pushed her husband out to mass every morning — he had gone twice, a lone man among women, and then taken to spending the hour in a café — had faithfully made meatless meals on Friday, and had gone with her mother-in-law almost every Tuesday evening for prayers to Our Lady of Perpetual Help.

The poor fellow had married her for her romantic sighs, her worldly work, her Englishness. Eventually he rebelled. Their quarrels became increasingly bitter. In the end he called her a nun and

259

she taunted him about his Indian blood. *It all became so twisted!* Gwendolyn lamented. *'Cause I like Indians. That's what I first thought was attractive about him.*

Robert sighed and glanced at Nia, but she seemed to be evasively refolding diapers into a small-enough size. *Well,* he said *differences invite trouble.*

But it wouldn't have made any difference if I'd actually become Catholic, Gwendolyn went on *because when the baby was born —* she was gently bouncing the crying child in her arms to the beat of her statements, which seemed to distract it — *my father-in-law grumbled about it being a boy, 'cause property will be going out of the family'. For them I was a total loss! Oh, I'm so fed up. Excuse my French, but f— them!*

Robert was amazed. Gwendolyn's eyes, which had always bulged slightly, now looked enormous, ringed as they were with bluish shadow, the lashes heavy with mascara. And her hair had lost its straw colour. Dyed an even yellow, it was parted in the centre, looped over her ears and gathered in a loosely-braided bun. Her nails gleamed, her dress, dark and smart, was tight over her enlarged bosom.She seemed a long way from the little field flower who had brightened Eldon's office. *Why did you* he said, rather rudely *come to Toronto?*

Well, she replied, laughing *where Nia leads . . .*

And how will you manage? I mean, with expenses.

Oh, she said *that's okay. My father died a few months ago, but before that he sold the farm for a housing development. My share, in installments, brings me much more than I was making at the Board.*

She lowered the baby, now asleep, into a wicker basket lined with soft blue blankets.

Darling — Nia whispered *we'd better go.*

At the fond term a sudden brightness shone from Gwendolyn. And at the door, when she had kissed Nia good-night, she impulsively seized Robert's hands and kissed him too.

*

The following Friday, in front of Hugh's building, when Robert and Nia were about to leave for the cabin, and she was already waiting in the car, to which Robert was carrying the laundered and neatly-folded bedclothes, the janitor came out and said he had a parcel for him. It was an almost square, bulky object covered with kraft paper and tied by twine. Correctly addressed, it had been delivered from the city's largest department store while he had gone to get Nia. Robert pried open a corner of the wrapping: inside was a galvanized washtub.

A washtub! he said to Nia. *I told him to send it back. We both had a good laugh.*

Well, you're both stupid! Nia said. *That's my bathtub.*

*

But when she tried to sit in it, at the cabin, it proved too small.

Darkness brought rain, and then the night was swept by thunderstorms. Robert woke to immense rolling crashes that shook even the solid log walls. Nia was already awake, cowering under the thin woollen covers. Between lightning flickers and ear-rending roars, fusillades of water beat on the roof, making them feel they were inside a drum. *Darling,* Nia said *maybe you'd better shut the windows —*

He did, then sheltered her in his arms. She was trembling. And it pleased him, when he kissed her, that she had not got up to brush her teeth. Though her mouth was almost always sweet, she was normally quick to erase the effect of sleep. But now, too frightened, she huddled against him. *It's all right,* he said *it'll be over soon.*

I wasn't worrying about us. It was Joel —

You're being irrational. It might not even be raining there.

I mean in the larger sense. If anything was to happen to me — he has no one else. Mother's too old —

He has me. I'd look after him. It was easy to say, and to enjoy the swell of pride that came with being protective. For an instant he even saw himself and the boy as father and son, and was charmed

261

by the idea of having a child, particularly one partly grown. And the fleeting notion of an absent Nia even, just then, pleased him.

*

Overhead, the rumbles were retreating. The drumming had let up, and been replaced by a soft steady hiss. Nia sighed deeply, then kissed his bare shoulder.

What is it? Robert said gently.

I think — you're the only man, other than my father — who's ever really loved me. And he — she added after a moment *didn't love me enough to stay.*

26

With stability came discontent. Robert grew conscious of small faults in Nia. Her figure had filled out a little more, making it slightly less lithe and alluring. Her breasts, though still stunning, had started to sag; now, he noticed, they fell forward a bit when she removed her brassiere. Her face, as beautiful as ever, and always fresh, was becoming a fixture, merely confirming what he expected from it, as if it were a painting. Her love for him, which was continually expressed in words, looks, touches, began to be cloying. Sometimes he longed for other women, and, when inside her, would recast her into Betty or Gwendolyn.

He felt fate had misled him. On meeting and winning Nia, he had been so struck by her looks and spirit, he could never have imagined, had he even suspected, that she would become such a bundle of inner frailties and fears. True, she had warned him from the start, but he had been blinded by his own cravings.

Nia was taking it as it comes. She knew that Robert was growing disinterested, but felt that her charms were enough to hold him, and that his passion for her had to wax and wane. She now kept from him most of the details of her home life, preferring to have him see her only as an agreeable companion. Her fearful physical lapses she seldom referred to. Besides, Joel, who was growing, was becoming delightful and took up much of her time after work.

However, in midweek, whenever she had no early afternoon appointments, Nia joined Robert for lunch at the apartment. Before eating, or after it, they would briefly make love. The weather had been very warm. For days thin clouds had partly obscured the sun, promising the relief of rain, but had only increased the humidity and heat. Just now the sky was a dull whitish glare, and in that flat light, as they lay on the cot, everything in the room looked stark and strange. Robert could see pits and cracks in the plaster, splits and splinters in the thin parquet. All seemed reduced to rubble, dross, decay. On her chest Nia had beads of moisture. When he entered her, his rage burst.

Gripping her arms, breasts, belly, he drove her to one climax after another. Straddling her, pressing her thighs apart, he thrust with fury, while she, provoked to an equal pitch, tore at his ears, clutched his neck and shoulders, dug her nails into his skin. Frantic for something more, he turned about, seized her ankles, and fell with bared tongue on her furrowed mound. Locked like that, each mouthed the other until, mutually, the convulsion came. There was embarrassment, disgust, foreboding, but he meekly drank what was left of her fluid, and she his.

Then lying by her side, Robert felt how disagreeable this had been. Not the act itself, though neither had ever done it before, but that what should have been tender and loving had been brutally spoilt. He peered closely at her face, and observed what he had long feared to see — an aging woman. There was even a tiny blonde hair sprouting from her upper lip!

The phone rang.

Surprised and annoyed, Robert got up and padded to the bookcase. He was entirely nude.

Hello? he said.

Mr. Aronson? It was a strange male voice.

263

Yes.

Are you Robert Aronson, the movie director?

Yes . . .

How are you . . . how's the weather up there?

Sure now he was being mocked, Robert's irritation increased. *It's lousy* he said. *How's yours?*

Oh, it's sunny here the man chuckled. *It's almost always sunny, above the smog.*

Where're you calling from?

The coast. The man said he was a producer, and the studio he named was one of the majors, known for its family films. *Hey,* he said *we screened your whale-hunt footage.*

Yeah. . . ?

It's the best directing of whales I've seen.

Well, I didn't exactly direct them . . .

No, but your handling of the scenes. You know what I mean. Listen, we have a story about a whale. It's kind of a kid's story, but with adult appeal. I'd like to talk to you about it.

About directing it. . . ?

Yeah. Can you come down here, to Los Angeles?

The walls suddenly whipped away, and he, exposed to the world, was standing bare, bathed in sweat and slime. *Well . . .* he said *I d'know. When? I'm working on a picture now.*

A feature?

A television feature. Adult drama he added.

Uh-huh. Can you not get away for a day? Or, listen, I have to be up near Canada at the end of the month. I'll be in Seattle for a few days. Could you come there? Or I could even slip up and meet you in Vancouver, if that would help.

Yes Robert said, instinctively pretending importance. *I think it would. I'm in prep now but maybe I can get away before we start shooting.*

Okay. They exchanged addresses and confirmed phone numbers. *Now,* the producer said *Vancouver . . . I'll be at . . .* He gave a hotel and a date. *We'll see you there . . .*

After Robert had hung up and related this to Nia, she said *It's your break. Take it.*

They sat on the cot, their stickiness drying. He was excited, but disturbed. It could mean such sudden changes. And then there was the irony that the idea of his directing a kid's movie should have been derived from such savage slaughter.

I don't know . . . he said.

Don't be foolish again! You may not get another chance — She was firm, though nothing in this news, as they both knew, boded well for her.

And something else troubled him. *The guy said 'We'll' see you. Was that just the editorial we?*

No. He'll have a lawyer with him — *or maybe a business manager. If they hand you a contract look at it then* — *and say at once what you don't like about it. Because those become talking points. If you just go away with their boilerplate it'll be much harder to debate it later.*

*

While she was showering, he thought about that. When Nia came out, dressed in her white underclothes and slip, with her hair combed, looking, he decided, remarkably beautiful, he was bursting with a new idea. *Darling, you're at home with Hollywood people and their ways. Why don't you come with me?*

To Vancouver? No. I won't fly —

We don't have to! We can drive. A week there, a week back . . . say another week for contingency. Or for just stopping where we like. Seeing places.

Nia shook her head. *There's Mother* — *and Joel is just out of school and we haven't made summer plans yet* — *and there's work* — She wasn't convinced she was up to such a car trip, but didn't want to say no. *I'm not sure I can even get away* —

Will you check? Please. Because we've never had that long a time together.

She was silent for a long moment, then said *I suppose we could take the train* —

Oh, but the train would be expensive, and we'd always be with strangers. With the car we can camp along the way, have picnics, cook out. I still have the Coleman stove.

Nia seemed to soften. The stove was a potent symbol.

27

Yes, CBC Personnel told her, according to their records she had three weeks of unused holidays in the current year. And when she talked with Joel he said that for the summer there was a daily puppet programme at a nearby park he thought he would like to attend.

Wilma, though, was wary; she insisted on first seeing her several doctors and getting their consent before giving her own. Nia's reason for possibly being away three weeks was concocted from her earlier one: the novelist's drama now being finished, she said, he and his wife were going on a driving tour and had asked her to come along. One by one the barriers of resistance crumbled.

The most looming obstacle, however, was Adams. Nia felt she could not repay his kindness with a lie.

Hal, she said *it was sweet of you to get me — give me — the time off — and I want to use it. And I don't want you to ask how —*

Adams stared at her, then dropped his gaze. He was good at concealing his feelings, but when he looked up again his hollow mask bespoke hurt as much as any words could have. *As you wish* he said softly. Nia sighed, and had to crinkle her eyes to keep from crying.

*

Robert regretted his hypocrisy but managed, with some discomfort, to modify it. He knew Nia suddenly looked better because he needed her, but told himself that if they had just met he would anyway be almost as deeply moved by her as, he could see, other men still were. And if she was now, inescapably, an *older woman*, well, then he must resign himself in the *richer or poorer* sense. Besides, when he pictured himself with any more ordinary woman, Betty, or Gwendolyn, or Martha, though each had some allure — or even Myra, the most attractive of the four, Nia was undeniably in a different class, and it would be madness, after all they had gone through, to give her up. And as well, their present pattern, by which he did not have to be with her day and night, suited him. As for driving to Vancouver, where she was sure to impress the Hollywood people, for that he would be especially grateful, especially good to her.

*

She was sorting out clothes to take, checking to see what needed cleaning, when Joel told her there was a man at the door. Nia went down; it was Steve! Surprised, she said *How did you know where to find me?*

He grinned. *Telephone information. I talked the girl into giving me your address.*

Well — come in. She led him through the house to the back garden, where the sun was now hidden behind the next street, but had left an afterlight on the white wooden lawn chairs. *Is it about the cabin — ?*

No, not at all he said, smiling. *That whole property belongs to Martha.*

Would you — like a drink?

She went to the kitchen to mix rum and sodas. Wilma was at the dining room window, watching Steve talking with Joel, who had gone around by the side alley to join him. When Nia came out they were walking along the planted beds, in which the boy was pointing out the graceful garlic that was his personal project. It was evident from Joel's liveliness that he liked Steve. Apart from Francis, whom he adored, and a few of her other friends, her son, despite his lack of a father figure, did not readily take to many men.

What, no drink for me? Joel gasped as she handed Steve his.

No — and no ham either she said. Joel giggled, and so did she. When the boy left on his bicycle, and she had yelled after him to be back before dark, she turned to the tall, grinning man. *Well —?*

I've come to woo you.

And —?

Just that. You and Robert are a bad match.

Really. You don't imagine — do you — that it's any of your business?

Oh, but it is he said, still smiling. *I don't think you're entirely happy, and happiness is my business.*

Over the rim of her glass Nia looked at him askance, because she could see that behind his tomfoolery Steve was serious. That made him a menace.

*

Indeed, it was only after his divestment that Steven Carey began truly caring about his calling. He had the necessary qualities: an assurance as smug as stupidity, excellent health, and utter self-centredness when carrying out his task. Moreover, Martha's inheritance allowed him to live without working. He took his cases where he found them, and his methods, though crude, were effective. Tearful sufferers often became smiling friends. There was no payment; at most he would accept a meal or two, or, from a woman — if it was comfortable and agreeable to them both — other favours. He was generous with his time and what money he had, but Martha, who resented his adulteries, kept him from having much. Occasionally, when his ministering grew into a full-blown affair, and he needed more money, he would take a temporary job driving a cab.

*

Ever since I was a kid, Steve went on *I've been searching for richness in life. Not riches — but richness in spirit, looks, mind, body. You've got them all. You were meant to enjoy life to the fullest. And this thing with Robert is wrong. He's too young for you. You'd be*

268

much better with me. In fact . . . he said, grinning *you and I would be fabulous!*

Well — ! And what about Martha?

He shrugged. *She doesn't have to know. And if she finds out, I'll make it up to her.*

So — Nia said *you've reduced all the complexities of life to a simple formula — which suits you.*

Yeah . . . That's what all religion does.

And you have no doubts about what you're doing — ?

Fundamentally, no.

You're a fanatic— Nia said with scorn. *I —*

She was interrupted by her mother, who had opened the screen door. *Dear,* Wilma called *I've made tea. Why don't you come and have it . . .*

Nia was slightly startled. It was unlike her mother to take such interest in a stranger. They went in. Wilma had set the dining room table; there were place mats, the best china and silver, a plate of cake.

A breach had been opened and Steve stormed through it.

He turned his entire attention to the delighted Wilma, calling her *pink rose,* shamelessly suggesting she could still *whittle a stick,* and declaring he would have her ahead of any *vernal gal.* Their hilarity was infectious; Nia, usually the foil of these ribald rubs, had to smile too. The old lady, thrilled to be favoured ahead of her daughter, laughed so hard she made herself damp. Both women were in a much better mood than before he came; Nia even appreciated his having animated her mother.

Steve too was pleased. He believed he had sapped some promising weak points, which would soon give.

*

In her room Wilma pinned to a hanger the long cotton panties she had rinsed in the bathroom sink. Like a budding girl, she had been too embarrassed to put them in the wash. The sensuality Steve had stirred came from a twisted source. Her own mother had started receiving callers not six months after the girl's father died, and Wilma, young as she was then, had known what those callers wanted, just as she had always irritably known what her daughter was up to with all her men, in spite of the insulting pretense and elaborate excuses she was expected to believe.

Only with her mild and staid father had Wilma ever felt quite safe. When he died in the smallpox epidemic of the 1880s, she fiercely expected everything else to stay the same. The kind, friendly man her mother married, following — whatever the *wench's* desires — a decent widowhood, could never get from the hurt girl, or later the stiff young woman she became, more than bare courtesy. For her father's sake, as she imagined it, had she afterwards adopted the pince-nez, the erect posture, the furrows in her high brow that were her little shields against licentiousness. Her husband-to-be had won her with his dream of going west, because it meant a far remove from that *wallowing pair*; then when Nia became her mainstay Wilma easily resumed the somewhat pained, leech-like role she had grudgingly enjoyed before her marriage.

Yet she liked to laugh. During her first years in Portage, when Nia's father had been stage manager of the town hall, she had gone to every visiting vaudeville show, and when they acquired the movie theatre *Aurora*, and she led the accompaniment to the antics of Charlie Chaplin or Harold Lloyd, she was sometimes so diverted she came close to missing cues. Nia and Joel told her jokes; occasionally all three spewed their food because of merriment during meals. But she had been dry a long time. Her husband had left one morning when Nia was eleven, after about four years of not touching. They had never heard from him again. Since then only Steve had roused her. In bed, thinking of his tall figure, his boldness and wit, she yielded to a lurking impulse, and crossing her legs, improvised a lover quite a lot like him.

A week later, Nia's morning headache was the worst it had ever been. Joel, already up, brought her a compress, aspirins and tea. When he went to get a towel she lit a cigarette. Returning, the frightened boy snatched it away, sure that smoking was causing all her ills. Nia ordered him to give it back, and as he bent to put it to her lips he heaved a desperate sigh. Both of them, though she was coughing, began to laugh.

Lucy, Joel said *you're driving me crazy.*

Well — welcome to the family, Charlie Brown!

When she heard their voices Wilma shuffled in. She had slept badly, was cold and cramped, and had not yet composed herself. Her grey-white hair hung to her shoulders in lank shags, her mouth, without its dentures, was puckered like a pale prune. She sat on the edge of the bed and complained of her back, hinting that her own pain was worse than any the younger woman could have. However she felt the compress, wiped Nia's cheeks, and sent Joel to fill the water bottle with ice.

Maybe, dear, she said *we should call the doctor.*

No — he'll only tell me to get more rest.

And indeed Nia had been labouring every night to clean, cook, and stock the house so that all would be in order when she left, three days from now. She really was tired, exhausted; she could feel fatigue tingling in every part of her, as if it had taken possession and was zestfully living a life of its own.

It was already eleven before she felt well enough to call a cab; then she rode to the office in a fever of dread, afraid she would not get through all she had to do. Actually, at the moment there was nothing particularly pressing about her work, nor would it be much set back by the three weeks she was about to be away. But that made it doubly important. Her promotion owed more to her background than to Adams' patronage. He had seen that the future of TV drama lay in film, and though Robert was at present the only director able to deliver a first rate result, he knew filmed programmes would attract other experienced people. He needed Nia, or someone like her, to select stories, plan ahead, and generally oversee the productions. On her desk she had a pile of books and scripts she was reading, and she intended to take several on the trip.

Driving past buildings that were a blur, she tried to go over her day. Betty had wanted to have lunch, and it was perhaps too late to put her off. At two she was meeting with Adams to bring him up to date on what she had done, at four she and Robert were to exchange the washtub and choose a tent and sleeping bags, and at night she had to deal with all the collected family laundry.

She dragged herself to her desk, which was spotted with pink message slips. Blessedly one was from Betty, cancelling the lunch. The rest, with people busy, or out, or calling back, took up the time before she had to see her boss.

What the hell . . . he said *you look awful! Are you sick?*

No — only a little tired.

Well, you shouldn't have come in. This can wait till you get back. For God's sake, go home.

I can't, Hal. I have to feel that I'm doing my job. Please — don't push me.

All right . . . he said with a sigh. *But let's cut it short.* And he invented another urgent meeting.

*

It was just past the appointed hour when Robert drove slowly up to the drama-department building. He was apprehensive. Always before, Nia and he had met at the corner, to avoid notice, but she had earlier called and asked him to come to the front door. And of course she wasn't there. Never on time! She usually came hurrying out five or ten minutes late, laughing and responding to the calls of acquaintances. But as he passed the entrance — a patrolman was writing tickets, he noticed, huddled back in the shaded portal, a bent, lumpish person, clothed in brown, about whom there was something familiar . . . and then realized with fright that it had been Nia. Unable to reverse or U turn, he went around the block, which gave him a little time to absorb the shock.

Nia's ailments had surfaced with a vengeance. She hadn't the energy to care much about how she looked. They drove in silence to the department store.

Can we stop at a supermarket Nia said. *I'd like to get the things that won't spoil. And one or two other places —*

I won't have time for other places Robert said. Which was quite untrue, but he felt he might not be able to endure it. The store they were going to, with its related buildings, occupied a whole city block. He parked at a meter on the side street. He carried the tub and Nia followed, clutching the front of her brown duster. *We'll go through here* he said.

Where — there are buildings all along —

There's a passageway.

I've never seen a passageway here —

Well there is one all the same he said curtly. Annoyed about the way she was dressed, he thought *Why a coat, in all this heat?*

However, it was windy, and the gusts were swirling papers and dust. They all but tore the tub from his grasp. Nia was hanging onto his arm, dragging a little.

Don't walk so fast —

What's the matter? He could see she was not well, but it was the meter he was worrying about.

Just don't go so fast.

Yet he kept on almost as before. He was impatient with her for being ill, for getting old.

The store doors shut out the fierce hot wind. Inside, the atmosphere was controlled, perfumed, smelling of fresh fabrics, leathers, wood, tremulous with ambling motions, low voices, the ping and rumble of cash registers. High overhead soared the sprinkler-studded ceiling, resting on marble columns that would have graced a Roman forum, while spread below were goods from all the

273

Earth. Robert's senses had always been excited by this floor, but now, pulling Nia, he went to the basement, where sports and house-wares were.

There's the exchange he said, hurrying towards the green light.

You go — I'll stay here.

A saleslady took the tub and went to get him the largest size. He turned back, unsure of where he and Nia had parted. Among the shoppers and the maze of counters he could see no sign of her. *Christ, I hope she hasn't wandered off!* he thought. He searched the aisles, growing steadily angrier. At last he came on her — just where she had stopped. She was staring blankly, and noticed nothing until he was at her side.

Can we go? she said, taking his arm.

No! We're waiting for the tub. Meanwhile, let's look at the tents.

Not moving, she gazed unsteadily at him. *I — don't think — I — can sleep outside —*

Okay, he said, repressing his rage *we'll stay in motels.*

He found the saleslady in an inner service room. Through the doorway he could see her leisurely folding large sheets of paper around the tub while talking across the table with another woman who was wrapping tumblers in tissue. They had time. Damn. It only increased his agitation. At last he had the tub in his hands.

Nia had not moved. She felt incapable of exertion. *If I just breathe* she thought . . . Then she curtailed thinking. It too required an effort. She also shut out feeling, which dulled Robert's rude-ness. She had a sense of wanting to be like the little violet that had survived the seasons; if she shrank enough within herself even this terrible one might pass.

When Robert returned he took her elbow and steered her rap-idly towards the elevators.

Please — not so fast —

He was afraid the meter had run out, and at first grimly main-tained his pace, but then, with a heavy sigh, said *Okay. . .*

I'm sorry — she whispered. *I can't walk any faster —*

He muttered *It's okay, okay. . .*

I'm sorry I'm holding you back —

And he said with choler *It's okay!*

A small crowd was already waiting. Robert halted Nia at the rear of it, and put down his bulky package. Then over the shoulders of those in front he glared at the shut shafts, as if by fixed rage he could force the doors.

Waiting there, Nia opened herself to awareness. Her mind, she felt sadly, was suddenly clear. *I guess —* she said, quietly enough for only him to hear *you don't love me anymore.*

He remained savagely still, thinking he was choked by that love.

I hurt — from the soles of my feet — to the top of my brain. This isn't me — my body — I don't want to live like this — And you'd like me to die — she added.

Robert frowned angrily, swift hope confused with fear.

Goodbye, darling —

He turned to her then, and caught the last colour draining from her face. She seemed about to faint. And there leapt into his mind her words about the pneumonia, that she had almost *willed* death. Frozen, conflicted, torn between wild hate and tenderness, he was swept by nameless terror. His heart stopped.

Hers already had. The eager joy in living that had buoyed her since birth had come to an end.

Two elevators arrived. The shoppers milled forward, and Nia, with a long sigh, shuffled after them.

*

Going back through the passageway, her arm in his, Robert held Nia tightly and walked with deliberate, slow steps. The meter had long ago run out and he was resigned to seeing a ticket. There was none, which raised his spirits, and restored a semblance of warmth.

Nia felt she was in a dream. As if, at the moment when she had yielded up her life, she had really died and this was some kind of a life after death. But outwardly it seemed ordinary. And offered no obvious choice but to follow the plans already made.

In the supermarket she seemed to rally slightly. By leaning on the handle of the cart she gradually moved along the rows. Robert waited until she appeared to be proceeding on her own, then slipped away and ran swiftly down the street. At a swanky drug store he bought a gold-boxed bottle of their *best* bath salts. It cost more than the tub, in which he hid it, but the extravagance assuaged his guilt. He was back before she reached the check-out.

At her house he wanted to take her in, but she declined. When she had climbed the front steps, he drove away. In the trunk was the carton of foods she had selected for the cabin and the trip.

*

Joel met her at the door. *He's here again!* he said excitedly. *Who?*
Steve. He brought wine and flowers!
And Carey, grinning widely, got up quickly from the fireside chair. Wilma, looking grotesque in bright lipstick, was sitting kittenishly on the sofa, her thin legs doubled under her. In her lap lay a single, pink, long-stemmed rose. The rest of the half dozen were in a vase on the mantelpiece. Jester was jumping about Nia's feet, joyously barking and wagging his tail. *My dear . . .* Wilma said to her daughter, like a character in a drawing room comedy *I knew you'd want Steven to stay.*
But I have so much to do! Nia cried.
I'll help you Steve said. And he did. He made the salad, set the table, poured the wine. With his long arms he passed the plates. And all the time, even with his mouth full, he chatted with infectious good humour, now and then making everyone laugh with one of his extravagant puns. Wilma's alabaster bowl, a gift from the *Aurora's* ensemble, he described as *marbelous*, and when she snuffed the candles, and both stubs went on smoking, he declaimed *Your candle sperms at both ends . . .* at which she shrieked and slapped his hand. Then he did the dishes, carried the laundry hamper to the basement, filled the washer, and hung the sheets

276

and pillowcases on the clotheslines that were stretched below the plumbing pipes. Nia tried to hang the smaller things but raising her arms soon tired her and she had to sit down on the camp cot. There were a few comic books on it. Joel and his friends sometimes retreated there when banished from the upper floors. Steve removed them and sat beside her. He lit a cigarette and put it to her lips.

It's good of you to do all this —

No, he said *I'm glad to. You look like you should be in bed.*

Yes — I'm totally beat —

Well, here, he said, rising *get your feet up . . .* And he stooped and raised them. Then he stood looking down as she lay full length. *I'd love to make love to you.*

Something of her old self came back. Amused, she said *I know —*

He dropped to his knees and reached across her, lightly cradling her waist.

Here — ? she said wryly.

Steve grinned. *Why not? Nobody can see us . . .* And indeed he had hung the bed linen so that it blocked the small side windows and the view from the kitchen door. With the cot against a stone supporting wall, and the three other sides curtained by sheets, they were in a custom-built enclosure. Joel had gone to his room, and though Wilma was still on the floor above, she seldom risked the steep basement steps.

Like under the stairs in Portage — Nia said.

What?

Where I grew up — I'd sneak down the back stairs to meet boys.

Well . . . He brought his mouth close and kissed her cheek. Their voices were low, intimate.

But I'm no longer fifteen —

Of course you are! Inside we all are. Or maybe sixteen, seventeen. Not more.

Let's just talk — talk to me —

I will. I certainly sure as hell will. Another time.

You want it all —

Steve grinned. *All is best. C'mon, what can you lose?*

Nothing — she thought. But aloud she said *Don't be absurd. And anyway, I'm too tired* — She was; too tired even to resist.

It won't cost you any effort. I'll be very gentle . . .

Suddenly from above came the crashing chords of the wedding march, segueing into a medley of familiar tunes. Wilma, seated at the piano, was vigorously calling up what she could remember of her repertoire. Jealously avid for Steve's company, she was summoning her swain from the depths.

Nia began to laugh. And Steve knew it was fatal to his suit.

God damn you! he thought when he walked away that night, unsure of whether he meant Nia or Wilma or both. *The Lord make thee like Zedekia and like Ahab . . .* The curse was a remnant he liked to recall. It relieved his feelings, and he assumed the Old Rogue never heard him anyway.

29

The next morning Robert phoned Nia's house and was told she had gone to work. He was reassured, but felt deeply troubled about her. Her behaviour yesterday was too real for comfort, and he was frightened by having provoked it. However much he might want at some point in future — at any rate after Vancouver — to be free of her, and he was now certain of that, he did not like to think of himself hurting her.

*

Driving to the cabin, Nia was quiet, but she was no longer so sick looking. Glancing at her Robert saw that in spite of age and illness she was still very good looking. She was staring out. Across the low bank of the road a large corner of the field's spring wheat crop appeared to have turned brown. *That was starting the last time we came by* — Nia said. *It's spreading fast. Darling — I'm seriously worried about that rust.*

And instantly, Robert noted, the field of some unknown farmer had leapt to life and become particular and personal. Nia's immediacy always amazed him, adding to his conflicts.

Almost invariably now, when he was away from her, his ambition was paramount, and he easily fantasized directing feature films, moving in the circles of the very successful, having many younger, even more-beautiful women. In that sense Nia was a scourge he had to be rid of. But when he was with her all that imagined future lost form, and he was mainly aware of the moment-to-moment delight she drew for him from everything around them.

*

When they arrived Martha was revving a black Jeep station wagon, and about to go. *Car trouble* she added, replying to his look. *It's never been right. I'm taking it to the dealer.*

Oh, hey, somebody's painted the boat! he said. It was lying upside down near his small dock. With Steve's permission he had earlier repaired the broken board.

I did Martha said. *This morning. It's still sticky, but it should dry soon.* She blushed and added *I put a paddle under it.*

Robert could not help thinking what a dear, shy soul she was — in an attractive body.

Nia had gone right into the cabin. She was glad that Steve, whom she had seen by the woodshed, was courteously keeping out of the way. By the time Robert brought in their bags, the groceries, the rum, scotch, wine and a half case of beer they had bought for the trip, it was too late for an elaborate supper, so Nia made a salad and opened a can of clams. With milk and seasonings, and a little flour for thickening, it made a hearty chowder.

Robert did the dishes, and when he joined her in bed she was wearing a nightgown, but without his asking she slipped it off and nestled into his arms. They made love sweetly and, spoon fashion, eased into sleep.

*

Nia's eyes were still shut when he re-entered the cabin after his morning exercises. He quietly prepared his own breakfast, and then placing a cup of hot coffee beside her, took his sketch pad and pencils and went out to the porch. For the next hour he drew scenes for the drama film, for he also liked being his own art director. It was only when he was distracted by the smell of cigarette smoke that he looked in. Nia was sitting up in bed, smoking and sipping the coffee.

Would you like me to heat it? he said.

No — it's all right. Go on with your work —

He sketched for almost another two hours, roughly visualizing his mental images. Then again there was a wafting of cigarette smoke, this time mingled with the warm smell of food. Nia, in her robe, was at the kitchen range, lifting the edge of an omelet with a long spatula. In her other hand she held a tall glass of beer, and Robert noticed with alarm that three empty bottles stood on the counter.

Is anything wrong?

Last night I think I swallowed a bit of clamshell she said. Poking a finger between her breasts, she complained *It seems to have stuck here —*

Robert was annoyed that these two days, which had been meant to be carefree, should be marred by such a trifle. Lunch, overhung with tension, was largely silent. However, seeing the amount of white rum Nia was drinking, on top of all that beer, and her guarded, absent glances, he suspected more was at issue than the clamshell. *Probably weighing our life together* he thought, and though he could understand that, he wished she would not spoil the present by dwelling on the past or future.

But then she took up the yellow curtains she had earlier started to stitch by hand, and finished them.

How about a swim? Robert said.

Put these up first, please —

Actually welcoming the break, he threaded a wire through the loops of the curtains and strung them across the loft windows. *Leave them closed* Nia said, and he did, though the sun was already well around the other side. When he came down she handed him a drink, and they sat out by the little dock, sipping the white rum, lime and soda.

I don't feel quite up to swimming Nia said. *But you go ahead* —

And with Martha gone, and her daughter, as she had told them, away at riding camp for the month, he stripped his clothes where he stood and dived into the pond. Nia watched while he swam swiftly across in a straight-arrow way and then lazily back, parting the small swells with a slow, sensuous breast stroke.

＊

After supper, which they had on the porch, Nia wanted a bath. Robert put big pots of water to heat on the range and stove, then began unwrapping the washtub. He caused as much noise as he could with the paper, but Nia indifferently kept putting away dishes. Then he held out the open tub to her, saying *Here . . .* But she still did not understand. Finally he tipped the tub towards her until she had to see the package inside. *That's for you.*

Oh, I love little presents — Nia laughed.

And when the tub, resting on newspapers in front of the stove, was ready for her, she poured in some of the salts, which instantly formed a buoyant film of shiny, effervescent bubbles. When she got in she found that with her legs drawn up she could sit comfortably. With the stove warming her and candles shedding a soft light, she sponged herself with a large bar of perfumed pink soap and her blue washcloth. Robert, on a chair between the tub and the bed, read to her from a book she had bought about using for food many of the woodland plants that grew wild around them. Nia had her hair pinned up, but some slipped down, and when Robert washed her back he had to tuck the strands up again. The water was silky and fragrant and slid smoothly over her. *Now I do feel like a queen* — she said.

You are! Joking and laughing with her, Robert had an instant of such rapture it seemed to him no one else could have ever experienced the like. For a moment he felt he and Nia were the only people in the world with this loving feeling.

*

After her bath, wrapped in a fresh robe, her feet in slippers, and quite warm from the heated water and the stove, Nia said *Let's sit on the porch* —

Robert lay down on the cot but she sat on the edge of it, staring out at the pond. On the far shore fireflies were glowing in the fading light, a frog croaked, fish were jumping and sending out rings. The small of her back was against his thigh. He took her arms and drew her down. And she came melting into him, her lips moistly on his mouth, her hair, released, caressing their cheeks, her whole body flowing into his. Happy, harking back to those first days when she had been awkward to his touch, he said playfully *You have changed...*

She sat up then, drawing herself apart from him, being, he felt, single, perhaps for the last time, and still looking out at the water, said *I guess when you belong to somebody, you belong completely.*

*

They made love that night in an unhurried, varied way, including even what had been ruined before. But this time done gently, tenderly, and imbued with sentiment. As Robert sank into sleep all his troublesome thoughts of the future were stilled. Snuggled against Nia's soft forms he was aware only of how gorgeous she was, and how much he loved the vital life in her.

30

They awoke to a golden glow coming from the sun-struck curtains. The loft was radiant, the room full of diffused sunshine. Shimmers of light darted up from the sparkling pond, across which low-flying swallows were swooping. Everything around was green and moist and gleaming from dew. Bare above the waist, Robert exulted in the breeze-stirred air. Doing push-ups on the grass, he breathed in the smell of the earth. With each lowering it grew richer, more pervasive, until it became intoxicating — and then, dropping flat, from sheer gladness he hugged the ground! When he rose he spread his arms to embrace it all, pond, cabin, Nia, all that the valley held, and murmured *Good-morning beauty...*

*

While he was having breakfast, Nia groaned.

He brought coffee to the bed. *As bad as usual?* he said.

Worse — she whispered.

The cup was still untouched when she got up, in her nightgown, and tottered to the toilet. When she came in, trying to brush her hair, but giving up after several strokes, Robert said *Is there anything I can do?*

There's nothing you can do — she replied, painfully kneeling, then sitting, then sliding into bed. *You're involved with an old woman* —

She was turned away and seemed to be sleeping when he picked up his papers and went out to the porch. There he sat in a chair and continued drawing his sketches, sometimes tipping the chair back until it touched the broad logs behind him. Determined to be done with this today, so as not to be distracted on the trip, he went on working without a break. Once, sometime late in the morning, he saw Nia come to the screen door with the binoculars, then he noticed that the bed sheets had been hung out to air, and later he was indistinctly aware of sounds of activity inside the cabin.

Nonetheless, when he finished he was surprised to find their whole household tidy and clean. Scattered clothing, utensils, the tub and pots of the bath, all had been put in their places. The floor had been swept, and, most unusual of all, the bed had been made.

I feel wonderful — ! Nia said. *My headache is gone and so is that thing in my chest. I've never felt so good in my life!*

You look great . . . Robert exclaimed. *You're . . . you're beautiful!*

And she was, with a glow like that of a young girl. He began to laugh, for though he had seldom thought of her as less than beautiful, she now had a freshness, a shining softness, that was astonishing. She was dressed in spotless white shorts and a white halter top, and her hair, brushed until it too shone, had been gathered back in a loose coil and tied with a black ribbon. Her mouth was bright with lipstick and her skin looked smooth and tan tinged.

Darling — the energy is coming back! I can feel it. I'm mad with hope again — !

She threw her arms around him, he pressed her to his breast. It did seem a miracle, this phoenix-like recovery; it evoked the magic of their early love. His heart, like hers, began to pound.

Oh, darling — we've made it! I have such a sense of freedom. Free — not only from pain — but from everything which is petty — which interferes — and I love you so very, very much!

Holding her, when her warm body, so lithe and alive, was one with his, when she seemed like a fount of bliss, and all he might ever want of a woman, Robert again felt, despite his former fears and fantasies, that this was as perfect as it could ever be.

*

At lunch they talked excitedly about the trip. Nia was now bubbling with ideas about pleasurable visits they could make and picnics they would have, and they promised each other to be packed and in bed by dark, so as to be well rested and ready for an early start.

When they got up from the table Robert said *What about a walk? Or . . . a boat ride?*

Oh — can we use the boat? That would be wonderful — !

While she got ready — having decided to oil her skin against the hot sun, Robert launched the boat and brought it to the dock. It smelled of paint, but not unpleasantly, and though the new board leaked a little, the water felt agreeably cool under his bare feet. He had stripped to khaki shorts and rolled up the pant legs until the pockets showed. Bareheaded, sitting on the bow, he wielded the paddle effortlessly, the way he had been taught as a boy at camp.

Darling — Nia laughed *you look like a boatman from the tunnel of love* —

She got in, bringing a drink, her cigarettes, an ashtray, polish for her fingernails, and the binoculars, all of which she settled around her on the broad stern seat. She too was barefoot, but she was wearing her wide sun hat, whose bright red ribbon matched both the colour of her lipstick and the polish she at once began to apply. These brilliant touches and the white shorts and halter vividly set off her lightly-tanned skin, now glistening softly from the oil. She looked stunning, Robert thought, and above all, blissful.

Now sit still, Robert said *and put the strap of the binoculars around your neck.*

Aye, aye, sir — But she went on painting on the polish, and the binoculars continued lying on the seat beside her.

Robert could not help being deeply pleased. As a youngster he had often paddled alone, wishing, imagining, he had a pretty girl with him, and his passenger was now much more than that. Yet he was no longer a *bumbling boy* unable to love, but a man who had loved and suffered, and was at last coolly able to assess the costs. And to manipulate them. But when he looked at Nia he found her so freshly alluring that everything in him stirred, and he was tempted to start a heady new affair with her. Frowning slightly, he went on stolidly plying the paddle, as much in a whirl as the water in the wake of his strokes.

They made a slow circuit of the other shore, edging into little bays and shallows that had been far from them before. Frogs jumped and small fish darted swiftly at their approach, but the water plants and long slim bulrush leaves bent to their touch. Then they entered the quiet soft bay where they had seen deer come down to drink, and indeed there were hoof marks on the moist leafy beach. Nia smiled. Robert sighed and relaxed, yielding to the lush sensuousness, gently drugged by soothing colours, pleasant scents, liquid sounds.

They moved on, stern first, into the narrowing inlet where the swift stream splashed out of the woods and entered the pond. The boat scraped bottom, and Robert rested the dripping paddle across his knees, and looked at the loveliness of Nia and of the overhanging forest. The sun was sending slanting shafts between the tall dark trees, and birds, brightly lit for a moment, were flitting by against the dappled dimness of the woods.

Nia had the binoculars to her eyes, and was turned away. She had taken off her hat, and it seemed to Robert that her hair was gathered at the back like it had been the first time he had seen her, all that long time ago. She said *I see a darling little one* and twisted round as she followed its flight across the stream. When she had completed the circuit she suddenly, with no sound, slid off the seat and fell backwards in the boat.

He thought she had lost her balance.

She lay there, legs drawn up a little, still holding the glasses, looking up at Robert with a startled, contorted expression. Her mouth was partly open; on the left side her upper teeth hung down slightly: he could see their tips below the lip. Her voice, when she spoke, was faint and surprised. *I was watching a little bird —*

Though distorted, it was like the lisp of a child, which she sometimes affected in fun.

Are you all right? Robert said, vaguely registering the question's triteness.

Nia touched her fingers to her right temple, as if a thought had just occurred to her.

Well, get up Robert said. *Come on, I'll lift you.* He tried to raise her to a sitting position, but she was slippery from the oil. Moreover, she seemed unwilling to help. The boat was rocking under them. *Put your arm around my shoulders . . . around my neck. Nia . . . around my neck.*

All right — But she was not doing it.

Robert took her left arm and put it over his neck. Then he caught her around the waist and lifted. Yet she made no effort and slid down again. *You're not holding on to me!* he cried.

I'm trying! Her speech was still distorted.

Robert seized her arm, put it over his neck again, and held on to its wrist with his left hand. Then he put his right arm around her and pulled her up. They wavered unsteadily, three legged — for Nia's left foot was suspended a little above the floor of the boat.

Stand on both feet.

I am —

No, you're only standing on one foot. Stand on both feet. Both feet!

They were swaying unsafely in the rocking boat. Robert was becoming alarmed. He let go of Nia's arm and tried to push her left leg to the floor. She fell against him and he staggered violently with her, attempting to stay upright, but her weight toppled him and both went down heavily on the gunwale. Wildly tipping, the boat took in a flood of water. Robert saw the binoculars slide into it. *Oh, damn!* he thought. Nia had, of course, failed to secure the strap.

Thrashing in the pitching water and clutching at Robert, she half rose with him. The boat rolled and they fell out into the stream.

Robert grabbed her hair to keep her face up. He was frightened now. Though the channel was only knee deep he knew she could drown in it. Abandoning gentleness, he pulled her up by force.

Nia began to cry. Large round tears slid down her oiled skin, mingling with the water running from her hair.

Stand on your feet! Robert shouted. *Both feet!* He wanted to walk her out.

I am — Nia sobbed. *I am* — *!*

But her left leg was hanging as before.

I'm sorry, I have to get you out of this! Taking her wrist with one hand he swung her across his bent back, encircled her legs with his other arm, lifted, and carried her sacklike up the bank. Bent double, dead weighted, he ran along the trail to the cabin. With each step his shoulder jogged sharply into Nia's midriff. *I'm sorry!* Robert gasped. *I've got to get you home!*

He flung open the screened kitchen door, turned into the inner room, and dropped her, as lightly as he could, onto the neat bed she had meticulously made up a few hours ago.

He took off her wet things and dried her quickly with a towel. Her right leg was now twitching in a jerky, uncontrollable way. *Falling . . . being under water . . .* he thought. *Two things she's normally afraid of . . . together they've probably brought on shock.*

She was shivering, and he got her under the covers, but the shivering continued and her right leg was still twitching, beating against the blankets. Robert tore off his wet shorts and got into bed with her, putting his warm body against her chilled one. He kissed her and stroked her breasts and belly, and wrapped his legs around hers, to stop that unruly limb. But the impulse went on, though the leg was unable to move. He half believed, half hoped, passion would cure her. *Does anything hurt?* he said.

Here — she said, tapping her temple with her fingertips.

I think you'll be better soon, once you're warm. With those words came a cold creeping fear, but he held it back. Soon it seemed to him Nia was growing calmer; he thought he could even detect a slowing of her rapidly-beating heart.

I want to go to the bathroom — she said.

Robert noted wryly that she was not too shocked to recall her usual euphemism for the chemical toilet.

The bathroom — she said irritably. *I have to go to the bathroom* — *!*

With some pulling and pushing, Robert succeeded in getting her into a nightgown. Then he quickly dressed in a dry shirt and trousers and put on the kettle for tea. *Now*, he said *d'you think you can get up?*

Yes — Nia said, still in that lisping, distorted way *if you'll help me* —

All right. Let's try.

Her left arm, however, did not respond to what she thought she was doing with it. It hung limply at her side. And again she was standing on only her right foot. Without his support she would fall. *Nia, you can't go to the bathroom.*

I can! she cried, becoming angry. *If you'll help me. You're not helping me!*

You can't, Nia. You can't walk.

And the fear he had been resisting suddenly raced through him. With sickening certainty he realized her left side was paralyzed. *Yet it's just shock!* he thought. But his attention was drawn to the bed: Nia had urinated under her nightgown.

There, he said, unable to suppress disgust *you've gone to the bathroom.*

She seemed not to know it. But when he had helped her onto the dry side of the bed, and had covered her, she drew herself together and began a tearless whimpering, a broken, almost inaudible keening, while her right leg went on spasmodically twitching.

Desperate to hold on to some order, Robert set about changing the bed sheet. To move Nia onto the clean one he had to roll, then pull, her over.

Stop the boat — she said.

Nia, he said gently *you're not in the boat.*

Oh, stop the boat — *please* —

He lay down and bundled her into his arms. *Nia, dear, you're in the cabin . . .* She had closed her eyes. *Nia, you're all right now. You're in bed, in the cabin.*

In the boat — she said, whimpering in that strange voice. *I hit my head on the boat. My head hurts* — *the boat* —

He held her, becoming impatient, wanting to shake her. *Nia, open your eyes. Look, look up. What do you see?*

Logs — boards —

That's right, the ceiling, the roof of the cabin. Now you know you're in bed in the cabin, don't you? Now, where are you?

In bed — she said, her eyes closing. *On the ceiling — in the cabin — in the boat — the boat —*

Terrified, Robert got up. *I must get a doctor!* he thought, moving abruptly to the door.

No — don't leave me! Nia called.

And agitated as he was, Robert remembered, or felt, he had once promised, in word or thought, never to do that.

Listen, he said *I'm just going to Carey's, to phone. I'll only be a minute. I'll be right back.*

No — don't leave me! Oh, please don't leave me!

He paused in the doorway, panicked and torn. *Nia, I want a doctor to come and see you. I'll just phone for a doctor . . .* And with that he swiftly crossed the kitchen and opened the screen door.

At the clack of the door catch Nia began to shriek.

Robert could not bear it; after a few steps he halted. He felt he would sooner spill his own blood than hear those heart-rending shrieks — and worse, some of them were ominously muffled.

I'm here! he shouted. *I won't go any farther.* Then he turned towards the log house and screamed, over and over, *Steve! Steve. . . ! Steve!*

After a moment Carey stepped out.

Come here, please, quickly! Robert yelled. Steve started to run.

Robert rushed back to the bed. The chaos was dreadful. Nia, in her terror, trying to scramble up, had thrown off the covers, and now, soaked in tears and sweat, her hair horribly dishevelled, panting, face flushed, she lay tangled in the sheets, the fresh one twisted together with the — soiled, for she had wet herself again.

He had barely time to lift a blanket before Steve burst in. Robert was ashamed to have Nia — his beautiful Nia — seen like that.

The tall man stood by the door, his face drawn. Robert explained that Nia had hurt her head when she fell. But Steve was not listening. He was thinking that his treacherous God, in whom he had never really believed, might have heard him all too well.

I'm sorry . . . he said.

Robert thought he was apologizing for seeing her in that state, and took it as just tribute to the splendid woman she was.

31

Instead of coming, the doctor Steve called sent an ambulance. Robert was holding a glass of scotch to Nia's lips when it came around the corner of the log house: a shiny white van that looked much too large for the narrow trail. But the driver's assistant got out, and with the help of his signals, and repeated calls of *Watch it, watch it!* the vehicle was safely brought ahead, turned, and backed up to the cabin door.

Robert had tidied the bed, wiped Nia's face with the blue wash-cloth, combed her hair. He had imagined, while Steve was phoning, that a physician would arrive bag in hand, would carefully examine the patient, would perhaps have a cup of tea — he had kept the kettle on simmer — and would finally give Nia a sedative from whose lulling effect she would wake cured of her phobia and her pain. He even hoped that by late morning they would still be able to start on the trip.

Word that an ambulance was coming had changed that. Now he expected Nia might be kept overnight in the district hospital, that he would stay nearby in the old hotel — he had glanced into the lobby through the glassed front door the day of the long scarf, and recalled the antimacassars and polished spittoons — and from there he would go to see her, carrying flowers and magazines, and would sit at the side of Nia's bed, and, smiling, listen to her complain about being confined. Their schedule for the trip included a contingency of about a day and a half; at worst they would be consuming it at the start.

And quelling his anxiety, he had packed Nia's overnight case. Pleased to have charge of her things, he had chosen fragrant panties and a bra —they had lain next to her perfume —nylon stockings, shoes with medium heels, and a sensible blouse, sweater, and skirt. And in her handbag, which he also placed in the case, he put her comb, brush and toothbrush, cigarettes and matches, and the little black, red capped, bottle of Joy. Then he had taken a new pajama top — white, with cheerful tomato-red stripes — from a pair Nia had brought for the trip, and had put it on her, over her nightgown. And finally, before giving her the sip of scotch, he had shoved his oilskin pouch of shaving things into the pocket of his jacket.

Ignoring his account of what happened, the ambulance men immediately lifted Nia onto a stretcher, covered her with a heavy red blanket, and buckled two wide straps across her. They would have driven off without him, if Robert had not shouted *I'm going too!* He was afraid they were ill disposed, but when he climbed into the van with Nia's case he found that a stool had been freed from its fastenings and placed beside the raised stretcher.

They drove swiftly up through the shaded forest and then down the snaking sandy road, where the low western sun was sending fingers of light through the grass and making the sumacs glow crimson. *This road,* Robert thought, *has never looked so incredibly lovely,* and as he put his arms around Nia his mind suddenly mutinied and he wondered when they would travel it again. Then thoughts of all but the immediate crisis retreated. He stroked her hair and kissed her closed lids and soft lips, which smelled of whiskey from the drink he had given her in the cabin.

She stirred, and speaking in that thick distorted whisper, said *I'm thirsty — my throat is so dry —*

We're going to the hospital Robert answered. *We'll get you a drink soon.*

Give me some scotch, please —

I haven't any here.

It's right there — on the table. Why won't you give me a drink? My throat is so dry — I want a drink — !

The assistant turned around. *How is she, sir?*

Just hurry Robert said, feeling afraid again.

The road became wider; their speed increased. Poles, houses, fields streaked by. Loose gravel clattered against the mudguards; the siren broke into a wail whenever another vehicle appeared. The two drivers crouched forward, intent on their task. Robert bent over Nia, thinking *Hurry . . . Oh, hurry!* He felt all would yet be well, if only they could get to the hospital. . .

*

There he was told to go at once to the Administration Desk and have a form filled out. The admitting officer was alone, and amiable; she smiled slightly as she typed in each answer. But she kept turning away to take phone calls, and then to speak to a messenger, and even to gossip with a passing nursing aid about their plans for the evening. Robert endured it all; he was so glad Nia had been got there in time. At last he was allowed to sign.

He rushed to the Treatment Room — a young doctor was just leaving, while two white-clad nurses were drawing a sheet over Nia. *Is she all right?* he cried.

The older nurse, solid, erect, grey, stared at him with displeasure. Then she took a thick black fountain pen from behind her bib and began to write on a large chart. *I suppose you can give me some information* she said sourly. *Her religion?*

None.

Catholic or Protestant? she snapped, and made an obvious effort to control the angry shaking of her chin.

Robert looked at the wide black band across her starched cap, the sturdy shoulders, the small medal of some sort pinned to her uniform and thought *The hospital rests on her. Patients are an assault on the system.* Aloud, he muttered *Uh . . . Protestant.*

Married?

Divorced . . . He felt that Nia was being taken from him, that the hospital was intervening.

Dentures?

He did not understand.

False teeth!

He thought the question preposterous, but before he could answer Nia suddenly murmured *Yes — a bridge.*

They all looked at her. She lay as before: skin pale, eyes shut. The teeth attached to the bridge still hung a little below the upper lip.

A door opened — the younger nurse stepped back. An old man in a white coat approached. He was slow, short, a bit bent, and his face, wrinkled like a soft ball of crumpled linen, was over-shadowed by a large pockmarked nose. This was the Chief of Staff, whom Steve had called. In earlier years he had sometimes paused between patients to sit for an hour by Carey's pond.

With his thumb the old fellow gently lifted one of Nia's eyelids, then the other, and let each close again. *Does it hurt anywhere?* he said.

My head — Nia said. *I hit it on the boat —*

It hurts here, does it? he said, touching her right temple.

I didn't see her hit it . . . Robert began, but the doctor silenced him by holding up a finger. Then he ordered a small dose of decongestant and took Robert into the next room.

Well, it's brain damage of some sort.

Brain damage! *W-what will that involve?* Robert stammered.

The physician lowered his white head. *If the paralysis was caused by the fall it may be possible to remove the block by an operation. If it caused the fall, then I don't know* . . . *It depends on how extensive the damage is. She needs a specialist. She'll have to go to Toronto as soon as possible. The best man I know is Purcell at the Line.*

Robert heard *the Line* with horror — it was a hulking, soot-blackened building surrounded by dilapidated houses and shabby stores. The grassy Township Line it had been named for had long been overrun by the suffocating sprawl of the city. *I want her to have the best of everything!* he exclaimed.

The doctor nodded. *Purcell is the best. I'll try to get him on the phone, shall I?*

*

The ambulance men were waiting when Robert returned to Nia. *You!* the older nurse said to him. *Are you responsible for her? There's a bill to pay.*

Across from the cashier's window hung a public telephone. Robert got some coins and gave Betty's number.

Oh, Lord! she blurted.

Don't tell her mother or anyone yet, Robert said *until we know how bad it is. I'll call you from the Line.*

How are you?

The question disconcerted him. *Oh, okay* he said, and sensed Betty's basic toughness. Derived from peasant forebears and her harsh upbringing on a prairie farm, it sometimes escaped her surface appeal. And it tended to put off suitors.

*

We won't have an escort, the ambulance driver told Robert *but I've got clearance for number ten.*

Robert had no idea of what that meant but he got in and the ambulance swung into the street. Immediately the siren started. They sped into the main street, past the glass-walled booth Nia had phoned from, around torpid traffic, and out onto Highway 10, going south. Then they opened the throttle, their speed climbing from seventy to eighty, ninety, and beyond, with the siren screaming above the piercing whistle of the air stream. There were a lot of cars on the road, and though the siren wailed continuously, most were sullenly slow moving aside. Time and again when the driver had to brake, Robert thought they were about to crash, but at just the last minute the car ahead would start to pull over and the ambulance would swerve around it and go on. Robert became morbidly fascinated by this battle of wills, but at the same time anxious, because of Nia, to avoid an accident. That the drivers and he might also be hurt did not enter his head.

Nia said *Darling* — ?

Yes, yes, I'm here he said, surprised that they had not sedated her.

Darling — *hold me. My throat is dry* — *so dry* —

She was strapped only across her legs and waist. He took her in his arms and kissed her, while cursing himself for not bringing water. To the others he said *You haven't anything to drink, have you?*

No, sir, I'm sorry the assistant said, without looking around. Both men, concentrating on their driving, were silent, except to *damn*, quietly, each of the cars refusing to clear the road.

All at once it became rough. Nia was shaken on the stretcher.

Oh — *hold me!* she cried.

Yes, love, yes Robert whispered. He held her tighter and put his face against hers.

Oh, dry — she moaned.

Robert filled his mouth with saliva, and kissing her, let the moisture run down between her lips. She swallowed. He did it repeatedly.

Now they were both being thrown about. Robert looked ahead and saw that the road had been torn up; new lanes were being carved out. Bulldozers had pushed topsoil into huge mounds on both sides, some jutting far into what was left of the asphalt. The ambulance began to dart among them, braking, skidding, then sharply turning and careening on. The siren screamed and throbbed, while a lone watchman lazily moved out of the way. Farther on, immense earthmovers appeared to be blocking the road. *We'll hit them for sure!* Robert thought, but the mass of machinery had been parked with enough of an opening for the van to plunge through. It went on, bucking through rubble and mud, the siren screeching, the motor roaring, and Robert holding tightly to Nia.

She was quiet now, with her eyes shut, but her right leg had begun kicking against the blanket again. Robert kissed her passionately, and fed her more spit. He no longer cared how that might look to the drivers.

Suddenly the van lurched out of the broken section and zoomed ahead on smooth pavement, its speed mounting higher and higher until it was on a swift, straight, steady course.

Thank God! Robert thought. *The worst is over. We'll be at the hospital soon.*

Just then there was a grating noise at the front end. A metallic clapping began. The ambulance lost momentum, moved off the road, and ground to a halt. *Sounds like . . .* the driver said. The two men got out and burrowed under the hood. One of them said *Yeah . . . a valve.*

A valve, what d'you mean, a valve? Robert thought. *Get this thing going!*

I'm afraid we've burned out a valve, sir the driver said. *We'll have to call for another ambulance.*

Robert stared at him; it seemed unreal. *Well, do it!* he said at last. *Do it as fast as you can!*

With a clatter like lances beating on cans the vehicle was backed along the gravel shoulder and into a farm laneway, beside a fragrant, partly-mown field of hay. From beyond the house, where cattle were milling in the barnyard, came a strong stench of manure. The air was moist, twilit, hot from the fiery disk sinking behind the horizon; while the blank sky above was beginning to flame. Robert stayed with Nia. There was a roaring tumult in his head. The swish of passing cars, the mooing of cattle, the buzzing of the flies invading the van seemed a thousand times amplified. *This will pass . . .* he muttered, as if all would come right if only he could endure.

The men returned; another ambulance was coming from a village *just twenty miles* off. They were followed by the farmer, whom curiosity had drawn from his tractor. He wiped his perspiring face and peered in at the odd sight of a tousled man stubbornly stroking an inert body. All at once he was startled — Robert had asked him for a drink of water.

Please, sir . . . Robert said, for the Samaritan had not budged. *She's very thirsty. Please . . . please . . .* But when the water came it all ran out of Nia's mouth, wetting the pajama collar.

Now the driver came over with a clipboard. *It's twelve dollars, sir* he said to Robert. *Seven into town and five service fee. We won't charge for this part of the trip.*

Anything was becoming believable! In an inside pocket Robert had traveller's cheques, but he took out his wallet: it held thirteen dollars. The driver handed back a signed receipt. Robert remembered to thank them both, realizing, through the confusion of his thoughts, that it was not their fault, no one could have done more.

*

The relieving ambulance arrived; it was a converted station wagon. To Robert's horror there was talk about changing blankets. *We're not supposed to . . .* the first driver said. But then, gazing at Nia, he relented. *Oh . . . Okay, we'll get our stuff later.* They managed to fit the stretcher into the smaller vehicle only by forcing it up against the front seat. The rising dust when it started was turned blood red by the nearly-set sun.

The new assistant leisurely looked back. Nia appeared to be unconscious, except for the occasional, strange twitching of her leg. Over the ear-splitting siren he said, idly *How is she?*

Just keep moving! Robert replied. Nia seemed completely gone from him, beyond his reach, and for the first time he felt she might die, right there in the ambulance. Tortured thoughts assailed him. *True, I wanted to be free of her, but not like this! No, no, God, I didn't want it to end like this! God, please . . .* However, he held on, fighting for control.

32

At the Line, Nia was immediately placed on a gurney and wheeled into the last of a series of grey painted, closed stalls. Robert followed, but was told to keep out, and he sat down on a wooden bench facing the cubicle's door. Nurses passed him to enter and leave, then a resident doctor came; then they all went away. The bench could have been empty for all the notice they took of him. When the corridor was clear he got up and looked into the stall. Nia was lying to the side of it, face up, her eyes shut, limbs composed. Even the rebellious leg was still. *My sweet love...* Robert whispered, and it seemed to him, to his delight, that her lips trembled in response. He heard footsteps approaching and quickly resumed his seat.

A fair haired, fine-featured man in a navy blue suit was coming along the row, opening each closed door, glancing in, and going on to the next. His nonchalance, the elegant cut of his clothes, the almost feminine grace with which he moved set him apart from the bustling staff, yet he was checking the rooms as if it was his right. *An administrator . . .* Robert thought. *Busybody! What's he doing here, so late?*

But then a nurse, hurrying after the man, said *No, doctor, in here . . .* and took him to Nia.

That can't be Purcell! Robert thought, and knew at once that it was.

The examination took ten minutes... fifteen... twenty. Pacing restlessly, Robert caught sight of his own reflection in the glass of a fire-hose cabinet. How unkempt he looked! Above the rumpled shirt his head and neck glistened darkly from sweat and oil — oil that had rubbed off Nia, and his unshaven face, streaked with dirt, was deeply lined by tension. His hair was wild. He had packed a comb for Nia, but in the rush had forgotten his own.

Purcell came out. *You're not the husband . . .* he said politely.

No Robert replied. *But I brought her in. She's with me.* And, armed now, he added *I'm responsible for her.*

The doctor nodded. *Well, it's a bad stroke, but we can't tell yet how serious the damage may be. I think she'll rest quietly for the night, and then we'll do tests and X-rays in the morning.*

Robert saw that Purcell's hair was more grey than blond, and that the suit he was wearing was new, or in any case little used. He understood then that the doctor had come in specially from some social evening, and he felt an unspoken kindness emanating from him. Grateful for it, Robert began to see him in an altogether different way. He watched the gesturing of his firm, freckled hands, and suspected that the doctor's casual manner, in which there had seemed something effeminate, came from being sure of what he was doing, and that it deliberately covered a shy, perhaps embarrassing, gentleness.

Can you tell me . . . Robert said *what the chances are?*

Well, Purcell said *she's very young for this kind of thing. Just judging by appearances, I think there's a good possibility of recovery. We'll know better tomorrow.* And turning to go, he said *You can come back to see her whenever you like.*

Robert looked in at Nia again. The nurse with her smiled encouragingly. *They gave her something to make her sleep* she said. *We'll be taking her up to a ward soon.*

I brought a small case of her things.

Yes, we have it.

All at once Robert felt useless; he could think of nothing more to do. Yet he was certain that now all would be well.

*

Betty was waiting for him at the entrance. He had forgotten! But she dismissed that. *Come to my place* she said.

And only then did he realize how solitary it would have felt to have gone alone to the apartment.

*

They sat up most of the night, discussing Nia's future. Betty considered what Nia's friends could do — *Those famous friends!* Robert thought — but it seemed this one was busy, the other away, that unable . . . none could be of real help. No, Robert alone . . . *Good!* It was the verdict he wanted.

After three o'clock Betty made up a bed for him on the living room sofa, then kissed him good-night. The touch of her lips was cool; he had been unaware of how feverish he was. Until dawn he lay awake struggling with the sensations of the day; even when he dozed fitfully he went on hearing the searing wail of the siren.

33

Soft sunlight was brightening the sky as he quietly let himself out. The fine summer morning made him feel that the world was peaceful, tolerant, surely good. At the apartment he enjoyed his shave and shower; then he dressed in a crisp white shirt, a jaunty tie, his clean seersucker suit. It was a recent purchase, and he had debated about packing it for Vancouver; now he was pleased he had left it behind. As for his appointment there, he decided to wait. If Nia rallied enough for him to be away overnight he might still fly out in time. But he had to speak to Hugh. He phoned and asked to see him later at the office. Hugh wanted to know why, and Robert told him what had happened.

Oh, boy! the builder said as he reentered his bedroom. He remembered his father, and was disturbed by this early return of darkness. Sally drew him down beside her on the bed and delicately asked for details. Her breath was sweet; she kept a freshener in the bedside drawer and used it on waking whenever Hugh was still home. He explained, adding with a sigh that Robert would probably want some sort of support.

Don't give him any! she said. *And don't you dare give him any money. This is the best thing she could have done for him! Otherwise, God knows how long he would have been tied to that old screw.*

You don't know her . . . Hugh said defensively. *You didn't even meet her.*

I know what she was doing to him. And if you have any regard for him, and for his future, you just let him cut loose. Sally had heard about the call from L.A. She had already pictured Robert in Hollywood and intended to talk Hugh into taking her there. *Remember,* she added for emphasis *not a . . . nickel!*

Hugh sighed again. He was not naturally cruel, but on the other hand he had never learnt to like charity, and he suspected that Sally was probably right.

*

At the hospital Information Desk the ample receptionist sniffed through her hoop of cards, found Nia's, and trembled with power. *No visitors! Are you a relative?*

Robert meant to be amiable; with the hospital he wanted only harmonious relations. He tried to smile, and said *I'm her common-law husband.*

Oh . . . The pudgy face stiffened. *Well, third floor south.*

The ward was a long open room with beds on both sides of a centre aisle. Near the end of it, a square space had been screened off by green curtains, and there, at a small table, sat a nurse.

Have you come to see Mrs. Wilson? she said. *Are you Robert? She's been calling for you. We have her in here.*

He parted the curtains. The light inside was dim green, as if the enclosure were under water. Nia was lying in a bed to which barred sides had been added, like those on a child's crib, and her right leg, which lay exposed — *Because I have good legs!* — he remembered, showed ugly bruises where she had been beating it against the bars. But on the near side they had been lowered. Over them a thin little nurse was trying to feed her orange juice through a bent tube.

Nia seemed insensible, but the nurse said *She's taken a little.*

Can't you put some padding on those bars? Robert said.

The nurse looked at him in surprise, but went out and came back with a blanket.

When Robert and Nia were alone again he said softly *Hi . . . can you hear me?* Her head straightened and she opened her eyes. They were an intense blue with very enlarged pupils, not quite black. *She can't focus* he thought, and aloud, said *Do you know who it is?*

Yes, darling — She groped towards him with her right hand. He gave her his and she held it. They stayed that way. Then she whispered *Darling* —

Yes. . . ?

But she did not answer. He hoped she was thinking about their life ahead, as he was. *Nia,* he said *I have to go away, to look after things . . .* Yesterday she had cried out *Don't leave me!* and he was uneasy about doing it now. This time, however, it really couldn't be helped. *I'll be back soon . . .*

She gave no sign. She seemed to have fallen asleep.

*

I guess she's slipped back into a coma Purcell said. *She's been in one most of the time. But she seems no worse than last night.* He was now wearing a white coat; Robert had caught up with him in the hall, near the X-ray Department.

I'd like to tell you about yesterday morning Robert said. *The change in her was amazing! She felt so good . . .*

That's always the way. The doctor shook his head with a sad smile. Robert couldn't tell whether this was whimsy or a medical statement, until Purcell added *They always seem to have a kind of euphoria, just before it happens.*

The *they* sank into Robert like a stone, ominous and oppressing. Yet he was certain Nia's case would prove special, even easy to cure, once all its details were known. And he told Purcell about her headaches, her drinking and smoking — the fall in the boat.

Oh, the fall . . . the specialist said. *I don't think there's any question that her condition caused the fall. There's nothing to indicate an outside injury.*

That means . . . Robert said, filling with fear.

Listen, Purcell said *I know how anxious you are. But I can't tell you anything for sure until I've seen X rays. We're going to take them now.* And as they stood there Nia was wheeled past.

Robert scarcely recognized her: a supine form, covered to the chin, eyes closed, skin pale, hair disordered — like some impersonal thing mechanically moving through a machine. *Do you think there's hope?* he cried.

Look, Purcell said sharply *she's had a serious stroke. The only thing in her favour is her age. A person that young generally has a good chance.*

Then, doctor, how long . . . *before she's fully recovered?*

Oh, it varies. But not less than six weeks, I should think.

*

Purcell's confidence restored his own, and Robert left the hospital cured of doubt. Indeed, he was delighted, as he made his way to meet Betty, that all deceit and connivance were about to end. Finally, forced by circumstance, how straightforward it all was!

His plans for directing the feature, for discarding Nia, had been pushed to the back of his mind. It was the immediate emergency that mattered. His love for her had returned with force. Though he couldn't be sure, if he had tried to analyze it, what part was love of her and what was propelled by an image of himself acting decisively in a crisis.

34

Betty had phoned to say they were coming; Wilma opened the door. *Something's wrong with Nia!* she said.

Yes, dear, Betty said. *She's in the hospital, but she's going to be all right.*

When they were seated, the old woman said *I'm not surprised. I knew it would happen, the way she lived. And mark my words, Francis Findlay will be next!*

Stupefied by this outburst, Robert sat silent while Betty and Wilma went on talking about how *it* had happened. Only when he noticed that Joel had come in from the garden, and was about to listen, did he get up and ask the boy to go out again, saying he would join him soon. Then he turned to Wilma.

Mrs. Peterson, he said *Nia was there with me. For the past two years, every time your daughter has been away from home, she's been with me.* That wasn't absolutely true, but he thought in essence it was. However he felt he was being too stiff, and tried to unbend. *We're in love... Very much in love.*

A small smile moved across the older woman's mouth. *Nia's been in love many times ...* she said.

Robert thought *I mustn't dislike her ... I mustn't, or none of this will work. Well,* he said aloud *I'm sorry you have to learn about it this way. The only reason we didn't tell you sooner was that Nia wanted to work out everything first, so as not to worry you.* It seemed such a reasonable excuse that he began to believe it. *Now I'm going to look after everything.* And he broached his plan of giving up the apartment and moving in with them.

Well, we've lots of room ... Wilma said. *But ...* She seemed to ponder, and her grimace deepened. Robert cringed, expecting another moral judgment.

Willie, dear, Betty said *Nia will need all kinds of special attention. You really won't be able to look after her, and Joel, and the house ...*

Oh, certainly not! Wilma said. *It's just that . . . I . . .* She burst out *I broil all my meats! Joel eats them that way too. I don't like . . . I can't . . . But you . . .*

Oh, no! Robert cried. *I don't want anything different! I'll be happy with whatever you have!*

Well . . . After a moment she smiled, and then giggled. *I guess we'd get along!*

Oh, God, Robert thought *if not for this childish, narcissistic creature . . .* But he knew that Nia's and his involvement had never been quite that simple, and, laughing too, he excused himself and went out to Joel.

*

The boy was holding a galvanized watering can from which he was sprinkling the flowers. Robert quietly, in the plainest terms, told him everything. *But they expect her to recover,* he said *and when she comes home she's going to have to be looked after . . . and, you know, your mother convalescing won't be any sweet-tempered patient. We'll all have to try very hard.*

Joel had started to cry but now he bravely laughed through his tears. *It's the smoking!* he said. *I told her she was smoking too much. If I ever see another cigarette in her hand I'm going to knock it right out!*

Good! And Robert felt the beginning of a bond between them.

When they went in the telephone was ringing: it was Martha! She was still in the city. Steve had given her Nia's number and she wanted to know what she could do. Robert thought of his car, which had been left at the cabin. He would need it for trips to the hospital, shopping, moving . . . Martha at once agreed to drive him, and Joel, who was appealing to be taken too. She would pick them up later, after lunch.

Betty stayed to make it. Wilma laid out her pink linen napkins; Joel brought in fresh flowers. They all became unaccountably merry.

*

Robert had to leave before the meal was finished. He hurried downtown and found Hugh eating a sandwich at his eight-foot desk.

I'll need twenty thousand Robert said. *Or maybe more, if I have to hire a home nurse.* He had mentally made a rough budget, as if it were a film. *Maybe twenty-five, at the outside.*

Hugh stared at his marble pen stand. It had been given him by an engineering firm. All the oddments in his office, even the carved ebony heads, had been gifts from companies eager to supply services to him. They were a crude, inconsistent assortment, but Hugh didn't care; the office, he felt, was only a tool for raking in cash. *I don't know* . . . he said.

Why? When we were younger, and one of us was in need, did we ever worry about whose money it was? Money means nothing if it can't be used to help a friend. And I'll pay you back, Robert said fervently *even if it takes a lifetime. But it won't* he added, forcing a laugh.

Oh, I could give you the money Hugh said. *But I don't think I should. You're losing all sense of proportion. What about your meeting in Vancouver?*

I don't know if I can make it.

You have to. How's it going to look to them, when they're thinking of trusting you with a major movie, if you go to pieces over a woman? Who isn't even your responsibility.

Of course she's my responsibility! Whose is she, if not mine?

Nobody's. It's just one of those things. Hugh finished chewing, then swallowed. He took a sip of his iced tea and assumed an even more philosophical tone. *Nobody* he said *is ultimately responsible for anyone else.*

Robert stared at him. Where was his kind friend?

*

Martha came by in an old but immaculate Cadillac. *Oh, I borrowed it!* she said. *Mine's still with the mechanics.*

Robert waited until they were close to *Singing Vale* — her pet name for the property, and then hoping that Joel, who was in the back seat, wouldn't overhear, quietly asked her to lend him some money. She put it off until they were at the log house. There they had a few minutes alone, while Joel and Steve went ahead to the pond. Martha picked up the ginger cat and nervously cradled it.

If I had known earlier . . . she said. *I was at my broker's this morning. Now . . .* Like most wealthy people, Martha had *no money* — all of it was invested. She lived from the monthly interest. Besides, another difficulty was swelling her breast, unsettling the cat, which leapt from her arms. *And anyway,* she exclaimed *I'm too fond of you to get so close!*

In another moment, if Steve and Joel had not been coming back, she might have confessed the thoughts Robert figured in. This was the result of the appraising glances he had cast at her. From those casual cues had come this ill-fated tangle.

Joel asked Robert if he could take out the boat. It was drawn up on the shore in its original place, to which Steve had discreetly returned it. And in the cabin Robert found the bed made, the binoculars hanging to dry, and on the table Nia's glass, ashtray, and nail polish. Watching her son paddling on the tranquil pond, he was confused by painful memories.

*

It's the most perfect place I've ever been! Joel said. They were having supper on the porch; the boy was sitting where Nia had sat two nights before. Robert smiled happily. This really was like a dream . . . his dream of reconciling all incongruities.

For their main dish he had sautéed two thick patties of chopped steak, but in haste — he had been packing the perishable food — he had seasoned the meat with only salt and pepper. Joel took a mouthful, then slowly stopped chewing. *No garlic . . .* he said. And added, with his winsome smile *A bit flat, isn't it?* How like Nia he was! Robert loved him with an intensity he had to hide.

*

In the hospital the ceiling lights were not yet on. Here and there bed lamps brightened the waning dimness of the ward. Outside the curtained enclosure, at the small table, the duty nurse, a different one, finally exasperated by the patient's futile cries, put down her pen. *I've told you ten times,* she said, looking in. *He's not here. He left hours ago. Now try to sleep...*

But Nia, ignoring her, rasped out again *Robert — Robert —*

Oh my God the nurse sighed. *He's not here... Not in the boat, not in the ... what is it? The ceiling? No, he's gone.* She railed under her breath, her voice rising *You can hear me, can't you? He's gone... Gone!*

The cries faltered, then stopped. *Gone —!* The thin thread that had held them faltered, and broke. The green watery space Nia stared at unseeingly gradually descended to a darkness into which she went silently screaming.

35

Driving home, Joel and Robert talked gaily about all the things they would do together. When they arrived there was a taxi waiting outside the house. Coming down the steps were Betty, Wilma, and — Francis Findlay! Betty had phoned him that morning and he had immediately flown from New York.

There's been a call from the hospital Betty said. *We're to go right down.*

Robert, you'll stay with Joel, won't you? Wilma said sociably. *Francis is taking us.*

No! Robert cried, startled by her lack of understanding. *Francis, you stay!* he commanded, and pushed the women into his own car.

⋆

309

The green curtains had been flung aside and Nia's bed pulled into the aisle, where piercing emergency lamps were spotlighted on it. A cluster of white-clothed doctors and nurses were bending over her, their movements frantic, their polished instruments blinding in the cold brilliance. At her side, where it was making a steady pumping sound, stood a large shiny tank containing a big bellows; from it a thick black hose snaked to a moulded mask that was being held over her nostrils. *Oh, the poor thing!* Wilma said. She and Betty had stopped halfway down the aisle. Robert advanced to the bed — it seemed to him that Nia was being dissected alive.

From the huddle over her a doctor's head shot up. *Wait outside, will you!* he shouted. He was still young, but he had a squarish dark moustache that was meant to make him look masterful, and did.

Later he opened the door of the little room to which they had been shown, where the three of them were sitting. *My name is Coutts* he announced in a clipped English voice. *Are you her relatives?*

Wilma adjusted her pince-nez. *I am her mother.*

Well, she had another stroke just before we called you. We don't know what caused it. Her condition is very critical now.

He left. They sat on, silent, not looking at one another, oppressed by the mindless perplexity of a misfortune too great to comprehend.

Suddenly the door opened again; they looked up: it was Gwendolyn!

I phoned and phoned, but your line kept ringing busy she said to Wilma. *Finally, Mr. Findlay . . . Oh, how is she?* Sobs shook her; she shielded her eyes with her hand. *And I wanted to know if I could reach her on the tour!*

Betty and Gwendolyn had not met; Wilma introduced them. Then she said *Dear, why were you calling Nia?*

Oh, it doesn't matter . . . My husband wants me to go back to him.

Wilma, who had not heard the details of Gwen's separation, looked at her with the greatest interest, but the young woman was evidently distraught.

Is she very bad? Then she gasped, with emphasis *My God, what a thing to happen!*

It was a phrase Nia had often used: Gwendolyn was understudying her idol. Indeed, she kept trying to intercept Robert's gaze, to convey to him her sympathy and love. But he sat apart, staring morosely at the hard tiled floor. Gradually she too became subdued. Time went by, and the three women, sitting together on a section of the folding wooden seats that were the only furniture, began to look like three large birds drooping wearily on their perches. Occasionally Wilma emitted a long, drawn out sigh.

Willie, Betty said *I don't think it's doing you any good just to sit here. I think we should go.*

Well... the old woman said, pleased to be once more the centre of attention *if I could do anything... But I guess we can only wait.*

We might as well wait at home. It's getting late and Joel has to go to bed. Betty stood up and said to Robert *Will you drive us?*

No he replied, giving her his car keys. *I'll stay here. And Gwen, why don't you go with them? There's nothing...*

Oh, no! the girl exclaimed. *She sat up with me when my mother di... I had the flu... I couldn't go to her. Nia stayed all night. No, no... it's the least I can do.*

Betty's slight shrug demolished this snivelling sentimentality. She took Wilma's elbow and turned to look at Robert; their eyes met. He felt how dependable she was. Yet behind it he sensed a dawning triumph, a patiently-awaited victory over the despot who had so long dominated her. And he wondered, morbidly, to what extent he felt that too.

They left, and then he abruptly remembered he had forgotten to tell Betty to take the food from the car. *Oh, let it spoil!* he thought despondently, though it went on troubling him, as did the degree of his distraction. He had simply assumed that the brisk, efficient Betty could drive.

Gwendolyn's excited words had brought on fresh tears. They were becoming to her, making her eyes glisten hugely in the heated face. A few were falling on her dress, causing dark stains above the milk-swollen breasts. Robert had to stifle an impulse to wipe them away. Ashamed, he muttered *I'm going to see what's happening,* and went out.

He had not far to go. Nia had been moved into the next room, to which the door was open.

She was lying on a stretcher table, covered to her bare shoulders with a white sheet. The big shiny tank with the black bellows was beside her, the thick hose leading to a nozzle that had been thrust between her lips and held there by crossed strips of white tape. Hanging upside down on a hooked pole extending up from the table was a bottle of clear liquid, and from it a thin red tube fed into Nia's left arm, which lay outside the sheet. Around the upper part of the arm was wound the broad black band of a blood-pressure gauge, and a nurse, all in white, was taking a reading. Dr. Coutts was there too, watching. Robert waited outside the door.

*

When the doctor came out he walked with him down the hall. *As you can see,* Coutts said *we have her under artificial respiration.*

Has Dr. Purcell seen her?

Yes, he was in earlier, and we can call if we need him. Coutts pressed the elevator button. The doors opened. As he stepped in he said *But we don't expect her to last very long.*

Robert felt that brusqueness was because of some personal problem of the doctor's, some insecurity he was covering up. He was not to be taken literally. Nia wasn't going to die.

*

36

Do you mind my being here? Robert said. He had returned from talking with Coutts and was gently stroking Nia's hair.

No, not at all the nurse said, giving him a shy smile.

She was young and attractive. *Really quite sweet* Robert thought, as he watched her take and record, which she did every few minutes, Nia's blood pressure and pulse.

Yes, fairly steady she said, answering him.

That's a good sign, isn't it? he said. He was sure Nia would make a last-minute recovery, that they would yet laugh at all this. He felt he could almost will her to live. Then came again the shattering recall that she had *willed* her pneumonia, and he wondered, with terror, if she had possibly brought this about, and if he, with his impatience, indifference, antipathy, had pushed her to it.

Two white-coated doctors walked in. One was the senior resident, a big balding man with slumping shoulders and a kindly face, the other a gangling intern. The resident studied the chart and handed it back without comment. Then he looked curiously at Robert.

We don't usually allow . . . he said. *We don't think it's a good idea.*

I know what you mean. You expect me to be upset by this Robert said, indicating the respirator and the tubes fastened to the patient. *But I feel they have to do with the hospital. They haven't anything to do with her.*

The resident glanced at Robert's hand, which was still on Nia's hair. *She's not conscious of anything.*

I know Robert said, though he did not believe it. *But I'd like to stay with her.*

The resident was silent for a moment. He understood that something inordinate was going on, and knew he ought to stop it, but as he gazed at the wretched lover there rose in him muddled feelings of superiority, admiration, envy . . . Robert's manic misery touched his. *Okay* he said, and with a covert sign to the intern, who was accompanying him on his rounds, he walked heavily out of the room.

The inverted bottle was emptying; the nurse went to get another. For a few minutes Robert and Nia were alone. He went on caressing her, slowly stroking the hair back from her forehead and temple, and recalled how impetuously she used to toss back those same locks with her left hand, the hand now pierced and pinned by the red tube. And he wondered what she was thinking about. *Even if she's not thinking . . .* she would know, he felt sure, the feel of his hand, and he went on sliding it over her soft warm skin. Her chest was moving up and down in response to the steady rhythm of the bellows, and as he looked at the curved bulge of her wonderful breasts under the sheet, and followed the low swell of her belly down to the rising of her thighs, desire began to build in him, but with it a corrosive fear about how long it might be before he could possess that lovely body again.

Someone stopped in the doorway, a man dressed in moccasins, loose slacks and sport shirt, his hands shaking, his lean face graven by grief. His mouth dropped open at what he saw, and Robert and he, both dumbfounded, stared starkly at each other. Robert barely nodded, and then, becoming cold, deliberately turned back to Nia. He was absolutely unwilling to share her with Adams!

The nurse, returning, showed the new visitor to the adjoining room, where Gwendolyn was.

Adams vaguely remembered the secretary from a meeting with Eldon he had once had at the Board, and he listened in amazement to her poignant account of the great amour now ending on the other side of the wall. Gwendolyn stopped short of inventing details, but she interpreted many that had earlier been unclear, and with choked ardour told a story of love and longing as she honestly would have liked it to have been.

Adams had been one of the last recipients of Findlay's phone calls. Utterly staggered, without pausing to reflect, he had thrown on the clothes just taken off and raced to the hospital, to . . . to pay homage to his own emotion, to the purest passion of his life. Rushing across the lobby, coming up in the elevator, he had imagined a deathbed recognition, had hoped for some disclosure of devotion, and trembling in anticipation, had found, like a foul canker on fruit, like filth on snow — Aronson! He felt demeaned, deceived, cheated. Worse even, besmirched.

An hour passed, then two. Gwendolyn had long since stopped talking and was ill at ease. Her breasts had engorged and she was wondering whether her baby had been given a bottle. Adams, mournfully angry, was unsure of why he had stayed, but was unwilling to be the first to leave.

Robert looked in and asked if they wanted a sip of coffee; the nurse, returning from her break and seeing that the cafeteria was closing, had brought him some in a paper cup. Adams curtly refused. Gwendolyn took a little, and fawningly accepted from *Vincent* a light for her *ciggy-poo*. Perhaps she was only trying to fog the enmity between the two men, which she could hardly help but feel. Then all at once she yawned: a prolonged, widening, unbreakable yawn.

Gwen ... go home, please Robert said. *You've helped all you can. And*, he added with sudden inspiration *she'd worry about the baby ...*

Oh! she said. *Yes. I left him with my next-door neighbours. He might be kee ... ping them u ... u ... u ...* She was caught up in another irrepressible yawn.

Come on, Adams said kindly *I'll take you*. His courtly graciousness to Gwendolyn, who was crying again, to mark her leave-taking with tears, conveniently masked his rancour and bitterness towards Robert. In the morning he intended to examine the director's current contract, and break it if he could. In any case he was determined that Robert would never work for him again.

*

37

For several hours, as regularly as the pressure and pulse readings, and the steady pumping of the respirator, Robert went on stroking Nia's forehead and hair. Despite the resident's remark Robert recklessly believed she knew his touch, and that it was keeping her awareness alive. He felt that whatever Nia's relations with others had been, or what Adams' claim, which rankled, might be, he alone now had her life in his hands, and between him and her there existed a fervent bond that totally excluded everyone else.

Yet gradually, through the tired glances exchanged across the body on the gurney, there developed a tender intimacy with the nurse. He liked her slim fingers, the soft hollow of her neck, the delicate fringe of her lashes when her eyes slid shut. *What are you thinking about?* he said.

She sighed. *The date I was supposed to go on last night.* He encouraged her with a small smile. *My boyfriend . . .* she began, and then her voice trailed off.

A little beyond the open door, in a crisp uniform whose starched shining whiteness defied the hallway's gloom, stood an older, frowning figure. But she smiled benignly as she stepped in and said to Robert *Why don't you go home now . . . I'm sure you need some rest.*

Instantly wary, Robert said *I'm all right, thank you.*

No, no, you should get some sleep. Her mouth was working tensely, as if unused to being stretched by a smile. *Go, go on now.*

Please . . . I want to stay.

No, you shouldn't be here! she said. Her eyes were beginning to glitter. *It's against the rules!*

The doctor Robert answered quietly *said I could.*

Paling slightly, the woman looked at him a moment longer, then stalked from the room.

The night supervisor . . . whispered the nurse.

What a frustrated old maid Robert thought, but twenty minutes later, when she was back, he saw with surprise that she wore both an engagement and a wedding ring. She had been, plainly, pretty once. And might, in other clothes, be quite pleasing now, if her face, grown sharp with time, was not further distorted by rage.

You should go and lie down somewhere she said shrilly.

Please . . . I'm all right.

But you mustn't be here all the time! she shrieked. She seemed close to losing control. Inured to the least love, the woman was shamed and revolted by this dumb devotion to an unconscious body.

I'll go soon Robert said, to pacify her.

*

Presently he went down to the darkened lobby and lay on a padded bench. A maintenance man wiping the chairs worked around him. Before long Robert went back to the room and resumed his vigil. Nia's chest was continuing its even rise and fall. The nubile nurse, red eyed, was sighing for sleep; when she answered it was seldom above a whisper. One more quiet hour passed.

I thought you'd gone! It was the supervisor again, and then, behind her, the resident appeared. *Doctor,* she murmured, drawing him back into the hall *may I have a word?* They spoke out of earshot, but it was the last Robert saw of her.

The resident reappeared and leaned his bulk against the doorframe, fixing his gaze on the hand that was caressing Nia's hair. Because of his size and authority he seemed older than Robert, but was actually a little younger, and much less confident. He was uneasy about having overruled the supervisor. She would probably make trouble, and on the face of it she was right. *There's really nothing you can do* he said severely.

I know Robert said. *I may not be helping her, but . . . she's helping me.* He hesitated; he had just realized that. *I'm sorry the nurse was upset. But I want to be here.*

The doctor nodded, reassured. Lonelier than Robert, he felt this intense worship warranted respect.

She's a very great woman Robert said, for he had sensed the resident's attitude and wanted to fill the role reflected in it. *We've been i . . .*

Do you know . . . the doctor said suddenly, cutting him off, afraid, indeed, of any disclosure that might be disillusioning *do you understand what happened to her?* Robert shook his head. *Well, the X rays —*

Oh — Robert interrupted *what did Dr. Purcell say about them?*

The resident pinched his nose, as if it were itching. *He said he had seldom seen a heart so deteriorated. He didn't know how she had gone on for as long as she had.*

Robert was silenced, torn between these facts and what he felt.

Anyway, the doctor continued *the pictures showed that her heart had been damaged earlier in life, maybe when she was a child.*

Rheumatic fever! Robert said. Nia had once told him . . . He had forgotten!

Yes . . . very likely. But whatever it was, when the heart is damaged scars form, and impede the free flow of the blood. He was on surer ground now, and pleased to see the young nurse listening too. *When there's a barrier eddies occur, and with the blood going round and round like that sometimes a piece of the scar breaks off and floats into the blood stream. Then it's carried along until it gets to a place too narrow for it to pass, and gets stuck there. In her case, the brain.* He paused. The nurse respectfully dropped her eyes. *We think that's what happened. We . . . don't know what caused the second stroke.*

Robert looked down and touched Nia's shoulder with his fingertips. The doctor began feeling self-conscious again. He knew he should avoid further compromising himself, but was reluctant to cut his link with this extraordinary love. *Well, if you must stay . . .* he said, blushing for the remark's redundancy *then come with me and have a cup of coffee.*

They went down to the cafeteria; it had reopened minutes earlier, at six, and was serving breakfast. Both men took some, and they sat at a table apart, but the empathy that had grown easily in Nia's small quiet room soon perished in this large busy one. They needed a subject, and Robert asked about the orderlies coming in. The resident explained the shift routine, and, to Robert's surprise, that he, as senior resident, was on duty all the time, eating and sleeping only when he could. Then, their food finished, Robert thanked him gratefully, got a container of coffee for the nurse, and went back to Nia.

A thin morning light was coming through the window facing her. *My darling Nia,* he thought *you've lasted through the night. Maybe you'll make it yet.*

Ward workers were beginning to go by the room; the hospital was taking on its daytime bustle. *Damn,* he thought, rubbing his bristled face *I shouldn't be with her looking like this.* The nurse was worn too, but her coffee remained untouched. He didn't know it then, but she had been called in specially for this, and he was paying her. And for the second ambulance, the hospital stay, and all the attentions Nia had received. He glanced enquiringly.

She said *I'm not supposed to drink it here.*

Go to the washroom. . .

No, it's okay. My shift will be over soon.

Mine won't, Robert said *but I'm leaving for a little while to get cleaned up, and then I'll be back.* He wanted to make some sort of tender gesture to her, a token of what they had shared, but nothing seemed appropriate. *Thanks for everything* he said.

That's okay she replied.

38

In the street the air was cool, and seemed, by contrast, fresh. Robert breathed it greedily, whole lungfuls of it, as if to drive out the heavy menace of the hospital. He knew what he had to do, merely reequip himself to go on helping Nia through the crisis, and he felt almost cheerful about having such a clear, uncomplicated task.

But at the apartment he found he had no clean shirt. Glad of a pretext to garner sympathy, and despising himself for it, he went up to the penthouse. Hugh responded to the knock. Hugh was still half asleep, blinking, barefoot, wrapped in a red terry-cloth robe. *How is she?* he said.

She's going to die. The words were out without thought, stunning Robert. He stood there bewildered, feeling deeply guilty.

Hugh hastily gave him a white shirt, one he had carelessly bought at a clearance sale. *Keep it* he said. *What about Vancouver?* he added distinctly, as he was about to shut the door.

I can't think about it now.

You're making a big mistake. You should break off this business, and go.

Robert regarded Hugh carefully, registering his features, because he knew he would never see him again.

And he just managed to reach his own apartment before a sob was torn from his throat. Another, more savage sob followed. He stumbled, and strange squealing sounds burst from his mouth. But these were unwanted, as was the horrible flow of moisture running from his eyes and lips. Yet he was helpless to stop it, and sobbing desperately, groaning and whimpering, he fell to his knees. Over and over, his head beating on the hardwood floor, he cried *She's going to die! She's going to die!*

However he soon got up, showered, shaved, dressed cleanly, and returned to the hospital.

In the full light of morning Nia looked more at peace. Nothing else in the room had changed, except that the door had been closed and a new nurse was attending. Robert asked her, expertly, whether the blood pressure had fallen. *Only a little* she said.

Dr. Purcell came in, followed by a retinue: Coutts, then the senior resident, the gangly intern, a second intern, and another nurse. *Good morning* Purcell said. He looked at the chart, frowned slightly, and turned to Robert. *We'd like to make an examination* he said. *Would you . . . in the next room, please.*

*

Even the small waiting room seemed fresher by morning light. The window was open, and though it looked out on an air well, sounds of traffic came up from the surrounding streets. Over the hospital roof Robert could see a bit of blue sky. He thought of the cabin, and the singing valley.

The door opened; Purcell, white coated, entered alone. He was polite and concise. *We've made a thorough examination. She's completely paralyzed. All response is gone. Only the most primitive part of her brain is still functioning, and it's keeping the heart going, because we're helping with the respirator. We could keep this up . . . indefinitely, until the heart simply wears out.* His manner changed; all the man's kindliness came out. *If she was my wife,* he said softly *I'd want to stop it. But it's up to you. I'll do whatever you say.*

Robert heard this murderous kindness and had to hold the doctor guiltless. *I alone,* he thought *will have to kill her.* Yet he recalled parting from Nia twice before, each time ostensibly for good, and insanely there flickered in him a feeling that neither was this the end. *Yes . . .* he nodded *stop it.*

Wait here Purcell said. *We'll call you.*

*

One of the interns came for him. All the apparatus had been removed, the room looked tidy and bare. And Nia too was cleaned up, but her lips were slightly parted where the nozzle of the hose had been inserted. And there were marks on her hand and arm where the intravenous had punctured her skin. Otherwise she seemed quiet and composed. She was still breathing lightly; there was a small but perceptible rise and fall of her chest.

It will take a few minutes the resident said. He was standing across from Robert, with Nia between them. The gangling intern was at the resident's side and the attending nurse had stationed herself at the foot of the gurney. The rest had left.

They watched the gradual weakening movement of the chest. When Robert thought it had stopped it suddenly started again, and when he was sure it was still going he was surprised to see the resident place his stethoscope over the heart. Then the resident lifted her wrist, held it, and let it slip from his fingers. *That's it* he said. Robert stared: she looked no different than she had a moment ago.

The others started to shuffle out. *I'll be along in a minute* Robert said. And for the last time he was alone with Nia.

It seems I have to say good-bye he thought. He touched her forehead and it was cool, not cold. It felt smooth and soft. Then he noticed that the wrinkles that had been in it were gone. Down the cheeks and around the mouth her skin had all smoothed out, and she looked young, very young again. Her body appeared to be completely relaxed, with her feet pointed together in that little girl way he had seen only a few times before. She seemed a young, young woman, ideal in sleep. *No one will ever know* he thought *all that she was.*

And fed by memories, there flared up in him a pure, overwhelming sense of Nia's aliveness, beauty, and pain. He was in love again, and the searing agony of it, driven by anger and remorse, left him burnt and numb, dry eyed, steady as a stone.

It was indelible. She had at last the abiding love that had evaded her all her life.

Good-bye my darling Nia Robert whispered, and kissed her on the mouth. He had almost expected something disagreeable, but her lips were soft, as they had always been. Her skin even had that familiar, faintly-perfumed smell. *Where is death, then?* he thought, and kissed her again.

Then once more he stroked her hair, and kissed her forehead. It hardly seemed right that this should be all, but there seemed nothing else to do. He looked again at the gentle, composed figure. After all their breaks, it seemed this couldn't be the last. He had never loved her more.

Good-bye darling he whispered, and went out.

*

In the hall Steven Carey was standing with Dr. Coutts. Robert was unruffled; he was beyond reasoning.

Who's the next of kin? Coutts said as Robert came up.

Her mother . . . I guess. Why?

We'd like permission to do an autopsy.

No! No! Why?

We'd like to know Coutts said in his clipped, commanding voice *what caused the second stroke.*

And you want to cut her up? No! Robert cried. *It would offend all that's beautiful!* Coutts, irritated, gazed at him coldly, and Robert, a Jew, realized it would be impossible to make Coutts, with his inherited prerogatives, his confidence, his correctness — to make him understand. *Do you have to?* he said wearily.

It may save another life.

Her mother is an old woman . . . Robert said. *She's been through enough. Don't ask this!*

It can't make any difference to her, Coutts said *and it's important to us. I'll call . . .*

No, Robert said *let me ask her.* And seeing the doctor redden, he added quickly *At least let me prepare her for it. Give me half an hour.*

All right Coutts said. But he picked up the phone as soon as Steve and Robert were out of sight.

*

323

At Steve's car Robert stopped. *We should call the house . . .*

I have Steve said. And just before he switched on the ignition, he said *She was very much loved.*

Robert thought he meant that everyone had loved her. Perhaps Steve did; he had been meeting Nia's friends.

39

The house was full of them. Betty was busy supervising the serving of drinks and snacks, while Wilma, roving through the crowd, was regally accepting everyone's tears and regrets. There was a ripple of surprise when Steve and Robert entered. Most of the friends had already met Steve, who had recognized in these actresses, writers and others of Nia's fascinating *family* a rich and ready field, but they looked curiously at Robert. However, before Findlay could introduce him steps and voices were heard coming from the porch, and the door was flung open by one of those who had gone to the airport to await Buddy Wilson. At once the band leader was surrounded. This was his first visit in years; most were eager to greet him.

Robert slipped into the kitchen, looking for Joel. He found him in the back garden, cradling Jester. In a moment a woman, a beauty too, if a trifle faded, came out and wanted to take the boy to meet his father. Joel refused, and turning his face to the fence began to cry.

*

My life with Nora was finished long ago, Wilson said the next day to Robert, with whom he had urgently asked to speak privately *and I wouldn't have come now if it wasn't for my son. He's my only child. My second wife didn't have any, and my current one can't. We would very much like to have him, but he won't come with me. And he's as stubborn as . . .* He meant *as his mother,* but was afraid of offending the lover. *He says he'll stay with you.*

Earlier, hearing with exultation that Joel had chosen him — *us!* Robert cried inwardly, he felt Nia had won. But the friends were shocked, and Betty — who, declaring that Nia would have wanted a cheerful wake, had the night before given a small, *brilliant* all said, evening for Buddy Wilson, from which Robert had stayed away — bluntly confronted him. She said, about the boy *It's nonsense, and you know it!*

So that now, faced with the father's claim, Robert felt his own grow weak.

I have to leave for New York and L.A. in a few hours Wilson said.

*

Robert took Joel to a small park, where they sat under a pine tree and nervously built little huts from the dried needles. Both held back their tears. The poor boy sensed he was already condemned. And Robert, utterly wretched, felt he was losing his only child, Nia's and his. While he told Joel his father and step-mother would truly welcome him, he vowed to himself that he would never betray Nia again.

*

Because of the autopsy, which had been inconclusive, the coffin remained closed. No recent photograph of Nia could be found, so the undertaker placed on the box a picture taken at the time of her marriage to Wilson. Wilma behaved with dignity, supported by Steve, who seldom left her side. Later he saw her off to her cousins in Woodstock.

Robert spent the day at the cabin. He felt that the funeral, like the hospital procedures, did not concern him. The evening was calm, as most had been. When he got up from the cot he looked for a final time at the pond, and walking slowly through the cabin, shut the door behind him. His car, dark against the darkening foliage, was waiting.

My darling Nia, he whispered *I loved you, and I take you with me. Yet I am leaving many tokens. Sun hat, clothes, blue wash cloth, pink soap, binoculars, good-bye. Good-bye my sweet. Nia, oh Nia, good-bye!*

He had it all within. And he gazed around, at everything that had been all to him.

Good-bye, beauty . . .

*This book is set in Minion, a typeface designed by
Robert Slimbach in 1990. Minion is inspired by classical,
old style typefaces of the late Renaissance, a period of elegant,
beautiful, and highly readable type designs. Created primarily
for text setting, Minion combines the aesthetic and functional
qualities that make text type highly readable with
the versatility of digital technology.*

Printed on 55lb., 100% PCW HiBulk FSC® Natural

FSC
www.fsc.org

MIX
Paper from
responsible sources
FSC® C016245